# The Lucky Penny

Dilly Court is a No.1 *Sunday Times* bestselling author of over forty novels. She grew up in North-East London and began her career in television, writing scripts for commercials. She is married with two grown-up children, four grandchildren and three beautiful great-grandchildren. Dilly now lives in Dorset on the Jurassic Coast with her husband.

To find out more about Dilly, please visit her website and her Facebook page:

www.dillycourt.com
f /DillyCourtAuthor

## Also by Dilly Court

Mermaids Singing
The Dollmaker's
Daughters
Tilly True
The Best of Sisters
The Cockney Sparrow
A Mother's Courage
The Constant Heart
A Mother's Promise
The Cockney Angel
A Mother's Wish
The Ragged Heiress
A Mother's Secret
Cinderella Sister
A Mother's Trust
The Lady's Maid
The Best of Daughters
The Workhouse Girl
A Loving Family
The Beggar Maid
A Place Called Home
The Orphan's Dream
Ragged Rose
The Swan Maid
The Christmas Card
The Button Box
The Mistletoe Seller
Nettie's Secret

Rag-and-Bone
Christmas
The Reluctant Heiress
A Thimble for
Christmas

### THE RIVER MAID SERIES

The River Maid
The Summer Maiden
The Christmas Rose

### THE VILLAGE SECRETS SERIES

The Christmas Wedding
A Village Scandal
The Country Bride

### THE ROCKWOOD CHRONICLES

Fortune's Daughter
Winter Wedding
Runaway Widow
Sunday's Child
Snow Bride
Dolly's Dream

# Dilly Court

## The Lucky Penny

HarperCollins*Publishers*

HarperCollins*Publishers* Ltd
1 London Bridge Street
London SE1 9GF

www.harpercollins.co.uk

HarperCollins*Publishers*
Macken House, 39/40 Mayor Street Upper
Dublin 1, D01 C9W8, Ireland

First published by HarperCollins*Publishers* 2024
2

A catalogue record for this book is available from the British Library

ISBN: 978-0-00-858077-3 (HB)
ISBN: 978-0-00-858087-2 (PB)

Typeset by Palimpsest Book Production Limited,
Falkirk, Stirlingshire

Printed and bound in the UK using
100% renewable electricity at CPI Group (UK) Ltd

MIX
Paper | Supporting
responsible forestry
FSC™ C007454

This book contains FSC™ certified paper and other controlled sources
to ensure responsible forest management.

For more information visit: www.harpercollins.co.uk/green

*For Jean Munday, a good friend for
so many years I've lost count*

# Chapter One

The chilly east wind that rampaged up the Thames from the North Sea was no respecter of persons. It tugged at the fashionable ladies' bonnets and tossed the gentlemen's top hats off with carefree vigour, sending them bouncing down the steps of St Paul's Cathedral to land at Flora's small feet.

'Pick it up and give it back to the man.' Gert Fox gave Flora a shove that almost toppled the tiny six-year-old over. Used to such treatment, Flora ran after the expensive top hat and snatched it up. She glanced over her shoulder at Gert, who scowled and jerked her head in the direction of the hatless gentleman, who was standing outside the imposing entrance.

Obediently Flora climbed the flight of steps and handed the hat back to its owner.

1

The gentleman took it with a smile. 'Thank you, my dear.'

'Aren't you going to give the child something, Arthur? See how thin and pale she is. I doubt if she's had a decent meal in days.' The pretty lady who stood at his side smiled down at Flora and her husband put his hand in his pocket. He pressed a penny into Flora's outstretched palm.

'I'm much obliged to you, sir.' Flora repeated the words parrot-fashion. She knew that Gert was listening and if she failed to say the mantra she had been taught there would be trouble.

'How quaint,' the pretty lady said, smiling. 'What delightful manners for a street child.' She turned to the small girl whose hand she was holding and gave it a gentle shake. 'Are you paying attention, Arabella?'

'Why hasn't she got any shoes on, Mama?' Arabella stared at Flora's bare feet, which were turning a delicate shade of blue. 'And her dress is torn and dirty.'

'Hush, dear. It isn't polite to make remarks about other people's appearance.'

The gentleman tut-tutted behind his walrus moustache. 'We came to show our daughter the glory of St Paul's, Constance. I suggest we go in out of the cold.'

Arabella slipped her hands out of the fur muff that hung from a gold guard chain around her neck. She peeled off her woollen mittens and held them out to Flora. 'Here, put these on, girl. I have my muff.'

Flora took them, but she was unsure as to what

to do next and she glanced anxiously at Gert, who stepped forward, baring her yellowed teeth in a sickly smile.

'I'm sorry, your honour.' She cuffed Flora around the head. 'My girl got no right to go begging, sir. We're proud people even if my old man is serving time in Newgate.'

Flora looked up at her, aghast. 'No he's not, Gert. He's in the pub.' She received another clip, this time around her ear, which made her yelp with pain.

Arabella's mother took her by the hand and dragged her, protesting loudly, into the cathedral. The gentleman eyed Gert askance. 'I think you had this planned, madam. My name is Sir Arthur Stewart and I served several years as a magistrate. I've seen many of your kind brought before me in court, so you won't get another penny piece from me. Now take the child away before I call for a constable, and I suggest you treat her better in future.'

Gert backed away. 'I'm just a poor woman, sir.'

Shyly, Flora handed him the mittens. 'Ta for these, sir. But they ain't mine.'

'What's your name, child?'

'Don't tell nothing, Flora.' Gert stood at the bottom of the steps, beckoning frantically. 'You'd better come quick or you'll feel your dad's slipper on your backside.'

'You aren't fit to be a mother to this poor child,' Sir Arthur said angrily.

'She ain't my mother.' Flora felt safer with the wide flight of steps between her and her tormentor. 'And Sydney Fox ain't me dad.'

'It's lies, sir.' Gert clutched her hands to her flat bosom. 'I still remember the agony of giving birth to the ungrateful little brat.'

'She's not my mother.' Flora moved a little closer to Sir Arthur. She knew instinctively that she could trust the tall man with the bushy moustache and eyebrows to match. She had suffered enough knocks and bruises in her short life to know when someone was likely to lash out with their fists. Sir Arthur might look stern, but Flora suspected there was a soft heart beneath the stony exterior. And very few people stood up to Gert, even Sydney, unless he was very drunk – then sparks would fly and Flora would take refuge in the cupboard below the stairs that led up from the basement room where they lived. When there was a storm or an exceptionally high tide, water would trickle along a channel built into the brick floor. Sydney Fox had told Flora that it came from the underground course of the River Fleet, which was in imminent danger of flooding their one-room abode. Drowning was a punishment meted out to wicked children by the devil himself, which she would find out soon unless she did exactly what she was told. Flora was inclined to believe him, if only for the reason that Biddy Downs's nine-year-old son had fallen in the Thames and his body washed up on the foreshore two days later.

Everyone knew that Tom Downs was a bad boy, so the devil must have been at work there, too.

Flora dragged herself back to the present, torn between fear of Gert and hope that Sir Arthur might do something to save her from the inevitable beating when she went home.

Gert stomped up the steps and seized Flora by the ear. 'I've had enough of you and your lies. Wait till I get you home.'

The look on Gert's face told Flora she was doomed. She was about to succumb to the inevitable when Arabella stormed out of the cathedral and grabbed her father by the hand.

'Don't let the horrid lady take her, Papa.'

Constance Stewart emerged from the building, clearly agitated. 'Please do something, Arthur. People are staring.'

Sir Arthur placed himself between Gert and a terrified Flora. 'Come now, madam. Surely there is no need to chastise the child. She has done nothing wrong.'

'Nothing wrong, guv? She's just told you a pack of lies. I never laid a finger on me dead sister's child.' Gert covered her mouth with her hand, as if realising that she had just admitted telling a falsehood. Her dark eyes widened in horror. 'I mean, I always thinks of young Flora as me own. I was with me sister, Matilda, when she gave birth to this child, and she passed away with a sigh, but not before begging me to take care of her baby.'

Sir Arthur frowned. 'This is obviously a pack of lies.

It seems to me that you and your husband are not fit people to bring up a young child.'

'Who said he's me husband?' Gert gave him a gap-toothed grin. 'I ain't tying meself to the likes of him, sir.'

'You are unfit to have any child in your care.' Constance placed a protective arm around Arabella's shoulders as if afraid that some of Gert's malice might harm her daughter.

'I agree.' Sir Arthur took a step closer to Gert. 'Give me a reason why I should not remove this child from your guardianship and put her in the care of a respectable foster mother.'

A sly look replaced the fear in Gert's eyes. 'Are you offering to purchase the brat, guv?'

'You would sell your own sister's child?'

'Not sell, sir. More like recompense for the years of toil and hardship I've endured to bring her up to the fine specimen she is today. You won't find a nipper with a better set of toothy-pegs, or hair the colour of a flaming sunset as well as sea-green eyes that will one day lure a man to his death for love.'

Constance clutched her husband's arm. 'Pay her what she wants, Arthur.'

'Yes, Papa,' Arabella added urgently. 'Buy her for me. I would like a sister to play with.'

'There you are, guv.' Gert smiled triumphantly. 'Just as I said. She'd be a bargain at twice the price.'

'And what is that sum, exactly?' Sir Arthur towered over Gert, who cringed visibly.

'I think ten pound is a fair sum, sir.'

'You know what you're asking is illegal. I could have you arrested and locked up in prison for such a crime.'

'Flora Lee's not for sale, sir.' Gert sent a sly glance at Arabella, who was tugging at her father's sleeve. 'But I would gladly hand her over to you and your good lady for safekeeping. A small sum of money to cover me expenses would not be against the law, so I believe.'

Flora held her breath. She would do anything to go with the lovely lady and her pretty daughter, who was desperate to have a sister. Flora swayed on her feet. She had not eaten since the previous evening, and then it had only been one slice of bread smeared with beef dripping. She had tried to make it last by taking tiny bites, but all the while she had been tormented by the aroma of the hot meat pies and baked potatoes that Syd and Gert consumed so greedily. Suddenly their voices seemed very far away and everything grew misty. Flora felt herself falling into a dark abyss.

When she opened her eyes she could hear angel voices singing so beautifully that she was convinced she had died and gone to heaven. The smell of ancient hymnals and incense filled the still air and she was lying on something hard and unforgiving. She tried to sit up but was pressed down again by a gentle hand.

'You're all right, Flora. You are in the vestry,

thanks to one of the cathedral's staff.' Lady Constance Stewart stroked Flora's straggly rose-gold hair back from her forehead. 'You fainted, dear.'

'You were frightened by that horrid person.' Arabella perched on the edge of the settle, eyeing Flora with a puckered brow. 'I think my papa paid her for you, Flora. You belong to us now.'

Constance shook her head, smiling. 'People don't own each other, Arabella. Your papa paid Mrs Fox's expenses, and she was happy with that.'

Flora raised herself to a sitting position. 'Does that mean I can stay with you, Arabella?'

'Yes, of course.' Arabella wrapped her arms around Flora, but drew away quickly, holding her nose. 'You smell horrible.'

Flora shrank away, mortified. 'I'm sorry.'

'Don't be unkind, Bella,' Constance said severely. 'Flora hasn't had the advantages to which we are accustomed. Go and find Papa and tell him that Flora is well enough to leave. We need to take her home with us.'

'I can walk, missis.' Flora was suddenly conscious of the state of her clothes, and if Arabella said she smelled bad, that must be the case. In all her six years of life she had never felt so humiliated, but the lovely lady was smiling kindly and that brought tears to Flora's eyes. She was used to being ill-treated, but to be shown sympathy and understanding was overwhelming.

'There, there, dear.' Constance gave her a gentle hug.

'We'll soon have you washed and dressed in clean clothes, and I'm sure a good meal would not go amiss.'

'Thank you, missis.' Flora sank back onto the hard wooden bench, closing her eyes. This must be a dream and when she awakened she would be back in the damp basement with the River Fleet oozing mud across the floor.

The next thing she knew she was being lifted by strong arms and held tightly as Sir Arthur carried her out of the cathedral and down the steps to a waiting hackney carriage, where Arabella and her mother were waiting for them. Sir Arthur did not speak, but she could feel the warmth of his body and smell the scent of Macassar oil mingled with the fragrance of expensive toiletries and just a hint of cigar smoke. Flora was too overcome to say anything and when he lifted her into the carriage she huddled in the corner, too dazed by the sudden turn of events to fully understand what had just happened to her.

Arabella, however, was clearly excited and she chattered nonstop until her mother told her to quieten down, followed by a frown from her father, which silenced her for the rest of the ride to South Molton Street. As the cab drew up outside the imposing terraced Georgian property Arabella jumped to her feet.

'This is our town house, Flora. Just you wait and see what our place in the country is like.'

Flora gazed up at the tall house that seemed to

reach into the sky. She wondered if the family lived in the basement or had rooms at the very topmost floor, where surely only birds could roost. She waited quietly until everyone had alighted.

'Are you able to walk, Flora?' Sir Arthur peered into the cab.

'Yes, mister.' Flora scrambled to her feet and was about to put her foot on the step, but it seemed very far down and she was relieved when Sir Arthur lifted her to the ground.

'Come on, slowcoach,' Arabella called from the open doorway.

Flora could see a strange man standing behind Arabella. He was dressed in severe black and looked very disapproving. She hesitated.

'Go on, Flora,' Sir Arthur said, smiling. 'I know you will find all this strange, but that is Jefferson, our butler. There's no need to be afraid of him. Isn't that so, Jefferson?'

'If you say so, sir.'

'There you are then. Go indoors, Flora.'

Each step felt as if she were wading in deep water. Not that she was scared, but nothing seemed real. What was a butler when he was at home, anyway? And there was a young lady, also dressed in black, but her outfit was relieved by a spotless white apron and a frilled mobcap. Flora stepped into the vast entrance hall, gazing round in wonder.

Constance had been about to mount the curving flight of stairs but she hesitated and retraced her steps.

'Ivy, this is Flora Lee. She'll be staying with us for a while. Please take her to the servants' quarters and give her a bath. I suggest you burn the rags she's wearing. I'll instruct Miss Blount to find some suitable clothes for her.'

'Yes, ma'am.'

'You may bring the child to the drawing room after luncheon,' Constance added casually.

Ivy seized Flora by the hand. 'Come with me.'

'I had a bath once,' Flora said conversationally as they left the room. 'Are we going to the bath house?'

Ivy shot her a wary glance. 'No, of course not. Whatever gave you that idea?'

Flora was worried now, and she turned her head to give Arabella a pleading look, but her new friend simply waved and followed her mother upstairs. Ivy tightened her grip on Flora's hand and led her through a maze of corridors to the back of the house. When they came to a green baize door, Ivy opened it and Flora saw a flight of stairs descending to what must be the cellar. So, she reasoned, rich people also lived below ground. They simply gave the impression of having a whole mansion to themselves.

Below stairs was another world. Again there were long passageways to navigate with doors leading off into mysterious closed rooms. The floor was tiled but there was no sign of water, which was something of a relief. There seemed to be little likelihood of getting wet feet below ground in this part of town. Ivy tugged at Flora's hand and quickened her pace.

'Haven't got all day, nipper. Best foot forward.'

Flora did her best to comply, and they were greeted by a burst of heat and steam when Ivy opened the door to the kitchen. Flora came to a halt, staring in disbelief at the size of the room, the shelves filled with burnished copper pots and pans, and the huge range that took up the best part of one wall. Servants were scurrying around filling dishes with delicious-smelling hot food. In the other half of the kitchen there were joints of raw meat and baskets of vegetables, together with a brace of pheasants still in full plumage awaiting preparation for dinner that evening. The most junior kitchen maids were busy clearing the large table of dirty crockery, kitchen utensils and knives that looked terrifying sharp. Flora was already feeling faint with hunger and the tempting aromas that filled the steamy air made her stomach rumble so loudly she thought that everyone would be bound to hear the gurgling sound.

'Who's this?' A tall, bony woman enveloped in a stained white apron brandished a knife in Flora's direction. 'Are we taking in street urchins now, Ivy?'

'That one looks like a tiddler. Better throw her back in the river, Ivy.' The cheeky scullery maid received a clip around the ear from Cook, causing her to drop the saucepans she was carrying with a loud clatter. Eyeing Cook nervously, she bent down to retrieve them.

'Get back to them pots and pans in the sink, girl.'

'Yes, Cook.' The girl shot a malevolent glance in

Flora's direction, as if her reprimand was Flora's fault, and she darted into the scullery where she began banging pans together as if in protest.

'That's enough of that, too. Or you'll feel the back of my hand.' Cook glared at Flora. 'What are we supposed to do with her, Ivy?'

'Madam said to bath her and burn her duds.' Ivy held Flora at arm's length.

'Better take her to the washhouse then, Ivy. You can fill a tin tub and clean her up in there.'

'Madam said to ask Miss Blount for some of Miss Arabella's old clothes.'

'She'll be down to collect her luncheon very soon.' Cook turned to an older woman who was kneading bread dough. 'Remind me to do that, Cora.'

'Yes, Cook.' Cora gave the mixture an extra thump.

'Come on, young 'un.' Ivy propelled Flora through the kitchen and out through a door at the back of the building. It seemed as though she would have to stay hungry for a while longer.

The washhouse was a small extension leading off the scullery. Beyond that, as Ivy took pains to point out, there was the privy, and a small garden enclosed by a high brick wall. It was hot inside the washhouse with a fire burning beneath the copper.

'You're in luck, nipper,' Ivy said, grinning. 'I'll scoop out some of the hot water so you won't have a cold bath. Stand over there so I don't splash you.'

Flora was too fascinated to object and she moved

away, watching intently as Ivy rolled up her sleeves and used a pitcher to ladle boiling water into the zinc tub. She topped up the bath with cold water from the pump and tested it with her elbow. 'I know you ain't a baby, but you're all skin and bone. I don't want to scald you, nipper. Now get your clothes off and hop in.'

Flora thought about making a run for it, but there seemed to be no escape and the determined set of Ivy's jaw was accompanied by a martial glint in her grey eyes. Reluctantly, Flora peeled off her grimy garments. Ivy had a block of coarse soap clutched in her hand as she advanced purposefully towards Flora, who realised that resistance was useless. Arabella's shocked expression and words of disgust rang in Flora's ears and she allowed Ivy to lift her into the tub.

Soaped, scrubbed and having endured near drowning, or so it felt after the last jug of water was tipped over her head, Flora was eventually dumped onto the stone floor and wrapped in a large, fluffy towel. Ivy hurried off, telling her to stay put in no uncertain terms. Flora decided it was easier to obey than to argue, and she waited patiently until Ivy returned with an armful of clothes.

'Put these on quick or you'll catch your death of cold and the missis will be angry.'

Minutes later Flora was wearing clean underwear beneath a plain grey dress with a white lace collar. Arabella was of a sturdier build and the clothes were all a size too large, but they smelled of lye soap and fresh air, which was a pleasant change from the odours of the basement in Turnagain Lane. The boots that Miss Blount had found in a cupboard were a perfect fit and Flora felt she could walk to the moon and back with such expensive footwear. She had almost forgotten her hunger, but Ivy took her to the servants' hall, where she was given a bowl of lamb stew and a plate of bread and butter. Cora was seated at the end of the long table, and she eyed Flora, scowling.

'Where was you raised, nipper? You've got no manners.'

Flora almost choked on a piece of potato. 'I says please and thank you, miss.'

'I mean table manners, silly. You eat like a pig. They won't welcome you above stairs if you can't eat proper.'

'I-I'm sorry,' Flora said humbly. 'I don't know what table manners are, miss.'

Cora rolled her eyes and rose from her seat. 'Someone needs to take you in hand, but it ain't my job.' She picked up her plate and stomped into the kitchen.

Humiliated and close to tears, Flora stared at her plate. She had no idea what constituted bad manners at table, and no one to ask. She sighed. Life was difficult wherever you were, and this huge house filled with strange people was almost as hard to navigate as the drunken bouts of ill temper from

Sydney Fox, or the capricious whims and spiteful slaps from Gert. Maybe the big man with the moustache had a cane secreted about his person or a leather belt with a metal buckle that he might whip off at any given moment. Flora glanced around to see if anyone was watching and, satisfied that she was on her own, she gobbled the rest of the food until she was so full that she could not eat another mouthful.

Suddenly and without warning the servants' hall filled up with people chattering and laughing as they took their seats at the table, while the more junior kitchen staff brought in tureens filled with vegetables, mashed potato and salvers layered with roast meat.

Ivy beckoned to Flora. 'Madam wants to see you in the drawing room, Flora. You're to come with me.'

Conversation ceased and all eyes were upon Flora as she scrambled to her feet and hurried over to Ivy.

'Why are they staring at me, Ivy?'

'They're a nosy bunch, nipper. Don't worry about them as have no manners. You just mind what you says to Lady Stewart and maybe she'll let you stay here. Miss Arabella could do with some company of her own age, if you ask me.'

The chatter resumed immediately and Flora clutched Ivy's hand, following her obediently. There had been that word again. If she had no manners at table and the curious servants had no manners, what was she to think? Maybe Arabella had the answer.

Flora was still pondering the problem of manners when they reached the drawing room. Ivy knocked and waited for a response. 'Now be careful what you say, nipper. Mind your manners and you'll be all right.' She opened the door and thrust Flora into the room.

'Thank you, Ivy,' Constance said, placing her coffee cup back on its saucer. 'That will be all for now.'

Ivy bobbed a curtsey, giving Flora an encouraging smile as she left the room.

Arabella had been sitting on the floor playing with a china doll, but she leaped to her feet and ran to give Flora a hug.

'You smell better,' she said cheerfully. 'Come and play with me and Bertha, my best doll. Maybe I can find an old one for you.'

Flora glanced anxiously at Constance, who gave her an encouraging nod. 'That's right, play nicely, girls.'

Sir Arthur cleared his throat noisily. 'You don't really mean to take this child in as a companion for Arabella, do you, my dear? I mean, look where she came from.'

'She's very young, Arthur. Just a baby really, and they're more or less the same age.'

'Even so, she's come from nothing. Do you really want our daughter mixing with a child from the lowest of the lower classes?'

'Hush, Arthur. Not in front of the children.'

Flora shot a sideways glance at Sir Arthur. She understood what he was saying and she was ashamed of her lowly status. Someone who did not know what manners were was obviously not suitable to live in such a grand house. She sat cross-legged on the floor and allowed Arabella to do the talking.

'I doubt if the child understands what I'm saying, my dear.' Sir Arthur sipped his coffee, frowning. 'Surely we can find a more suitable companion when we return to the country next week?'

Arabella leaped to her feet. 'No, Papa. I like Flora. I want her to come home with us.' She thrust her doll into Flora's arms. 'Bertha likes her, so she must come and play with me.'

Constance smiled indulgently. 'Well, if Bertha wants Flora to come to the country house, perhaps we should listen to your doll.'

'If you think that the opinion of a china doll is more important than mine, I suppose I am outnumbered,' Sir Arthur said gloomily. 'However – and this is important – there is one person you haven't asked.' He leaned forward, fixing Flora with a penetrating stare. 'What would you like, young lady? Do you wish to return to your family in Turnagain Lane, or do you want to come and live with us as Arabella's companion?'

# Chapter Two

In the weeks that followed Flora learned that Arabella was thoroughly spoiled and prone to tantrums if she did not get her own way. Despite this, Arabella was affectionate and loyal. She took it upon herself to teach Flora how to treat servants and how to behave at table, although Sunday luncheon was the only meal they were allowed to have in the dining room with the adults. At other times they ate in the nursery with Arabella's governess, Miss Gough, in attendance. Of all the people living in the house it was Miss Gough whom Flora disliked the most, and she feared the whiplash of Miss Gough's spiteful tongue. It seemed that, being the daughter of a retired army officer, Jane Gough considered herself to be of a higher social standing than a child from the slums, as she put it. She was strict with Arabella but rigidly respectful;

however, with Flora she unleashed all the venom
that had built up in her soul over the years of genteel
poverty and subservience.

Towards the end of the week the servants were
busy packing up the family possessions that they
wished to take to the house in the country. Flora
could only sit back and watch as Ivy and the other
housemaids rushed around filling large wicker
hampers with items that Lady Stewart could not
live without. Miss Blount was in charge of the wardrobe, including that of the girls, but as Flora had
only a few outfits her valise was noticeably smaller
than the large trunk filled with Arabella's clothes.
There was another set aside for Arabella's collection
of dolls, together with drawing materials and school-
books. Miss Gough was in charge of the latter, which
she did with her usual tight-lipped expression of an
ancient martyr about to be burned at the stake. This
was Arabella's description of her governess, which
made Flora giggle, although she knew nothing about
the poor creatures Arabella described in such detail.
Maybe book learning was not such a good thing
after all. Such grisly details were probably best left
to history. She was thankful that she could neither
read nor write, but Miss Gough had other ideas. It
seemed, even after a few days, that Miss Gough's
main mission in life now was to force Flora to learn
to read, write and master arithmetic. Flora felt that
her head would explode if she had to sit hunched
over a slate scraping the letters of the alphabet again

and again until her vision blurred and her small fingers ached with cramp.

'When we go to the country there will be more time in which to turn you from an ignorant little urchin into a suitable companion for Miss Arabella,' Miss Gough said through clenched teeth. 'There will be fewer distractions at Nine Oaks.'

'What is Nine Oaks?' Flora whispered to Arabella when Miss Gough's attention was distracted by Ivy, who brought a message from Lady Stewart.

'That's our house in the country,' Arabella said, giggling. 'You'll soon see. We're off first thing in the morning.'

'Is it nice there?'

'Oh, yes,' Arabella said earnestly. 'It's much nicer than London. The gardens will be full of flowers and I can ride my pony whenever I want to.'

'But you still have lessons with her,' Flora glanced in Miss Gough's direction.

'Only for a month or so and then we have a few weeks to enjoy the summer, and best of all, Miss Gough goes to stay with her papa in Yorkshire, or her sister in Somerset.'

'Does she really? Don't we have to do any lessons?'

'Mama says that it's important to learn other things.'

Flora was mystified. 'Like what, Bella?'

'I don't know, just things. You'll see.'

Miss Gough turned away from Ivy to give the girls a stern glance. 'Practise your letters. You especially, Flora. You are an ignoramus.'

'What's that?' Flora asked innocently.

Miss Gough reached for the cane that hung on the wall behind her desk in the schoolroom, and she slapped it meaningfully across her hand. 'Get back to work. Don't make me use this on you. It hurts me more than it does you.'

Flora eyed her warily and was about to question this statement when Arabella nudged her hard in the ribs. Flora stifled a sigh. She could only hope that life in the country would be easier than it was here in the big house. And why was it wrong for Gert or Sydney to give her a few whacks, when Miss Gough was allowed to use the cane, even when she was stone-cold sober? Confused, Flora bent her head over the slate and made an attempt at copying the letters, but the scratching of the slate pencil seemed to infuriate Miss Gough even more. She waited until Ivy had left the room before advancing on Flora with malicious intent, however she wreaked vengeance on the slate instead, tossing it across the room with a cry of frustration.

'Is it time for my piano practice now, Miss Gough?' Arabella asked sweetly.

Miss Gough heaved a sigh and nodded. 'Yes, go to the music room. But you stay here, girl. Fold your arms and lay your head between them on the desk. You will recite the alphabet in your head until I return. Come with me to the music room, Arabella.'

Flora did as she was told and closed her eyes. Moments later she was fast asleep.

She was awakened by a gentle hand resting on her shoulder. 'Flora, dear. Are you supposed to be sleeping?'

Flora opened her eyes and lifted her head to find Constance smiling down at her.

'No, missis.'

'No, ma'am.'

'Arabella has gone for a piano lesson, ma'am. I'm learning the letters, but they jumble up in front of my eyes. She's going to whack me again, missis – I mean ma'am.' Tears trickled down Flora's cheeks.

'There, there, Flora. There's no need to cry. You have only just started learning. Arabella has had many lessons. I'll speak to Miss Gough.'

'No, please. She don't like me, ma'am. I'll try to learn me letters.'

Constance put her arm around Flora's shaking shoulders. 'You are little more than a baby. No one is going to hurt you in my house. I want you to be my daughter's companion. I'm not worried about your progress in class. You'll learn in your own good time. I'm afraid Miss Gough is being a little over-conscientious.'

Flora wiped her tears away on her sleeve, but noting her ladyship's raised eyebrows she realised immediately that this also was not done in the best of households.

Constance took a lace-trimmed handkerchief from her pocket and handed it to Flora. 'You wipe your eyes with a hanky, dear. Not on your sleeve.'

'I'm never going to learn to be like you or Arabella.'

'You have no need to copy anyone, Flora. From what I've seen of you it's enough to be yourself. You will learn manners as well as having enough education to see you through life's difficulties, but it will take time. If you are in trouble at all you must come to me.'

'Yes, ma'am,' Flora said meekly. She leaned closer to Constance, inhaling the now familiar scent she wore. It was hard to resist reaching up to stroke the petal-soft skin of her cheek, but Flora managed to control the urge. She was still nervous and afraid of doing the wrong thing, although she knew instinctively that she was safe with Arabella's beautiful mother, which was a new experience. In Flora's short life she had learned to distrust everyone, including those closest to her.

'Good girl.' Constance smiled and patted Flora on the shoulder as she turned to leave the schoolroom.

Flora picked up the slate pencil and did her best to copy the letters in the primer that Miss Gough had laid on the desk for her use. She would not give the dreadful woman the opportunity to call her lazy as well as stupid. The sound of brisk footsteps in the corridor outside the schoolroom heralded the return of Miss Gough. Flora did not look up but she could feel Miss Gough's frustration, and she worked even harder, knowing that the shrieking noise of the pencil on the slate board would grate on anyone's nerves. Eventually Miss Gough sighed and slammed her hand on the desk.

'All right. That's enough for now, Flora Lee. You may go to luncheon.'

'Yes, miss.' Flora wiped her slate with the damp cloth provided for the purpose. She took care to put it away in the desk she shared with Arabella. It was all too easy to upset Miss Gough and she reached for the cane at the slightest excuse. Arabella rarely incurred Miss Gough's displeasure, but Flora lived in constant dread. Miss Gough was a termagant, but her expression could alter in a matter of seconds if she thought that Sir Arthur or Lady Stewart were in the vicinity. Flora made her escape and went in search of Arabella.

On the day of the move to Nine Oaks, South Molton Street was lined with carriages, wagons and a wagonette as the servants rushed around packing everything needed for the journey. To Flora it seemed that the Stewarts took everything apart from the furniture when they moved from one residence to another. Flora had been glad to leave the house as the closed curtains left the rooms in semi-darkness and the chairs draped in Holland covers took on a ghostly appearance. Even so, she was afraid she might be forced to travel with Miss Gough, but fortunately Arabella insisted that Flora should sit next to her in the family barouche, while Miss Gough was relegated to travel in another carriage with Miss Blount and Jefferson. The rest of the servants piled into the wagonette, leaving a caretaker to keep an eye on the house, which was closed until the family chose to return.

As the coachman flicked his whip over the horses' ears and the vehicle trundled off at a sedate pace, Flora was excited at the thought of moving to the country, but slightly scared. Born and bred in the city, she could barely imagine what green fields and forests were like other than in the picture books she had studied avidly in the schoolroom. Flowers, as far as she knew, came in boxes delivered to Covent Garden Market or were sold on street corners by children and old ladies. Vegetables came in baskets piled on top of porters' heads and ended up on market stalls or costermongers' barrows. Arabella laughed at this idea and told her that vegetables came from the walled kitchen garden at Nine Oaks, where dozens of gardeners worked hard to bring the products of their labours to the table. Flora only half believed her, but she was looking forward to finding out.

It took the best part of a day to reach Nine Oaks, which was some eleven miles away. They travelled through the East End and crossed the River Lea, stopping briefly to water the horses and allow the passengers to alight and take refreshment at an inn. It was late afternoon when they reached Nine Oaks, which was situated on the periphery of Epping Forest. Flora and Arabella had fallen asleep, leaning heavily on each other, but Flora awakened first as the carriage came to a sudden halt. She gazed dazedly out of the window, blinking hard in case she was still asleep and dreaming, but she was definitely awake and the grand mansion with white stucco gleaming in the sunshine was definitely real. Wide stone steps led up to a portico over the front entrance and servants stood on either side to greet the master and mistress on their return. Flora had thought that the house in South Molton Street was smart enough, but Nine Oaks was like something out of a story-book. Surely it was the place for a princess to live and not a humble child from the slums. She was suddenly afraid. Perhaps Miss Gough was right about her after all. However, everyone was stirring and Arabella had woken up, yawning and stretching.

Sir Arthur alighted first and handed his wife to the ground, leaving Arabella to be assisted by the footman, who then proffered his hand to Flora. She glanced up at his good-natured face, suspecting that he was laughing at her, but she saw only sympathy in his eyes and an encouraging smile on his lips. She accepted his help.

'Thank you, James,' she said politely.

He acknowledged her words with a wink. 'Best follow them indoors, miss,' he said in a whisper. 'Just do as Miss Arabella does and you won't go far wrong.'

Taking his advice, Flora followed Arabella up the steps, keeping her eyes downcast so that she did not have to meet the curious gazes of the new set of servants. The grandeur of the entrance hall with its curving staircase leading up to a galleried landing, crystal chandeliers and oil paintings in gilt frames was almost overpowering. The delightful scent of the garden roses spilling out of silver urns was quite intoxicating, especially after taking deep breaths of fresh country air. Used as she was to the sooty and often putrid smells of London, Flora was almost overcome. She came to a sudden halt, not knowing what was expected of her now. Should she go upstairs with Arabella, or was she relegated to the servants' quarters? No one had bothered to explain her status in these circumstances.

Sir Arthur was speaking to Jefferson, who had appeared as if by magic from somewhere deep in the house, and Lady Stewart was in conversation with a woman who wore a severe grey gown with a chatelaine hung at her waist. Flora was impressed with the amount of keys dangling from the silver chain as well as a tiny pair of scissors, a thimble and a small silver box. The keys clanked together with each movement the housekeeper made. Flora realised that she must be the topic they were discussing as the grey lady eyed her in a manner that reminded Flora uncomfortably of Miss Gough. Then, as if conjuring up the devil by mentioning his name, Miss Gough strode across the marble-tiled floor to stand respectfully a few paces away from Lady Stewart.

'Ah, Miss Gough. I trust you are not too tired after the journey from South Molton Street,' Constance said, smiling. 'Please take the girls up to the nursery suite and settle them in.'

'Yes, my lady.' Miss Gough beckoned to Arabella.

'Will I send supper for two to the nursery, my lady?' The lady with the chatelaine stared pointedly in Flora's direction.

Constance turned to her. 'Yes, Mrs Fellowes. Perhaps they should have it a little earlier than usual. It's been a long day for everyone.'

'Very well, my lady.' Mrs Fellowes shot a suspicious glance at Flora. 'Is the young person to have a room of her own?'

Arabella had been about to follow Miss Gough upstairs, but she stopped and turned to her mother, frowning. 'No, Mama. I want Flora to share my room.'

Constance smiled fondly. 'If you so wish, my dear. I'm sure a bed can be put up for her. Your room is certainly large enough.'

'Very well, my lady. I'll make sure it's done.' Mrs Fellowes folded her arms across her ample bosom. 'Will there be anything else, ma'am?'

'No, I'm sure you have everything well organised. I'm going to my room to change.'

Miss Gough grabbed Flora by the shoulder and pulled her aside to allow Constance to pass. 'Where are your manners, you dreadful child?'

Flora sighed. There was no answer to that and

both Miss Gough and Mrs Fellowes were glaring at her in mutual distrust. Now she had two people to contend with instead of just one. Not for the first time, Flora found herself wishing she could return to the familiar streets she had always known. At least she knew how to survive in Turnagain Lane and its environs, although if she did go back she would take care to avoid Gert Fox and Sydney.

'Come on, slowcoach,' Arabella called as she raced up the stairs, passing her mother and receiving a mild scolding. Flora noticed that Arabella got away with virtually everything. However, she could not find it in her heart to be jealous. Arabella was a good friend and happy to share everything. Flora was certain they would be together forever, or that's what Arabella told her. She followed obediently up two flights of stairs to the nursery suite, which consisted of one large schoolroom, a separate room for Miss Gough, and a large airy bedroom with views over parkland at the front of the house.

'You can count the nine oaks from here,' Arabella said, kneeling on the window seat and pressing her small nose against the windowpane. 'They were planted by my great-great-grandfather, so I've been told. There's a portrait of him hanging over the fireplace in the drawing room. I'll show you when we go downstairs to say goodnight to Mama and Papa.'

'Maybe I shouldn't come with you,' Flora said shyly. 'I mean, I'm not your sister.'

'You are my sister as far as I'm concerned. My parents bought you to keep me company, so they must want you, too. Don't take any notice of old Gough, she's a misery.'

'She doesn't like me.'

'She doesn't like anyone. She's only polite to Mama and Papa because they pay her wages.'

'You said she will go away soon.'

Arabella laughed. 'Not soon enough. But you're right, Flora. She goes to stay with her sister in Somerset for three weeks this summer. When she's gone, you and I can begin to enjoy ourselves.'

'What do you do in the country? There are no houses or shops that I could see, and no water. I'm used to the river being close by with the docks and all the ships.'

Arabella climbed down from the window seat and did a twirl. 'There's plenty to do. Tomorrow I'll show you the grounds and maybe we can find a pony for you to ride.'

'I don't know how to ride.'

'Then I'll show you, or rather Dobson will give you lessons. He taught me to ride almost before I could walk. Don't worry, Flora. You'll be perfectly fine. I won't let anything bad happen to you.'

Next morning Ivy served breakfast in the school-room. She placed a tray on the table and set out two bowls of porridge, boiled eggs and a rack of toast, plus a dish of butter and another filled with strawberry jam. 'These stairs are going to kill me, Miss Arabella. I declare they're worse than the ones in South Molton Street, and they were bad enough.'

'I'm sorry,' Arabella said gently. 'Perhaps Mama will allow us to eat in the dining room soon.'

'We can but hope.' Ivy pulled a face. 'Seems likely you both have a day off from lessons. I heard that Miss Gough has taken to her bed with a sick headache.'

Flora pulled up a chair and sat down at the table already laid out with cutlery and napkins. She waited for Arabella to start eating; at least that was one thing she had learned during her time in South Molton Street. As to table manners, that was another matter. She tried hard to eat properly, although in Miss Gough's presence this often ended in a sound scolding for eating with her mouth open or slapping her lips when something tasted really nice. If she slumped in her seat that was wrong, but if she sat too upright that also received a frown. Arabella was a better teacher and more patient, although today she seemed preoccupied and ate so quickly that even Flora could not keep up with her. They had barely finished their meal when Arabella jumped up from the table and headed for the doorway.

'Come on, Flora. We can go where we like today. There's no one to stop us.' She darted from the room and made her way to the servants' staircase at the back of the house. Flora could do nothing other than to follow her. As she suspected, Arabella was intent on visiting the stables, which were situated a few hundred yards from the main house. Flora was amazed to find that the horses lived in almost as palatial surroundings as the family. Arabella rushed through the covered archway into an open cobbled yard and was greeted by a middle-aged man with a face wrinkled and brown like a walnut. He came towards them, grinning.

'So you're back for the summer, Miss Arabella. I suppose you want to see your pony.'

'Yes, indeed, Dobson. Right away, please.' Arabella followed him into one of the stables where a pony whinnied at the sight of her and nodded his head up and down in excitement. Arabella reached up to stroke his soft muzzle. 'Star, I've missed you so much.' She turned to Dobson with a persuasive smile. 'Flora can't ride. I said you would find her a nice quiet pony and teach her like you taught me.'

'Does she want to ride, Miss Arabella? She don't look too keen to me.'

'You do, don't you, Flora?' Arabella fixed Flora with a stern stare.

'Oh, yes. Please teach me, mister.'

Dobson eyed her curiously. 'Well now. I'll see what I can do.' He beckoned to a stable boy who was filling up the water trough. 'Fetch Sunny for the young lady and saddle him up while I get Star ready for Miss Arabella.'

The boy nodded and hurried off into a stall further along the row. Arabella was practically dancing with excitement while her pony was being made ready for her to ride. She allowed Dobson to lift her onto the saddle, and she held the reins as if she had been riding all her life as she guided Star out into the stable yard. Flora waited nervously but eventually Sunny was brought to her and Dobson placed her firmly on the saddle. He led the pony out into the sunshine, much to Arabella's delight.

'We can go for a ride in the park,' she cried excitedly. 'It's easy, Flora. Just hold on.'

'Not so fast, Miss Arabella.' Dobson shook his head. 'The child isn't safe on her own.' He summoned the stable boy once again. 'Here, Ted. Take the leading rein. Don't let them go too far.'

Ted nodded and grinned. 'Right you are, sir. Hold on, miss.' Leading Sunny, he followed in Arabella's wake. She urged Star to a trot but Ted held Sunny back. 'Don't worry about Miss Arabella. She's a good rider, you just hold tight, miss.'

Flora needed no second bidding. She was thrilled and terrified at the same time as she clung to the saddle for dear life. Ted walked Sunny very slowly and gradually Flora's fears eased. She could see Arabella with her dark curls flying in the breeze as she allowed Star to canter and then gallop across the grass deer park. She wheeled him round and came back to them at a more subdued trot.

'You'll soon be galloping alongside of me, Flora. We'll go round once more, Ted, and then you can let Flora try on her own.'

'I dunno about that, miss. I was told to bring her safe back to the stables.'

'You'll do as I say,' Arabella said imperiously. 'Now take her round once again, if you please.'

Ted mumbled something beneath his breath, but he did as he was told and when Arabella was satisfied she instructed him to return to the stables. Ted obeyed, albeit reluctantly.

'Now you're free,' Arabella said proudly. 'Come on, Flora. Follow me.' She dug her heels into Star's sides and they went off at a brisk trot.

'Please, Sunny,' Flora whispered. 'Please walk slowly.' She flicked the reins with little hope of success, but Sunny was well trained and he plodded slowly forward. Flora began to feel more confident but she was not prepared when Star cantered past her with Arabella shouting.

'Giddyap.'

Sunny lurched forward and broke into a trot, taking Flora by surprise as they headed towards the red brick of the walled garden. She screamed in fright as they hurtled towards the open gateway and, as if fleeing from Arabella's gleeful shouts, Sunny cantered into the vegetable garden. Seeming to realise his mistake, he came to a sudden halt and Flora found herself flying through the air. She landed with a dull thud in a bed of lettuces where, shocked and gasping for breath, she lay on her back staring dazedly up at the cloudless sky.

'Are you all right, miss?'

Flora raised her head just a little. 'I don't know.' She blinked hard, peering at the suntanned face that seemed to be disembodied as it hovered above her. As he came into focus, she realised it was a freckle-faced boy just a few years older than herself. 'Who are you?'

He grinned, revealing a row of even pearly teeth. 'I'm Daniel. Who are you?'

'I'm Flora. Where's Arabella?'

'I dunno, miss.' He helped her to a sitting position. 'Your pony is eating all the lettuces. I'd best see to him, if you're not hurt.'

'I'm all right.' Flora scrambled to her feet and brushed the dirt off her skirt. 'Don't tell Arabella that I fell off. She'll laugh at me.'

Daniel took the reins and dragged Sunny away from his unexpected feast. 'You are too little to be riding out on your own. I ain't afraid to tell Miss Arabella so meself.'

'Please don't. I do want to learn to ride.'

'There's ways of doing it right.' Daniel led Sunny out of the garden. 'Like as not I'll get the blame for the ruined vegetable bed because I didn't shut the gate.'

Flora followed him outside and closed the gate behind her. 'I'm sorry to have caused you bother, Daniel. I'll tell them it was my fault.'

Arabella rode up to them before he had a chance to answer. 'What happened? You were behind me and then you vanished.'

'She was thrown, miss,' Daniel said, frowning. 'She's just a little scrap of a thing, not fit to be out riding on her own. You should have known better.'

Flora stared at him open-mouthed. No one ever scolded Arabella. She glanced anxiously at her friend, waiting for the inevitable cry of anger, but to Flora's astonishment Arabella seemed at a loss for words.

'I fell off onto the bed of lettuces,' Flora said hastily. 'Daniel helped me, Arabella. He says he'll get into trouble for the ruined crop, but it was my fault.'

Arabella took a deep breath. 'No one is going to be in trouble. Help her back on the horse, Daniel. You may take the reins and lead her back to the stables. I'll find the head gardener and tell him what happened was actually my doing. From now on you'd better have proper lessons, Flora. Some of us are natural riders and some, like you, are not.' She rode off, leaving both Flora and Daniel staring after her in amazement.

'I'll bet that's the first time she's ever taken the blame for anything,' Daniel said, laughing. 'Come on, Miss Flora. Let's get you and the animal back to the stables.' He lifted her back onto the saddle. 'There's nothing of you, missy. How old are you?'

'I'm six, but I'll be seven next month. How old are you, Daniel?'

'I'm ten, but I'll be eleven in a couple of days' time. I'm strong for me age, miss. Now hold on, please. I don't want you toppling off again.'

Flora held on tightly but somehow she was not afraid. 'Maybe I can come and help you put right the damage I did when I fell?'

'I don't think that would be possible, miss. You are from the big house. I'm a servant here like me pa who's a gardener. He'll help me put things right. You don't mix with the likes of me.'

'I am the likes of you, Daniel,' Flora said, sighing. 'And that's the truth.'

# Chapter Three

*Nine Oaks, late April, 1877*

Flora perched on the window seat in the library, her head bent over a copy of *Great Expectations* by Mr Dickens, which was proving to be her favourite book ever. She had discovered the ability to lose herself in a good story when she had first mastered reading at the age of seven. Perhaps she had something to thank Miss Gough for, but it certainly was not kindness nor understanding. It had been a relief when Miss Gough was forced to retire due to her sister's chronic illness, and she had gone to live in Somerset to care for her. Flora had been ten when the torment she had received from Miss Gough ended. She had done her best to be a good pupil, unlike Arabella, who flouted every rule, daydreamed through lessons and did badly in every subject, and yet received copious amounts of praise for the slightest achievement. Flora had learned from the start that life was not fair and her place in the scheme of things was well below that of her dear friend. Arabella was, of course, her closest confidante and ally, but when faced with extreme difficulties, Flora would seek refuge in the walled kitchen garden.

Her somewhat spectacular arrival, when she was tossed over Sunny's head and landed in the lettuce patch, had been the start of an enduring friendship with Daniel. He might be four years her senior, but they had much in common, and a similar sense of humour. No matter how cross or sad she was feeling, Daniel could say or do something that would make her laugh. He taught her everything he knew about plants, whether grown for the table or purely for their intrinsic beauty. He knew the names of all the garden birds and in spring he showed her their nests filled with tiny eggs. When Arabella was enduring a piano lesson or fittings for her many gowns, Flora would make her escape and go in search of Daniel. Sometimes they went fishing in one of the brooks that ran through the estate, or else she would help him in the greenhouse, pricking out seedlings into clay flowerpots. It was an endless source of fascination to see the tiny green shoots grow big enough to plant in the soil. Arabella knew of Flora's friendship with Daniel but she shrugged it off as being a childish whim. After all, she was a few months older than Flora and therefore so much wiser. Flora did not agree but she kept her thoughts to herself.

She glanced at the grandfather clock that stood to attention in the corner of the large, airy room. Arabella would burst through the door at any minute, flushed and breathless from hurrying. If there was anything Arabella hated it was having to stand still for hours while the dressmaker completed the fittings for the gowns she would wear during the London season. Arabella was to be presented at Court at Queen Charlotte's Ball in a week or so, with all the fuss and bother that went with a debutante's coming out. Flora was very glad that she was not included in all the madness, which was supposed to culminate in a good match for the young ladies concerned. She placed a marker between the relevant pages and closed the book. At the last stroke of midday, as predicted, the door opened and Arabella marched into the room.

'Well, that was a waste of a morning. You don't know how lucky you are not to have to endure all this fuss, Flora.' Arabella slumped down on a small sofa. 'We're off to London on Monday and then it will be one party after another.'

'You'll have a wonderful time. You know you will.'

'Some of them will be tolerable, but others will be so tedious, especially the visits to the opera. I hate that awful screeching with everyone putting on a show of enjoyment when really they are bored to tears.'

'It's not so bad. Maybe we can get Ralph to take

us to a music hall. You know he'd do anything for you, Bella.'

Arabella tossed her head. 'Ralph is a dear, but if he thinks I'm going to marry him I'm afraid he'll be very disappointed. I'm going to marry an earl at least. Anyway, I don't think Papa would be pleased if I threw myself away on the first man to fall in love with me. I plan to cut a swathe through the available gentlemen and break a few hearts in the process.'

Flora laughed. 'You are incorrigible, Bella. I pity your poor suitors.'

'But what about you, Flora?' Arabella was suddenly serious. 'I mean, it's all very well my parents going through this expense and to-do, but no one seems to have given a thought to your future. You've become so much a part of the family that you go unnoticed.'

'That's the best way, as far as I'm concerned. I'm truly grateful to your parents for giving me so much, but I never forget that I was taken on as your companion. When you get married my position here terminates. I fully expect that.'

'But that's awful.' Arabella's dark eyes widened in dismay. 'You are my sister, Flora. Maybe not officially, but we've been together for most of our lives. You will have to come and live with me when I get married.'

'I don't think your prospective husband, whoever he is, would be very happy with that arrangement.'

'No matter,' Arabella said firmly. 'He will take us both or I won't agree to marry him.' She rose to her feet, holding out her hand. 'Come. It's time for luncheon and I am starving. We won't talk about this again. My mind is made up and you know how stubborn I can be.'

'I most certainly do.' Flora clasped Arabella's hand and rose to her feet.

Luncheon was a light meal, especially when Sir Arthur was away on business, as he was at present. Flora and Arabella sat at the vast dining table with Constance, and inevitably the conversation turned to the growing list of invitations to balls, parties and soirées already received. Flora had little interest in the social side of the season and she would miss her daily visits to the walled garden where she was sure to find Daniel hard at work. Even so, she was looking forward to spending some time in town. Whenever she was in London she took every opportunity to visit the museums and art galleries, while Arabella was more interested in taking tea at Gunter's or spending hours exploring the new department stores. It was not that Flora had anything against shopping or having new clothes, but she had only a small allowance from Sir Arthur, which she considered very generous in the circumstances, but she had to be careful how much she spent. Arabella was very generous in passing down clothing she had probably only worn once or twice, and they took

the same size in shoes and gloves, which Flora appreciated. It would be nice to be more independent but
there was little chance of that and no opportunity
to earn money for herself. Constance would have
been horrified had Flora suggested that she might
find a paid position elsewhere, and Arabella would
have thought it a huge joke. Flora had realised long
ago that she was trapped by their kindness and
consideration, as much as by love. She owed the
Stewarts everything, but she would never allow
herself to become complacent.

After the meal ended, Constance spirited Arabella
off to the drawing room, where they were to discuss
the final details of the coming-out party to be held
in South Molton Street. Flora was invited to particip-
ate, but she knew they would get on better without
her. She made an excuse and went to the room she
had to herself since Arabella declared she was too
old to share. Flora put on her straw bonnet and lace
gloves, which she considered totally unnecessary, but
she might bump into Mrs Fellowes on the way out
and the housekeeper was a stickler for doing things
properly. As soon as she was clear of the house Flora
tucked the gloves into her pocket and quickened her
pace as she headed for the walled garden.

Daniel was there, as she had hoped. He was hoeing
the soil between rows of feathery carrot tops when he
spotted Flora and he stopped to give her a cheery wave.

'What brings you here at this time of day, Flora?
You don't usually get away so early.'

Flora strolled over to him, smiling. It was always a pleasure to be in his company, and with the prospect of a few weeks' separation it was even more important to spend a little time with him now. 'I can't stand any more chitchat about the London season. It's quite mad in the house. The servants have started packing trunks and boxes ready to leave on Wednesday morning.'

'Then you've come to the right place. There's nothing like the plants, fresh air and birdsong to make everything feel right.'

'You are so lucky, Daniel. I envy you your job and your place in the world. I don't seem to fit in anywhere properly.'

Daniel's smile faded and he dropped the hoe, placing his arm around her shoulders. 'Don't ever think that way. You may not be one of them fine debutante ladies, but you hold a place in all our hearts, especially mine.' He enveloped her in a hug that almost took her breath away.

She smiled up into his weather-beaten face. He was not what might be described as handsome, but his regular, open features, firm chin and pleasant expression drew people to him, and his tall, well-built physique was undoubtedly attractive. His amber eyes seemed to reflect the warmth of the sunshine as his concerned gaze melted into a smile.

'That's better. I hate to see you sad.'

Flora laid her head briefly against his shoulder, but withdrew quickly. Such a sign of weakness would be looked down upon by the family. Strength was in keeping a stiff upper lip, as she had been told so many times while growing up. Certainly the times she remembered when living with Gert and Syd had been harsh, and even though she had been a small child, crying for any reason was punished by a sharp slap. 'There's something to cry for,' had been Gert's favourite maxim. It was something that Flora would never forget.

'I'm only a little sad, and that's because I won't be able to come here and be with you for quite a while.'

Daniel retrieved the hoe and leaned on it, frowning thoughtfully. 'I'd forgotten you were all off to London so soon. Don't go, Flora. Tell the mistress you want to stay at Nine Oaks.'

Flora laughed. 'She might agree, but Bella would never forgive me. She wants me at her side to hold her hand when things get difficult.'

'Knowing Miss Arabella, I imagine she will be too busy to bother about anything other than what gown she is going to wear next.'

'You're wrong about her, Daniel. She's really nervous and she needs me to support her. You can't imagine what some of these parties are like. I've only been a bystander at one or two, but you have to smile until your face freezes, and trying to remember the names of all the important people is a nightmare.'

'All the more reason for you to stay here.'

'You know I would if I could, but I owe the Stewarts everything. Anyway, it's only for a few weeks and then we'll be returning to Nine Oaks.'

'You might get swept off your feet by someone with a title and bags of money.'

'I don't think those sort of gentlemen are looking for a girl from Turnagain Lane, because that's where I came from. You know it and it doesn't matter, but to people like the Stewarts breeding is everything, money comes second.'

Daniel frowned thoughtfully. 'You shouldn't be thinking that way, Flora. I tell you what, I have an idea for your last day of freedom before they carry you off to the city.'

'You make it sound as if I'm going to prison. I promise you it's not as bad as I've been making out. I know I'll miss home, that's all.'

'Leave things to me, Flora. Tomorrow is the first of May, meet me here at dawn and I promise you a day to remember.'

'Really? Are you serious?' Flora met his smiling gaze with a half-smile. 'Are you teasing me, Daniel?'

He held his hand to his heart. 'On my honour. You have nothing to fear, my lady. Never mind the rich toffs in London, I will be your knight for the day.'

Flora was about to reply when she heard her name being called urgently. She turned her head and saw Edna standing in the gateway. She was waving frantically.

'Miss Flora. You're wanted in the drawing room,' she said breathlessly. 'Come quick or I'll be in trouble with Ivy for loitering, although I run as quick as I could.'

'I have to go, Daniel,' Flora said with a rueful smile. 'But I won't sleep a wink tonight for wondering what you have planned.'

'First light, Flora. Don't forget.'

She blew him a kiss as she turned away to follow an agitated Edna back to the house.

'I'm sorry, miss,' Edna said as she led the way into the house through the servants' entrance. 'This is the quickest way.'

'It doesn't matter. I've used this entrance when it suited me. Why all the hurry, Edna?'

'I couldn't say, miss. I just answered the bell and Lady Stewart told me to fetch you immediately.'

'It's all right, thank you, Edna. I'll tell her ladyship that you had to search for me. Don't worry, you won't get into trouble on my account.' Flora hurried on through the twisting corridors until she came to the main part of the house. She knew that Edna had been exaggerating, but then she remembered that Edna had climbed her way up the employment ladder, which was precarious at the best of times. Mrs Fellowes was an efficient but strict housekeeper. She expected nothing but perfection from her staff and a small misdemeanour could send Edna scurrying back to the scullery where she had started years ago.

Flora entered the drawing room to find Arabella and her mother in deep conversation.

'Ah, there you are, Flora.' Constance motioned for her to take a seat. 'We were just discussing the supper dishes to serve at the ball.'

'Yes, you're so much more practical than we are,' Arabella added eagerly. 'We could leave it to Cook, but she has no imagination. What do you think?'

Flora picked up the notebook but the page was blank. 'It doesn't look as if you've got very far.'

'No, we started talking about how I should wear my hair,' Arabella said, giggling. 'And we forgot all about the food.'

Constance leaned back in her chair, sighing. 'I feel quite exhausted by all this. Perhaps you would like to sort it out with Cook, Flora? You always get on so well with the servants and you have a better idea of what is needed than either myself or Arabella. Alas, we are not very practical souls, are we, darling girl?'

'No, Mama. I'm afraid not. I do hope the man I marry doesn't expect me to be well versed in everything. I will need a cook who knows exactly what food to produce for every occasion, and a butler like Jefferson who knows absolutely everything.'

'Whereas you were born to manage servants, Flora,' Constance said with an affectionate smile. 'The man who marries you will be very lucky, but I hope you won't leave home too soon. I don't know how I would manage without your good sense.' She paused, frowning. 'By the way, have you got a new gown for Queen Charlotte's Ball? I know you are not a participant, of course, but Bella will need you there to keep her calm.'

'And to remember the names of all the other young ladies,' Arabella said, pulling a face. 'I simply don't have female friends and I can't be expected to remember each one individually. Whereas you have an amazing ability to put names to faces.'

'I will be there to help, of course, and I have the gown you gave me last winter, Lady Stewart.'

'Ah, yes. I always loved Bella in that one. I remember it now. I think it will do again. All eyes will be on the girls, so the rest of us will pass unnoticed.'

'Quite so,' Flora said calmly. It would have been nice to have a gown designed and made for her personally, but the one Arabella had only worn on a couple of occasions was extremely beautiful. If she were to be honest, Flora considered that the emerald green was far more suited to her auburn hair and green eyes than it was for Arabella, who was a raven-haired beauty with pansy-brown eyes. 'Shall I go and speak to Cook now? Before we get into the fuss and bother of moving everything to the London house?'

'Yes, indeed. You are always so practical, Flora. Thank you, my dear.' Constance closed her eyes. 'You could tell Cook to make me some of the chamomile tisane as I have one of my heads coming. It's all the extra work that the season entails. I will be glad when it's over.'

Next morning, the first day of May, Flora left the house just as dawn was breaking. She managed to get away without being seen by any of the servants, who were going about their normal duties silently in order not to disturb the family. She went straight to the walled garden where Daniel was waiting for her. He eyed her bonnet, shaking his head.

'That's not the right thing to wear on May Day, Flora. Will you take it off for me?'

She laughed as she untied the ribbons. 'What would Mrs Fellowes say?'

'We're going to be pagans for one day.' Daniel tweaked the pins from Flora's hair so that it hung loose around her shoulders, and he placed a crown of wildflowers on her head. 'Now you're my Queen of the May. Just for today, you understand.'

Flora touched the delicate petals of primroses, daisies and the lacy fronds of cow parsley. 'What a lovely thought, Daniel. I didn't know you were so romantic.'

'You'd be surprised. I, of course, am the Green Man, but I'm going in disguise as Daniel Robbins.'

'You are indeed the heart and soul of the Green Man.' Flora laughed. 'This is all very exciting, but where are we going now?'

He took her by the hand and led her out of the

garden to where he had a pony and trap waiting. 'My cousin Ted is in on the secret. He persuaded Dobson to let us use the trap and old Bosun for the day. We'll go in style, Your Majesty.' He handed Flora onto the driver's seat and climbed up to sit beside her. 'We're going to join your subjects in their May Day celebrations.'

'I've seen the maypole they erected on the village green.'

'That's just part of it.' Daniel took the reins and urged the old horse to walk on. The scent of spring flowers filled the air, mingling with the aroma of damp earth and grass crushed beneath the cart wheels. The sun had risen in the east and a warm breeze fanned Flora's cheeks. She shot a sideways glance at Daniel's strong profile and she smiled, remembering her seventh birthday, the first one she had spent at Nine Oaks. With Sir Arthur and Lady Stewart away on a business venture, there had been nobody to organise any kind of celebration for Miss Arabella's young companion. Arabella had asked Cook to bake a special cake, but Cook had deferred to Miss Gough, who had refused to agree to such an extravagance. 'Don't get above yourself, Flora Lee. You are a child from the slums. Never forget that.' Miss Gough's words still rankled and at the time they had almost reduced Flora to tears, but she had endured worse and she managed to hold them back until she reached the walled garden. Daniel had sensed her distress and he had taken her to his grandparents' cottage. His grandmother had given Flora bread and honey and allowed her to play with the last kitten left in a litter of five, the others having found homes. That kitten had been a lifeline to the young Flora, and had earned its place now, lazing in the sun or in front of the fire. Flora still visited her feline friend, taking him small treats she had purloined from the kitchen. The old cook had left years ago and her successor was much more easy-going and a generous provider.

'What are you thinking of?' Daniel asked, smiling. 'You are transparent as a raindrop, Flora Lee.'

She laughed. 'Happy thoughts really, Daniel. You always bring out the best in me. Are we nearly there?'

'Almost.' Daniel flicked the reins and the horse obliged with a slow trot. Minutes later they emerged from a wooded area into the wide-open space of the village green, where girls in white dresses and flowers in their hair were assembled around a chair covered in moss-green velvet. Behind the chair stood the make-believe Green Man, dressed in rather a ragged costume that had seen better days, with fronds of fern stuck in his hair.

'Who is that?' Flora asked eagerly. 'I don't recognise him.'

'It's Tom Polley, the blacksmith. He's going to crown the May Queen.'

'Where is she? I can't see her.'

'She's coming. You can hear the music.'

Flora listened and sure enough she could hear the sound of a tambourine and a drum, accompanying the high-pitched tones of a flute. Moments later the procession, headed by a pretty girl wearing a flowing white gown and a blue cape, walked with her head held high and a happy smile curving her lips.

'I know her,' Flora said in a low voice. 'That's Elsie Root, the scullery maid at Nine Oaks.'

'Well, she might be a scullery maid in real life but today she's the Queen of the May.' Daniel leaped from the driver's seat and walked round the cart. He lifted Flora to the ground as easily as if she had been a feather. 'Today it's all about make-believe. You are my lady, Flora, and I am your servant, Daniel Robbins.' He bowed from the waist, making Flora giggle. She tapped him on the shoulder.

'I dub you a knight of this fairy-tale realm. Arise, Sir Daniel.'

He straightened up, looking into her eyes with a tender smile. 'I am yours forever, my lady.'

'What happens now?' Flora asked hurriedly. She had a feeling that a boundary had been crossed, although she could not explain why.

'The Green Man is about to crown Queen Elsie, and then we will watch the maypole dance. The festivities will go on all day. The morris men will come soon and there'll be games, a hog roast and dancing.'

'I never knew all this existed, Daniel.'

'The family always spirited you off to London at this time of year. You just happen to be here now and I knew you would enjoy it.'

Flora's response was drowned by the sound of a trumpet fanfare, played slightly out of tune by a young man who had mastered the flute but could do with a little more practice when it came to a brass instrument. Whatever the merits of his music, the queen was duly crowned, and the dancers took their positions. The band struck up a tune that Daniel said knowledgeably was called the 'Blackberry Quadrille', and the dance began. Flora found her feet tapping in time to the music and somehow she was holding Daniel's hand in their mutual enjoyment of the moment. They broke apart only to clap at the end of the dance. Then there were tumblers, one of whom Flora recognised as Daniel's cousin, Jim, who was also a gardener on the Nine Oaks estate. The fire eater was Mick Ellis, the baker, whose wife, Annie followed him round with a wet flannel to dampen his beard when it started to singe.

The morris men arrived next and their lively performance, complete with bells and batons, was greeted with enthusiastic applause. By this time Flora had given up trying to put names to faces and she concentrated on enjoying herself. When all the entertainers had performed it was time for everyone to join in the dance, which was led by the Green Man and the May Queen, Daniel whirled

Flora into a lively jig followed by a polka and then a gallop.

The music ended, although there was so much chatter and laughter on the village green that it was some time before the dancers realised their dance had come to an end. Flora leaned against Daniel, breathless and laughing, but the sight of Arabella on horseback, accompanied by Ralph Pettigrew, brought her back to earth with a jolt.

Arabella reined in, controlling her lively horse with an expert hand. 'Flora! What on earth do you think you're doing?' Her gaze fell on Daniel and she frowned. 'You ought to know better, Robbins. You had no right to bring Flora to this pagan festival.'

Daniel held his head high. 'Begging your pardon, Miss Arabella, this is a traditional May Fair. Perfectly respectable.'

Ralph Pettigrew edged his thoroughbred stallion between them. 'Who is this impertinent fellow, Arabella? He should be thoroughly disciplined for speaking to you in such a disrespectful manner.'

'Don't interfere, Ralph,' Arabella said crossly. 'This man is one of the ground staff at home. He'll be dealt with in the proper manner.' She turned to Flora, frowning. 'You look absolutely frightful. Take those silly weeds from your hair. And you, Robbins, see that she gets home safely. I don't doubt that you brought her here.'

Daniel inclined his head. 'I did, Miss Arabella.

And I will see her safe home, but only when she asks it of me.'

'Don't be insolent.' Ralph lashed out with his riding crop, catching Daniel across the side of his face, which left a scarlet weal on his cheek. Acting on impulse, Flora jumped in between them and grabbed the whip, almost unseating Ralph, but he was too strong for her and in pulling his crop free he sent her tumbling to the ground. Arabella's horse reared and Flora was in danger of being trampled beneath its flailing hoofs, but Daniel dragged her to safety.

'Is that how you toffs treat young ladies? Get down off your horse and we'll sort this out like men.' Daniel set Flora back on her feet. He fisted his hands. 'Come on, sir. Or are you too scared to fight a common man?'

Ralph controlled his agitated mount with expert ease. 'I wouldn't stoop to exchange blows with a fellow like you.'

Arabella held up her hand. 'That's enough. You're making a spectacle of us, Ralph. Ride back to the house now.' She wheeled her horse around. 'As for you, Flora. I'm ashamed of you. Go home at once.'

'I don't wish to leave yet,' Flora said defiantly. 'You can't make me, Bella.'

'I think you're forgetting your place. Go home or you may find you haven't got a home to go to. Do you understand?' Arabella dug her heels into her horse's flanks and rode off at a spanking pace, following in Ralph's stormy wake.

'I'm sorry, Flora,' Daniel said earnestly. 'All this was my fault. She's right, I shouldn't have brought you to this place.'

'Nonsense.' Flora tossed her head. 'I am not a servant. I do as I choose, and I want to stay and enjoy the May Fair. What comes next?'

# Chapter Four

Flora stayed on at the May Day celebrations, but some of the enjoyment had been dulled by Arabella's unreasonable behaviour. It was not as if her friendship with Daniel was a secret. Arabella had known from the start that Flora's escape from the somewhat rigid rules that governed their day-to-day life was to spend time in the gardens with Daniel and his family. There had never been a problem until today, although Flora suspected that Ralph Pettigrew's unexpected presence might have something to do with Arabella's sudden change in attitude. Sir Arthur had made it very clear that he expected Arabella to marry well, and Ralph's family pedigree went back to William the Conqueror. Their fortune had been eroded over the centuries but as Sir Arthur said, breeding was everything and Ralph was first in line for a title and a crumbling castle in the West Country.

Arabella would inherit the Stewart family fortune, and even if it had been accrued in trade, it would save Pettigrew Castle from falling into total ruin.

By dusk the gathering was becoming rowdy. Cider and beer had been flowing all day, thanks to the local innkeeper and his wife, and by now everyone was very merry. The music grew wilder and the dancing more vigorous. Couples wandered off into the green depths of the woods only to emerge later looking guilty, smug or simply embarrassed.

Daniel drew Flora aside as a drunken reveller tripped and fell just inches away from them.

'I think perhaps I should take you home, Flora. I don't want you getting into trouble on my account.'

Flora shrugged. 'I don't take any notice of Arabella. She'll have forgotten all about it by now.'

'You don't believe that and neither do I.'

'Well, perhaps not, but I'm not a child.'

'Of course not, but that's all the more reason why I should take you back to Nine Oaks. Whether you like it or not, you depend upon Sir Arthur.'

She met his earnest gaze with a sigh. 'You're right, Daniel. I do depend upon the family for everything, and they could cast me out on a whim. I've been educated above my station in life, but I am not trained to earn my own living.'

'You could get married, Flora. I'll marry you, if you'll have me.'

She shook her head. 'Thank you, Daniel. But that isn't the way.'

'I've always loved you, Flora. You know that.'

'And I love you, Daniel, but it wouldn't work. I've been raised like a lady, not the wife of a gardener. Can you imagine what it would be like if I had to live in your tiny cottage?' She laid her finger across his lips as he was about to argue. 'I would try my hardest to fit in and you would do everything in your power to make me happy, but it would end badly. I don't know how to do the simplest household tasks. I can't cook or sew anything other than fancy embroidery. I don't know how to wash clothes or even how to make a bed. I've had everything done for me since I was six years old.'

'But we love each other.' Daniel took both her hands in his and held them tight.

'We do now, but I'm afraid it wouldn't last. I still have memories of life in Turnagain Lane. I know how poor people scrape a living and end up hating each other.' She wrenched her hands free from his warm grasp. 'I'm sorry, Daniel. I must go home. You stay here and enjoy yourself.' She started off towards the main road but Daniel followed her.

'I don't agree with anything you've said, but you are not going to walk back to the house on your own. Come with me and I'll hitch Bosun to the cart and see you safe to the door. It's no use arguing.'

Flora knew better than to gainsay him in this mood and she went with him to where Bosun was tethered with the other horses. She said little during the drive back to the house and they parted outside the servants' entrance.

'Thank you for today, Daniel,' Flora said softly. 'It's something I'll always remember and treasure.'

He kissed her on the cheek. 'I wish things were different.'

'I know, but perhaps it had to be said. My feelings for you will never change, but it's better to part as friends than enemies.'

'That would never happen. I'll always love you, Flora. No matter what happens.'

She climbed down from the cart and hurried in through the servants' doorway, knowing that it would not be locked until much later in the evening. Tempting as it was, she did not look back. It had cost her dear to refuse Daniel's offer of marriage, even though it had been made on the spur of the moment. One day she would marry, although not yet. There was so much to do before she settled down to married life and rearing a family, but she could not expect Daniel to understand how she felt. It upset her to think she had hurt him, but better that than to agree to his proposal and live to regret a hasty decision. She braced her shoulders and hurried past the open kitchen door where she could see the scullery maid tiredly mopping the floor. The sound of chatter in the servants' hall and the clatter of cutlery on china reminded Flora that she had missed dinner, and that would not have gone down well with Lady Stewart or Arabella. She owed them an apology for staying out so late. A lovely day had been spoiled by her argument with Arabella and now she must face the consequences. Feeling like a naughty schoolgirl, Flora made her way to the drawing room where, to her surprise, she found Lady Stewart drinking coffee and Ralph Pettigrew seated by the window with a brandy glass cupped in his hand.

'I'm sorry to interrupt,' Flora said awkwardly. 'I was looking for Arabella.'

'You may well look guilty, young lady.' Ralph placed his empty glass on a small drum table at the side of his chair. 'You've upset your friend more than you can imagine.'

Constance frowned. 'It's not for you to say, Ralph. Arabella was put out by today's events, but she went to her room because she had a headache.'

'With all due respect, ma'am, you weren't present this afternoon,' Ralph said stiffly. 'There was a very unpleasant scene and if I were Sir Arthur I'd sack that impudent gardener right away.'

'Well, you have no say in how we manage our staff, Ralph,' Constance said tartly. 'I will handle this in my husband's absence.'

'You'll forgive me saying that, in Sir Arthur's absence, and as Arabella's intended, I feel I should be a protector of both you ladies.' Ralph shot a venomous glance in Flora's direction. 'And I do not mean you, Miss Lee. I suggest you retire to the servants' quarters or wherever it is you sleep at night.'

'I am not a servant, sir.' Flora fought back the desire to tell him exactly what she thought of him. 'I am Arabella's companion, and it's up to me to apologise to her for any upset my behaviour might have caused.'

Constance nodded. 'Quite right, Flora.' She turned to Ralph. 'And you, sir, have gone too far. Please remember you are a guest in this house. And as for Arabella, I don't think she has actually accepted your offer, has she?'

'No, not yet, but I live in hope.' Ralph rose to his feet. 'It seems I have offended you, and for that I apologise, ma'am. I have Sir Arthur's permission to request your daughter's hand in marriage. Arabella is taking time to think about it, but I assure you the outcome is a foregone conclusion.'

'We'll see about that.' Flora backed toward the doorway. 'Don't be too sure of yourself, sir.' She turned on her heel and marched out of the drawing room. Angry beyond words, Flora made her way up the wide staircase to Arabella's room and entered without knocking. She stood in the doorway, arms akimbo.

'If you are stupid enough to accept that man's offer of marriage, I wash my hands of you, Arabella Stewart.'

Arabella had been lying on the bed, fully clothed, with a damp cloth pressed on her forehead. She sat up, staring dazedly at Flora. 'What are you doing here? I thought you were having a wonderful time with the commoners.'

'I did have a lovely day, until you and that awful man turned up and ruined everything. What possessed you to speak to me like that, Bella? I thought we were friends.'

'We are friends.' Arabella choked on a sob. 'Don't be mean to me, Flora. I've had a terrible day. Papa seems determined that I should marry Ralph.'

'Since when have you obeyed your father in everything, Bella? You were always the rebel, not me.'

'Ralph will inherit a title from his uncle, who is old and not likely to last the year out, according to Papa. I will become a titled lady if I marry Ralph, but we'll live in a draughty old castle miles away from anywhere. I'll get fat and ugly from child-bearing and Ralph will fritter away my fortune.' Arabella threw herself down amongst the pillows, sobbing loudly.

Forgetting her own feelings, Flora climbed onto the bed to comfort her. 'There, there, it won't be as bad as that. You'll never be ugly, Bella. Even if you get fat, you'll still be beautiful.'

Arabella raised her head with a reluctant giggle. 'You do say such silly things. You always make me laugh.'

'I don't know why I should be nice to you after what you said when you found me on the village green. I was having a lovely time until you and that man arrived. You were quite horrid to me, Bella.'

'I know and I'm truly sorry. I suppose I was taking it out on you because of the awful time I had with Ralph. He used to make me laugh, but he's changed and become so persistent.'

Flora put her arms around Arabella and gave her a hug. 'We'll be in London on Monday. You won't have time for him then, and you'll have suitors by the dozen clamouring for your favours.'

Arabella managed a watery smile. 'You always know how to make me feel better. I am so sorry I was hateful to you. I suppose I was jealous because you looked so happy and you were obviously having a wonderful time.'

'It's forgotten, Bella. We all say things we don't mean at times. You get into your nightclothes and I'll go downstairs to the kitchen. If Cook isn't there, I'll make you some hot chocolate. It's the only thing I know how to do properly.'

'Just ring for Edna, she'll do it for you.'

'They were all at supper when I came in through the servants' entrance. Let her have a break for a change. I might even steal a couple of cakes if there are any, like we used to do when we were younger.'

Arabella's eyes twinkled. 'And jam tarts. I remember you burned your tongue on one because you couldn't wait for it to cool down.'

'I won't make the same mistake again.' Flora headed for the door. 'I'll be as quick as I can.'

Flora slept well that night in spite of the upset caused by Ralph Pettigrew. She got up next morning, washed, dressed and coiled her long hair into a bun at the nape of her neck before going downstairs to the dining room. She was ready to face Ralph and tell him exactly what she thought of a man who tried to bully a young woman into marrying him, but the dining room was empty apart from Edna, who was filling a silver breakfast dish with crisp bacon and devilled kidneys.

'Am I the only one up this early?' Flora said casually.

'Her ladyship is taking breakfast in her room and the gentleman has gone. He left early this morning.' Edna sniffed, making her opinion of Ralph Pettigrew perfectly clear without the need for words.

Flora sighed with relief. She knew if she saw him again she would not be able to keep her feelings hidden, but now she could have her breakfast in peace and Arabella would be able to relax. Flora went to the sideboard and helped herself to a generous amount of bacon and devilled kidneys. Only now she realised that she had eaten very little the previous day, but, despite the emotional turmoil, she had not lost her healthy appetite. She smiled to herself as she sat in solitary state at the huge table, enjoying the delicious meal. Not for her the fastidious pecking at her food like some of the young ladies she had met. She had a good appetite and dim memories of near starvation as a small child were always with her.

'Shall I bring some more toast, miss?' Edna asked with a hint of a smile.

'Yes, please, Edna. And will you make sure a tray is taken up to Miss Arabella? Lady Stewart won't be pleased if we're late getting ready.'

'Yes, miss. Of course.' Edna bustled from the room leaving Flora to savour her meal in peace. When she had finished, she went upstairs to Arabella's room to make sure she was up and dressed.

Arabella greeted her with a wide smile. 'You were right in what you said about Ralph. I hardly slept a wink for thinking about it, but what you said was true. He's not the man for me. I never wanted to be a baroness anyway. Besides which, if his aged uncle finds a closer relative to leave everything to, Ralph will still be a penniless fortune-hunter. I intend to enjoy my coming-out season, and you will share it with me.'

The move back to London went smoothly enough. The servants were used to making the change between town and country, and as far as Flora and Arabella were concerned it was simply exchanging one luxurious bedroom for another. The only difference from their usual routine were the frequent visits to the modiste for final fittings of the gowns that Arabella would wear to all the different functions. Then there were dancing slippers, fans and lace shawls to purchase, requiring many pleasant hours of shopping in the new department stores and small boutiques.

Arabella was in her element but after a couple of

days Flora began to tire of shopping interspersed with afternoon teas taken at some of the grand houses they would be visiting later on for balls and elegant dinners. It seemed to Flora that the young ladies of Arabella's acquaintance were all weighing each other up in order to decide who would be the most challenging rival when it came to snaring a rich husband. Flora was glad to be on the sidelines merely observing the competitive natures that had come to the fore. Old friends were suddenly on opposing sides, uttering sly comments with claws barely sheathed. Worst of all were the mothers of the debutantes, who bristled with ambition and would have frightened the redoubtable Duke of Wellington had they been the opposing army. However, there were many occasions during the first couple of weeks when Arabella was otherwise occupied and that left Flora with little to fill the time other than reading.

She had discovered Hatchards in Piccadilly when she was much younger, and had spent what little money she had left from the allowance that Sir Arthur had given her on purchasing books. Arabella had always teased her and called her a 'blue stocking', but Flora took it all in good part. There was nothing she enjoyed more than getting lost in the imaginary world of a great storyteller. She never felt lonely when she was immersed in a tale about characters who became like real friends, and she was always sad when the book ended and she had to part with them.

The fine May weather gave her a perfect excuse to take an early-morning walk, often stopping for a while in Hatchards, and continuing to Green Park. She liked to stroll amongst the fresh greenery, or sit in the shade of the trees and read a couple of chapters of the book she had brought with her, or one she had purchased that morning. Flora knew exactly how long she had before she must leave the oasis of calm and return to the house in South Molton Street. Arabella would be dressed ready for the first social appointment of that day, and Flora knew better than to be late. Arabella's diary was organised with military precision and timed to the last few seconds, but none of it worked without Flora, who was her companion and chaperone to daytime engagement. Lady Stewart would take on the onerous duty when it came to soirées, dinners and balls. Flora was used to being in Arabella's shadow at such events. She was there to fetch and carry or to fend off unwanted admirers, which she did with a sympathetic smile or a sharp word, if all else failed. The only person with whom this strategy failed miserably was Ralph Pettigrew. He seemed to be everywhere and was an obvious favourite with the society hostesses. Ralph knew how to make himself agreeable, but every so often the mask would slip and his true self would emerge. Flora had personal experience of this, and it made her wary of him. She did her best to keep him away from Arabella, but Ralph was persistent and seemingly oblivious to hints, however broad.

Invitations continued to arrive and sometimes there were several parties to attend in one evening. Flora was kept busy helping Arabella in and out of the family carriage, taking care that the skirts of Arabella's expensive gown did not trail in the dust. The last of these invitations was to a ball in a Park Lane mansion. The host was a wealthy businessman whose wife had social ambitions for their only daughter. Constance Stewart had been going to turn down the invitation, but Sir Arthur had insisted they should accept, as Sir Brandon Barclay was thinking of backing a project close to Sir Arthur's heart. Flora had been listening to the conversation that had taken place at luncheon, and was eager to learn more, but Sir Arthur insisted that business was for the City and not the dining table at home. Arabella and her mother seemed to agree, but Flora was frustrated. Why, she wondered, had the Stewarts bothered to pay for an expensive education for herself and Arabella, when they were not expected to use the brains that God had given them? She broached the subject to Arabella when they were getting dressed for dinner that evening.

Arabella picked up a silk rose and held it to the side of her head as she gazed at her reflection in the dressing-table mirror. 'Do you think I should wear this in my hair, or the pearl hair comb?' Arabella twisted her head, holding up a glittering barrette. 'Or this?'

'The pearl comb,' Flora said, sighing. 'Why do

they treat us like simpletons, Bella? What do you think?'

Arabella selected the comb and handed it to her maid, who was standing patiently waiting for her to decide. 'Yes, I think you're right. The pearl comb is perfect. What was the question? I've quite forgotten.'

'It doesn't matter.' Flora perched on the edge of the bed, smoothing the cool silk skirt of the evening gown she was wearing. 'We are treated like ornaments, that's all.'

'You should forget all that stuff you get from books, Flora. Try to enjoy yourself. I know I will.' She examined her appearance once again. 'Yes, thank you, Mary. That will be all for now.'

'Yes, miss.' Mary bobbed a curtsey and hurried from the room.

Arabella rose from the padded stool and picked up her fan. 'I do hope Ralph isn't at the ball. Although I doubt if he would stoop to attend a function held by someone with new money. Ralph thinks he's already got the title and the castle, but his relative might live on for years.'

'In that case he's angling to marry you and live off your papa. I can't stand that man. If you weaken and marry him, I'll never speak to you again.'

Arabella laughed. 'I'll never speak to myself again if I should be so foolish. Come on, Flora. Let's have a pleasant evening.'

\*

After dining at the Fortescues' mansion in Piccadilly, the family went on to the palatial home of the Barclay family in Park Lane, where the guests were already filing past the host and hostess. Their plain daughter stood at their side, her lips compressed in a tight line and deepening frown lines on her forehead, which did nothing to enhance her appearance. Arabella gave her an impetuous hug, which drew a look of disapproval from Lady Barclay.

'I love your gown, Jane,' Arabella said enthusiastically. 'You must give me the name of your modiste.'

'I hate all this.' Jane cast a sideways glance at her mother. 'I'd rather be in the country. I prefer horses to men.'

'Hush, Jane.' Lady Barclay tapped her daughter with her furled fan. 'People will think you're serious.'

'I am,' Jane said behind her hand. 'Deadly serious.'

Flora gave Arabella a gentle nudge. 'We're holding up the other guests. Maybe we should move on.' She gave Jane a sympathetic smile. 'If it's any consolation, I agree with you.'

They moved on, following Sir Arthur and Lady Stewart to a row of gilded chairs set against the far wall, but Arabella was claimed for the grand parade before she had a chance to sit down. The orchestra had tuned up and Sir Brandon Barclay led his daughter onto the floor. Flora felt for poor Jane, who looked flushed and uncomfortable as she tried to keep up with her father. Arabella was swept onto the dance floor and it would be like this for the rest of the evening. Flora did not expect to be inundated with dance partners, and she sat next to Constance, folding her hands in her lap as she settled down to watch the spectacle. The gowns were lovely and the gentlemen looked elegant in their evening suits. Flora had a couple of dances marked off on her card, but for most of the time she was content to be a spectator. She could not help comparing the formality of the ballroom with the wild abandon of the May dancers on the village green. But that brought back memories of Ralph Pettigrew which settled on her like a cloud, and that cloud had barely lifted when she saw him making his way towards them through the throng of dancers. The stately grand parade had finished and the orchestra struck up a waltz.

Flora tried to look inconspicuous when Ralph stopped to talk to Sir Arthur and paid his respects to Constance, who smiled up at him with undisguised enthusiasm. Flora hoped he would walk away and pick on some unfortunate young woman who had not been selected as a partner, but Ralph turned his attention to her.

'Good evening, Miss Lee. You are looking particularly charming this evening.'

Flora eyed him suspiciously. 'Thank you, sir.'

'Might I have the pleasure of this dance, Miss Lee?'

Flora could hardly refuse without appearing churlish, and most likely upsetting Constance into

74

the bargain. She allowed him to help her to her feet. 'Thank you, sir.'

Ralph took her in his arms, holding her at a decorous length as he led her into the waltz. The floor was so crowded that there was very little space in which to gyrate, and the babble of voices and subdued laughter made conversation difficult.

'You don't like me, do you, Flora?' Ralph squeezed her hand until it became painful.

'No, I don't,' Flora said honestly. 'And neither does Arabella. I wish you would leave her alone.'

'Could it be that you are jealous? Perhaps you have a desire to become a baroness?'

'Definitely not.'

'Or perhaps you would rather jump over the broomstick with the young gardener?'

'You are insulting, sir.'

'At least I've roused your interest.'

'You've proved to me that you are no gentleman.'

Ralph threw back his head and laughed. 'But you are no lady, are you, Flora Lee?'

'I make no pretence of being something other than who you see now.'

'You were born in the workhouse, so I've discovered. Your mother was no better than she should be and you were raised in a slum.'

Flora bit back a sharp retort. 'You seem to know a lot about me.'

'I make it my business to find out things that might be useful in the future.'

'I am just Arabella's companion. What possible interest could that be to you?'

'You have more influence over her than you know. If I find an object, or a person, in my way, I deal with them. Do you get my meaning?'

'Are you threatening me, sir? If you are, I feel bound to tell Sir Arthur. I don't think he would want his only child to marry a man who resorted to such tactics in order to gain her hand.'

'Which is the reason why you are a danger to my future plans, Flora. Either you change your attitude to me or I make use of the information I have about you.'

The waltz ended and the dancers drifted off in pairs, leaving Flora and Ralph standing together. He was still clutching her hand and she could not break away without making it obvious and creating a stir.

'Let me go, sir,' Flora said in a low voice.

'Not until I have your word that you will refrain from making adverse comments about me in Arabella's presence.'

Flora had no intention of pandering to his bullying tactics but she sensed that he was in deadly earnest. She looked round in desperation and was suddenly aware of a stranger edging his way through the crowd, and he seemed to be heading for them.

As if sensing his approach, Ralph turned his head. 'Gabriel! I thought you were dead.'

# Chapter Five

Flora shot a speculative glance at the handsome stranger. Although in evening dress, as were all the men present, this man seemed to exude an aura of authority. He was definitely not someone to be toyed with. Flora could see that Ralph was genuinely shocked, but the newcomer was smiling urbanely.

'I'm sorry to disappoint you, Cousin. Won't you introduce me to your beautiful companion?'

'But your ship went down with all hands, Gabriel. Or so we were informed.' Ralph eyed him warily.

'The news was greatly exaggerated.' Gabriel turned to Flora with a charming smile. 'Since my cousin is not prepared to make the introduction, I am Gabriel Cutler, master of the *Ariadne*, which is unfortunately at the bottom of the Atlantic Ocean. That part was true, but I and my crew escaped, more or less unharmed.'

Flora proffered her hand, which he took and raised to his lips. 'How do you do, sir? I am Flora Lee, a nobody.'

Gabriel laughed. 'I don't believe that for a moment, Miss Lee.'

'Don't waste your time flirting with the girl,' Ralph said crossly. 'She wasn't lying. She is a charity case. A paid companion to Miss Arabella Stewart.'

'Unpaid,' Flora added with a wry smile. 'Sir Arthur and Lady Stewart took me in as a young child. They raised me with Arabella so that we are now more like sisters, but your cousin is quite correct. I was born in poverty and raised by brutes and bullies until I was six years old. I make no pretences as to my origins.'

'Then we have something in common, Miss Lee,' Gabriel said seriously. 'My cousin and I grew up together in a crumbling castle perched on a clifftop. Our esteemed uncle beat us regularly and fed us mainly on gruel, until we were both old enough to be sent away to school.'

'Uncle Peregrine wanted us to be men. Anyway, he's old and not expected to live long now. I would hazard a guess that is why you have come back from the dead to claim your inheritance, but the title and the castle are coming to me.'

Flora glanced round anxiously. 'This isn't the time or place for family arguments. Please keep your voice down, Ralph.'

He turned on her furiously. 'Who are you to tell me what I may or may not do?'

'I said before that I am a nobody, but if you wish to impress Arabella you had better curb your tongue, sir.' Flora returned to the seat next to Constance, who eyed her anxiously.

'What is going on, Flora? Who is that young man? I don't recall meeting him, but he seems to be arguing with Ralph.'

'It's a family matter, ma'am.'

'I don't want a scandal, Flora. Can you do something to stop them making a scene before Arabella returns? I don't want her to see Ralph like this.'

It was on the tip of Flora's tongue to tell Lady Stewart that her daughter already had a very poor opinion of Ralph Pettigrew, but she merely nodded. 'I'll do my best, ma'am.' She walked back to where Ralph was still berating his cousin, although in a more subdued manner. She tapped Gabriel on the shoulder.

'Excuse me, Captain. But I have your name on my card for this dance.'

Gabriel's taut expression melted into an amused smile and he proffered his arm. 'How churlish of me to forget. May I have the pleasure of this polka, Miss Lee?'

She laid her hand on his arm. 'I'd be delighted, Captain Cutler.'

Gabriel whirled her onto the dance floor and the lively tempo of the dance made conversation almost impossible. However, he proved to be an excellent dancer and Flora was enjoying herself for the first time that evening. She was sorry when the music stopped and the couples wandered off to rejoin their respective parties.

Gabriel proffered his arm. 'I see that my cousin is making himself agreeable to that lady, who I guess must be the mother of your friend, Arabella.'

'Yes, she is. That is Lady Constance Stewart. Her husband, Sir Arthur, is not far away, and I can't see Arabella at the moment. I imagine she is doing her best to avoid Ralph.'

'He is not a welcome suitor?'

'Arabella has a mind of her own. I'm sorry to speak ill of your cousin, but she can't abide him, and neither can I.'

'Your honesty is commendable. I don't like him either.'

Gabriel's whimsical smile made Flora giggle. 'Thank goodness for that.'

'Shall we venture into the supper room? That way we can avoid Ralph and I can keep your admirers at bay while we get to know each other.'

'Arabella is the one with a full dance card, I am what you might call a professional wallflower.' Flora laid her hand on his sleeve and they walked slowly towards the room set aside for refreshments. There was quite a queue by now, but Flora was in no hurry. There was something about Gabriel Cutler that was both fascinating and exciting.

'Now that I do not believe. But if the other gentlemen here are too interested in fortune hunting,

I will put my name down for every last dance on your card. They will be the losers.'

Flora shot him a sideways glance. She was not sure if he was teasing her, but she was quick to see a flash of anger in his eyes and she realised that he meant what he said.

'Are all seafarers as bold as you are, Captain Cutler?'

'When one spends most of one's life at sea there seems to be little sense in wasting precious moments ashore with polite niceties.' Gabriel led her to a table. 'Why don't you take a seat and I'll fetch us both something to eat. What takes your fancy?'

Flora sank down on one of the spindly gilt chairs. 'I'll have whatever you're having, but only a little. We had dinner before we came here.'

'Don't worry. I'll finish off what you can't manage. I'm starving.' Gabriel joined the group of gentlemen who clustered around the table set with a tempting array of delicacies. Flora did not think she could eat anything, but she did accept a glass of champagne from a passing waiter. She sat sipping the wine as she watched Gabriel move effortlessly between the other men, who made way for him without question. Normally sceptical, Flora was impressed, and eager to learn more about the sea captain who had suddenly come into her life. She waited until he returned with the plates of food and set them on the table.

'What happened at sea?' Flora asked eagerly.

'Were you caught in a storm, or boarded by marauding pirates who sank your vessel?'

Gabriel took a seat opposite her. 'The latter would have been more exciting, but it was a storm in the Bay of Biscay that sent my poor *Ariadne* to the bottom. We did everything we could to save her, but in the end I had to give the order to abandon ship.'

'That must have been a terrible experience. How did you survive?' Flora picked at a small helping of lobster in aspic and a slice of cold chicken, while Gabriel tucked into game pie, ragout of lamb and slices of roast beef.

'We manned the lifeboats and were eventually picked up by a French fishing boat.'

'What happens now that you've lost your ship?'

'A good question. I'm hoping that Sir Brandon will have a vessel for me. The *Ariadne* belonged to his shipping company.'

'Oh!' Flora glanced round the room, but there was no sign of Sir Brandon or his wife. However, Jane and one of her sisters were seated at another table enjoying the company of several young men. Flora turned back to Gabriel. 'A match with one of those young ladies might prove helpful in finding another ship.'

Gabriel smiled, shaking his head. 'I'm no fortune hunter, Flora. In fact it was Lady Barclay who invited me.'

'Perhaps she had you in mind as a prospective son-in-law?'

'I don't think a relatively poor seafarer would be her idea of a perfect match. She is a very nice lady and I think she took pity on me because I am on my own.'

'Is Ralph your only relative?'

'Apart from our uncle, yes. Ralph and I were orphaned when our parents died within months of each other. Mine lost their lives in Meerut at the beginning of the Indian Rebellion. Ralph's mother died in childbirth, and his father succumbed to cholera in the same year. That's why we both ended up in Pettigrew Castle with Uncle Peregrine.'

'I'm so sorry, Gabriel. That's such a sad story.'

'We were both very young. I was eight years old and Ralph a few months younger. Anyway, we survived. That's the main thing, as did you. It seems we have much in common, Flora Lee.'

She laughed. 'I don't know about that, but I'm glad we met. I wasn't looking forward to tonight, or any of the other functions, if I'm to be honest.'

Gabriel sat back in his chair, eyeing her closely. 'So where would you rather be?'

'I love the house in Essex. Daniel, the head gardener's son, took me under his wing when I was a small girl. He taught me about plants and birds – all sorts of things.'

'You were lucky to have such a good friend.'

'Yes, although it's not so easy now. Lady Stewart is very kind, but she doesn't approve of me mixing with the servants, even though I am a servant of sorts.'

'Surely that's not how Miss Stewart treats you?'

Flora shot him a sideways glance. 'Is this what it's all about, Gabriel? Are you being nice to me in order to get close to Arabella? I wouldn't blame you if that was so. She's a great catch and she'll inherit a large fortune one day, besides which, she's a sweet girl – most of the time, anyway.'

Gabriel's winged eyebrows shot together in a frown. 'No! That most certainly is not my ambition, Flora. I'm not looking for a rich wife, or any wife, if it comes to that. The woman who married me would have to live for months or even years on her own while I am at sea. She would never know when I was coming home, if at all.'

'You are a merchantman,' Flora said thoughtfully. 'I believe wives often sail with their husbands. Is that not so?'

'They do, sometimes. Even so, it's no life for a gentlewoman.' Gabriel rose to his feet, holding out his hand. 'I believe they are playing a waltz. As my name is on your card for every dance, I believe this is mine. Shall we?'

Flora rose to her feet. 'You said that you are older than Ralph. Doesn't that make you in line to inherit from your uncle? You could purchase your own vessel then.'

'Ralph should be next in line, but I believe Uncle Peregrine disinherited his brother, Ralph's father, after a bitter family quarrel. I don't personally care. What would I want with a leaky old ruin and a useless title? Ralph is welcome to both.' Gabriel took her by the hand and led her back to the dance floor.

He was as good as his word and danced every dance with Flora until the very end. Many people had already left, but Sir Arthur seemed reluctant to leave his business associates. Flora was surprised to see Lady Stewart in a militant mood as she prised her husband away from the group of gentlemen. Ralph had stayed, although with little encouragement from Arabella, who in the end simply turned her back on him and refused to be drawn into conversation. Flora and Gabriel exchanged meaningful glances.

'I should be leaving now,' Gabriel said in a low voice. 'But I need to make sure that my cousin doesn't make a fool of himself.'

'You feel responsible for him?' Flora gave him a searching look. 'Why should you? He doesn't appear to be pleased that you survived the shipwreck.'

'Are you always this direct, Flora?'

'Only when I'm stating the obvious. If Ralph had any affection for you he should be shouting your return from the rooftops. I know I would.'

Gabriel took her hand and raised it to his lips. 'I believe you.'

'Flora!'

Constance Stewart's voice made Flora turn with a start.

'Yes, ma'am.'

'It's time to go home.'

Flora realised that Gabriel was still holding her hand and she snatched it free. 'Yes, ma'am. I'm coming.' Flora turned to see Arabella standing with her father and, judging by the sulky expression on her pretty face, she was not too happy.

'Goodnight, Flora,' Gabriel said softly. 'May I call upon you tomorrow?'

'That would be lovely,' she said over her shoulder as Constance gave her a gentle nudge towards the doorway.

'Don't encourage him.' Constance shot a wary glance at Gabriel as she led a reluctant Flora to join Arabella and Sir Arthur. 'Men with the sea in their blood make very poor husbands, my dear. And I believe he is penniless. You can do better for yourself.'

Flora could think of nothing to say and she could see that Arabella was scowling at her. 'What's the matter with you?' Flora demanded as they followed Arabella's parents out through the grand hall to the waiting carriage.

'You monopolised the only interesting man for the whole evening.' Arabella tossed her head.

'You were surrounded by eager young men, no doubt the cream of society. Why would you begrudge me a few dances?'

Arabella sighed. 'I had to keep Ralph at bay. That's your job, Flora. He would not take the broadest of hints.'

Sir Arthur cleared his throat noisily. 'That's enough, girls. I don't want to hear any more bickering.'

Arabella huddled in the corner of the seat, gazing out of the window, leaving Flora to enjoy the memories of that evening. She could still hear the music and feel the strength of Gabriel's arms around her in the waltzes and the polkas. Even so, she could not prevent a feeling of guilt intruding on her pleasurable thoughts. Until now the only man in her life had been Daniel, but this evening she had forgotten him completely. It felt as if she had betrayed her dearest friend.

'We're home,' Constance said wearily. 'It's been a very long evening. Wake up, Arabella. It's time you were tucked up in bed. We have another busy day tomorrow.'

'It is tomorrow already, my love.' Sir Arthur rose from his seat as the footman opened the carriage door and pulled down the step. Sir Arthur alighted and held out his hand to help Constance alight. They entered the house together, leaving Arabella and Flora to make their own way.

'I'm sorry if you were upset,' Flora said softly as they crossed the entrance hall, pausing at the foot of the staircase. 'I didn't think you would be interested in a man like Gabriel.'

'I'm not.' Arabella shrugged. 'But you were having such a wonderful time. I suppose I'm not used to seeing you enjoying yourself.'

Flora giggled. 'You mean you're used to seeing me sitting out each dance like the wallflower I truly am.'

'Yes, I suppose I am,' Arabella said with a reluctant smile. 'It was mean of me. I am sorry, too, Flora. You deserve to have some fun, and your captain was the most dashing man in the ballroom.'

'He didn't know anyone at the ball, and I think he wanted to provoke his cousin. I don't think he likes Ralph any more than we do.'

'I'd like to get to know your captain, especially if it upsets Ralph. To be honest, I'm already rather bored with the young men I meet every day. Captain Cutler seems very interesting.'

'I think it's time we both got some sleep,' Flora said hastily. She knew that Arabella's affections were fickle when it came to men. She had broken a few hearts already and somehow Flora did not want her to inflict similar pain on Gabriel, even if unintentionally. Arabella was never cruel, but her pampered existence had led her to believe that she could have anything and anyone she wanted.

'Goodnight, Arabella.' Flora picked up a candlestick and ascended the stairs. All she wanted to do was to go to bed in her own room and dream of dancing in the arms of a handsome man.

'Wait for me,' Arabella said plaintively. 'I am desperate to hear everything that passed between you and the sea captain.'

'I'm afraid you'll have to wait until morning, Bella.

I'm too tired to think, let alone talk. I really must go to bed.' Flora hurried on despite having sore feet. She did not stop until she was in her room. With a sigh of relief she closed the door and started to undress. Unlike Arabella, Flora had no maid to wait upon her, but she was used to looking after herself, and she valued the quiet moments she spent alone in her room. She slipped on her nightgown and climbed into bed. She lay down and closed her eyes but, in her mind she was transported back to the ballroom. The strains of the orchestra playing a waltz lulled her to sleep.

When Flora awakened next morning she was struck with a feeling of guilt. She could have spent time with Arabella before going to bed, and perhaps she ought to have shared what little she knew of the captain with Bella. They had never had any secrets from each other until now. However, Captain Cutler had been present at the Barclays' ball with the intention of speaking to Sir Brandon about a replacement for his lost ship. He had made it very clear that he had not been there in search of a wife. Perhaps she should share that piece of information with Arabella, who was a hopeless romantic, and might already have imagined herself in love with the enigmatic stranger. Flora washed, dressed and put up her hair before going downstairs to the dining room where she hoped to find Arabella, but there was no sign of her and Flora breakfasted on her own. She was just finishing her last cup of coffee when Arabella walked into the room.

'You won't believe the nerve of the man,' Arabella said crossly. 'Ralph has just left his card, asking me to meet him for luncheon today. As if I had no other appointments. Who does he think he is?'

'You don't have to give him an answer.' Flora dabbed her lips with her napkin. 'Sit down and have some breakfast.'

'I'm not hungry, but I will have some coffee.' Arabella slumped down on her usual chair at the table. 'Of all the gentlemen who were at the ball last evening, why did it have to be Ralph Pettigrew who left his card?'

'He's determined to court you, Bella. I suppose it's flattering in a way.'

'Nonsense. He's just after my money. Now if Captain Cutler had asked me to luncheon, that would have been different.' Arabella gave Flora a searching look. 'He hasn't contacted you, has he?'

'No, of course not. I told you, Bella, he only danced with me because he didn't know anyone else at the ball. It was Ralph who introduced us.'

'I want you to do something for me,' Arabella said earnestly. 'I need you to speak to Ralph and tell him that, no matter how many castles he might have, I have no intention of marrying him. He could be a prince and I still wouldn't look at him twice.'

'I don't think he'll take any notice of me, Bella. You've already made it perfectly clear that you aren't interested in him.'

'You must try. Please, Flora. If word gets round that I'm seeing Ralph Pettigrew it will put the other young men off, especially his handsome cousin.'

'But I don't know where Ralph lives.'

Arabella produced a gilt-edged visiting card that she had tucked into the neck of her morning gown. 'It's here. You must take a cab and go there in person. Please, Flora, do this small thing for me.'

Flora realised that to argue would be futile. Once Bella had made up her mind there was very little that would sway her from her purpose. 'All right. Give the card to me. I'll do it, but I doubt that anything I have to say will make a difference.'

Arabella smiled delightedly. 'I knew you would help me. You are my sister in all but blood. Thank you, Flora dear.' She clapped her hands. 'Actually, I think I might manage to eat something. Will you ring for Ivy on your way out? I want more coffee and fresh toast.'

With the visiting card tucked into her reticule, Flora left the house and was about to hail a cab when one drew up at the kerb and Gabriel Cutler alighted. He doffed his hat, giving her a smile that lit up his blue eyes so that they sparkled in the early morning sunlight.

'Good morning, Miss Lee. It seems that I am just in time to catch you before you go out. Although shouldn't you be accompanied by a maid?'

Flora felt the blood rush to her cheeks. His smile was even more devastating this morning and she was momentarily at a loss for words. She shook her head and took a deep breath.

'Good morning, Captain Cutler. I'm on an errand for Miss Stewart.'

'Might I accompany you? I find myself with a little time on my hands this morning. I was hoping to see you again.'

'Surely it's Arabella you wish to see, sir? I am just her companion.'

'She is a very lucky young lady, and no doubt very charming, but it was you I came to see.'

Flora had a sudden vision of Arabella's expression if she knew she had been passed over for a girl with nothing other than her looks to commend her. She and Arabella might bicker occasionally, like real siblings, but Flora was genuinely fond of Bella and would do nothing to hurt her.

'I really have an important mission, sir. Perhaps another time.' Flora started walking but Gabriel fell into step beside her.

'I hope you won't mind if I make sure you get to your destination safely, Flora.'

She came to a halt, turning to give him a straight look. 'You aren't used to being denied anything, are you, Captain? Well, this time you must respect my wishes. I have a personal errand to run for Miss Stewart, so please allow me to go on my way.'

He took a step backwards, his brows drawn together in a frown. 'I beg your pardon. I didn't realise I was intruding.'

Flora was tempted to tell him the truth, but as Ralph was his cousin it might complicate matters. She hardly knew Gabriel Cutler, but it was better if she did what she had to do on her own. She inclined her head in a polite nod and walked on, hoping he would not follow. She resisted the temptation to look back. Even so, as she hurried along the busy London streets she had a feeling that he was following at a discreet distance.

It was not very far to Hay Hill, but she was hot and out of breath from hurrying when she reached the address on the visiting card. The property in question was a five-storey house just off Berkeley Square. Flora stood with her hand on the door knocker, momentarily losing her nerve. She did not relish the thought of a confrontation with Ralph Pettigrew. Despite his urbane exterior, she had a feeling he could turn nasty if crossed. But she had promised Bella and she could not simply walk away. She rapped on the door and took a step backwards, half hoping that no one would answer. However, the sound of approaching footsteps put a stop to her retreat. The door opened slowly.

'Well. What d'you want?' An elderly woman glared at Flora. She looked more like a cleaning woman than a housekeeper. Her white mobcap was askew on a head of thinning grey hair, and she wore a grubby white apron over an equally grubby cotton blouse and skirt.

'Is Mr Pettigrew at home?'

'I dunno. I ain't his servant.' The woman was about to slam the door when a booted foot placed strategically over the doorstep made her look up in alarm.

Flora turned to see Gabriel standing at her side. 'You followed me.'

He shook his head. 'I was on my way to visit my cousin. I didn't know this was your destination.'

'Get off me front step,' the woman snarled.

'If you won't tell Mr Pettigrew that we are here, I suggest you let us in and we'll do it for you.' Gabriel towered over her and she shrank back into the hallway.

'Top floor. Cheap attic room. Tell him to pay what he owes me in rent.' The woman stomped off and her footsteps echoed off the high ceiling.

'Are you sure you want to do this, Flora?' Gabriel followed her to the foot of the stairs. 'I could give Ralph a message for you. Unless you really want to speak to him yourself.'

'Were you truly on your way to see him?' Flora eyed him curiously. She could not quite make him out.

'I did intend to see him at some point today, but I merely followed you to make sure you reached your destination safely.'

'I know my way about London,' Flora said stiffly. 'I have a message from Miss Stewart that I must pass on in person. She'll want to hear his response from me.'

'After you, then.' Gabriel stood aside while Flora ascended the steep flight of stairs. It was quite a climb to the top floor, and if she were to be honest she was glad that Gabriel was with her. The house had definitely seen better days, but now it was dilapidated, dirty and the smell of blocked drains permeated the whole building. There were several doors leading off the small top landing and Flora hesitated, unsure which one belonged to Ralph. Then, without warning, the door opposite flew open and Ralph ejected a rough-looking man with unkempt wiry hair, streaked with grey, and garments that smelled as bad as they looked.

'Get out and don't come here again,' Ralph said angrily. 'You'll have your money when you do the job I paid you for.' He broke off, staring at Flora and Gabriel. 'Why did you bring her here, Cutler? You should know better.' He lashed out at the scruffy individual, causing him to stumble. 'Get out of here now.'

Flora took a step backwards, staring in dismay at the man as he scrambled to his feet. She had not seen Sydney Fox for twelve years, but she would never forget that face.

# Chapter Six

Gabriel took her by the arm and guided her into the dingy attic room. The only light filtered through dirty panes in the roof window, and the lingering smell of an unwashed body mingled with a hint of stinking cockroaches and stale beer.

'Are you all right, Flora?' Gabriel asked anxiously. 'Did he knock you as he barged past?'

Flora shook her head. 'I'm not hurt.' She was afraid she might be sick at any moment and the heat beneath the sloping ceiling was suffocating. 'Who was that man?'

'Yes, Ralph. I don't think much of your choice of friends.' Gabriel pressed Flora gently onto the only chair in the room that did not seem to be broken.

Ralph slammed the door. 'I don't know the fellow.'

'But you were talking to him, Ralph. You must know him or you wouldn't have let him into your room. What's going on?' Gabriel faced his cousin with a set jaw. 'What mess have you got yourself into this time?'

'I admit that funds are somewhat short.' Ralph perched on the edge of the iron bedstead. 'You can see the dire position in which I find myself, thanks to the stinginess of our illustrious uncle.'

'You could find some employment, Cousin. I have.' Gabriel glanced round the squalid room with an expression of contempt. 'You're living like an animal.' He turned to Flora. 'Let me take you home. This isn't a fit place for a lady.'

'I didn't ask either of you to come here,' Ralph said testily. 'Take her away and fill her head with nonsense if you will, but don't believe everything he tells you, Miss Lee. My cousin is a liar and a fortune hunter.'

'Miss Stewart asked me to come here.' Flora took a deep breath. 'She doesn't want to see you again, sir.'

Ralph curled his lip. 'But her papa is very keen on his daughter marrying into the nobility, and he has the money to procure a titled husband for her.'

'You delude yourself, Ralph.' Gabriel held his hand out to Flora. 'No man in his right mind would want his daughter to marry you.' He turned to Flora with a sympathetic smile. 'Please allow me to take you home.'

Flora rose somewhat unsteadily to her feet. A cold shudder had run down her spine at the sight of Sydney Fox.

'Yes, I want to go, but first I must know why that man was here.'

'Are you certain you've seen him before?' Gabriel said gently. 'You could be mistaken.'

'I think it was the same person, but it's many years since I last saw him.'

'That man was trying to extort money from me. It was a gambling debt that I had overlooked.' Ralph eyed Flora keenly. 'Are you sure that Miss Stewart sent you here, Flora, my dear? Could it be that you have an ambition to become a baroness?'

'Certainly not, sir.' Flora forced herself to sound calm. 'The message from Miss Stewart is perfectly clear. She does not want you to contact her again.'

'I need to hear it from her own lips, not yours.' Ralph turned to his cousin. 'Why are you here, Gabriel? Are you trying to ingratiate yourself with the heiress by looking after her companion?'

'No such thing, Ralph. I happened to meet Miss Lee on the way here. I was simply going to tell you that I have no interest in claiming the title or the estate when our uncle passes away.'

'You are the elder by a couple of months it is true, but I was always his favourite.'

Gabriel threw back his head and laughed. 'You suffered as many beatings as I did – I remember our uncle calling you a nasty little sneak. But you are welcome to the inheritance. I want none of it.'

Ralph turned to Flora. 'There you are, Miss Lee. You are a witness to my cousin's decision.'

'It has nothing to do with me,' Flora said firmly. 'I've delivered the message I came with, so I'll bid you good day.'

'You can tell Miss Stewart that I don't give up so easily.'

'I'll see you safely home, Flora.' Gabriel paused in the doorway. 'We're leaving, Ralph. I suggest you either seek financial help from our uncle, or you look for gainful employment. I want nothing more to do with you. That's what I came to say.'

Flora managed the flights of stairs even though her knees were shaking and she felt as though she was suffocating. Gabriel was close behind her and he opened the front door.

'You're very pale. Flora. Are you sure you're all right?'

She took deep breaths of fresh air. 'I will be in a few moments.'

'Did you really recognise the man who was here when we arrived?'

'I don't know. I was only six when the Stewarts took me in as I told you before. But he did remind me of the man who taught me to pick pockets and made me beg on street corners, no matter what the weather was like.'

'I am so sorry. Your early years must have been hell on earth.'

'I knew nothing different. Syd was bad enough,

but I seem to remember that his wife was even worse. She would smile as she pinched and slapped me, as if she enjoyed being spiteful.'

'It doesn't bear thinking about. It was bad enough for us boys to be beaten, but I don't know how anyone could be so brutal to a defenceless little girl. Come, Flora. I'll take you home. You've done what you set out to do.' Gabriel stepped off the kerb to hail a passing hansom cab.

Flora glanced round nervously but there was no sign of the man who had brought back such unhappy memories. The fact that he reminded her of Syd Fox was probably a coincidence. She was grown up now and neither Syd nor Gert could do anything to harm her. She climbed into the cab and made room for Gabriel to sit beside her. Her emotions were still in turmoil as the memories of childhood came flooding back. In the ensuing years she had pushed them to the back of her mind, helped to a great extent by Daniel. He had shown her the wonders of nature and the soothing properties of observing plants and wildlife. He could find something of interest in all seasons, even in the depths of winter. Daniel had understood her moods without the need for long explanations.

'Flora, you haven't heard a word I just said.'

She turned her head to give him an apologetic smile. 'I'm sorry. I was miles away. What did you say?'

'It's all right. You've obviously had quite a shock,

but if you are worried about that man just say the word and I'll seek him out.'

'Thank you, but it was probably my imagination. As I said, it was all a long time ago.'

'I'm at your service, should you need me, Flora.'

She shot him a sideways glance. 'I'm sure you have more pressing things to do, Captain. You must be anxious to find another ship.'

He laughed. 'Not particularly. I was just a boy when my uncle paid the captain of a merchant ship to take me on as an apprentice, leaving Ralph to finish his education at Oxford. I had very little choice in the matter.'

'Your uncle doesn't seem to be a very fair-minded man.'

'He never wanted children but he found himself looking after two small boys, so I suppose he did the best he could. I've no complaints about my life at sea, although there are disadvantages to being away for years at a time.'

'From what you said to your cousin, it sounded as if you should inherit from your uncle.'

'Ralph is welcome to it all, including the debts that go with it, and the upkeep of a crumbling ruin. He is in desperate need of a rich wife. You should warn Miss Stewart.'

'Arabella knows that,' Flora said firmly. 'She wants nothing to do with Ralph.'

'We're here,' Gabriel said as the cab drew up outside the house in South Molton Street. 'I'll wait until you're inside and then I'll be on my way.' He alighted from the cab and held his hand out to assist Flora. 'I hope to see you again. May I call on you tomorrow morning?'

Flora met his steady gaze with a smile. 'Please do. I'll look forward to it, Captain.'

He raised her hand to his lips. 'It's Gabriel, please.'

'Very well. I'll see you tomorrow, Gabriel.' Flora could see the footman holding the front door open, leaving her no excuse to loiter. She crossed the pavement and stepped into the entrance hall to be met by Arabella.

'I saw you with Captain Cutler. Why didn't you ask him in?'

'It's not my place, Bella. You would be the first to complain if I took advantage of my situation.'

Arabella tossed her head. 'I would not. You are my sister, Flora. You know that very well, and I wanted to get to know the handsome captain. He is so different from the type of young man I meet daily during the season.'

'He asked if he could call on us tomorrow morning.'

'What did you say to that? Don't tell me you refused because of some silly misconceived sense of duty?'

'No, I said he would be most welcome.'

Arabella gave her a hug. 'Come into the morning parlour and tell me everything. Did you see Ralph? What did he say? And how did you come to be in a cab with Captain Cutler?'

'I'll tell you in private, unless you want everyone to know your business.'

'Of course.' Arabella took her by the hand and dragged her across the hall to the morning parlour. As soon as they were inside she closed the door. 'There, no one can hear us now. Tell me everything.'

Flora peeled off her lace gloves and undid the ribbons on her bonnet. She needed time to compose herself. She decided against mentioning Sydney Fox, after all, it might not have been him. Gabriel had been quite right in advising her to put him out of her mind, although it was not going to be easy. The memories of early childhood that she had tried so hard to forget had been brought back with a suddenness that was both alarming and shocking. It could serve no useful purpose to confide in Bella, and to talk about it would make it seem more real. 'I met the captain quite by accident,' Flora said casually. 'He was on his way to visit his cousin.'

Arabella listened intently while Flora gave her a brief account of her meeting with Ralph. 'So Ralph understood that I do not wish to see him again?'

'I hope so, but you never know with someone like him. I told him that you didn't want anything to do with him, and Gabriel confirmed it.'

'Gabriel? You are already on first-name terms?'

'He asked me to call him by his first name. I don't have to follow the strict etiquette laid down for you, Bella. You're a lady and I am just me.'

Bella laughed. 'You are funny, Flora. You know

very well that gentlemen admire you. Sometimes I am quite jealous.'

'You need not be. I have nothing to offer any of the young men who are looking for wives this season. Their parents would be horrified if they knew about my background. I don't really know who I am, and I don't want to think about those early years before your mama saved me.'

Arabella gave her a hug. 'You will always be my sister. If you can't find a rich husband you will have a home with me. You can be a lovely aunt to my children and they will run to you when I am cross with them. They will confide their troubles in you because I will be too busy being the wife of someone very important.'

They both subsided in fits of giggles but were interrupted when the door opened and Constance marched into the room.

'Why aren't you girls dressed ready for luncheon at the Hamiltons'? You know we were invited last evening, Arabella. Did you forget to mention it to Flora?'

'No, it's my fault,' Flora said hastily. 'I'm afraid I forgot all about it. We'll be ready in five minutes.'

'Better make that ten minutes,' Arabella added as she headed towards the door. 'Or even fifteen.'

Luncheon at the Hamiltons' mansion in Sloane Square was pleasant enough with the usual selection of guests, most of whom Flora knew by sight, although she was content to remain in the background while Arabella did all the socialising. The food was delicious, but most of the ladies picked at their meals, perhaps worrying that their expensive gowns might get a little too tight if they over-indulged. Or even worse, that they might be accused of gluttony. Flora observed all this without comment, but it did seem unfair that so much food might go to waste when there were people starving on the streets in the poorer parts of London.

That evening there was a visit to the opera, which Arabella hated and Flora quite enjoyed, followed by a late supper at Rules in Maiden Lane. It was well past midnight by the time Flora fell into bed, exhausted by a day of contrasts. The brush with someone who could have been Syd Fox's double had disturbed her more than she cared to admit, and as she lay down to sleep she was afraid she might relive the past in a series of bad dreams. The best part of the day had been meeting Gabriel again, and she would be seeing him again in just a few hours. With that soothing thought uppermost in her mind, she closed her eyes and fell into a deep sleep.

Next morning Flora was surprised to find Arabella had risen early. She sashayed into the dining room for breakfast, dressed in what was really an after-noon gown with a rather daring décolletage for so early in the day. However, she brushed aside Flora's suggestions that she might change into something that would escape Lady Stewart's notice and, having eaten very little, she went to the morning parlour ready to receive their guest.

Gabriel arrived as the long case clock in the entrance hall struck eleven. Arabella had been peering out of the window and she announced his arrival with a flurry of excitement.

'Really, Bella. I don't know why you are so interested in Gabriel,' Flora said sharply. 'He's a sea captain without a vessel at the moment.'

'I can enjoy a little flirtation with an exciting man, can't I? I'm not planning to marry a penniless seafarer, Flora. That's more your destiny than mine.'

'That was unkind, Bella. It might be true but there's no need to rub it in.'

A knock on the door preceded James, who stood to attention. 'Captain Gabriel Cutler, miss.'

Arabella greeted him with a wide smile and an outstretched hand. 'Captain Cutler. We met briefly at the Barclays' ball.'

He bowed over her hand. 'Good morning, Miss Stewart.' His gaze strayed to Flora and his smile widened. 'Miss Flora.'

'Good morning, Captain,' Flora said primly.

'Ring for a servant, Flora.' Arabella sank gracefully onto the sofa, patting the space beside her. 'Do take a seat, Captain. I'm so eager to learn about your life at sea.'

Flora tugged at the bell pull. She was used to seeing Arabella in her flirtatious mood but it had never bothered her before. It did now, but she did her best to keep the feelings of hurt and annoyance at bay. There was little she could do other than to take a seat and listen to Arabella's skilful attempt at flirting, although Gabriel seemed not to notice anything out of the way and he replied to her questions with polite good humour.

Edna duly appeared and Arabella ordered coffee and cake, having first offered Gabriel something stronger, which he declined. Edna left the room to return minutes later with a tray of coffee and a plate of small cakes.

'You may pour, Flora,' Arabella said graciously. 'I want to ask the captain about his plans for the future.'

Gabriel gave Flora a sympathetic smile as she passed him a cup of coffee. 'Thank you, Flora.'

'Your new vessel, Captain,' Arabella said firmly. 'Have you one in mind?'

'I'm making enquiries, Miss Stewart. Sir Brandon was very helpful, so I think we might be able to do business. But surely this is rather dull talk. Wouldn't you rather tell me about yourselves?' Gabriel turned to Flora, who was about to sip her coffee. 'I daresay your social diary is rather full?'

'Not really. Arabella is the one in demand.'

'I would expect nothing less,' Gabriel said gallantly. 'I'm sure your time is precious, Miss Stewart, and I wouldn't want to take you away from your more exciting engagements.' He turned back to Flora. 'But perhaps you might be free to accompany me to the zoological gardens tomorrow afternoon, Miss Flora?'

'I'm sure she would, and I daresay I could find a gap in my appointments for such an exciting outing,' Arabella said airily. 'When shall we say, Captain?' Without waiting for his reply, she stood up and went to a small escritoire by the window. She took a diary from a drawer and flipped through the pages, sighing. 'I am so very busy, but it so happens that I have only a dressmaker's appointment and I can put that off. Does that suit you, Captain?'

Gabriel nodded. 'That will be delightful. What about you, Miss Flora? Would you enjoy a trip to the zoological gardens?'

'Yes, indeed. I will look forward to it.' Flora managed a smile.

'Then it's settled.' Arabella took a pen from an inkstand, dipped it in the inkwell and made a show of writing in her diary. She replaced both pen and diary with a flourish. 'It will be lovely to spend time in the outdoors. I find it quite suffocating going from one drawing room to another.'

Gabriel put his cup and saucer on the table beside the sofa. He rose to his feet. 'I look forward to it, ladies. But I'm afraid I must leave you now. I will pick you up at two o'clock tomorrow afternoon, if that is convenient to both of you.'

'Of course it is,' Arabella said, smiling. 'I will look forward to it immensely. Ring the bell please, Flora. Edna will see you out, Captain Cutler.'

He shook his head. 'Please don't get up, Flora. I can manage quite well without bothering the servants. I will see you tomorrow at two o'clock.' He left the room, closing the door behind him.

'What a charming man, and so handsome, too. I can see why you like him, Flora.' Arabella clasped her hands together, smiling. 'I think I'm a little in love with him already.'

'You only say that because you know I like him and he likes me,' Flora said warily. 'Haven't you got enough young men to choose from, Bella? Why did you have to make such a fuss of Gabriel? He's neither rich nor titled. Are you just playing with him like a cat with a mouse?'

'That's mean. Just because you think he's interested in you personally. Like all my suitors they only make a fuss of you to get closer to me. I think Captain Cutler could be my devoted swain, if I chose to make him so.'

'Your papa wouldn't like it, Bella. He has plans for you that don't include a penniless sea captain.'

'Papa would buy Gabriel a new ship, or a fleet of vessels, if I told him to. You know I always get my way in the end, Flora.' Arabella crossed the floor and gave Flora a hug. 'You are a silly girl. I don't want Captain Cutler. I just enjoy flirting and I'm sure he does, too. You are a deal too serious, my girl.'

'Life isn't a game, Bella. You are playing with people's feelings and emotions.'

'Nonsense. You can have your bankrupt seafarer. Although I'm sure that he will return to the sea and you will never see him again.'

'You can't know that, Bella.'

'It's a fair assumption, my love. As is the fact that I will snare a nobleman with a fortune equal to my own. But you need not worry, Flora. I will always look after you and we will live happily ever after.'

'You don't care how many broken hearts you leave on your way to such riches?'

'Hearts don't break. It's a myth.' Arabella strolled over to the window. 'I do hope it's a nice day tomorrow. Maybe I ought to purchase a new bonnet for our trip to the zoological gardens. We need to go shopping. If we leave right away, we should have plenty of time.'

After spending the rest of the morning scouring the shops and new department stores for a bonnet, they arrived back at home laden with bandboxes and packages. The shawls, bonnets and gloves were mostly for Arabella, who was extravagant to a fault, but she was also generous and there was a new straw bonnet trimmed with pink silk roses and a matching chiffon scarf that she insisted were for Flora.

'Only you could get away with that shade of pink, Flora. Some people might say that a woman with red hair should not wear pink, but I disagree. The bonnet is most becoming.'

Flora smiled. 'Thank you, Arabella. You always

have perfect taste when it comes to knowing what to wear. Shall I take the packages up to your room?'

'I'll come, too. I want to try on the two bonnets again so that I can choose which is the most flattering. I want to make a favourable impression on Captain Cutler.'

'I'm sure you will without the need for a new bonnet. You know very well how pretty you are, Bella.' Laden with packages, Flora headed for the staircase with Arabella carrying a bandbox in each hand.

They reached the first landing and were met by Constance, who was dressed for outdoors.

'Where have you been, Bella? Have you forgotten that we are taking tea at Brown's with Lady Mallory and her two daughters? And tomorrow afternoon we are going to have lunch with some of the other debutantes and their mamas, to ensure there will be no mistakes at Queen Charlotte's Ball.'

'I don't like those silly girls, Mama. Anyway, I can't go with you. I'm going to the zoological gardens with Flora and Captain Cutler.'

'No you are not, my girl.' Constance bristled with annoyance. 'You will come with me now and also tomorrow. You haven't time to change, but you look reasonably presentable. Flora, please take my daughter's shopping up to her room.'

'Isn't Flora coming with us?'

'No, Arabella. This doesn't concern Flora. She would only feel left out of the conversation if she

111

accompanied us.' Constance managed a weary smile. 'You do understand, Flora, dear.'

'Yes, ma'am. Of course.' Flora attempted to take one of the bandboxes and in doing so dropped two of the smaller parcels.

Constance beckoned to Edna, who was hovering anxiously by the front entrance. 'Help Miss Flora, please.'

'Yes, my lady.' Edna rescued the bandboxes and packages. 'I can manage these, miss.' She stood back to allow Flora to ascend the stairs and followed on at a respectful distance. Flora glanced over the banisters and saw Arabella staring up at her with a resigned expression on her pretty face. Flora raised her hand in a sympathetic wave. Arabella might wrap her father round her little finger but she knew better than to go against her mother. Constance Stewart appeared to be mild-mannered and gentle, but beneath the sweetness and charm there was a will of iron. Although rarely used, the family knew when it was unwise to disobey her commands. Flora was sorry for Arabella, but she was delighted to think she would have Gabriel's undivided attention for a whole afternoon. There was no one to insist that she needed a chaperone. There were definite advantages in not being born a lady.

Next afternoon at precisely two o'clock, Flora was dressed in her best walking gown with the skirt draped into a neat bustle and the green tussore bodice enhanced with tiny mother-of-pearl buttons and deeper green ruffles at the neck. It was last year's fashion, passed down by Arabella, but the soft sea-green matched the colour of Flora's eyes and the perky little hat decorated with iridescent feathers complemented the outfit. Flora pulled on her lace mittens before picking up her reticule and frilled sunshade. She was determined to make the most of this outing, which would give her the chance to get to know Gabriel better.

She was on her way downstairs when the clock struck two and James opened the front door to admit Gabriel. He took off his top hat and stared at her with undisguised admiration.

Flora was suddenly shy and she knew she was blushing as she descended the last few steps.

'I'm afraid Arabella is unable to join us, Gabriel,' she said breathlessly. 'She had forgotten a luncheon appointment and her mama insisted that she should accompany her.'

'I will try to bear the disappointment,' Gabriel said gravely.

Flora thought that James sniggered, but he turned it into a cough and stared down at his highly polished black shoes.

'She was very disappointed.' Flora laid her hand on Gabriel's sleeve as he proffered his arm and escorted her out of the house.

'I hired a cabriolet,' Gabriel said as he helped her into the vehicle. 'I thought we would do it in style.'

The man in the driver's seat was hunched over, his head bowed and a cap pulled down over his eyes. Flora experienced a sharp stabbing pain of pure fear. She recognised him even before he turned his head to give her a gap-toothed, malicious grin.

'Gabriel.' The word had barely left her lips when the driver whipped the horse into a frenzied leap forward and Gabriel was flung to the ground. 'Stop,' Flora cried. 'Please stop.'

# Chapter Seven

'Stop, please stop.' Frantic with fear and concern for Gabriel, Flora stood up in the well of the cabriolet, but the driver whipped the poor horse so that it broke into a gallop and Flora was thrown back onto the seat. She leaned over the side, tempted to jump to safety, but the vehicle was weaving perilously in and out of the traffic and such a leap could prove fatal. She sank back against the squabs, clutching anything that came to hand. All around them there were shouts of derision and foul language from the cabbies, carters and pedestrians alike. By now the horse was so terrified that there was no stopping it, even if the man handling the reins tried his hardest.

Flora could hear a woman screaming and then she realised it was herself. She could hardly breathe as the air was sucked out of her lungs and then, suddenly, the horse broke free from its harness. The vehicle toppled over onto its side and Flora felt herself flying through the air into oblivion.

Every part of her body hurt. Each small movement was like torture. Flora opened her eyes but she was not in her lavish bedroom in South Molton Street. This place was dark, damp and smelled of foul drains and every kind of rotten thing mixed together. Her lips were cracked and her mouth was dry.

'Water,' Flora croaked in a voice that did not seem to be her own. 'Water, please.' She tried to sit up but fell back onto the straw-filled palliasse with a yelp of pain.

'So you've come round, have you?' A woman's voice came from somewhere above her. It was horribly familiar.

'Where am I?'

'You've come home, dearie. Where you belongs.'

'Gert?'

'Oh, so you do remember your dear old auntie.' Gert Fox bent down to lift Flora's head just enough to allow her to sip from a cup of water. It did not taste good but it was wet and it moistened her cracked lips and dry throat.

'It was Syd, wasn't it? The driver, I mean.'

'Yes, it was your uncle, come to rescue you from them rich folk what have been spoiling you for the past twelve years. Quite given up on you, we had, until my Syd spotted you at the house on Hay Hill.

Never forgets a face does my Syd. He knew it were you from the moment he set eyes on you.'

'Where is he?'

'Don't worry your head about him. He's in the pub as always. Got to get a few tots of rum inside him to cope with the pain. All your fault it was, spooking the poor horse. He's never been seen again. Probably running at Newmarket, I should imagine.' Gert laughed hoarsely at her own joke.

'Why did he bring me here? My family will be anxious. I must go home.'

Gert's smile froze and her face assumed a mask-like quality. 'You are home, dearie. With your real family. Them as took you are not related to you like we are.'

'They've been kind to me and educated me to be a lady. What do you want with me?'

'Well, now. That's the question. What are you fit for now, Flora Lee? You ain't never going to be a proper lady, but you are going to make up for abandoning your real family. That's a promise, dearie.'

With a huge and painful effort, Flora raised herself on one elbow. She realised that she was wearing a grubby chemise and nothing else. 'Where are my clothes? You can't keep me here. I'll report you to the police.'

Gert snorted with laughter. 'You won't see hide nor hair of a copper round here. They're too scared to come into this neighbourhood. As to what you was wearing, they fetched a few bob in Petticoat Lane. You'll wear what you're given now that you're one of us again.'

'You sold my clothes? That's stealing. You can't do this to me.'

'Already done, my duck. Spent the money in the pub. Had a good night out on your smart duds.' Gert squatted down beside Flora so that they were face to face. 'We're working out what you're going to do to make amends for the trouble you caused us good people.'

'Good people? You're devils,' Flora said faintly. 'Captain Cutler will find me. Sir Arthur will notify the police and they will be searching for me.'

'They haven't found you yet, have they? You been lying there dead to the world for over a week now. They'll have given up days ago. Their sort don't really care about anyone else. You're better off back with your own people.'

Flora struggled to sit up but Gert took a small bottle from her grubby pocket and tipped it into the glass of water. She forced Flora's mouth open and poured the liquid into her mouth. 'Swallow that and the pain will go away for a while. Sweet dreams, dearie.'

Flora struggled in and out of consciousness. She had no idea how long she had lain on the uncomfortable bed in the damp cellar, and she was weak from lack of food. Gert acted like a prison warder, doling out sips of water when Flora was conscious, but adding drops from the little brown bottle she kept in her pocket whenever Flora surfaced enough to speak. Gradually, however, when the pain from her injuries lessened, Flora realised what Gert was doing and remained silent when she regained conscious-ness. She was passive and pretended to be too weak to move, which was partly true. When the mist caused by laudanum cleared from her brain Flora knew that she must find something to eat or she would never regain her strength. It was impossible to say how many days or even weeks she had spent in a semi-comatose state, but if she was to escape from this dreadful place she needed to make Gert think she was going to cooperate. Quite what Gert and Sydney had in mind for her was a mystery, but Flora suspected that they were going to put her to work for them as they had when she was a child. She was too old to get away with picking pockets and lifting wallets from unsuspecting gentlemen, but there were other ways a young and attractive woman could earn good money, and none of them were legal. Flora might have had a sheltered upbringing with the Stewarts, but she had seen and heard things in her early years that she knew no child should experience.

She had been conscious for some time and had managed to sit up, taking in the details of the room in which she had been detained. At first she had thought it was a cellar but it was a basement area with a tiny window at street level that allowed shafts of daylight to filter through the city grime. The only furniture was a small table and two chairs. A shallow flight of stone steps led to a door. Flora had heard the key turn in the lock each time Gert left the room. She assumed that her aunt and uncle, if that's what they truly were, lived on the other side of that door. Occasionally she caught a hint of tobacco smoke or the fumes of rum and gin. Sometimes the aroma of fried fish or sausages wafted into the room. She remembered only too well that Gert was no cook. They had lived on whatever they could scavenge or food bought from the street vendors.

Every day when Gert and Syd were out, Flora forced her cramped muscles to work. She stretched her limbs until pain forced her to rest, and sometimes she managed to get onto her knees. The only way she had of knowing the time was when it grew dark, but there was a street lamp on the pavement outside, and the pale yellow gaslight gave her a little comfort through the long night hours. Sometimes she wondered if Gert and Syd were going to leave her to die as a punishment for deserting them, but common sense asserted itself with each dawn and she assumed that they had a definite plan. This was confirmed when, one morning, not long after sunrise, Gert entered the room followed by Syd.

Flora kept her eyes closed, feigning sleep.

'Just look at her, Gertie,' Syd said worriedly. 'She's all skin and bone. A skeleton is no good to us.'

'I'll ease up on the laudanum and give her some

food.' Gert prodded Flora's side with the toe of her boot. 'Wake up, you lazy slut. I know you can hear us.'

Flora groaned and opened one eye. 'Who are you?'

'Don't pretend to be off your head. I knows you too well, Flora Lee. Open your eyes.'

Reluctantly Flora obeyed. She knew she could only push Gert so far. 'What?' she demanded weakly.

'So you have got a tongue in your head after all. It's time you got up and started earning your living, my girl.'

'I can't move,' Flora said weakly.

'What will we do if she's crippled?' Syd asked urgently. 'She's no use to us if she's got broken bones that won't heal.'

Gert stood arms akimbo, glaring down at Flora. 'She's all right. She just needs to eat and get her strength back.'

'I can't eat,' Flora murmured.

Syd drew Gert aside, speaking in a loud whisper. 'Look what you've done. She's no use to us dead.'

'Shut up, you fool. She can hear you.' Gert dragged her husband up the steps and gave him a mighty shove into the room above.

Flora lay very still, wondering what was going to happen next. She did not have long to wait. Gert reappeared carrying a mug of hot tea and a slice of bread scraped with butter.

'Here, you. Sit up and eat this. I'm not having any more of your nonsense. We've kept you for three weeks and now your injuries are healed you can start working and earning your keep.'

Flora had intended to throw the food in Gert's face, but she was quite literally on the brink of starvation and she sank her teeth into the bread, eating ravenously. She drank the tea and sank back on the bed, exhausted from the effort.

Gert snatched the empty cup with a triumphant grin. 'There now, dearie. We'll soon have you back on your feet.'

'You can't keep me here against my will,' Flora said defiantly.

'Where do you think you'll go if you leave here? Them rich folks won't want you coming back in the middle of the party season, especially looking like you do without your fine clothes. Oh, they'll probably take you in, but you'll be kept out of sight in the servants' quarters and made to scrub floors and clean the privy.'

'They wouldn't treat me like that. I have friends.'

Gert curled her lip. 'Like that sea captain fellow, I suppose?'

'What do you know about him?' Flora eyed her warily.

'For a start my Syd saw you with him at the house in Hay Hill, and you was calling for someone called Gabriel when you was under the influence of laudanum. I might not be an educated person like you, Flora, but I know what's what. He'll be off on his travels before you can say knife.'

Flora said nothing. She barely noticed Gert leaving the basement as she struggled to come to terms with what she had just been told. Gert was speaking out of spite, but there was an element of truth in her words. Perhaps the Stewarts would be too embarrassed to take her back, and her reappearance might cause a scandal that would harm Arabella's chances of making a good match. The mention of Gabriel's name had shaken Flora to the core. She had clung to the hope that he might still be looking for her, but Gert's words had made that seem unlikely. It was true that they were only just getting to know each other, but his priority would have been to find another ship to command. Perhaps he had forgotten about her, although she knew she would never forget him. It occurred to her suddenly that maybe Gert and Syd were right. This was where she really belonged. She lay back on the palliasse, overcome by weakness and mixed emotions. Of one thing she was certain, she must regain her strength and she would lull Gert and Syd into a false sense of security. If they thought she was going to comply with their wishes they might grow complacent and then she would make her move.

Flora grew stronger as each day passed. Gert brought her food, although it was a poor substitute when compared to the diet Flora had enjoyed while living with the Stewart family. She exercised whenever she was certain that neither Gert nor Syd would walk into the basement. By this time she had a rough idea of their daily routine. The walls were thick but Gert and Syd were noisy and constantly bickering, which often led to violence. Flora could hear screams and shouts followed by splintering wood or breaking china. Even so, they were creatures of habit and Flora could judge the time of day by their comings and goings. With Syd it seemed that he was bound for the pub, while Gert went about her business. Flora suspected that the police might be interested in Gert's activities as she seemed to have enough money to purchase food and other necessities without actually having to work.

As her weakened muscles regained their strength, Flora concentrated on finding a possible way of escape. She knew that Gert locked the door each time she left the basement, but one day when she did not hear the click of the metal lock, Flora knew that Gert had forgotten. She waited, hardly daring to breathe until she heard Syd leave and minutes later there was the encouraging sound of the outer door closing. Very carefully and quietly Flora opened the connecting door and stepped into the one room that Gert and Syd called home. It was almost exactly as she remembered it, only much smaller. She smiled to herself. She had been a tiny six-year-old when she lived in such cramped conditions. It was obvious that Gert was no housekeeper. Flora suspected that some of the dust in the shadowy corners had been undisturbed for years. The fireplace spilled over with ashes and there were scraps of mouldy cheese and stale bread on the table. Flies buzzed around a jug of sour milk, and cockroaches scuttled across the stone floor, disappearing into holes in the brickwork.

Flora was hungry, but even the flies had abandoned efforts to eat the hard heel of cheese or the greenish blue mould on the crust of bread. Flora's main aim was to find something to wear, but a quick search provided nothing that would fit her, and she was barefoot into the bargain. She opened the outer door and found herself in a long, dark corridor, which she remembered led to the backyard and the privy. Not only that but there was a pump and she could finally have a proper wash. She forgot all about Gert and made her way carefully to the rear of the building. The door was unlocked and she stepped outside into the relatively fresh air, tainted slightly by the smell emanating from the privy, but her sights were set on the pump. The feel of cold water on her skin was wonderful, and she found a scrap of lye soap that someone had accidentally dropped, with which she washed her hair. It was a hot day and the sun's rays managed to penetrate between the crush of tall buildings. She had no towel but she shook her head like a dog that had just emerged from a pool and raised her face to the sun, feeling its warmth like kisses on her skin.

The flapping of a garment hanging on a washing line caught her eye and she realised it was a simple cotton frock, the sort that a young serving maid might wear. She did not think twice about unpegging it, but then she was seized with a fit of conscience and she took off the chemise that she had been wearing and hung it from the line in return for the dress. It was hardly a fair swap, but Flora was desperate and she hoped the previous owner of the dress would forgive her. She hurried back into the building and closed the door. She was tempted to make a dash for freedom, but she would not get far without anything on her feet and not a penny to her name. She made her way back to the room and came face to face with Gert.

'Where do you think you're going, miss?' Gert stood arms akimbo, barring Flora's way.

'I found the privy and I had a wash. Do you begrudge me a simple thing like that?'

'You was trying to escape.'

'I thought about it, but it looks as if you might try to stop me, and you sold my shoes.'

Gert's croaky laughter echoed off the ceiling, causing the cobwebs to move stealthily in the draught. 'For good reason, and I got a fair price for them, too. Now get back in your room.'

Flora shook her head. 'No. I will not return to that filthy prison. I am younger than you, Gert. If you choose to fight me, I promise I will give as good as I get. You haven't got Sydney to back you up now.'

Gert's eyes narrowed. 'So you think you could get the better of me, do you?'

'I will certainly try. I'm not a six-year-old child now, and I'm not afraid of you or Syd.'

'All right then. Supposing you knock me down and you make it out onto the street. Where will you go? You've no money and it's a long walk back to South Molton Street, especially barefoot.'

'What do you want from me, Gert?' Flora demanded angrily.

'We want recompense for all the years we was deprived of your company.'

'You know you don't mean that. You didn't want me in the first place. You treated me badly and made me pick pockets and steal wallets. I hate to think what you would have made me do when I was growing up.'

'Well, you'll never know, will you?'

'You can't keep me here.' Flora barged past Gert, catching her off guard so that she stumbled into the room. But as Flora reached the front door it opened and Syd strolled in accompanied by a tall, well-built man wearing a blood-stained leather apron. His broken nose made him look like a retired prize fighter and a livid scar creased the side of his face, marring his otherwise good looks.

'Where do you think you're going?' Syd grabbed Flora by the arm, twisting it behind her and causing her to cry out in pain. He pushed her into the room, giving her a shove that sent her sprawling onto the floor.

'So this is the girl, is it, Syd?' The man in the apron eyed Flora curiously. 'She's a bit skinny.'

'She's stronger than she looks and she needs to work. We can't keep her. You can have her for a reasonable price.'

'That's right,' Gert added hastily. 'Flora can wash dishes and scrub floors with the best of them.'

'Wait a minute.' Flora scrambled to her feet. 'What are you talking about? You can't sell me, and I'm certainly not going to work for him. He looks like a butcher.'

Gert grabbed Flora's arm and pinched it hard. 'You'll do as you're told, my girl. Tulliver won't stand for any of your backchat.'

'I ain't certain I'll take her on,' Tulliver said doubtfully. 'I don't want a skivvy who's not willing to work. I run a respectable establishment. We get toffs from the City eating in my bar.'

'Then make her wait on tables,' Gert said silkily. 'She's got a pretty face and neat little figure. She'd be popular with the gents, if you get my meaning.'

'She's worth five guineas of anyone's money,' Syd added hopefully.

'You can't sell me,' Flora protested angrily. 'You kidnapped me. You'll both go to prison for that.'

Gert prodded her sharply in the ribs. 'We cared for you when you come here nigh on a month ago, like a broken doll. Tulliver is just going to pay our expenses. Ain't that right, Ted?'

Tulliver looked Flora up and down. 'Where's her shoes? Her hair's dripping wet. She looks like something washed up on the foreshore.'

Syd took Tulliver aside. 'We had to sell her duds to pay for the doctor and the medicine. She's better now – she just needs feeding up.' He spoke in a low voice but Flora could hear every word.

'They're lying to you, Mr Tulliver,' Flora said firmly. 'I was abducted outside my home in South Molton Street. If you take me back there I'm sure that Sir Arthur Stewart will reward you handsomely.'

Tulliver shifted from one foot to the other. 'I dunno. I don't want to get mixed up in shady dealings with the gentry. I rely on the toffs from the West End when they come slumming and eat fancy food in my pub. I got a reputation to keep up.'

Gert moved to his side and took him by the hand. 'Ted, look at her. She's a beauty when she's tidied up a bit, and she talks proper. She's been educated like a lady and she will attract the gents like moths to a flame, if you get my meaning.'

'You can't make me do it,' Flora said stubbornly.

Tulliver eyed her warily. 'She would be a draw, I'll give you that.' He put his hand in his pocket. 'Three guineas and that's my final offer.'

'Four guineas,' Syd insisted. 'She's a quick learner.'

Flora eyed him with distaste, but even though she hated the idea of being bought and paid for by Tulliver, she saw a way of escape. If she was put to work in a public house she would have a better chance of regaining her freedom. She met Tulliver's curious look with a hint of a smile.

'I've changed my mind,' she said sweetly. 'I suppose

I could give it a try. Anything is better than being cooped up here in this rat's nest.'

'Here, you! That's enough of that talk.' Gert raised her hand and slapped Flora's face. 'Mind your manners when you speak about your family. We raised you from a baby.'

'Never mind all that,' Tulliver said hurriedly. He took another couple of coins from his pocket and thrust them into Syd's hand. 'There's your money. Now where are the girl's shoes?'

'They sold them.' Flora rubbed her sore cheek. 'You can see what I have to put up with, Mr Tulliver. Working for you will be a pleasure after being here.'

'That's good enough for me.' Tulliver picked her up and flung her over his shoulder. 'You've got a deal, Fox. She's mine now.'

Gert snatched the money from Syd's hand. 'Ta, Ted. You won't regret it, but if she gives you trouble send her back here and we'll deal with the baggage.'

Tulliver grunted in response and opened the front door. 'Lucky for you that I came in my wagonette.' He dumped Flora unceremoniously on the driver's seat and climbed up to sit beside her, taking the reins. 'Walk on.'

Flora glanced over her shoulder and shuddered at the sight of a carcase resting on a bed of sawdust. 'You're a butcher as well?'

'I came straight from Smithfield meat market. You see, Flora, I'm a cook first and foremost. People come for miles to sample my food.' Tulliver shot

130

her a sideways glance. 'You look as if you need feeding up yourself.'

'Why did you buy me?' Flora met his amused gaze with a straight look. 'You know it's against the law. You aren't a stupid man. I can tell.'

'You're wise beyond your years,' Tulliver said, grinning. 'I need someone to help me run my restaurant. I got ambitions beyond being the land-lord of a pub in Play House Yard. I want to be famous and when Sydney sat in my bar, running on about the young woman he'd raised who had been taken by a rich family and brought up to be a lady, I paid attention. You're one of us, but you've been polished like a diamond. You can be very useful to me.'

'But you've paid good money, so that means I'm a slave.'

Tulliver shook his head. 'Call it an apprenticeship. I'll teach you how to earn a living and you'll teach me how the upper classes go about things.'

He drove on past Ludgate Hill railway station and Flora concentrated on the route they had taken, committing it to memory as a possible way of escape. They passed Apothecaries' Hall and turned into Play House Yard. Tulliver reined in outside an ancient-looking, half-timbered building. Above the door was a sign painted with the dual masks depicting comedy and tragedy.

'This is it,' Tulliver said proudly. 'The Play House Inn. There was a theatre here many years ago, erected on the site of an old monastery built by the Dominican monks.'

Flora eyed him curiously. For such a tough-looking individual he seemed almost poetic in his appreciation of history. 'It looks very old,' she said, nodding.

'The monks were known as the black friars because of their black habits, and that's how Blackfriars got its name. It's said that Shakespeare trod the boards in the original theatre, and he had a house nearby in Ireland Yard.'

'How do you know all this, Mr Tulliver?'

'I made it my business to find out. I never had much education, but I find it fascinating, although not many people round here agree with me. All they are interested in is drinking and eating and pleasure of the flesh. Although you, being brought up in a genteel manner, wouldn't be familiar with that sort of thing.'

Flora shrugged. 'The family who took me in as a child have a house in the country. I used to spend most of my time with the gardeners and the local people. I'm not a lady, Mr Tulliver, but I'm not a servant either. I will work for you until I've paid off the money you gave Sydney Fox, and then I consider my debt to be done. I will be a free woman. Do you agree?'

'I can't argue with that.' Tulliver climbed down from the driver's seat. 'But I'll work you hard, Flora. Don't think of trying to run away because I'll catch you and bring you back. I expect a good return for my investment.'

'Treat me well and I'll earn my keep. I'm willing to learn.'

Tulliver lifted her to the ground. 'Fair enough.' He opened the pub door. 'Moses! Stop whatever you're doing and unload the wagon.'

Flora stepped aside as a youth lumbered past her. He shot a wary glance at his employer before reaching into the wagon with arms that seemed too long for his skinny body. Flora was amazed to see him heft the carcase onto his shoulder as if it weighed next to nothing. He made as if to go back into the pub but Tulliver caught him by the scruff of the neck.

'Go round to the back, boy. How many times have I to tell you that?'

'Aye, boss.' Moses shambled off, muttering to himself.

'Go inside, Flora.' Tulliver ushered her into the taproom. 'Moses is a bit backward in all things, but he's harmless.'

'He's very strong,' Flora said cautiously.

'Strong in the arm, weak in the head, as the saying goes. The poor chap was abandoned as a baby. I had a pub in Stew Lane, overlooking the river. Early one morning I'd gone for a walk on the foreshore and I spotted a wooden crate floating close to the shore. I didn't take much notice until I heard a baby crying, so I waded in and found a wizened scrap of humanity, mewling like a kitten. Nobody thought the boy would survive, but he did.'

'And you never found his mother?'

Tulliver shook his head. 'Never expected to. There was an accident when two ships collided on the river with a terrible loss of life. Someone wanted their son to be saved but we never traced his parents. He had nothing to identify him, so we called him Moses, like in the bible.'

Flora swallowed hard. She felt a surge of fellow feeling mixed with pity for Moses.

Tulliver beckoned to a plump, dark-haired woman who was washing tankards behind the bar. 'Coralie, my love. Come and meet our new helper.'

She lifted the hatch and walked towards them, her hips swaying as if she were dancing to a melody that only she could hear. She was perhaps in her early forties and still handsome with dark eyes and a voluptuous figure.

'You didn't tell me you was looking for more staff, Tulliver.'

'It happened on the off-chance, my love. I'll tell you everything later, but this is Flora Lee, and she is in dire need of something decent to wear, especially shoes.'

Coralie looked Flora up and down, shaking her head. 'Another of your waifs and strays, Ted Tulliver. I swear we ought to run a home for the homeless and hopeless. She looks as if a puff of wind would blow her over.'

Tulliver took his wife aside, speaking in a low voice although Flora could still hear every word he said.

'That rogue Syd Fox tried to sell her to me.'

'Sell her?' Coralie's arched eyebrows drew together in a frown. 'That's illegal.'

'Of course it is, and I would have told him where to go in no uncertain terms, but then I saw the poor girl – half-starved and still dripping wet having tried to wash herself at the outside pump.'

'But she must have a family somewhere, Ted. We have to return her to her own people.'

'It's not as easy as that, my love. Apparently she was raised by a wealthy family who took pity on her as a small child. They brought her up to be a companion for their only daughter.'

'Then she should be returned to that family.'

'She says she doesn't want to go back. I'll leave her to explain it to you herself, but she has special qualities, Coralie. She will bring a touch of class to our establishment.'

Coralie eyed Flora askance. 'I'm not sure about that. She'll think she's too good for a common pub in the East End.'

'Not at all. We've agreed that she will undertake an apprenticeship and after that she is free to leave if she pleases. I'm going to train her in the kitchen and you can show her how to wait on tables.'

'I suppose it could benefit us. She does look as if she needs someone to take care of her, and she has no shoes.'

'That's right, my darling girl. I knew you'd see it my way when you knew the full story. May I leave her in your capable hands? I have a side of beef to prepare for the table.' Tulliver strode off towards the back of the taproom and disappeared through an open door.

Coralie folded her arms, staring hard at Flora, who tried not to squirm beneath such intense scrutiny. 'Well now, Flora. I suppose my husband knows what he's doing, but you'll have to answer to me as well, and I'm much more demanding than Ted is.'

Flora held herself very erect. 'I didn't choose to come here, Mrs Tulliver. I heard your husband telling you about the wealthy family who took me in when I was a child. I've had advantages that no common girl could hope for, but I was abducted outside their home in South Molton Street.'

'I don't understand. Who would do such a thing?'

'You know that my so-called uncle is Sydney Fox?'

'Yes, he drinks here sometimes. I can't say I like the fellow. Is he really your uncle?'

'I don't know for sure. He and Gert both said I was their niece and that my mother had died, leaving me in their care, but I have no idea if that was true. I was lucky to be rescued from them by Sir Arthur and Lady Stewart.'

Coralie frowned. 'So why are you here? Why didn't you go back to those people, who obviously cared well for you?'

'I was injured during the kidnapping and when I regained consciousness I was imprisoned in a cellar with Gert acting like a wardress. I recovered eventually and I was about to make my escape – that's when Syd returned with your husband. He offered to sell me to Mr Tulliver.'

'Well, I'll be jiggered. I never heard the like.'

'Please don't send me back there, Mrs Tulliver,' Flora said earnestly. 'I promise I'll work for you for nothing until I've paid off the amount your husband gave Syd.'

'I'll have a few words to say to Ted. He knows better than to have any dealings with the likes of Syd Fox.'

'I think he took pity on me, Mrs Tulliver. I'm happy to be a sort of apprentice because I want to learn a trade and then I can be independent.'

'But the kind people who took you in and raised you as their own. Don't you want to go back to them?'

'Of course I do, but would they really want me? Arabella and I were like sisters, but she'll have been presented at court by now. I had plenty of time to think about it when I was imprisoned in that damp basement room, and I don't want to bring embarrassment to the family who were so good to me. A scandal might ruin Arabella's chances of making a good match.'

Coralie shook her head. 'It's like something out of a penny dreadful. I love reading them stories, but you seem to be living in one of them. If they're fond of you, they'll be happy that you're alive and well.'

'They would welcome me, I know that, but I'm

not their flesh and blood. Arabella will marry an earl or a duke and what would happen to me then? What sort of life will I have? I want to earn my own living and find the place where I truly belong.'

'Lord above us, you really mean that, don't you? I'll have to think about this, Flora. But first things first. You look as if you could do with a good meal, and then we'll see about getting you something to wear, and a pair of shoes.'

'I'm a fast learner,' Flora added in desperation.

'Come with me. We'll get you fed and clothed and then I'll find a room for you.'

'I haven't any underclothes,' Flora said in a whisper. 'I stole this frock from a washing line because Gert Fox sold my clothes and shoes.'

'I'll have words to say to that woman if ever I meet her. I never heard the like.' Coralie sashayed off, following in Tulliver's footsteps. 'Come along, Flora. Something to eat first and then we'll see to the rest.'

# Chapter Eight

Ted Tulliver had been right when he claimed to be an excellent cook. Flora had been virtually starved for almost a month and she could only eat a fraction of the meal that Coralie set before her, but it was delicious. Perhaps the manner of serving was clumsy and the table setting in the bar left a lot to be desired, but Flora could see enormous potential in Tulliver's ambition to provide excellent food and wine to a better-off clientele.

Coralie eyed the food left on Flora's plate with a frown. 'You don't eat enough to keep a sparrow alive, girl. We'll have to feed you up.'

Flora smiled. 'That was wonderful, Mrs Tulliver. Your husband is a remarkable cook.'

'So I keep telling him. We could go far, him and me. We could get one of them smart restaurants up West and make a fortune.'

'I think this is exactly the right place for you. There are plenty of over-priced places to eat in the West End, but you have a wonderful history here. Mr Tulliver was telling me about the Blackfriars monks and Shakespeare's connection to the theatre. You have a chance of running an eating place like no other. Rich people would come all the way across town just for a bowl of that stew.'

Coralie pulled up a chair and sat down, leaning her elbows on the table. 'You must have dined in them expensive eating places up West. What could we do to compete with them?'

Flora gazed around the taproom with its beamed ceiling and oak-panelled walls. It was cosy but hardly elegant, although that might prove to be an advantage, particularly in the winter when the fire in the inglenook welcomed people in from the bitter cold outside. She thought quickly. 'I don't think you should try to copy places like Rules, Wiltons or Kettner's. The Play House Inn should be something unique. An attraction in its own right.'

'What could we do, then? We want to lure people from the West End.'

'You need a lick of paint and a few pictures on the walls. Perhaps illustrations of what the place was like when the monks used the theatre for their choir. You need to find your own style, never mind what other places do. Above all, the inn should make people feel welcome when they walk through the door.'

'You seem to have good ideas, girl. I understand

what you're saying, but making it work won't be so easy.'

'I don't know about that. It seems to me that you are more than halfway there. The main thing is to make sure that people find out that you exist, and that it is a really interesting place to visit. Although it is rather out of the way.'

'I think it's going to be more difficult than it sounds, but it's worth a try.' Coralie rose to her feet. 'My husband is putting a lot of faith in you, Flora. Personally, I would hold back until we know you better, but Ted thinks you could help us.'

'I'll certainly do my best,' Flora said earnestly.

'I believe you. Anyway, first things first, Flora. If you've had enough to eat you can come with me and I'll show you where you'll be sleeping. Then, if you promise not to run away, you can borrow a pair of my shoes and we'll go shopping.'

'Why are you being so nice to me?' Flora demanded suspiciously. 'You don't know me. I could be telling you a pack of lies. I might be planning to rob you and run away.'

'I've been in this business for thirty years, love. You wouldn't think so to look at me, but I was only ten years old when I was sent to work in a pub near my old home. Apart from what Ted says and does, I think I'm a good judge of character. But if you turn out to be a wrong 'un, I'll eat my best hat, feathers and all.'

Flora stood up, giggling at the image that Coralie's

words conjured up. 'I promise you won't have to do that.'

'I hope not, but I warn you, I am not easily fooled and I expect the highest standards. Cross me, Flora, and you will find yourself in trouble. Do you understand?'

Flora nodded. 'I do.'

'Then come with me. Let's get you settled in so that you can start learning how we do things.' Coralie led the way through the bar to a narrow hallway at the back and a twisting staircase to the top of the building. Beneath the sloping roof were two attic rooms. 'This one is where I store things that have not much use any more, and the other is where you'll sleep. It's not very big but there's a bed and a chest of drawers. Maybe we can find some other things to make it more homely.'

Flora glanced around the room beneath the eaves with a small window overlooking Play House Yard.

'It's quite big enough for me, Mrs Tulliver.'

'Call me Coralie. We'll get along fine, Flora. Now, I'll give you some fresh bedding, but before that we'll take a walk to Petticoat Lane and get you some new duds. I can't stand to see you dressed in that awful frock that doesn't fit anywhere.'

After a successful trip to the street market, Flora and Coralie returned to the pub laden with packages. Flora took them upstairs to her bedroom and tore off the brown paper wrapping. The garments were all second-hand but that did not matter; in fact, Flora was used to having cast-offs from Arabella, although the clothes in Petticoat Market were a poor copy. However, they were clean and free from bugs, something that Coralie had been very particular about. She had examined the seams carefully and nothing missed her sharp eyes. It was not a huge wardrobe with two sets of underwear, a plain grey gown with a white apron for waiting on tables and a more serviceable skirt and a couple of blouses for day-to-day wear. Coralie had decided that Flora should keep to the kitchen at first and learn all there was to know about the type of food they served. Then, if she progressed well, she might work in the bar, washing tankards and generally cleaning up, especially after spills of wine or ale. Waiting on tables was to come later, although Flora suspected this would only happen when Coralie was certain that she would not make a break for freedom. The idea of an escape had occurred to Flora several times earlier that day, but she knew she must be practical and put such thoughts from her mind, for now at least. The Tullivers had been kind and generous so far, and for that Flora was grateful. However, she had a feeling she would have to work hard to earn her freedom.

She tidied her new clothes away and made up the bed with the sheets and blankets that Coralie had provided. There was no mirror in the small room, so she could only hope that the white-cotton blouse and plain dark-blue skirt looked reasonable. At least she felt comfortable and the undergarments fitted perfectly. She made her way downstairs to the kitchen and was greeted with a smile from Tulliver and a shy grin from Moses. However, one look around the kitchen was enough to make her heart sink. Tulliver might be a talented chef but he seemed to work in chaos. There was not a clear space on the huge pine table nor the dressers that lined the walls. The range was smoking and in desperate need of a clean and there were over-filled sacks, spilling vegetables, rice and flour onto the filthy tiled floor.

'You look better now, girl. Are you ready to start work?' Tulliver said cheerfully.

'What do you want me to do?' Flora asked faintly. Simply finding anything seemed like an impossible task.

Tulliver looked round with a sigh. 'Maybe you could tidy up a bit? I've got some meat to prepare in the cellar. It's cooler down there. I'll leave you to it. Moses – I want you to help Flora. Don't stand around lollygagging. Get on with peeling those spuds.' Tulliver snatched up a vicious-looking meat cleaver as he left the kitchen.

'You're very pretty,' Moses said shyly. 'I like you, Flora.'

She smiled. 'Thank you, Moses. I like you, too.' She unhooked a rather grubby apron from the back of the door and tied it around her waist. 'Now, where to start!'

Flora had never done any form of housework, let alone sorted out such a mess, but she made a start by clearing the table of vegetable peelings, empty jars, bottles and dirty crockery. Moses was a willing helper and he filled large pans with water from the pump at the sink in the scullery and hefted them onto the range. With hot water it was possible to wash the china, cutlery, pots and pans. When it was dry and sparkling clean, the crockery was replaced on the dresser and the gleaming cooking utensils hung from hooks above the range. Flora turned her attention to emptying the shelves that lined the walls. She worked methodically, sorting the rubbish and filling a large sack, which Moses took out into the backyard. Her next task was to clear out the larder, throwing away anything that had grown mould, smelled bad or was completely unrecognisable.

Flora scrubbed every surface until she was satisfied that it was clean. Then she replaced everything in neat rows. Moses stowed the sacks of vegetables, rice and flour in the larder, leaving Flora free to sweep the floor before mopping it with hot water and washing soda. She remembered having seen Daniel's mother use the same method on the stone floor in their cottage, and it seemed to work. She had just finished mopping up the excess water when Tulliver returned. He came to a halt in the doorway, his astonished expression almost comical.

'What's happened here? Have I come into the wrong kitchen?'

Moses rushed up to him and clutched his arm. 'No, boss. This is where we work. See what Flora has done. I helped her a lot.' He turned to Flora. 'I was a good boy, wasn't I?'

'You were such a great help, Moses,' Flora said gently. 'I couldn't have done it without you.'

'I don't know what to say.' Tulliver scratched his head, leaving his curly brown hair standing up in a quiff. 'Remarkable. I don't know if I'll be able to find anything, but you've done a good job, Flora. And you, Moses,' he added hastily.

'What now, boss?' Moses asked eagerly. 'Shall I help the missis in the bar?'

'Yes, good idea.' Tulliver slapped him on the back. 'Ask her what she wants you to do.'

Moses sloped off, repeating beneath his breath that he had done well.

'What about me?' Flora stifled a yawn. She was exhausted after working so hard, and the injuries she had suffered when the chaise overturned had begun to ache.

'Better rest awhile,' Tulliver said, nodding. 'I was forgetting you've been confined to bed in that cellar for weeks after the accident. You've proved yourself today, and I really do need someone organised like you. Go upstairs and rest. You can help me with the diners this evening.'

'Thank you, Mr Tulliver. I promised to earn my keep and I will.' Flora untied the apron strings and hung it back on its hook. She made her way tiredly upstairs to the tiny attic room, and lay down on the bed. It was surprisingly comfortable, especially when compared to the straw-filled palliasse that she had endured in the cellar at Turnagain Lane. It was quiet up here away from the noise and chatter in the bar. The sound of traffic in the street below was faint but strangely comforting. Flora closed her eyes, intending to rest a while, and slipped into a deep sleep.

It was the start of a journey that Flora could never have imagined. There was no comparison to the soft, pampered life she had led as Arabella's companion, but Tulliver was a good employer. However, he expected a lot from his workers and Flora was kept busy from early morning until late at night. She suffered from burned fingers and aching limbs, but she found the results of the hard work satisfying, especially when Tulliver trusted her enough to let her prepare a simple dish on her own. She was a quick learner and her knowledge of how food should taste and how it should be presented proved invaluable. Tulliver was an excellent chef but not too proud to learn. He respected Flora's sensitive palate and was quick to take up her suggestions if he thought they would improve his dishes.

Moses was Flora's ardent admirer. He followed her round like a loving, energetic puppy, and was willing to undertake the dirtiest of tasks if it earned a smile and a word of encouragement from her. Between them they kept the kitchen immaculate, which earned Coralie's approval. Late in the evening, when the last food had been served and the pine table scrubbed until it was like bleached bones, Flora was free to do as she pleased. However, she usually chose to go into the bar to help Coralie wash the tankards, which made a nice change from the heat of the kitchens. She was able to take stock of the customers and she tried to work out the best way to attract a different clientele. Most of the men who drank in the bar worked in the docks or were crews from ships or lightermen. Flora had a vain hope that one day Gabriel Cutler might chance by, although it was just a dream. He had most likely found someone to sponsor a voyage and was somewhere far away from Play House Yard. She remembered him fondly but with little hope of ever seeing him again.

Flora worked hard and found she had a natural talent when it came to cooking. She was eager to learn and Tulliver was an excellent teacher. She had found a friend in Coralie, but she missed Arabella. As the summer progressed she began to long for the cool green beauty of the Essex countryside, and in particular the walled garden where she had spent so much of her younger days. The scent of flowers grown for the house and the ripening peaches espaliered against the red brick walls was something she could never forget. She missed her chats with Daniel and the kindliness of his parents. Sometimes during a hot sleepless night beneath the thatched roof of the inn, Flora wished that she had accepted Daniel's proposal. Her excuse then was that she wanted to see more of the world and to discover her capabilities, but she realised now that the world away from Nine Oaks was not as wonderful and exciting as she had imagined.

Although neither Tulliver nor Coralie pressed the point, Flora knew she must do something to bring a more exclusive clientele to the inn, however it was not as easy as she had first thought. She came to the conclusion that the only way to attract the sort of customers that Tulliver had in mind necessitated a return to her old home. Besides which she was longing to see Arabella and explain the reason for her disappearance. Without telling the Tullivers her plan, she took the opportunity of a quiet afternoon in July to make the journey to South Molton Street, taking two omnibuses and walking the rest of the way. It was a hot, airless day and the streets were relatively quiet. There was no guarantee that she would find Arabella at home and if she was not there then Flora's journey would have been for nothing. However, if that were the case Flora knew she must try again. Her need to speak to her adopted sister was growing stronger each day.

Flora reached South Molton Street and her nerve almost failed her. After all, Arabella might have gone to Nine Oaks to get away from the heat in the city, or she could have accepted an invitation to a house party in the country. Flora forced herself to walk up to the house, but hesitated on the doorstep. She took a deep breath and knocked on the door.

Jefferson opened it and his eyes widened in surprise. 'Miss Flora?'

'Is Miss Arabella at home, Jefferson?'

He swallowed hard, resuming his customary mask-like expression. 'I'm afraid not.' His eyes flickered over her plain attire. 'The family are out of town, Miss Flora.'

Despite her previous misgivings, Flora was bitterly disappointed. She had not realised quite how much she missed her adoptive family until this moment.

'Have they gone to Nine Oaks, Jefferson?' Flora tried to sound casual but there was a break in her voice as she fought back tears.

'No, miss. They're visiting a family in the country.'

'Do you know when they will return, Jefferson?'

'I'm sorry, Miss Flora. I haven't yet been informed of their plans.'

'Thank you, Jefferson.'

'Is there any message, Miss Flora?' There was a hint of compassion in Jefferson's clipped tones as Flora turned to leave.

'No message, thank you.'

'Very well, miss.' Jefferson closed the front door and Flora stepped down onto the pavement. She turned to leave, almost colliding with Ralph Pettigrew.

He doffed his top hat. 'Well, if it isn't the errant

Miss Lee. You've chosen to return to us. Where have you been all this time?'

'I think you know very well where I've been, sir.'

'I am as much in the dark as the kind people who took you in from the street all those years ago, Miss Lee.'

'You had dealings with Sydney Fox,' Flora said in a low voice.

'I don't deny it.'

'You told him where to find me.'

'I imagine he must have known that all along. The whereabouts of the Stewarts' town house is hardly a secret.'

'I blame you personally for what happened to me. I have nothing further to say to you.' Flora went to walk past him, but he barred her way.

'You're dressed like a maidservant on her day off. Where have you been, Flora Lee?'

She faced him angrily. 'You obviously haven't kept in touch with Syd Fox or he would have told you that he sold me to an innkeeper near Blackfriars Bridge. I am learning the trade, Ralph.'

'He sold you?' For once Ralph seemed genuinely shocked. 'Surely not.'

'He most certainly did. I was kept a prisoner to start with and then I was exchanged for money, but you say you didn't know about that.'

'I don't know anything about that. What tavern are you talking about?'

His dumbfounded expression confirmed the fact

that he knew nothing about Syd's deal with Tulliver, which was oddly comforting. Flora would have hated to think that Tulliver was friendly with a man like Ralph Pettigrew, title or no title.

She tossed her head. 'If you want to enjoy an excellent meal in unusual surroundings, I suggest you visit the Play House Inn, near the Apothecaries' Hall. You could bring some of your wealthy friends. I gather that young men about town often go slumming in the East End. You might be agreeably surprised.'

Ralph stared at her with narrowed eyes. 'Maybe I will. Just for the sake of amusement. I would love to see the high and mighty Miss Lee working her fingers to the bone, serving food and drink to the hoi polloi.'

Flora walked away with mixed feelings. She knew that Ralph would be driven by curiosity, although at the same time she was afraid that he might try to cause trouble. She decided not to say anything to the Tullivers when she returned to the inn. After all, Ralph might decide it was beneath him to spend an evening in the East End, although if he brought with him some of his wealthy friends it could be exactly what Tulliver was hoping for.

Several days passed and Flora had begun to think that Ralph had forgotten about their meeting. She had just finished in the kitchen one evening, and was helping Coralie in the bar when the door opened and Ralph Pettigrew sauntered into the taproom, followed by five well-dressed gentlemen who had obviously been drinking. Ralph walked up to the bar, ignoring Flora and greeting Coralie with an engaging smile.

'My dear lady, your tavern has been highly recommended to me. I've been told that the food served here equals anything I can get in the West End.'

Coralie smiled coyly with a hint of a rosy blush flooding her cheeks. Flora realised with something of a shock that Ralph Pettigrew could be quite charming when he chose.

'Well, sir. You heard right.' Coralie turned to Flora. 'Best fetch my husband. These gentlemen know what's what.'

'I should say we do,' Ralph said agreeably. 'Now then, girl. Do as your mistress tells you.'

Flora bit back a sharp retort and hurried to the kitchen, where Tulliver was supervising Moses as he washed the pots and pan.

'What is it, Flora? More food? I really have finished for this evening.'

'Mrs Tulliver wants you in the bar to speak to some rich toffs,' Flora said carefully. 'They've heard about your cooking and they're demanding food.'

'Gentlemen, you say?'

'Yes, I know one of them and I recognised a couple more. They are what they say they are, and it could bring the type of customer you want.' Flora chose not to give him any further details. It would be best if Tulliver were to speak to Ralph and his companions and form his own opinion.

'I'll have words with them.' Tulliver strode out of the kitchen, with Flora close on his heels.

When they entered the bar Ralph and his companions were seated around a table, drinking wine. Tulliver walked up to them, standing tall with his arms folded across his broad chest.

'You want food, gentlemen?'

Ralph eyed him curiously. 'Your reputation has reached the West End, landlord. What can you offer us?'

'It's short notice, gentlemen, but I have some excellent steaks.'

'Pretty run-of-the-mill fare,' Ralph said casually. 'I was expecting something more.'

Tulliver nodded. 'Then perhaps you would like them served with a Bordelaise sauce.'

Flora was quick to notice the surprised looks wiping the smiles off the faces of the men seated around the table. Ralph seemed momentarily lost for words, but he collected his thoughts and nodded.

'Sounds excellent, landlord,' Ralph said hastily. 'As we're in the East End, how about some chipped potatoes? I believe fish and chips is often served round here?'

'What about eel pie?' one of the less drunk men added, grinning.

'Not my speciality, guvnor,' Tulliver said evenly. 'I can make chips, if that's what you want, gentlemen.

Although I was taught to cook by a French chef and I prefer to serve sauté potatoes with a fine steak.'

'I'm starving, Ralph. Tell the fellow to stop talking and start cooking.' The man in the red waistcoat refilled his glass with wine. 'Another bottle, girl.'

Tulliver turned to Flora with a nod.

She fetched the wine and pulled the cork expertly, to Ralph's obvious astonishment.

'We'll have the pretty girl to wait on us, landlord. What are you waiting for, fellow? Six servings of your best steaks. If you make it reasonably tasty, I daresay I'll put the word round in the upper echelons.'

Tulliver inclined his head. 'How do you like your steaks cooked, gentlemen?'

Back in the kitchen, Tulliver made the Bordelaise sauce while the steaks were cooking, and Flora sautéed the potatoes, garnishing them with butter and chopped parsley.

'You'd best wait on them, Flora,' Tulliver said seriously. 'But if they give you any trouble, I'm right here. I don't care if they're lords or dockers, I won't stand for any bad behaviour in my dining room.'

Flora took the food to the table. She had the satisfaction of seeing the gentlemen's expressions change subtly as they ate hungrily, calling for two more bottles of wine.

'Excellent meal,' the man in the red waistcoat said loudly.

'A glass of port and a slice of a good Stilton would

go down well now.' Ralph glanced at Flora as she cleared the table. 'I don't suppose your kitchen can rise to those heights.'

'We have a good vintage port,' Flora said firmly. 'Would you like me to bring the whole truckle of Stilton?'

Ralph blinked and for a few seconds seemed to be taken aback, but he quickly regained his normal arrogance.

'Bring it here, girl. Let me see it. If it's riddled with maggots I'm not interested.'

Flora finished clearing the table and returned to the kitchen. She relayed the message to Tulliver, who went down to the cellar and returned with two crusty bottles of port.

'You fetch the cheese, Flora. I'll take the port to the table. It's going to cost his lordship dear.'

'Make sure they can pay,' Flora said anxiously. 'I don't trust Ralph Pettigrew, but the other gentlemen seem to be all right.'

Tulliver laughed. 'They won't cheat me. I've had years of experience in this business. If your friend thinks he can get the better of me, he's mistaken.'

Flora took the cheese to the table, leaving Tulliver to present the port for approval. She held her breath when he announced the price of each bottle, half expecting Ralph to change his mind, but he agreed with a tipsy grin. Flora could only hope that his wealthy friends would pay if Ralph turned out to be short of funds.

Coralie also seemed anxious. 'Are you sure they'll pay up, Flora?'

'I really hope so,' Flora said earnestly.

There was little she could do other than to help Coralie clear the tables after the locals had drifted off to their respective homes. That left Ralph and his party, who were all very drunk by the time they finished off the wine and two bottles of very expensive port.

'This is going to cost them a small fortune,' Coralie said in a low voice as she totted up the bill and handed it to her husband.

Tulliver checked the total. 'They'll settle up like little lambs. Flora, lock the door and give me the key. Just in case the gentlemen decide to make a run for it.'

Flora did as he asked and handed him the key. She stood beside Coralie and watched as Tulliver presented Ralph with the bill. There was a moment of silence as Ralph tried to focus his eyes on the total.

'There's some mistake, landlord. We can't have drunk all that wine. You're trying to take advantage of us.'

Tulliver loomed over him, his heavy brows meeting over the bridge of his nose. 'Are you calling me a liar, sir?'

The man in the red waistcoat, who seemed to be the least inebriated of the group, held out his hand and took the piece of paper. He studied it in silence and then nodded.

'No, this seems to be correct, Pettigrew. We've had a good evening, so you'd best settle up. It was your idea to come here.'

'I never offered to pay for you all,' Ralph said feebly. 'That's not fair, chaps.'

One of the others snatched the bill and read it. He laughed. 'You'll have to marry the heiress, Pettigrew. Or has she sent you packing?'

'Leave Miss Stewart out of this,' Ralph said thickly.

Flora was incensed. How dare he bandy Arabella's name about in a public bar? She made a move towards him, but Coralie held her back.

'Leave it to Ted,' she whispered.

Tulliver stood his ground. 'I don't care who pays, gentlemen. But someone needs to or you will spend the night in the police station.'

The man in the red waistcoat rose to his feet. 'Well, Pettigrew, are you going to pay or do you fancy a swim in the river?'

'I-I can't raise that sort of money, Carstairs,' Ralph said feebly.

The other gentlemen jumped up with a chorus of disgust and they descended upon Ralph, picking him up bodily. 'Which way to the river, landlord?'

'You're going nowhere until someone stumps up the cash.' Tulliver stood his ground.

Carstairs took a leather pouch from his pocket and counted out the coins. 'That's for the excellent meal, landlord. Now unlock the door and let us out.'

'Are you really going to throw him in the Thames?' Flora met Carstairs' amused gaze with a smile.

'I daresay we'll give him a good soaking, Miss Lee.' Carstairs smiled. 'I don't know what you're doing here, but you should go home. Arabella needs you.' He followed his friends out of the tavern with Ralph shrieking at the top of his voice.

Flora stared after him as he followed his companions into Play House Yard. That was the second time that evening that Arabella's name had been mentioned and it struck home with such force that it took her breath away.

# Chapter Nine

Flora was surprised and worried by Carstairs' parting words. She seriously considered returning to South Molton Street in a second attempt to see Arabella, but she dismissed the idea as being impractical. Even so, she could not help wondering what Carstairs had meant when he said that Arabella needed her. He had been drinking but had not been drunk. It was a puzzle that she had no means of solving without first speaking to Arabella. However, trade was picking up at the Play House Inn, largely due to the improvements that Coralie had made at Flora's suggestion, and word had spread about the standard of meals they served. As early summer drifted into a hot and humid August they were increasingly busy. Tulliver was delighted and gave Flora credit for their continued success.

In Flora's rare free moments she thought about

visiting Nine Oaks in the hope that the family had returned to their country house, but it was not an easy journey and if she turned up unexpectedly, what would she say? How would she explain the fact that she had not sent word nor tried to return home? Arabella had everything she could possibly want or need. She was a much-loved daughter of a wealthy family. She would make a suitable match and she would forget all about her childhood friend and surrogate sister. Flora knew that it would not be the same for her. She would always remember the happy childhood she had enjoyed, thanks to the generosity of Sir Arthur and Lady Stewart. One day she hoped she might have a chance to explain her absence and tell them how much she appreciated what they had done for her, but that would have to wait for a while yet.

Even allowing for the heartache, Flora had her sights set on making something of herself, and she was doing well. Both Tulliver and Coralie were pleased with her hard work, her useful ideas, and her progress in the culinary arts. Moses was her devoted servant, and she was popular with the locals and the passing trade alike. She had not seen Ralph since the night when his friends threatened to throw him in the river, but as far as Flora knew no bodies had been washed up on the foreshore recently, and she assumed that Ralph had escaped a watery fate. Not that she cared much what happened to him; it was Gabriel Cutler who occupied her dreams, although if he had really been her friend he would surely have made an effort to find her after the abduction. It seemed impossible that he had hired a vehicle and yet not recognised the driver as being the man who had made such a scene in Hay Hill. Much as it pained her to admit it, even to herself, the only conclusion she could draw was that he simply did not care. She pushed these thoughts to the back of her mind and concentrated on her work, learning as much as she could from both Tulliver and Coralie. However, she soon realised that to bring the Play House Inn to the attention of the rich and famous was going to take much more time than she had imagined. The long hot summer did not help as the city sweltered in the heat of August and those who could get out of town did so in droves. However, trade with the locals and the seamen from the vessels that plied the river was brisk. Heat meant great thirst and ale was the answer.

Flora was in the taproom one morning, mopping the stone floor, when someone hammered on the front door.

'It's open,' she called in exasperation as the knocking grew louder. 'Come in, do.'

The knocking continued and Flora lifted her skirts and made her way across the wet floor to fling the door open. She took a step backwards as Daniel raised his fist to knock again.

'Daniel, what are you doing here in the city?'

He tipped his cap. 'Good morning, miss. I've come all the way from Nine Oaks. There's someone who's desperate to see you.'

'Is anything wrong? Is someone ill?'

Daniel turned his head, pointing to a carriage at the entrance of Playhouse Yard. Flora recognised it instantly as the Stewarts' barouche.

'Miss Arabella,' Daniel said tersely. 'She's come for you.'

Flora stepped past him and ran to the vehicle. 'Arabella.'

Daniel had followed her and opened the door. 'I'd step inside if I was you, miss. I don't like the look of some of them characters hanging round here.'

Flora laughed. 'They're not as villainous as they first appear, Daniel. Best attend to the horses.' She climbed into the barouche and Arabella flung her arms around her.

'Flora. Why did you run away? Why didn't you let us know where you were?'

'I was kidnapped,' Flora said breathlessly as she disengaged herself from Arabella's clutching hands. She perched on the edge of the seat. 'I didn't choose to leave, but how did you know where to find me?'

'It's a bit complicated, but Jefferson told me that you had called at the house in South Molton Street several weeks ago. I was very cross that he did not take your address.'

'He said you were out of town, Bella. I didn't know where you had gone. I didn't try to get in touch with you before because I thought you were better off without me.'

Arabella's pretty mouth drooped at the corners and her dark eyes filled with tears. 'How could you think that? We were like sisters.'

'But we aren't sisters, Bella. That's the whole point. The people who abducted me were my aunt and uncle, the same persons from whom your mother and father rescued me when I was a child. They wanted to use me to make money for them, but in the end they sold me to the landlord of the inn.'

'You were sold! That's illegal. Are you being kept prisoner?'

'No, not at all. The Tullivers have been very kind to me. Mr Tulliver is training me to be a cook and his wife has taught me how to manage a bar and how to deal with customers.'

'But you've had a good education, Flora. You were brought up to be a lady, like me.'

Flora smiled. 'But I'm not really like you, Bella, dear. Scratch the surface and I'm a common girl. I can only be an embarrassment to you and your family now.'

'I suppose Ralph told you that. He's a mean and nasty man. I loathe him, but he still thinks I'm going to marry him.'

'Was it he who told you where to find me?'

'No, actually it was Robert Carstairs.'

'Ralph brought him and some of their friends

to the inn.' Flora gave Arabella a searching look. 'Carstairs said that you were in trouble. What did he mean?'

'I believe that my father has lost a lot of money because of a business deal that went terribly wrong. He went into shipping, you know.'

Flora shook her head. 'Not really, although I do seem to remember something of the sort.'

'Papa invested in tea clippers some years ago, so I've been told. Of course he never discusses business with us, as you know. Apparently steamships are the way forward now, but he hadn't realised that at the time. Anyway, we are not as rich as we once were.'

'I'm sorry, Bella. How does it affect you?'

'I now need to marry someone with money. Papa has lost interest in marrying me into a titled family. He just needs me to make a good match.'

'Is he forcing you to accept someone you don't like? I mean, I assume Ralph is not a good candidate now. He's poor as a church mouse.'

'No, it's not Ralph. Papa has connections in Devonshire. We've just returned to Nine Oaks from a month at Rockwood Castle.'

'Your papa always wanted you to live in a castle.'

Arabella smiled ruefully. 'Well, I won't be living in Rockwood. It was lovely meeting the family and we had a wonderful time, but I felt as if I was on show. The Careys and the Blanchards were kindness itself and they held a ball to introduce me to as many eligible bachelors as they could gather together.'

'I am so sorry, but surely that's what the London season is all about. You were happy with that.'

'I was a good catch then. I'm virtually a pauper now and everyone knows it. That's why my parents took me all the way to Devonshire to try to find me a rich husband.'

'But you're only eighteen, Bella. You have plenty of time to meet someone and fall in love.'

'I just feel so alone and so responsible for my family. Now everything depends upon me.'

'Perhaps your father's finances aren't quite as dire as you think. They are probably worried for your future. I know they love you dearly.'

'You are so good for me, Flora. Please come home. I really need you.'

'I can't just leave here. Tulliver paid my uncle a lot of money. He didn't want to buy me, but in the end he decided it was payment for an apprenticeship, so I can't just walk away. I have to honour my part of the agreement.'

'But surely you weren't a party to the arrangement. You were being held captive by your aunt and uncle.'

'That's true, but I saw it as my only way of escape.'

A warning cry from Daniel alerted Flora to Coralie's approach. She peered in through the open door of the carriage.

'Flora, what are you doing?'

'Bella, this is Mrs Tulliver, the kind lady I was telling you about. Coralie, this is my good friend Arabella Stewart.'

Coralie looked from one to the other. 'Well, don't keep the young lady hanging about in the street, Flora. You'd best come into the parlour.'

'Thank you, ma'am,' Arabella said eagerly. 'I would love to visit a tavern. It's something I've never done.'

'Then we will broaden your experiences, miss. However, we have to go through the bar, so just follow me and ignore any of the rude fellows who might speak to you.' Coralie marched off, leaving Flora with little alternative but to help Bella down from the carriage.

'Best walk the horses, Daniel,' Arabella said firmly. 'I won't be too long.'

'Yes, Miss Arabella.' Daniel climbed onto the box and took charge of the horses.

Flora gave Daniel a grateful smile. She could not help but be impressed by his skill. She knew he could handle a horse and cart, but he had obviously graduated to driving a carriage and pair with some expertise. Daniel was full of surprises. She left him reluctantly and led Arabella across the yard.

Inside the tavern a few of the locals had arrived and were leaning against the bar. They stared openly at Arabella, who looked fresh and pretty in a morning gown of white organdie sprigged with rosebuds. Her tiny straw hat was trimmed with pink roses and a narrow veil, set at a perky angle on her dark hair. Judging by the expressions on their faces they had never seen an elegant lady in such close proximity.

Her skin glowed with good health and her cheeks were rounded, unlike the pasty-faced women who struggled to survive in the poorest parts of town. Flora had been glad of the serviceable garments provided by Coralie, but now she was uncomfortably aware of her dowdy appearance, especially when compared to Arabella. Putting such unworthy thoughts out of her mind, she guided her friend towards the parlour, away from the curious stares of the workmen.

Flora had realised from the beginning that Coralie was extremely proud of her parlour, but now she was seeing it through Bella's eyes and she realised it must look garish to the point of vulgarity. The room was crammed with heavy mahogany furniture uphol-stered in purple velvet. The mantelshelf was swagged in velvet of a similar shade and decorated with gold tassels. A brass garniture with matching timepiece and candlesticks held pride of place between Staffordshire pot dogs and a ruby glass vase. Small objects that Coralie had collected over the years covered every available surface, shelf and small table.

'Do take a seat, Miss Stewart,' Coralie said in the manner of speaking she used for the professional classes or clergymen. 'May I offer you some refresh-ment? Tea, coffee, or perhaps a glass of sherry wine?'

Arabella sat gingerly on the nearest upright chair. 'No, thank you, Mrs Tulliver.'

'It's very kind of you to visit,' Coralie continued, smiling. 'Flora has told me all about you and how wonderful your family have been to her. Unlike them as is actually related to her, who are scum, if you'll excuse the expression.'

'Oh, yes. I agree with you entirely,' Arabella said earnestly. 'Flora has suffered greatly at their hands.'

'Might I ask the reason for your turning up here unannounced?' Coralie shot a wary look in Flora's direction. 'You know that Flora is our apprentice?'

'I have told Bella that,' Flora said quickly. 'She understands how much I owe you and Mr Tulliver.'

'Ain't I glad to hear that?' Coralie breathed a sigh, which could have been relief, or even a touch of impatience. 'Now that's settled, perhaps you two would like to have a chat before Miss Stewart has to leave?'

'Actually, Mrs Tulliver. I came to take Flora to the home where she belongs.' Arabella ignored the warning looks that Flora gave her. 'I understand that your husband paid a sum of money for her services, which is, of course illegal, as our solicitor would point out to you. There is no deed of apprenticeship, so it is not a proper arrangement. How much do you require in order to repay the debt?'

Coralie stared at her for a moment and then shook her head emphatically. 'I'm afraid my husband won't agree to that, miss.'

'I can't see why he would object,' Arabella said haughtily. 'It's quite obvious that Flora has been brought up to better things than slaving away in a kitchen.'

Flora laid her hand on Arabella's arm. 'I've learned

a lot since I've been here, Bella. Mr and Mrs Tulliver have been kindness itself. I can't let them down.'

A frown creased Arabella's normally smooth brow. 'I'm sorry, I do not see why they can't get another person to work in your place. I am more than happy to reimburse them.'

Coralie's cheeks flamed scarlet. 'Well, Miss High and Mighty, you know nothing about running a business like this. My husband and I have put a lot of time into training Flora. You can't pay enough to cover that.'

'Without any proper indentures you cannot prove that there was any such transaction,' Arabella said calmly. 'Papa has an excellent solicitor. I will contact him, if necessary.'

'Please stop.' Flora stepped in between them. 'Coralie – Mrs Tulliver, it's true I had little say in the matter, but it's also a fact that you and your husband have been very good to me. However, I owe everything to Sir Arthur and Lady Stewart. I doubt if I would have survived very long as a small child had I been left with my aunt and uncle. In actual fact I have no proof that we are related – I don't know who my parents were. In spite of that, the Stewarts took me in. If I am needed, then I must go to them.'

Coralie looked from one to the other. 'I'm going to fetch Ted. He'll sort this out, since neither of you seem to care what I think.' She bustled out of the parlour, calling loudly for her husband.

'So you will come with me, Flora?' Arabella clutched Flora's hand. 'Say you will.'

'Does it mean so much to you, Bella?'

'Yes, it does. You are my dear sister and I've been miserable without you to talk to. I can't bear to see you working your fingers to the bone for these people.'

'I am learning how to support myself. I haven't the advantages that are yours by right. When you marry, I will have no place in the Stewart household.'

'That is so untrue. You will always be my friend and confidante. I've told you that a dozen times, but you don't listen to me.'

The sound of booted feet on the stone floor preceded Tulliver as he erupted into the room, followed by Coralie.

'What is going on here? Can't a man work in peace without women squabbling?'

'That's not how it is, sir,' Flora said hastily.

'I've offered to repay the money you gave Flora's relations for her freedom, if you can call it that. Although, as far as I can see, she escaped from one form of prison to another.' Arabella drew herself up to her full height, but even then she only came up to the middle button on Tulliver's waistcoat. 'I've come to take her home, sir.'

'I've explained that Flora is an apprentice,' Coralie added angrily. 'But this young lady won't listen.'

Tulliver stood with his arms folded, looking from Arabella's flushed face to Flora. 'You aren't a prisoner here, Flora Lee. I don't want an unwilling worker.'

Flora faced him with an attempt at a smile. 'I've been happy working for you, sir. You've taught me such a lot in a very short time, and so has Mrs Tulliver. But it wasn't my choice to come here and I owe my very existence to the Stewarts. If they hadn't rescued me from my aunt and uncle all those years ago, I doubt if I would be alive today.'

'Flora is like a sister to me, sir,' Arabella said firmly. 'She is needed at home. Just tell me how much you want and I will refund the money you paid for her.'

Coralie threw up her hands. 'This is ridiculous. I'm shocked by your duplicity, Flora.' She stormed out of the parlour, slamming the door as she went.

'My wife is naturally upset,' Tulliver said slowly. 'She has placed a great value on Flora's experience of high-class establishments, as well as her hard work. However, Flora is free to choose, but I value her services, as well as her ability to attract a better class of customer. She is not just a servant – I think of her as one of my own family.'

'You have been very good to me, sir.' Flora was weakening. Much as she wished she could go back to her life of luxury and ease, she knew that she had found fulfilment in doing a hard day's work. Even in such a short space of time she had learned a lot from both the Tullivers. It would be easier had they overworked or bullied her, but she could not fault the treatment she had received at their hands.

'If you will allow her to leave, I promise to spread the word among my friends and acquaintances so that your name is better known,' Arabella said firmly. 'I am acquainted with a reporter on the *Daily Telegraph*. I might manage to persuade him to come here and write an article about your tavern. I can't say fairer than that.'

Flora gazed at her in admiration. Arabella seemed to have grown in confidence during their separation, or perhaps she had always had the gift of persuasion.

Tulliver looked from one to the other. 'What do you have to say for yourself, Flora?'

'I didn't choose this way of life, sir. I'm very grateful for everything that you and Mrs Tulliver have done for me, but I owe as much, or even more, to the family who raised me as their own child.'

'So you are going back to the rich folk who treat you like an unpaid servant?' Tulliver said angrily.

'Flora is my sister, sir.' Arabella slipped her hand through the crook of Flora's arm. 'We are going home. Just tell me how much money you want in order to release her.'

'What have you to say for yourself, Flora?' Tulliver fixed her with an unwavering stare. 'Speak up. You are among friends, whatever you say.'

'I'm sorry, Mr Tulliver,' Flora said earnestly. 'You did save me from whatever Syd Fox had planned for me, and for that I will always be grateful, but I do have another family. I can't let them down.'

'I value your services, Flora. You don't have to

go with this young lady.' Tulliver barred their way. 'I'm sure she is old enough to look after herself.'

Flora shook her head. 'It wouldn't be right if I were to stay here when I am needed at home, sir.'

Tulliver took a step backwards. 'I can see that your mind is made up, Flora. You are not a prisoner here and you're free to leave as and when the desire takes you, but I won't take the young lady's money.'

'That's truly generous,' Flora said, biting back tears. 'I'm sorry I've upset Mrs Tulliver.'

'Coralie will recover her good spirits when she's had time to think. Go now, if you must.'

'Come along, Flora.' Arabella tugged at Flora's arm. 'Have you anything to bring with you?'

'Everything I have here was bought by Coralie. It's only fair to leave the clothes here and she can sell them.' Flora followed Arabella out of the parlour, through the taproom and outside into the hot sunshine. Arabella signalled to Daniel, who drew the carriage to a halt at the entrance to Play House Yard. He leaped down to open the door for them.

'So you're coming home, miss?'

'Yes, Daniel, I am. For a while at least.' Flora smiled at him as she climbed into the carriage and made herself comfortable next to Arabella.

'I'm glad you're coming home. We'll all be happy to see you back where you belong.' Daniel closed the door and moments later the barouche moved off, leaving Play House Yard and the inn to fade into the distance.

Flora turned to Arabella, eyeing her closely. 'Now tell me the real reason you wanted me to come with you, Bella. It can't be because your papa has had a setback in business.'

'You're right. Though it was the truth, in part anyway.'

'Then tell me the rest.'

Arabella stared out of the window, avoiding meeting Flora's direct look.

'Well, it's a little complicated.'

'We have an hour or so before we reach Nine Oaks, so you have plenty of time to tell me what's been happening in my absence.'

'I think I've fallen in love, Flora.'

'Really? That's wonderful. Who is he?'

'I'd rather not say at the moment. No one knows, not even the gentleman in question.'

Flora laughed. 'Bella, it sounds like one of your penny dreadful romances. Is he a prince or a peasant?'

'Don't laugh at me. I'm deadly serious. He's neither, although he does have a title.'

'Is he rich or poor? There must be something wrong with him or you wouldn't be so reluctant to tell me who he is. Surely your parents would approve?'

'That's just it – he's a lot older than me.'

'Goodness gracious! Is he a doddery old gentleman who walks with a stick and has a bath chair for when he cannot move another inch?'

'Now you're making fun of me. I believe he's in his late thirties and I am not quite nineteen.'

'That doesn't sound too bad. Has he got a wooden leg or a patch over one eye, like a pirate?'

'I'm not telling you any more. You're just turning the whole thing into a joke.'

Flora wrapped her arms around Arabella and gave her a hug. 'I am truly sorry. All this has happened so quickly I'm feeling quite light-headed. I promise not to say anything to embarrass you. Tell me how you met this mature, titled, person.'

'He is a friend of the family we stayed with in Devonshire. He was also a guest there, and we danced together at the ball they gave in our honour. He accompanied us on several sightseeing trips and to a few parties.'

'So you got to know him quite well.'

'Yes, I did. He is so nice and kind, Flora. He actually listened to me and he was interested in what I had to say. Totally different to all the young men I've met.'

'He does sound very nice. What did your mother and father think of him?'

'They liked him enormously. I can't imagine anyone would dislike him.'

'So what is the problem? Is he poor?'

'Heavens, no! He is very wealthy. He owns a large country house and estate on the borders of Devonshire and Dorset, as well as a town house in Piccadilly.'

'I really don't understand, Bella. If your parents

and everyone else like him, and he's rich as well as titled, there doesn't seem to be anything wrong with your relationship.'

'That is the problem,' Arabella said with a heavy sigh. 'He isn't interested in me in a romantic way.'

'How do you know that? He might be harbouring a secret passion for you.' Flora held up her hands. 'I am being serious, Bella. Perhaps he does think he is too old for you, but that is something you have to disprove. You need to get to know the gentleman better. Might I know his name now?'

'No. Because you might give something away when you meet him. We are invited to a ball along with many other guests. I want your honest opinion of him before I tell you who he is.'

'That doesn't make sense. How will I do that if I don't know this person's identity?'

'You will just have to trust me, Flora. Can you do that? My whole life depends upon the outcome of the ball next week.'

'I hope you have some cast-off gowns I might wear.'

'All your belongings are exactly where you left them before you were abducted. I knew you would return one day, and now it's happening. I couldn't be happier, Flora. We're going home.'

# Chapter Ten

If Flora had been in any doubt about her welcome home she realised very soon that she had worried needlessly. Everyone, from Sir Arthur and Lady Stewart to the ground workers at Nine Oaks, expressed their delight and relief that she had returned. Her old room had been made ready for her on Arabella's instructions, and her clothes were pressed and aired. There were bowls of garden roses filling her bedroom with their scent and providing splashes of delicate colour. Cook had made her favourite chocolate cake as well as small tartlets filled with lemon curd, which she also loved.

Flora was quite overwhelmed, but after their arrival there was one person she did not see on her daily walks in the grounds, and she began to think that Daniel was avoiding her. One morning immediately after breakfast she made her way to the walled garden, hoping to find him there. However, the only person present, hoeing between the regimented lines of lettuce, spinach and carrots, was Jim Downs, Daniel's cousin.

Flora greeted him warmly, but Jim seemed slightly aloof, which was unusual for him as he was normally the friendliest of souls.

'Do you know where I might find Daniel?' Flora eyed him warily.

'He's helping with the harvest, miss.'

'I haven't seen him since the return journey to Nine Oaks. I think he's avoiding me.'

Jim stabbed the hoe into the dry soil and leaned on the handle. 'I don't want to speak out of turn, miss, but do you blame him?'

'I don't understand. What are you saying?'

'You went off without a word. None of us knew where you was, miss.'

'That's what I want to explain. It wasn't my choice, Jim.'

He pulled the hoe free. 'It's none of my business, but you are one of them in the top house. You aren't like the rest of us. Leave my cousin be, that's all I has to say.' He stabbed the head of the hoe into the soil and continued his work, putting an end to the conversation.

Flora was shocked by his attitude as much as by his angry words. Daniel had been her friend and companion since childhood, although their affection for each other had reached a new and dangerous level on May Day. Flora had known all along that Daniel had deep feelings for her but on that day, when their relationship reached a pivotal level, she had held back. Even though it was hard to admit, Flora knew that the difference in their social standing would eventually come between them, although Daniel was not the sort of man who would give up easily. However, her feelings for him had undergone a subtle change and it all stemmed from the ball held in Park Lane. Gabriel Cutler had come into her life and had occupied her thoughts during the time she spent in the cellar at Turnagain Lane, even though she had done her best to exclude him. Flora knew instinctively that the sea ran in his blood, and even if he returned her love he might never settle on shore. He had probably found another ship and she would never see him again. That was a penance she would have to suffer alone.

Flora left the walled garden and walked slowly back to the main house. She had come home at Arabella's request and now she must devote herself to helping her dear friend find true love with the wealthy older titled gentleman who had caught her fancy. However, Flora wanted to be certain that he was worthy of her surrogate sister, title or no title. Arabella was not going to waste her youth, beauty and sunny disposition on someone who did not deserve her. Flora was deep in thought when the rumbling wheels of a farm wagon made her glance towards the lane. She came to a sudden halt at the sight of Daniel sitting on a hay bale with his arm around Elsie Root, the scullery maid who had been the Queen of the May. Her cheeks were flushed and she was gazing up at him so adoringly that Flora had to turn her head away. So that was the real reason why Daniel had been avoiding her. It had not been because of anything she had done – Daniel had found solace elsewhere. Flora walked on quickly, not wanting to be seen, but she could not resist the temptation of a quick glance over her shoulder, and it was obvious that neither Daniel nor Elsie had eyes for anyone other than each other.

Flora walked into the house and was met by Arabella, who was dressed for an outing.

'You've forgotten, haven't you?' Arabella sighed. 'I told you last evening that I was going for my final fitting today. I want you to come with me, Flora.'

Flora forced herself to appear cheerful. It was hard to accept that Daniel had fallen for someone else in such a short space of time, but if she were being honest she had to admit that it was hurt pride and not a broken heart that bothered her now. She stifled a sigh. 'If it's already made you have obviously chosen the gown. Is there any point in asking my opinion?'

'If you put it like that I suppose not, but I want your company. I also want you to meet the young woman who has designed the gown and is having it made. It was Rosalind Blanchard who recommended her to me when we stayed at the castle.'

'You and your castle – are you sure you don't want to marry Ralph Pettigrew? You could have your own pile of crumbling stones as well as a title.'

'Stop teasing me, Flora. Come with me and you'll meet my new friends.'

'It's too hot to travel into town. Take Mary with you. She'll be looking after the gown when you bring it home.'

'No, I want you to come with me. Please go to your room and put on your best bonnet and your lace mittens. We're not going into town. My modiste has a house on the edge of Hackney Marsh. It will be pleasantly cool there and you can meet Amelia. We've become quite friendly since you weren't here to comfort me.'

'It wasn't my choice,' Flora said, exasperated. 'But I'll go and get my bonnet and my lace mittens if it pleases you,' she added hastily, noting the ominous trembling of Arabella's lips. 'I'd better look my best for your fashionable friend.'

'She's not at all pretentious, Flora. And she's getting married soon. It's all so romantic.' Arabella sighed. 'Do hurry up. I've sent for the carriage. It will be like old times.'

'You would think I'd been absent for a year or more,' Flora muttered as she headed for the grand staircase.

The house on the edge of the marsh was not how Flora had imagined it would be. Protected by a high brick wall, which no doubt stopped the marsh grasses and wild plants invading the neat vegetable garden, the half-timbered building sprawled comfortably amongst barns and outbuildings, lazing in the sun as if taking an afternoon nap. But the peaceful scene was shattered by the excited shrieks of a small boy, who was being chased by a girl of nine or ten. They came to a halt as the carriage drew up outside the main entrance. Flora was first to alight, followed by Arabella.

'It's Daisy, isn't it?' Arabella said, smiling.

'Yes, miss.' Daisy wrapped her arms around the small boy. 'This is Percy.'

'I remember.' Arabella patted his curly head. 'How are you, Percy?'

He answered with a growl.

'Don't worry, miss,' Daisy said hastily. 'He does that to people he don't know. He's a good boy really.'

'I don't doubt it. I have an appointment with Miss Sutton. Will you tell her that Miss Stewart is here?'

'Yes, miss.' Daisy eyed Flora curiously. 'Are you her maid?'

'Certainly not.' Arabella stepped in between them. 'Miss Lee is my companion. Not that it's any of your business, young lady. Now please do as I asked.'

'She looks like a servant,' Daisy muttered as she took Percy by the hand and led him into the house.

Flora laughed. 'I think little Percy is better than a guard dog.'

'He's Mariah's son. She is Amelia's housekeeper

and they seem to be really good friends. A bit like us, Flora. They rely on each other. It's really sweet to see.'

'Is Daisy her daughter?'

'No, Daisy is a child that Amelia took in. The poor little soul had been put into service far too young and was being ill-treated.'

'That was a good thing to do. She sounds like a nice person.'

'She is very caring as well as being such a clever designer. Mariah's daughter is a little older than Daisy, I think. Betsy helps in the sewing room. You'll meet them all shortly. Providing Daisy passes on my message.'

Almost before the words left Arabella's mouth the front door was opened by a flustered woman enveloped in a white apron with her sleeves rolled up to reveal floury hands and wrists.

'I do beg your pardon, Miss Stewart. Young Daisy still has a lot to learn about manners. I've been baking, so please excuse the state I'm in. ' Her gaze strayed to Flora, who stepped forward, holding out her hand. 'I don't think I know you, miss.'

'How do you do, ma'am? You must be young Percy's mama. He's a handsome little fellow – I can see the likeness. I am Flora Lee, Miss Stewart's companion.'

'How do, miss?' Mariah wiped her hand on her apron. 'Please come inside, Amelia will be with you shortly. I've sent Daisy up to the sewing room to fetch her.' Mariah showed them into a large parlour that was dominated by a grand piano.

Flora looked round at the eclectic mix of furniture, which although shabby and none of it matched, made the room look lived-in and homely.

'You have a musician in the family?' Flora said, smiling. 'Do you remember our piano teacher, Bella? She used to smack me across the knuckles with a ruler if I played a wrong note.'

Arabella smiled. 'I most certainly do, but I had the worst of it. You are a much better pianist than I will ever be.'

'Just wait here, ladies,' Mariah backed towards the door. 'If you'll excuse me, I have a pie in the oven and it should be done now.'

Flora took a seat at the piano and lifted the lid. 'May I?'

'Suit yourself, miss. I'm sure no one minds.' Mariah bustled out of the room just as Flora struck up a chord. She ran her fingers over the keys.

'It's in tune, so someone must love it.' She played a melody that had Arabella waltzing around the room, but she stopped as the door opened and a pretty young woman rushed into the room. Her glossy dark hair had escaped from the confines of a snood and her large violet-blue eyes sparkled with amusement.

'Please don't stop on my account. Hardly anybody plays the piano these days, and you dance divinely, Miss Stewart.'

Arabella's cheeks reddened but she laughed shyly. 'I feel silly now.'

'Not at all. I love to see people happy and enjoying life. You are just practising for the ball next week, I'm sure.'

'Yes, of course.'

Flora closed the piano lid and rose to her feet. 'That is a fine instrument, Miss Sutton. Do you play?'

'Not very well, although when I'm on my own I do play a little, just to amuse myself. Anyway, please come up to the long gallery. The gown is ready for the final fitting. I am rather delighted with it, even though I shouldn't say so.'

'I don't see why. You should be proud of your work.' Arabella followed her out of the room with Flora hurrying after them.

The entrance hall with its wainscoted walls and low ceiling was reminiscent of a bygone age. Flora could imagine ladies in farthingales and frilled ruffs parading from room to room with gentlemen in doublets and hose accompanying them. However, there was no time to loiter as Amelia took the stairs with the grace of a young gazelle and Arabella tried to keep up. They reached the second floor and entered the long gallery that took up the entire length and breadth of the sprawling house. The whirring of sewing machines echoed off the ornate plasterwork on the ceiling, and cotton dust danced in the sunbeams that filtered through the small windowpanes.

Flora counted six tables with women intent on their machines, while two others worked quietly, hand-sewing the final touches on shimmering lengths of silk and satin.

Amelia led them to a screened-off area. 'Nellie is my senior seamstress. She will bring the gown for you to try on, Miss Stewart, and I will be here to supervise any alterations, if necessary.' She returned to the main workroom and moments later a small woman joined them. She was half-hidden beneath a flurry of peach-coloured silk taffeta and lace but her proud smile lit up the room.

'Here you are, Miss Stewart. I think this is one of the best gowns I've had the pleasure in helping to create. If you'll permit me to assist, you may try it on, but I'm sure it will fit you perfectly.'

Flora stood back, watching in awe as Bella became a beautiful swan in the elegant gown. The fit was perfect and the delicate colour suited her peaches and cream complexion.

'You look wonderful, Bella.'

Arabella eyed her reflection in the tall cheval mirror and her hand went to her hair. 'Of course it will look better when I've had my hair done properly, but it is rather fine, don't you agree, Flora?'

'I most certainly do.' Flora clasped her hands, her eyes filling with tears. 'You look like a princess, Bella. It's the loveliest gown I've ever seen.' She turned to Amelia, who had just joined them. 'You are so clever, Miss Sutton.'

Amelia smiled proudly. 'Thank you, but I admit I'm delighted with the end result. You show it off to perfection, Miss Stewart.'

'I couldn't be happier.' Arabella did a twirl in front of the mirror. 'I will tell everyone what an amazing couturier you are, Miss Sutton. Although they will be able to see for themselves when I wear this gown to the ball.'

'Thank you. Word of mouth is the best advertisement that anyone in my profession can have.' Amelia shot a speculative glance in Flora's direction. 'Are you going to the ball next Friday, Miss Lee?'

'Yes, I will be there as chaperone.'

'Surely not? I know that Freddie would have extended the invitation to include you if you had met. He is the kindest, most generous man alive.'

'Do you know him well?' Arabella asked casually. 'I mean, we met in Devonshire and I danced with him several times. He seemed very agreeable.'

Flora turned away to hide a wry smile. Arabella's interest in the gentleman was ill-concealed.

'Yes, he chose to help me get started and for that I will always be grateful. I just cannot understand why such a nice, kind, good-looking gentleman with wealth and a title is still unmarried. I believe he has had his heart broken on several occasions, but that is just hearsay.'

'Perhaps he will find someone worthy of him one day,' Flora said tactfully. 'I'm looking forward to meeting him.'

Amelia angled her head, looking Flora up and down with a critical eye. 'Have you a gown for the occasion, Miss Lee?'

'I have several. Bella is very generous. You should understand that I am not family, Miss Sutton. I was taken in by Miss Stewart's parents at a very young age. They treated me like a second daughter, and I owe them everything.'

'Flora and I are the same size. She has my last year's gowns.' Arabella gazed dreamily at her reflection in the mirror. 'I am so excited about the ball. You could have a new gown if you really wanted one, Flora, but there isn't time now.'

Amelia gave Flora a calculating look. 'I have a beautiful ball gown that I made for a client who changed her mind. She's a very wealthy lady and ordered two of my creations, which she has actually paid for. I think it might fit you with just a little alteration, Miss Lee. It would certainly suit you.'

Flora hesitated. 'I don't know. I'm quite content with Bella's cast-offs.'

'What do you think, Miss Stewart?'

'Of course,' Arabella said hastily. 'It sounds perfect. Maybe she could try it on, if you have time.'

'Nellie.' Amelia pulled the screen back just far enough to look into the sewing room. 'Will you be kind enough to fetch the scarlet gown that Lady Sellers chose not to accept?'

'Of course, Miss Sutton.'

'I'm sure you'll love it as I do, Miss Lee,' Amelia

said enthusiastically. 'It's a bold colour, but with your auburn hair and rose-petal complexion you could carry it off beautifully.'

'And it would be another advertisement for your couture,' Flora said, smiling.

'Precisely so.' Amelia clapped her hands. 'And no cost to you. Everyone is happy.'

Minutes later Flora stood very still, gazing into the mirror. The gown fitted perfectly and the colour was flattering. It was a little too long, but Nellie was on her hands and knees adjusting the hem with young Betsy, Mariah's daughter, passing her the pins.

'It could have been made for you, miss,' Nellie said approvingly. 'I worked on this gown meself and I'm glad it's going to be worn, especially by someone with your looks and figure.'

'Thank you, Nellie.' Flora could hardly speak. She had never imagined she might look like this and it was hard to believe. 'What a glorious shade of red,' she added after a while. 'It reminds me of Christmas at Nine Oaks and the scarlet-berried holly bush at the entrance to the walled garden.'

Arabella doubled up with laughter. 'Now I'll think of that every time I look at you, but it is a wonderful colour and the gown looks lovely on you, Flora. You must have it.'

'You look beautiful, miss,' Betsy said shyly. 'The lady who ordered this was not half as good-looking as you.'

'We don't say things like that, Betsy.' Amelia shook

her head. 'But you're right, nonetheless. I'm so proud of that gown. You and Miss Stewart will be walking advertisements for Marsh House Modes. But you'll need dance slippers.'

Flora glanced anxiously at Arabella. 'You must have an old pair I could borrow. Mine are rather shabby.'

'I daresay Mary can find you a suitable pair,' Arabella said casually. 'You do look nice, Flora. I'm quite jealous, but that is not my colour.'

'Shoes are very important,' Amelia said with a wry smile. 'I could tell you a funny story about dance slippers, but I won't bore you.'

'Emmie had to wear her black boots to a ball,' Betsy said, giggling. 'They were painted with washing blue mixed with starch so that they matched her gown, but someone spilled wine on them and the dye ran. I saw them in the morning, they did look funny.'

'Thank you, Betsy. I don't think the ladies want to know about my most embarrassing moments.' Amelia shooed her off with a tolerant smile. 'But I will tell you that Freddie came to my rescue that night. He led me out onto the dance floor as if I were the Queen herself. He's such a dear man.'

'How did you come to meet him?' Flora stood very still while Nellie and Betsy worked on the hem of her gown. 'If you don't mind me asking, that is?'

'I'm sure it's none of our business,' Arabella said hastily.

'No, I don't mind at all.' Amelia eyed the seamstress's work critically. 'That's good, Nellie. Just the right length. What was I saying? Oh, yes, how did I meet Freddie? That again is another story, but my fiancé, Todd, is a doctor. He was born in London but grew up in Rockwood village and was close to the family at the castle. That's how he came to know Freddie, who was a constant visitor.'

'It all sounds very romantic,' Flora said, smiling. 'I can't wait to meet him.'

Arabella shifted from one foot to the other. 'Will someone help me? Much as I love this gown, I cannot wear it home.'

'Of course, how silly of me.' Amelia popped her head round the screen. 'Maisie, I need you to assist Miss Stewart. There are no alterations needed. The gown is a perfect fit.'

'The gown is wonderful,' Arabella said, sighing. 'I just hope I won't be eclipsed by my chaperone.'

'You didn't mean that, did you, Bella?' Flora asked anxiously as they settled themselves in the Stewarts' barouche.

'Mean what?'

'That I would take the attention from you at the ball.'

'No, of course not, but that gown is very bold and eye-catching.'

'I'll wear something else if it bothers you so much.'

Arabella shook her head. 'No, please don't take

any notice of me. I'm all of a twitter at the thought of meeting his lordship again. I'm used to being in control of my suitors but this time I am at a disadvantage, and Papa's financial situation does not help. It's not your fault, Flora.'

'Nor is it yours, Bella. What your papa does in business should have no bearing on whether a gentleman is attracted to you, especially someone who is wealthy in his own right. Anyway, I doubt if Lord Freddie will look at me twice. You will be the belle of the ball, and rightly so. I will melt into background and sit with the rest of the wallflowers and matrons.'

Arabella subsided into silence and Flora sat back, closing her eyes and imagining herself waltzing around the ballroom in the beautiful gown, but it was Gabriel Cutler who held her in his arms, not the mysterious Lord Freddie.

It was mid-afternoon when they arrived back at Nine Oaks and Flora was so hungry that her stomach rumbled uncontrollably.

'I am starving, Bella. We've missed luncheon. Will you send for afternoon tea? We could take it on the terrace.'

'I couldn't eat a thing. All I want to do is to lie down in a darkened room. My head is pounding.'

'I'm so sorry. Shall I send for Mary?'

'Yes, please.' Arabella moved slowly towards the staircase.

Flora turned to James, who was standing stiffly to attention. 'Will you send Mary up to Miss Bella's room, James? She'll know what to do.'

'Yes, Miss Flora.' James strode off in the direction of the servants' quarters.

Flora hesitated, wishing she had asked him to send tea and sandwiches to the terrace, but she decided to go to the kitchen. She had always been a favourite with Cook and there might be some chocolate cake or perhaps scones. She followed James but she could not keep up with his long strides. He was already in the kitchen when she opened the door and to her astonishment he was chatting amicably with a man who was seated at the table with his back to her.

'I'm sorry, Miss Flora. Was there something else?' James said awkwardly.

'No, it's all right, James. You may go.' Flora held her breath as the visitor rose to his feet and turned to face her.

'Flora?'

# Chapter Eleven

'Captain Cutler,' Flora stared at him in disbelief. 'Why are you here, and in particular why are you sitting in the kitchen?'

He laughed and his blue eyes crinkled at the corners. 'I'm waiting for Sir Arthur to return. To tell the truth, I'm more comfortable below stairs than I am in the drawing room.'

'Me, too, although I wouldn't admit it to just anybody.' Flora beckoned to Elsie Root, whom she had just spotted emerging from the scullery. She suppressed a desire to make a remark on Elsie's budding relationship with Daniel. It was, of course, none of her business. She managed a smile. 'Elsie, please send a tray of tea and cakes to the drawing room. Captain Cutler and I will await Sir Arthur there.'

Elsie shot her a wary sideways glance and bobbed a curtsey. 'Yes, Miss Flora.'

'We'd better go upstairs,' Flora said in a low voice. 'Much as I love the kitchen, it does put the servants out a bit if we invade their domain.'

'Of course. I should have thought of that.' Gabriel hurried to open the kitchen door that James had allowed to close behind him. 'It's so good to see you again. I was frantic with worry when that fellow abducted you. I should have recognised him as the shifty-looking individual we saw at Ralph's lodgings.'

She eyed him curiously. There were many questions on the tip of her tongue, but she forced herself to sound unconcerned. 'It all happened so quickly, Gabriel. Come with me, we can talk better in the drawing room.' Flora led the way to the drawing room. Her heart was pounding and she was certain that her cheeks were flushed. Seeing Gabriel again had brought back all the emotions she thought she had managed to conquer during the past few months. She took a seat by the fireplace.

'Won't you sit down, Gabriel. I don't know how long Sir Arthur will be and we might have to wait a while.'

He remained standing, gazing at her with a worried frown. 'Ralph told me that he found you working in a common tavern. I didn't believe him at first, but then I ran into Carstairs and he confirmed what Ralph had said.'

'Yet you didn't come to find me. Wouldn't that have been the action of a friend?'

'Yes, of course, but I had an urgent message asking me to visit my uncle at Pettigrew Castle. He has these sudden attacks and insists that the end is nigh, then miraculously he recovers, but while I was away I was offered a new command, which I could not refuse. I only returned last evening and I heard you had come home. It was such a relief.'

'Well, I'm unharmed, as you see, and I learned a great deal working for the Tullivers.'

He shook his head. 'I wish I could have come to London sooner, but I needed the money, so I had to return to sea.'

'There was nothing you could have done, Gabriel. I am quite capable of looking after myself. I owe a lot to the Tullivers, and I only left them because Bella needs me here.'

Gabriel strolled over to the window and gazed out at the sunny parkland with sheep grazing contentedly on the lush grass.

'I couldn't be in a more pleasant spot,' Gabriel said thoughtfully. 'No wonder you love this place.'

'I don't remember telling you that.'

'You did, and I knew by the fond way you spoke about Nine Oaks that you would rather live in the country than in the city.'

Flora laughed. 'You must be a mind reader. May I ask what your business is with Sir Arthur? I mean, we are well aware that there have been some difficulties regarding his venture into shipping.'

'Obviously I can't discuss business matters with

anyone except Sir Arthur, but I will say that the days of sail are coming to an end. Steam is the way forward.'

'Is that what you would like? A steamship to command?'

'I did my apprenticeship under sail and I will be sorry to see the old tea clippers fade into the history books, but steam engines are powerful and reliable. Wind is a fickle mistress, if you'll excuse the analogy.'

'I understand what you're saying, but how does all this affect Sir Arthur?'

'That is for him to decide. I do as I am bid.' Gabriel's eyes twinkled irresistibly and Flora smiled back.

'I doubt that very much.'

He was suddenly serious. 'But what about you, Flora? I know some of the story, but who was it who abducted you that dreadful day?'

'Do you remember following me to your cousin's lodgings in Hay Hill?'

'Yes, how could I forget walking in on that unpleasant fracas? But then Ralph has always made a habit of mixing with the wrong sort of people.'

'The individual who caused the unpleasantness was Sydney Fox, the man who claimed to be my uncle. I was raised by him and his awful wife until the Stewarts took me in. It was Sydney who abducted me on the day in question. He and Gert kept me prisoner in a dank basement room for weeks.'

'That's unbelievable. The police were called after

the incident, but I believe nothing came of their enquiries. I wish I could have done more to help you.'

'I blame your cousin, Ralph. If he hadn't had dealings with Fox none of this would have happened.'

'What did Fox hope to gain by kidnapping you?'

'When I recovered from the injuries I sustained in the accident I found out that he and his despicable wife planned to sell me to the highest bidder.'

Gabriel crossed the floor in two strides. He took a seat in the chair opposite Flora, taking both her hands in his. 'I can't believe that anyone would treat you so badly, let alone your family. But you must have escaped. How did you get away from them?'

'It was an odd series of circumstances. They had taken away my clothes and shoes and locked me in the cellar, but I managed to free myself. As strange as it may sound I stole a garment from a washing line in the backyard, and I was about to leave the house when Syd turned up with Ted Tulliver.'

'Tulliver from the Play House Inn?'

'You know him?'

'It was one of my favourite haunts whenever we were in dock. He's a good fellow. I can't believe that he would agree to purchase a young woman.'

'He could see the state I was in and he took pity on me. He gave Syd the money he demanded, although Ted insisted that it was to pay for my apprenticeship. He's an ambitious man and a brilliant chef. He thought I could bring in a better class of customer and my knowledge of eating out in expensive restaurants might be useful to them.'

'You were free then. You could have asked Sir Arthur to pay off Tulliver.'

'I could have, but I don't want to be beholden to the Stewarts forever. Coralie and Ted were both very kind to me.'

'Yet you returned here. What went wrong?'

'Nothing. It was Robert Carstairs who told me that Bella needed me, and then she turned up one day and persuaded me to come home.' Flora withdrew her hands from Gabriel's warm grasp. 'I had to put her first.'

He nodded. 'I understand. What an ordeal you suffered. It makes my experiences at sea pale by comparison.'

'I thought you would be gone for a long time. I must confess, I was surprised to see you today.'

'Sir Arthur had bought two vessels, one of which was given to me to command, but we had barely reached Santander when we had to put in for repairs. Unfortunately they proved to be so extensive that Sir Arthur refused to accept the estimate, and I had to let the crew go. I made my own way home.'

'At least you didn't sink mid-ocean,' Flora said earnestly. 'Wasn't the ship insured?'

'That's why I need to speak to Sir Arthur. There's a question of unpaid wages and my position in the company, as well employment for the crew, who did all they could to keep the old tub seaworthy.'

'I'm sorry, Gabriel. You must be very disappointed.'

'I was, but now it's given me a chance to see you again, Flora.'

'But you'll be off on your travels again soon, no doubt. You said that Sir Arthur owns two ships. Perhaps he will ask you to command the other one.'

'As far as I can see it is in as bad shape as the one left in Santander. I'm afraid it will have the same fate as its sister ship.'

'What will you do? Will you go to another company?'

'That depends upon a lot of things. I need to speak to Sir Arthur first and then I have to travel to Pettigrew Castle yet again to visit my uncle, who is apparently failing fast, or so the message said.'

'I thought you weren't interested in the inheritance.'

'That's right. The ancient building is crumbling into dust. It's Ralph who is desperate to inherit both the old ruin and the title. I am going to visit the old gentleman more out of duty than from affection. He did raise us both, but it was obvious that he did it because there was no one else to care for two orphaned boys.'

Before Flora had a chance to reply the door opened and Sir Arthur entered the drawing room. He stared at Gabriel, eyebrows raised.

'Captain Cutler. What brings you here today?' Sir Arthur's gaze turned to Flora and he smiled. 'I see you two have become reacquainted. However, this is business, Flora my dear. Would you mind giving us a few moments?'

Flora jumped to her feet. 'Of course, sir.'

'I believe my wife wants a word with you, Flora. The ball in Piccadilly has set everyone talking. I daresay it is something that requires urgent attention.'

'I hope all goes well for you, Captain,' Flora said as she walked past him, and she was rewarded by a charming smile. She left the room and made her way to the blue parlour where she hoped to find Lady Stewart and Arabella. Flora entered the room without knocking. Everything was very informal in the blue parlour. It overlooked the terrace at the back of the house and the parterre garden, which was Daniel's father's pride and joy. It was a cosy room with comfortable armchairs and a worktable where Constance kept her embroidery and an array of silks, as well as needles, scissors and the printed motifs she used in her latest craze of decoupage.

Constance and Arabella were seated together on the chintz-covered sofa, studying a fashion magazine.

'You wanted to see me, ma'am?'

Constance looked up, smiling. 'Yes, Flora. I believe you need a new pair of dancing slippers for the ball on Friday.'

'Mine will do, thank you, ma'am. I'm more than happy with the beautiful gown from Marsh House Modes.'

Constance nodded. 'It is splendid, although in my day a young woman like you would have been wearing a delicate pastel shade or even white. However, times change and we must keep up with them. After all, my dear, you are not a debutante, so I daresay the conventions do not apply in your case. It is a very fine gown and the colour will go well with your Titian hair.'

'Dancing slippers, Mama,' Arabella said gently. 'You were going to speak to Flora about them.'

'Yes, of course. Actually I have a new pair, not even worn, Flora. You may have them. Arabella tells me that you have the same size feet as I do. People used to remark on my dainty feet when I was a girl.'

'So I've heard, ma'am. But I can't take your new shoes.'

'Nonsense, Flora. It gives me pleasure to see you dressed well, and I'm so glad you are back with us. Bella missed you so much, didn't you, dear?'

'Yes, Mama. I am very glad she's safe now. We'll be the belles of the ball, won't we, Flora?'

'You will be. I will be respectfully behind you at all times.'

'That's settled then,' Constance said firmly. 'I'll tell Mary to take the slippers to your room, Flora. Now, girls. I want some help in cutting out some of these delightful little pictures of flowers and fruits for my decoupage.'

Flora was about to agree but Arabella rose swiftly to her feet. 'I'm sorry, Mama. But I've just remembered something very important I have to do, and I need Bella to help me.'

'Oh, dear!' Constance said, pouting. 'Are you sure you couldn't put it off until later, my love?'

'If I could I would certainly do so.' Arabella grabbed Flora by the hand. 'We'll go out this way and we won't bump into that wretched sea captain.'

'Who is that, Bella?' Constance picked up a dainty pair of silver scissors. 'Which sea captain is that?'

'The one who scuttled Papa's ship in Spain. As far as I can see, it is Captain Cutler who is to blame for our lack of funds. Don't look at me like that, Flora. I know you liked him, but you've been absent while Papa was going quietly bankrupt. I blame the captain for allowing Papa to purchase two ships that were only fit for firewood.'

Flora opened her mouth to argue, but Arabella dragged her out through the open French windows, stopping only when they were out of her mother's earshot.

'I'm sorry, Flora, but if we had agreed to help Mama cut out those horrid little pictures we would have been there until it was time for dinner. Now why were you looking for me?'

'I wasn't, Bella. I was told that your mama wanted to see me.'

'Oh yes, it was those silly slippers. Mind you, they are very pretty. Mama always buys the best of everything and, to be honest, they are too small for her, but she would die rather than admit it. You will be the best-dressed companion at the ball – just don't outshine me, please.'

'That would be impossible and you know it, Bella. I know my place and I won't let you down. However, I need to know the name of the gentleman who has taken your fancy. After all, I might say the wrong thing if I don't know who he is.'

'All right, you win, Flora. But only because the ball is being held at Freddie's London house in aid of charity.'

'He must be very wealthy.'

'Yes, he is, but that's not why I love him.'

'You love him? Really?'

'Yes, I do. He is so kind and considerate. He's funny, too. He can make me laugh even when I feel sad, and he's very good-looking. He has wonderful blue eyes, and when he smiles it feels as though the sun has come out, even if it's raining outside.'

'My goodness! That does sound like love.' Flora eyed her friend curiously. 'So tell me his name, and why your parents would disapprove of the match.'

'Well, to be honest he has never done anything to make me believe that he feels the same way I do, but he does pay particular attention to me whenever we meet.' Flora sighed. 'His name is Frederick Ashton, the Earl of Dorrington, and he's eighteen years my senior.'

'That is a big age gap, I must admit, but not insurmountable if you both love each other. Has he been married before?'

'No, never. Amelia knows him quite well and she told me that he has been unlucky in love. If anything, he is too nice and kind.'

'He sounds like an angel. I can't wait to meet him.'

'You won't say anything to him, will you?' Arabella's eyes misted with tears. 'I would feel such a fool if he thinks of me as a silly young woman.'

'I'm sure such a thought would never enter his head. I will be the soul of discretion. You mustn't worry about a thing.'

'You don't think he's too old for me, do you?'

'Not at all, there are many happy marriages with just such a difference in ages. But I will be better able to judge when I've met Lord Dorrington.'

'Freddie,' Arabella said with a tender smile. 'Everyone calls him Freddie. He's such a dear.'

'I simply cannot wait until Friday.' Flora gave Arabella a hug. 'I will be the soul of tact and diplomacy, so don't worry about me.'

'We will be staying at the town house, of course. It would take too long to get back here after the ball. We'll get dressed there, too.'

'It will be a wonderful evening,' Flora said firmly. 'Stop worrying. You'll get frown lines on your forehead.'

Arabella's hand flew to her face. 'No! Not really. Have they started already?'

'No, of course not, silly. Stop imagining things. Anyway, a few lines might make you look older, as you are so worried about the difference in your ages.'

'You are hateful sometimes, Flora,' Arabella said crossly.

'You know you don't mean that.' Flora tugged playfully at one of Arabella's dark curls and soon both of them were giggling like children.

In her old bedroom at the house in South Molton Street, Flora dressed for the ball in the scarlet silk taffeta gown. It was beautiful in its simplicity and there had been no need to embellish the lustrous material with beads, lace or fringing. It fitted perfectly and Flora could hardly believe that the lovely young woman gazing back from the mirror was her own image. Constance and Bella shared a personal maid, and it was Mary who coiffed Flora's auburn hair into a coronet of curls interspersed with cream rosebuds from the garden at Nine Oaks. The result was almost regal and Flora smiled ruefully as she recalled the ill-fitting cotton frock she had stolen from the washing line in Turnagain Lane. How things had changed since that day. She picked up her dance card, fan and long white gloves. This was going to be Bella's evening, and she would do everything in her power to make sure that Lord Dorrington paid attention to the young woman who had fallen in love with him. Flora went to Arabella's room and found her dressed and ready, but clearly nervous.

'Come along, Bella. Whatever happens we will enjoy ourselves. Just be yourself, and everything will fall into place.'

Arabella laughed nervously. 'Is that a promise, Flora?'

'It most certainly is. Lord Dorrington is a very lucky man. You are going to dazzle him with your beauty and wit. That's an order.'

Arabella was giggling as they left the room arm in arm as they headed for the staircase.

The grandeur of Lord Dorrington's house in Piccadilly left Flora feeling as though she had walked into a palace. She had been to many balls and functions, but the grandness of the mansion surpassed all her expectations. She sensed that Arabella was nervous and she tried to keep her calm, but as they waited to be announced at the top of a flight of stairs, Flora was alarmed to see the colour drain from Bella's cheeks. They were behind Sir Arthur and Lady Stewart, who were the next to be greeted by Freddie. Flora had a good view of him and she liked what she saw. He was not handsome, but his classic features had a healthy glow of a man who preferred the outdoor country life to that in the city, and his genuine smile of welcome lit his blue eyes. He greeted Arabella's parents as if they were old friends and he shook Sir Arthur's hands with a sympathetic smile.

'I'm sorry for your run of bad luck, Sir Arthur,' Freddie said in a low voice. 'I might be able to help, if you would care to call on me here, tomorrow at noon. We could discuss a matter which might well be to our mutual benefit.'

Sir Arthur clasped Freddie's hand. 'You are too kind, my lord.' He proffered his arm to his wife with a beaming smile and they walked on into the ballroom.

Arabella did not move. She seemed to have forgotten how to put one foot in front of the other and Flora gave her a gentle nudge. 'Bella.'

Freddie greeted Flora with a charming smile. 'I don't think we've met, Miss Lee, but Amelia mentioned you when I saw her yesterday.' He turned to Arabella. 'Miss Stewart, it's a pleasure to see you again.'

Arabella opened her mouth as if to respond and her lips moved silently as she crumpled to the floor in a flurry of silk and lace.

Freddie scooped her up in his arms. 'Make way,' he said in a clear voice.

The guests parted to allow them to pass and Freddie carried the unconscious Arabella to an anteroom with Flora following close behind. He laid her gently on a sofa. 'We need some smelling salts,' he said as he straightened up. 'Would you be kind enough to ring for a servant, Miss Lee?'

Flora could see that Arabella was coming round from her faint and she unfurled her fan, using it vigorously. 'She'll be all right in a minute or so, my lord. Perhaps it was the heat.'

Arabella opened her eyes, staring dazedly up at Flora. 'What happened?'

'You fainted, Bella.' Flora turned to Freddie, who was standing behind her, his brow creased in a frown. 'Might she have a glass of water, sir?'

'Of course. Don't worry, I'll send for someone.' He tugged at an embroidered bell pull and almost immediately a liveried footman entered the room. 'Fetch some water for the young lady, please, Malton.'

The footman inclined his head and retreated quickly.

'Can you sit up?' Flora leaned over Arabella and clasped her hand.

'Yes, thank you.' Arabella raised herself to a sitting position, blushing furiously. 'I am so sorry, my lord. I don't know what came over me.'

'Please don't apologise. I'm afraid you were overcome by the heat.'

'Yes, that must be what it was.' Arabella clasped her hands to her cheeks that were now flushed a rosy pink. 'I feel so foolish.'

'Nonsense. Would you prefer to rest here for a while? I really should return to my guests.' Freddie looked up as Malton reappeared carrying a glass of water. Freddie took it off him and held it to Arabella's lips. 'Take a sip or two, Miss Stewart.'

Flora was impressed by his gentleness and genuine concern for Bella's wellbeing.

Arabella did as he asked as obediently as a small child. 'Thank you, sir. I am quite recovered now. I do apologise.'

Freddie straightened up, handing the glass to Flora. 'It is I who must apologise for any discomfort you may have suffered.'

'Don't try to get up yet, Bella,' Flora said hastily as Arabella made an effort to rise from the sofa. 'I'll stay with her, my lord. We'll join the other guests when Bella has rested for a while.'

'Of course.' Freddie nodded. 'I'm afraid I have to leave you, but should you wish to return home, my carriage is at your disposal.' He gave Arabella a sympathetic smile as he left the room.

'Well, Bella, that was one way to get his lordship's attention.' Flora laughed at Arabella's stricken expression. 'I'm just teasing you. He's a very kind man and very wealthy, too. I don't wonder that you faint at the sight of him.'

'Stop it, Flora. I feel bad enough without you making it worse.'

Flora held out her hand. 'Come on then. You're looking much better. Try standing up and see how you feel. We should get back to the ballroom before your mama realises that you are absent and sends out a search party.'

Arabella accepted Flora's help to rise from the sofa. She stood for a moment, taking deep breaths. 'I'm quite all right now. But I don't know if I can face Lord Dorrington again. He must be thinking what a ninny I am.'

'Nonsense. Stop making things worse than they really are. He was sincere in his concern for you, Bella. And what's more he remembered you from when you last met. That is a very good sign.'

'And you don't think he's too old for me?'

Flora thought for a moment. 'No, I really don't. There's something very youthful about him. I'd say that he's really quite shy, although he hides it well. Come along, Bella. We're missing all the fun.'

'Stay close by me then, Flora. If Freddie speaks to me I need you to be there in case I faint again.'

Flora took her by the arm. 'No, you won't swoon. I refuse to allow it. You are going to be the most beautiful young lady at the ball.' Flora opened the door and led a rather reluctant Arabella to the ballroom.

They were met by Freddie, who must have been keeping an eye open for them. He came towards them smiling broadly.

'I am so glad you are feeling well now, Miss Stewart. I know I am not on your dance card, but may I have this waltz?'

Arabella allowed him to take her hand and lead her onto the floor. Flora watched approvingly. Bella looked beautiful and almost ethereal as she danced with Freddie. They were a perfectly matched couple and Flora was aware of the jealous looks being directed at them by ambitious matrons whose daughters had been overlooked. Flora glanced round, feeling suddenly very lonely and out of place. She knew many of the families by sight and had been entertained at their elegant homes when accompanying Arabella, but she had always been simply Arabella's companion and a person of no particular note. She received some pleasant smiles and nods but not a single invitation to join a group or to take a seat at one of the tables. It was, she realised, not out of rudeness or incivility, but in their minds she did not exist as an entity, she was like a shadow who followed in Arabella Stewart's wake. It was an alarming thought and she wondered if any of the society families had even noticed that she was missing after the abduction and her time working for the Tullivers. At least she had been a valued member of the staff at the Play House Inn.

'Flora, may I have the next dance?'

She spun round to see Ralph Pettigrew standing very close to her. 'I-I wasn't planning on dancing. I'm here to chaperone Arabella.'

Ralph curled his lip. 'Now that's an out-and-out lie, Flora. I've been talking to Lady Stewart, so I know that Bella is here with her parents. She seems to have caught the attention of our gracious host, too. I didn't give her credit for aiming so high.'

'Please go away, Ralph. Leave me alone. I don't want to dance with you.' Almost before the words had left her lips, Ralph had seized her round the waist and they were drawn into the waltz. 'You are no gentleman,' Flora added in an undertone.

'I am soon to join the nobility. My uncle is close to death, but it's obvious that Arabella is no longer interested in me.'

'She never was,' Flora said breathlessly. 'Why won't you give up, Ralph? Neither of us likes you.'

'Of that I am aware, but I need a wife quite

urgently, or someone who will agree to become affianced to me, at least until the old man meets his maker.'

The waltz ended and couples drifted off the floor. Flora broke free from Ralph's grasp.

'You had better find anyone who can put up with you.' She was about to walk away, but Ralph caught her by the hand.

'I need you, Flora. And I think you need me.'

'People are looking at us. Let me go.'

'Not until you hear me out, Flora Lee. I have something to say which will be to your advantage.'

# Chapter Twelve

'Leave me alone, Ralph.' Flora twisted free. 'If you don't go away, I will speak to Lord Dorrington and he will have you thrown out.'

'Look at you! Dressed like a duchess and undoubtedly the best-looking woman in the house, but you are on your own. I'm offering you the chance to become a baroness, a woman of property married into one of the oldest families in England. You would live in a castle overlooking the Bristol Channel.'

'Let go of me, Ralph. People are staring at us.'

'If you resist, I will announce our engagement,' Ralph said in a low voice. He forced a smile, baring his teeth. 'Agree to meet me tomorrow morning outside the Stewarts' residence in South Molton Street and I'll leave you alone now.'

Flora was panicking inwardly. She did not know

if he would go ahead with his threat, but she could not take that chance. 'All right. Go away and I'll see you tomorrow morning. We'll talk it over then.'

He nodded. 'Ten o'clock sharp. I'm a very punctual fellow.' He sauntered off into the crowd, leaving Flora to stare after him in disbelief. Had he really asked her to marry him in order to ensure his inheritance? At least she had bought herself time to think, but why had he chosen her? There must be dozens of impoverished young women who would agree to anything in order to marry someone with a title, let alone a castle.

There was, however, little time to brood over Ralph's shocking behaviour. Freddie and Arabella returned, both of them smiling happily and laughing at some shared joke. Flora could see that there was mutual attraction, and she was delighted. Bella deserved to have someone to love and protect her from the rest of the world. An older man might make an ideal husband for her, and Freddie appeared to be very caring and supportive.

'Thank you, Miss Stewart,' Freddie said gallantly. 'Might I have the pleasure of the next dance?'

'That would be lovely.' Arabella fanned herself vigorously. 'But perhaps we might have a glass of fruit cup first?'

'Of course, how thoughtless of me.' Freddie turned to Flora. 'I can recommend my steward's fruit cup, Miss Lee. He adds a special touch which he keeps secret, even from me.'

'Thank you, my lord. I would love to sample it.' Flora glanced round, hoping to find somewhere to sit that was less crowded.

Almost as if he read her thoughts, Freddie pointed to a table that had been vacated. Flora suspected that one look from their host was enough to encourage the less notable guests to beat a hasty retreat.

'Make yourselves comfortable and I'll be back in a moment.' Freddie walked off in the direction of the refreshment room, leaving them to take a seat.

'Isn't he splendid?' Arabella said dreamily. 'He is so kind and attentive. I felt as if I was floating on air when he held me in his arms.'

'He is a true gentleman and very charming, Bella. You are very fortunate to have found someone you could truly love.'

Arabella stared at her in surprise. 'You didn't think that earlier. I'm sure you thought I was a romantic ninny.'

'No such thing,' Flora said hotly. 'I could see that you were smitten, but now I've seen you together I understand.'

'What's the matter, Flora? You're not yourself. I always know when something is wrong.'

'Don't take any notice of me. I'm making something out of nothing.'

'I don't believe that for one moment. You are always the sensible, level-headed one. What happened while I was dancing with Freddie?'

'Oh, so you are on first-name terms already?' Flora could not help laughing.

'Don't change the subject. Has someone upset you?'

'Ralph Pettigrew was here. He annoyed me, but it's not important. Anyway, I think he left having done his best to infuriate me.'

'Why, what did he say? I won't allow you to keep it a secret even if it takes all night to get the truth from you.'

'He wants me to be his fiancée so that his dying uncle will leave everything to him. Apparently proving intent to marry is a condition that Ralph must fulfil if he wants the title and the estate.'

Arabella shuddered. 'The wretched fellow. That's why he wanted me, until he realised that I was no longer an heiress.'

'I have no fortune, so he must be desperate.'

'You sent him away, though?'

'Yes, of course I did.'

'There's something else. I know you, Flora. Tell me, do.'

'Not now, his lordship is coming with our refreshments. Don't spoil the evening, Bella. I can look after myself.' Flora had no intention of telling Bella everything that had passed between herself and Ralph, nor would she demean herself by meeting him as he demanded. The fellow was clearly deluded.

Freddie approached carrying two glasses of fruit cup,

which he placed on the table. 'The refreshment room is open if you would care to dine.'

Arabella drank thirstily, replacing the cup on the white tablecloth. 'If I may be so bold, Freddie. I would love to dance.'

His boyish countenance flushed with obvious pleasure. 'I'm not noted for my efforts on the dance floor, but I would be delighted to partner you again, Bella.' His smile faded as he glanced at Flora. 'Are you all right if we leave you here for a while, Miss Lee.'

'Of course. I'm here for Bella and I am only too happy to sit here and watch. She has been so looking forward to this evening.'

Freddie eyed Arabella warily. 'I fear I am monopolising you, Bella. There are many young gentlemen who would be honoured to dance with you.'

Flora jumped to her feet and, forgetting etiquette and everything that went with it, she took their hands and joined them together. 'It's obvious that you want to dance with each other. For goodness' sake forget everyone else and enjoy yourselves.'

Freddie shook his head, laughing. 'No one has spoken to me like that since my dear old nanny retired. I respect your judgement, Flora.' He slipped his free hand around Arabella's waist and led her into a lively polka.

Flora sat back, sipping her fruit cup. Freddie had been right, it was delicious and rather more intoxicating than the usual run of refreshments served at the various functions that Flora had attended. She looked up and saw Lady Stewart approaching her with a purposeful look on her face.

'Flora, I am most concerned.'

'About what, ma'am?' Flora half rose but Constance motioned her to remain seated.

'You know very well what I mean. I fear that Lord Dorrington is making a spectacle of my daughter. Bella is too young and inexperienced to realise that everyone will be talking about her.'

'I can't see the harm in a couple of dances, ma'am. Surely it's very flattering that an important man like Lord Dorrington pays so much attention to Bella.'

'Not if he's merely toying with her affections. Dorrington is old enough to be Bella's father. He might simply be amusing himself at her expense, and ruining her chances of making a good match in the process.'

'He seems sincere enough, ma'am. Bella is a beautiful young woman and a lovely person. He would be lucky to have earned her affection, if that were the case.'

'You know very well it is, Flora. She is infatuated with him. Whether it's the thought of his wealth or his title, I don't know, but he is very unlikely to be considering marriage.'

'I think you do him an injustice, ma'am. From what I gather he is a very sincere gentleman and in no way a Lothario.'

Constance raised her hand to her forehead, closing

her eyes. 'I have one of my heads coming on. Flora, dear, please fetch my husband. I wish to go home.'

There was no arguing with Constance when she was in this mood and Flora hurried off to find Sir Arthur. He was not at all pleased.

'I was close to doing a good business deal,' he grumbled as he followed Flora back to the table where his wife sat fanning herself vigorously. 'It's not often one gets a chance to talk over such things at a social event.'

Flora reached the table first. 'Are you feeling any better, ma'am?'

'No, I am not. I've had to watch my daughter cavorting in Dorrington's arms like a common hoyden. That's what my dear mama used to call women who danced the polka, which is a very vulgar spectacle. Heaven knows the waltz was frowned upon when it first came to this country, then the polka, which is even worse.'

'Now, now, Constance. You're getting yourself into a state, which is quite unnecessary. I take it as a great compliment that our esteemed host has favoured our daughter above all others.'

'Then you are more of a fool than I took you for, Arthur.' Constance rose to her feet. 'You will tell Arabella that she is to come home with us now.'

Flora sent an imploring glance at Sir Arthur, but he was already shaking his head.

'No, I will not. I don't know what foolish idea has crept into your head, Constance, but I refuse to ruin Bella's chances. Dorrington is an earl and incredibly wealthy. I thought you wanted our daughter to marry well.'

'If that is what is on his mind,' Constance said in a low voice. 'If you won't fetch her then Flora must.'

'No!' Sir Arthur's genial expression hardened. 'Flora will remain here to chaperone Bella. I will take you home.' He turned to Flora. 'I know I can trust you to do the best for my daughter.'

'Yes, sir. Of course.' Flora eyed Constance warily, but her ladyship seemed to have nothing more to say.

'Good girl. Tell Bella that I will send the carriage to collect you both at midnight.' Sir Arthur tucked his wife's hand in the crook of his arm and led her unprotesting from the ballroom.

Flora sat down and resigned herself to playing the part of a staid, middle-aged chaperone. However, she had obviously been noticed in her beautiful new gown and soon her dance card was full and she barely had time to catch her breath between mazurkas, gallops, waltzes and the occasional polka. She completely lost sight of Arabella, which was not what she was supposed to do, but Flora was enjoying herself and had put Ralph Pettigrew out of her mind. She met up with Bella in the supper room.

'Have you danced every dance with Dorrington?' Flora asked in a low voice as they seated themselves at a long table decorated with silver epergnes overflowing with fruit and flowers.

'Almost every dance,' Arabella said, blushing. 'We get on so well. But I haven't seen Mama or Papa. Have they gone home?'

'Yes, your mama did not feel well, but your papa said he would send the carriage at midnight.'

'Like Cinderella,' Arabella said, giggling. 'Shall I run down the stairs, leaving my slipper behind for Freddie to pick up?'

'I don't think you need to go that far.' Flora looked up as Freddie approached carrying two plates of food. 'He already knows who you are. I don't think he'll forget you in a hurry.'

'I certainly hope not.' Arabella beamed up at Freddie as he placed a plate on the table in front of her.

'Is anyone fetching supper for you, Flora?' Freddie asked anxiously. 'If not, you should have this one.'

'My partner for the mazurka was very gallant,' Flora said, smiling. 'He's bringing me something to eat.'

'Excellent.' Freddie pulled up a chair and sat down next to Arabella. 'As you are here, Flora, and I know you are Bella's official chaperone,' he added seriously. 'I have been invited to the wedding of someone you both know and I would like you both to accompany me as my guests.'

Arabella paused with a forkful of smoked salmon halfway to her mouth. 'Not Amelia and her handsome doctor?'

'Yes, precisely so. They are getting married next

Wednesday. As far as I can gather it will be a real country wedding, with the ceremony in the village church and the reception held in the grounds of Marsh House, if the weather permits.'

'I would love to come,' Arabella said enthusiastically. 'I'm sure that Flora would, too.'

Flora laughed. 'I can speak for myself, Bella. Yes, I would be more than happy to attend the wedding. How exciting.'

'Splendid.' Freddie picked up his knife and fork. 'I will be very proud to escort two beautiful young ladies to the wedding. I admire Amelia for the talented, hard-working young woman she is, and I've known Todd since he was a boy.'

At that moment Flora's partner reappeared, bringing their food, and she spent the rest of the time making small talk. He was a pleasant but rather boring young man who worked for his father's bank in the City. Flora was secretly relieved when they finished the meal and returned to the dance floor. She was immediately claimed by the next gentleman on her card and all too soon it was midnight and time to leave the ball. Freddie insisted on seeing them to their carriage and he held on to Arabella's hand a little longer than was necessary as he helped her into the barouche. Flora smiled to herself as she settled in the corner of the seat. It had been a good evening and for once she had felt she was at one with the rest of the guests instead of merely being Miss Stewart's chaperone. Arabella spent the journey home staring dreamily out of the window, as if reliving the wonderful time she had enjoyed at the ball, and her conquest of the most eligible bachelor in London.

Arabella was a bundle of nerves while she waited for her mother to get dressed and come downstairs next morning. It took all Flora's tact and patience to deal with her friend during breakfast and afterwards as they sat in the morning parlour. Constance always took her breakfast in bed and then Mary helped her with her toilette and coiffed her hair, which occupied the best part of the morning. It was almost time for luncheon when she finally swept into the parlour. Flora glanced at Arabella, who was unusually pale and tense.

'Well, young ladies. What have you to say for yourselves after the show you made of me and your father last evening?' Constance sat down gracefully, arranging her skirts around her.

'We did not make fools of you or ourselves,' Arabella said boldly. 'The very reverse. We both behaved impeccably. Didn't we, Flora?'

'We did nothing wrong.' Flora nodded.

'I will hear all about your antics when I meet Lady Sheldon and her daughter for luncheon, so you had better tell me now what transpired after your papa and I left, Bella. You need not speak, Flora. I know you will back my daughter no matter what she said or did last evening.'

Arabella took a deep breath. 'We danced with the gentlemen on our dance cards, and we enjoyed a delicious supper, escorted by our partners. Then we danced until midnight and Lord Dorrington saw us to the carriage. We came home.'

'There's more. I can tell.' Constance turned to Flora. 'I've heard my daughter's account of the evening, now I want the truth from you. Did Lord Dorrington continue to make a spectacle of Arabella?'

'No, ma'am. At least, it all depends upon how you view the situation,' Flora said carefully. She knew that beneath the sweet, calm surface, Constance Stewart had a mind as sharp as that of any court prosecutor. She could tie an unsuspecting person in knots verbally, and she was noted for showing no mercy even if her victim was reduced to tears. 'Lord Dorrington behaved exactly as you would wish, ma'am. However, he invited us both to the wedding of our couturier and her fiancé. It will be held in a country church and afterwards at Marsh House. There will be very important people amongst the guests.'

Constance took the information with such a serious expression that Flora thought she was going to forbid them to accompany Freddie. She was silent for a moment or two and then she gave Flora a straight look.

'If I allow you both to attend the wedding, do you think that Amelia will design a wardrobe especially for me? I would not wish to see anyone else wearing a similar outfit.'

Arabella nodded eagerly. 'I am sure she would, Mama, but not until after the honeymoon.'

'I suppose I cannot refuse, then. You may accompany his lordship. I will inform your papa. He will no doubt be delighted. I believe that Dorrington mentioned something to him that would help save his business from collapsing into bankruptcy.'

Arabella jumped up from the sofa and gave her mother a hug. 'Thank you, Mama.'

'Don't crush my gown, Bella. Lady Sheldon is always so immaculate. I'm sure she makes a note of everything she can find lacking in my clothes and general appearance. I always feel as if I am a soldier on parade when we meet.'

'Then why are you friends with her, Mama?' Arabella asked boldly.

'We are not friends, Bella. I choose to be seen with her because she is a leader of fashion, as I will be when Marsh House Modes take me on as a client. I believe it is quite difficult to be accepted unless known to Miss Sutton, and this would be a perfect opportunity.'

'Lady Sheldon will be green with envy,' Arabella said with a wry smile.

'You may laugh, Bella, but keeping up to date with current fashion is vital if one is to keep one's place in society.'

'I understand, Mama. I will tell Dorrington when I next see him.'

'That might be sooner than you expected,' Flora

said as she looked out of the window. 'That smart carriage and pair has what I believe is his coat of arms emblazoned on the door.'

Constance turned to examine her reflection in a wall mirror, patting an imaginary stray hair into place. 'I will see him on my own. Make yourselves scarce, girls.'

Flora was about to comply but Arabella stood her ground. 'No, Mama. I will remain here. It concerns me and I will not be sent out of the room like a five-year-old.'

Constance stared at her daughter wide-eyed with surprise. 'Bella, don't speak to me in that tone.'

'I'm sorry, Mama. But you must treat me like a grown woman and not a child. I know my own mind and I count myself very fortunate if a gentleman like Freddie is taking an interest in me.'

Flora glanced out of the window again and watched as the footman handed a large bunch of roses to Freddie and two smaller posies, one of which might be gardenias, although it was impossible to be certain. Whatever they were, Freddie had his arms filled with blooms as he crossed the pavement to the front door. Moments later James knocked and entered the parlour.

'Lord Frederick Dorrington to see you, my lady.'

'Send him in, James.' Constance waited until he had left to pass on her message. 'Allow me to do the talking, Bella. You might think you are an adult now, but I am still your mama and you will abide by what I decide.'

'Yes, Mama,' Arabella said softly, but the determined set of her chin and the golden glints in her dark eyes were at odds with her meek demeanour.

Freddie burst into the room without waiting to be announced and, to Flora's surprise, he presented the large bouquet to Constance.

'Good morning, Lady Stewart. How kind of you to see me. I had these sent up from my estate in Devonshire by train this morning, so they could hardly be fresher.'

Constance accepted the bouquet with a gracious smile. 'How kind and thoughtful, Lord Dorrington. They are beautiful.'

Freddie turned to Arabella and proffered a delicate posy of gardenias and forget-me-nots. 'Thank you for a wonderful evening, Miss Stewart.'

Arabella took them with a shy smile. 'Thank you, sir.'

Freddie turned to Flora with a boyish grin. 'I hope the most captivating chaperone at the ball will accept these sweet peas.'

'Thank you, my lord. They are one of my favourite flowers. Daniel used to plant some especially for me.'

'Daniel?' Freddie raised an eyebrow. 'He sounds like a good friend.'

Constance tut-tutted impatiently. 'He is a gardener at our country house, my lord. I thought that Flora had outgrown that childish attachment.'

'I don't know, ma'am. Some of my best friends

are gardeners. I am never happier than when I am at home in the country. I've always found great solace in communing with nature.'

'Your estate sounds like heaven,' Arabella said dreamily. 'I much prefer the countryside to living in town. Isn't that so, Flora?'

Flora knew that this was not strictly true but she nodded anyway. It was clear that Bella had her sights set on Lord Dorrington and he seemed to be equally smitten. It would be a marriage made in heaven, if only Lady Stewart could see it.

Freddie seemed oblivious to any undercurrents. 'I hope you will accept an invitation to stay at Dorrington Place, Lady Stewart. I usually entertain a house party at the end of August, and it would be my pleasure if you and Sir Arthur would be my guests. Miss Arabella and Miss Flora, too, of course.'

'I will have to ask my husband,' Constance said stiffly.

'Of course. I understand and I will have an official invitation sent to you. But now the purpose of my visit this morning.'

'I thought that was obvious,' Constance said coldly.

'Is there anything wrong, ma'am?' Freddie met her gaze with a straight look. 'I was merely going to suggest a trip to the zoological gardens. Perhaps you would care to join us?'

Constance beckoned to Arabella. 'Take the flowers

and see that they are put in water. I would like a few words in private with his lordship.'

'Mama, please . . .' Arabella gave her a beseeching look.

'The flowers, Arabella!'

Flora jumped to her feet and took the bouquet from Constance's hands. 'Come, Bella. We don't want our lovely posies to wilt in the heat.' She gave Freddie a conspiratorial smile as she walked past him to open the door. 'Bella!'

Pouting, Arabella followed her out of the room. 'Why did you do that? I want to hear what Mama has to say to Freddie.'

'Don't be a ninny. She's going to ask him what his intentions are, of course.'

Arabella clapped her hands to her flaming cheeks. 'How embarrassing.'

'Not at all. Your mama loves you and she doesn't want to see a man of a certain age taking such an interest in you unless his intentions are honourable. Just because he has a title and great wealth doesn't necessarily make him a gentleman.'

'But who could doubt that Freddie is sincere?' Arabella buried her face in the posy of gardenias. 'He gave me these. I know the meaning, do you?'

Flora shook her head. 'Daniel used to tell me a lot about the flowers grown at Nine Oaks, but it was more about planting and nurturing than their spiritual meaning.'

'Well, white gardenias are a symbol of purity as

well as secret love and joy, and we all know what forget-me-nots stand for.'

'Or maybe he simply loves gardenias. Perhaps you are getting over-romantic, Bella.'

'Well, sweet peas mean "thank you", so there! He thanked you for being such an understanding chaperone.'

'Which is going to annoy your mama even more. She'll know that I didn't do my duty by you. I allowed you to dance with him all evening, while I was enjoying myself.'

'Oh dear. What will we do now?'

'We'll find a servant and have the flowers put in elegant vases, while we wait to be summoned to the parlour.'

'I know what Mama can be like when she is set on something. She will talk him out of seeing me again.'

Flora pulled a face. 'If I were a betting person, I would put my money on Freddie. I am sure he will persuade her that his intentions are entirely honourable.' She beckoned to a new and very young housemaid.

'These bouquets need to be put in suitable vases.'

The maid bobbed a curtsey. 'Yes, miss.'

'Thank you,' Flora said, smiling.

'You don't have to thank the servants,' Arabella said wearily. 'They are paid to wait upon us, Flora.'

'They are still human beings with feelings of their own. I had a little experience of dealing with people at the Play House Inn. Good manners apply to everyone, I don't care what their station in life might be.'

'Mama is right. You do spend too much time with Daniel and the rest of the servants. You're beginning to think like one.'

Flora was saved from responding by the parlour door opening. Freddie stepped out of the room. 'I have your mama's permission to take you and Flora to the zoological gardens today, Arabella. If you would care to accompany me, that is?'

'Yes, I would love to,' Arabella said enthusiastically. 'It will take me just a few minutes to put on my bonnet and gloves.'

'And better still, your mama is very happy for you both to attend Amelia's wedding next week.'

Arabella hurried towards the staircase, but Flora held back. She met Freddie's wide smile with a searching look. 'Promise me that you won't break her heart.'

'If anyone's heart is going to be broken it is likely to be mine, Flora. I am, to quote Shakespeare, like Othello, a man who loved not wisely, but too well.'

'I'm sorry,' Flora said earnestly, 'but Bella is my main concern. If you are sincere then I am happy, but if you are merely entertaining yourself I will "Cry 'Havoc!' And let slip the dogs of war" and that is Shakespeare, too. Mark Antony, I believe. Our governess, Miss Gough, was very fond of the Bard.'

Freddie took her hand and raised it to his lips. 'You are a good friend to Bella. I respect you for that, Flora. You have my word that I will do nothing to upset or hurt Bella. Now, might I suggest you get your bonnet, too?'

# Chapter Thirteen

The outing to the zoo proved very enjoyable. Freddie was such good company that Flora forgot their previous conversation and the awkwardness caused by Constance's suspicions. Arabella was clearly in her element and the afternoon passed without anything to spoil her pleasure in Freddie's company. Flora was content to take second place, as always.

The next day Freddie called again, and this time they had tea at Gunter's and Freddie invited them both to the theatre the following evening. Arabella was ecstatic and Freddie was her only topic of conversation, which Flora found rather tedious, although being a good friend she tried to listen and make suitable comments. The wedding at Marsh House was the only engagement approved of by Constance. She insisted on helping Arabella choose what she should wear, although she seemed to assume that Flora was capable of selecting her own outfit. It was just another instance that underlined Flora's position in the household. She knew that Constance was not ignoring her deliberately, it was simply a matter of precedence. Arabella was her daughter and Flora was a convenient companion.

The Stewarts were due to move back to Nine Oaks, but Sir Arthur was involved in a business deal that he hoped would rescue the family fortune, and Constance did not want to leave London without him. Flora might long for the green countryside and the fresh air, but Arabella was delighted to remain in South Molton Street with Freddie calling on them every day without fail.

The day of the wedding dawned bright and sunny although the heat would be oppressive later on. Flora, Arabella and Freddie travelled together in the padded luxury of the Dorrington landau. Flora sat back and allowed the conversation to flow over her head. Freddie had a way of telling stories of his past experiences that were both interesting and amusing. Flora was certain that he tried hard to keep Bella amused. It was as if her laughter was like music to his ears, and Bella blossomed from his constant attention. Not only that, but Freddie knew exactly how to treat Bella when she had one of her moods, and his pleasure in her company was obvious. If ever a man had fallen head over heels in love it was Freddie Ashton, and Bella responded with equal fervour.

Much as Flora delighted in their happiness, it was

very one-sided as far as she was concerned, and it was a relief when they reached the village church. There were several carriages standing in the shade of oak trees heavy with their dusty summer foliage, the horses pawed the ground and snorted to each other as if having a chat while they waited. Having helped Bella and Flora alight, Freddie escorted them into the cool interior of the church. They were met by a big man, looking rather hot and uncomfortable in his Sunday best clothes.

'Good day, Farmer Allen,' Freddie said in a respect-fully low church voice. 'Where do you want us to sit?'

'This way, my lord.' Farmer Allen indicated a row of empty pews and they sat down.

'Who is that man?' Flora asked in a whisper.

'He farms the land near Marsh House. I believe that he and Mariah are also going to get married. The marsh seems to be a romantic place,' Freddie said, smiling.

Flora glanced round at the other guests, although she could only see their backs, including a variety of best bonnets and waving ostrich feathers. Someone was playing the organ reasonably well, and the groom stood at the end of the aisle with his best man, while the vicar waited patiently for the bride to arrive. The familiar church smell of musty hymnals mingled with the scent of garden flowers that had been lovingly arranged in vases, which were placed strategically so that the vibrant colours glowed in the shadowy nooks and crannies of the ancient building. Then there was a sudden rustle and heads turned. An excited murmur rippled along the pews as the organist struck up the Bridal March and Amelia entered the church on her father's arm. At least, Flora could only assume that the dignified gentleman of senior years was related to Amelia. His proud demeanour was enough to convince her, although the hold of his head could have been due to his starched shirt collar and an overly tight cravat. However, Amelia looked beautiful in a gown of ivory silk with Valenciennes lace ruffles and a long train. Her veil was held in place by a coronet of roses, but it was the happy look on her face that turned her prettiness into real beauty. Close behind them was Mariah, looking almost regal in a lilac silk gown and matching bonnet, followed by Betsy and Daisy dressed in white organdie, with flowers in their hair and posies of rosebuds clutched in their small hands. Of little Percy there was no sign, which Flora thought, after his antics when she had seen him before, was probably a good thing. Somebody at home was undoubtedly struggling to keep him amused.

The ceremony proceeded with much sniffing and handkerchief use by the ladies. Flora was surprised to see Freddie wipe a tear from his cheek, and his hand sought Bella's, clasping it surreptitiously. Flora was glad that Lady Stewart was not present as she would have considered this behaviour totally unsuitable. As it was, the atmosphere when the happy couple were declared to be man and wife was joyous and one of the women, whom Flora recognised as being one of Amelia's seamstresses, actually cheered. She was immediately silenced by a glowering look from Nellie, who obviously had standards of behaviour close to those of Constance Stewart.

Then the ceremony was over and the wedding party processed down the aisle and out into the hot sunshine. The bridal carriage, decorated with swags of greenery and white roses, was summoned and everyone headed for Marsh House either riding or on foot. It was a slow journey as the carriage went at an ambling speed so that Amelia and Todd could wave to the bystanders along the country lane. Todd threw coins for the children and the other coach drivers had to go even more carefully for fear of running over the youngsters who risked their lives as they attempted to retrieve the money. Flora found herself wondering if she would ever find such happiness as that shared by the bride and groom. Although she had imagined herself to be in love with Daniel, she realised that it was something she had outgrown. Not so her feelings for Gabriel Cutler. They were more complicated but also less likely to come to anything. A man like Gabriel was married to the sea and unlikely to change. When he found another ship to captain she might never see him again.

The wedding party finally reached the gates of Marsh House. The sight that met Flora's eyes banished any negative feelings or emotions she might have felt. The grounds had been transformed to a fairyland of flowers and paper lanterns, which would glow wonderfully after dark. Amelia and Todd had obviously hoped for a fine day and been rewarded by blue skies and constant sunshine. The grass had been neatly clipped and the old dead tree in the centre of the lawned area had been hung with garlands of paper roses and bunting, which Flora suspected had been made from oddments of silks and satins in the workroom. Chairs and tables were set at intervals around the tree and several music stands suggested that an orchestra of some sort had been booked to entertain the guests. On either side of the carriage sweep there were poles decorated with ribbons and flowers leading up to the front entrance.

The bride and groom had already arrived and there were several carriages depositing guests. However, instead of entering the house itself, they were escorted across the yard to what had once been a huge cow shed. When Flora followed Bella and Freddie into the barn she was amazed to see that a purely functional farm building could look so splendid. Not only had it been scrubbed and cleaned until there was not a speck of dust or straw to be seen, but it had been transformed into a summer wonderland with flowers and swathes of white muslin. Some of Amelia's workers were bustling about laying platters of cooked meat, cold roast chicken, pies, pasties and salads on trestle tables covered in pristine white cloths. Another was laden with jellies, trifles and jam tarts, but in pride of place was a three-tiered wedding cake, beautifully iced and decorated with crystallised violets and rose petals. On the other side of the large barn were tables set with barrels of ale, cider and a punch bowl filled with the ubiquitous fruit cup. There was also wine, sherry and a case of champagne. It seemed that no expense had been spared.

Amelia and Todd were standing just inside the entrance, greeting their guests, while Mariah supervised the many helpers, eager to make Amelia's day memorable.

'Freddie.' A young woman called his name. She was dressed in a cream silk gown with a fashionable bustle and gold frogging on the bodice. A perky hat with a small veil rested on top of her soft flaxen curls. She was so elegant that she might have stepped out of a fashion plate, but she rushed up to Freddie and kissed him on both cheeks.

'I might have guessed that you would be here, Freddie.' She eyed Bella curiously. 'How do you do? I see I must introduce myself. I am Dolly Baker, an old friend of Freddie's.'

Freddie smiled. 'You didn't give me a chance to get a word in, Dolly. But allow me to introduce you properly. Arabella Stewart, I would like you to meet Adela Baker, or Dolly as she is known to her friends and family. Dolly, may I introduce you to Miss Arabella Stewart and her companion, Miss Flora Lee.'

Dolly gave them each a charming smile. 'How do you do? You must tell me how you met Freddie, but that will come later.' She turned and beckoned to a handsome couple who had just finished congratulating the bride and groom. 'I'd like you to meet my uncle, Sir Tommy Carey, and his wife Nancy. Both of whom are amongst my most favourite people in the whole world. If it hadn't been for Aunt Nancy, Todd would never have met Amelia, but that's another story altogether.' Dolly reached out to clutch her aunt's hand. 'Aunt Nancy, I'd like to introduce Arabella Stewart and her companion Flora Lee. There, that's done, and now we can all be friends.'

'How do you do?' Nancy said, smiling. 'It's a pleasure to meet any friends of Freddie's.'

'It is indeed,' her husband added. 'I'm delighted to meet you, ladies. We must get together properly, but in the meantime I am parched. Is anyone in charge of that barrel of ale, Freddie?'

Freddie laughed. 'I think Dr Sutton has his eye on it too. That's Amelia's papa. He's a physician at the London Hospital, which is how Todd and Amelia met in the first place.'

'There is so much to catch up on.' Nancy slipped Flora's hand through the crook of her arm. 'I'm sure that Freddie will take care of Miss Stewart. What do you say to a glass of punch? I'm sure I would love one.'

Flora eyed Nancy Carey curiously. 'I would like

some, of course, but surely you wish to speak to all the other guests first?'

'Why should I not want to spend time with you, Flora Lee? You are Miss Stewart's companion, but I think you are not just that. I've been observing you and I feel we have much in common.'

'I doubt that, my lady.'

'Humour me, Flora. As an outsider, I would say you two are more like sisters.' Nancy strolled over to the table and filled two glasses with the punch. She walked back, handing one to Flora. 'Am I right?'

'You are very astute, ma'am.' Flora took a sip of the punch. It was delicious but heady and she could imagine that the party would become very lively later.

'I wouldn't say that, but I have met a great many people from different walks of life. I like to think I'm a good judge of character.' Nancy put her head on one side, studying Flora with a sympathetic smile. 'Tell me your story, Flora.'

'There's not much to tell, ma'am. Bella's parents took me in when I was a child and raised me as their own. I would be nowhere had they not rescued me from poverty.'

'I'm sure you're being too modest. What were the circumstances, if you don't mind me asking?'

'It's no secret, ma'am. They found me living in a damp cellar with two people who claimed to be my aunt and uncle. I know next to nothing of my true parentage, but the Stewarts treated me like a daughter.

I grew up with Flora. We shared the same nanny and then a governess. We are like sisters, as you say, and I'm very fond of her.'

'You and I have much in common, my dear. I was a foundling, taken in by the Careys. I know what it's like to be with a family, however kind and welcoming, but you are not part of it by blood.'

'Sometimes I wonder who I really am.'

'I understand. Maybe you will find out one day. Even so, I can see that you are an intelligent, beautiful young woman, and a good friend.'

'I would like to hear more of your story, ma'am.'

Nancy smiled and patted Flora's hand. 'And I would be more than happy to tell you, but a little later. We really ought to circulate. I would love to get to know Miss Stewart. She seems to be very fond of Freddie.'

Flora was suddenly wary. 'You don't approve?'

'It's not that, Flora. It's just that Freddie is a wonderful person and I'm very fond of him. He's too tender-hearted for his own good and he's suffered heartbreak too many times to be good for him. I wouldn't want to see it happen again.'

'If you're thinking that Bella is flighty then you are terribly wrong,' Flora said firmly. 'She has genuine feelings for Freddie. In fact, I would go so far as to say she is falling in love with him. I think he returns her affection, too.'

Nancy gave her a searching look. 'But there is a problem. I can tell by the tone of your voice.'

'Lady Stewart thinks that Freddie is too old for her daughter. I'm sorry to put it so bluntly, but there it is. She is afraid that he is merely amusing himself with a much younger woman, and that sooner or later he will become bored and walk away, causing a scandal and ruining Bella's chances to make a good match.'

'That is very blunt,' Nancy said thoughtfully. 'But it is not Freddie. He is usually the one who gets hurt.'

Flora shook her head. 'Not this time, ma'am. I'd stake my life on it.'

'That's all I wanted to hear. Now, I need to go and congratulate the happy couple. I see that my husband is already doing so and I'd better join him. It was lovely to talk to you, Flora. We'll speak again later.' Nancy strolled off to join her husband, who was with Todd and Amelia.

Flora stood a little apart from the guests who were congregating in the barn. The sound of laughter and the drone of voices seemed to merge into the background as Flora sipped her drink. She was a little dazed after her conversation with Nancy Carey, who was obviously very fond of Freddie. It might be natural for his friends to be suspicious of Bella, but it should be obvious to anyone with any sensitivity to see that her feelings for him were genuine. Flora fanned herself with her free hand. It was hot in the barn and she needed to go outside into the fresh air. She placed her empty glass on the nearest table and was about to head for the double doors when someone laid their hand on her arm. Flora turned to see Dolly Baker smiling at her.

'I was about to come to your rescue, Flora. I could see that you were being cross-examined by my aunt. She's a darling, but she can be quite forceful sometimes. Aunt Nancy is very protective of Freddie. We all are.'

Flora sighed. 'I hope you aren't going to question me as to Bella's sincerity. It's usually the other way round, isn't it? I mean people demand to know the gentleman's intentions.'

'You are quite right, but as I said we all love Freddie. He and Aunt Nancy were very close at one time, but she chose to marry Uncle Tommy. None of us want to see him get hurt again.'

'It won't be Bella who breaks his heart,' Flora said firmly. 'Please tell your family to stop worrying. In any event, I think Freddie is old enough to look after himself. It's Bella I worry about.'

'Don't, that's all I can say, Flora. She is in good hands. I would love to see Freddie happily married with children of his own. He simply adores my baby, Blanche, who is already eight months old.'

'Is she here? I would love to see her.'

Dolly shook her head. 'I thought it best to leave her in Rockwood with my mama, but I will be travelling home tomorrow.'

'You must miss her very much,' Flora said cautiously. 'Your husband isn't here today?'

'No, Gus is in the army. However, I plan to join him very soon. I'll be travelling to India in January and we'll be reunited. I simply can't wait to see him again.'

'Being separated for long periods must be very hard.'

'I only stayed in England because I was so close to my confinement when he had his orders to join his regiment, but I think that Blanche will be old enough to undertake the long journey after Christmas. I might even go sooner if Gus has found accommodation for us.'

'You are very brave.'

'No, I'm just an army wife, and I love Gus too much to stay at home. One day you will feel like that about someone, Flora.'

'My romances seem doomed to end badly.' Flora smiled ruefully. 'I'm resigned to being a spinster aunt to Bella's offspring.'

'I don't believe that for a moment.' Dolly glanced over Flora's shoulder. 'I think that handsome gentleman approaching us is looking for you, so I'll go and join my aunt.' She patted Flora on the arm and walked off, heading for the bridal couple.

Flora turned slowly, thinking vaguely that Dolly was teasing her, when she saw Gabriel Cutler heading in her direction. She went to meet him.

'Gabriel, I didn't think you knew the bride and groom.'

He shook his head. 'I don't and I wasn't invited,

but there was no one at the gate to stop me so I came in to look for you.'

'But how did you know I was here? It's a long way from South Molton Street.'

'I was in Sir Arthur's office. I went there to collect my pay, since there is no ship for me to command. I asked after you and he told me that you had accompanied Arabella to a wedding.'

'I still don't understand,' Flora said, frowning. 'It's not that I'm not pleased to see you, but why are you here? It's a long way from town.'

He drew her to one side, lowering his voice. 'Have you seen Ralph recently, Flora?'

'Ralph? He accosted me at a ball in Dorrington House. He made some ridiculous suggestion that I should accompany him on a visit to your dying uncle. He wanted me to pretend to be his fiancée so that he could be certain of claiming the inheritance.'

'And you refused.'

'Of course, but . . .' Flora paused, her hand flying to cover her mouth. 'Oh dear, I remember now. He wanted me to meet him the next day. I had no intention of doing so, but I actually forgot all about it. I was so caught up in Bella's romance with Lord Dorrington that all thoughts of your cousin went out of my head.'

'Ralph came to see me last night. He was very drunk and he was ranting on about how you didn't keep your appointment. I think he is planning to take you to Pettigrew Castle whether you want to go or not.'

Flora rolled her eyes. 'You mean he plans to abduct me? Why would he do that, Gabriel? I am just an ordinary young woman with no family and no fortune.'

'For precisely those reasons, I should think.' Gabriel took her hand and held it in a firm grasp. 'I hate to say it, but my cousin is a dangerous man. He's determined to inherit our uncle's money, the castle and the title, even though I am the eldest. If he's to stand a chance he needs to convince our uncle that he has changed.'

'That doesn't answer my question. Why me?'

Gabriel glanced round the barn, which was filling up with people who were intent on helping themselves to the food and drink. 'Come outside, Flora. I saw some tables and chairs under the dead tree. We can speak more privately there.'

Flora allowed him to take her arm and guide her outside into the hot sunshine. They found a table in what little shade the skeleton of a tree gave.

'Now tell me why you came here so urgently.' Flora sat down on one of the chairs. 'What could Ralph do to me?'

'He's virtually bankrupted himself by his gambling and he's desperate.'

'Surely he should be there for the dying man who might not have been the best guardian, but he did clothe, feed and educate you.'

'Yes, that's true. I agree, but Ralph always has to win. He was the same as a boy and quite ruthless when it came to getting his own way. He has convinced himself that his only chance is to portray himself as a respectable man who will keep the family traditions and provide heirs, ensuring that the line does not die out.'

'Then he must find someone else. I refuse to be a part of such a scheme.'

'Don't underestimate him, Flora. I believe it was Ralph who instructed your uncle to abduct you, but the accident put paid to his immediate plans. By the time you had recovered, your uncle and aunt had fallen out with my cousin. Hence their decision to sell you to the highest bidder.'

Flora sank down on a seat, her knees suddenly refusing to support her. 'This all sounds like the plot in a gothic novel, Gabriel. I find it hard to believe.'

'People do strange things when they are desperate for money. Ralph has brought it on himself, but I do know he will stop at nothing to get what he desires. All I want is to protect you, Flora.'

She eyed him warily. 'Did you come all this way just to tell me that? Why should I believe you, Gabriel?'

'I am totally sincere in my regard for you, Flora. I hardly slept last night for thinking about the situation. I believe that Ralph is poised to act very soon, but I have a suggestion.'

'This is Amelia's wedding day and we are attracting

attention. Just tell me what it is and then I think you should leave.'

'This sounds quite mad at first but I think it might be the only way to stop Ralph from doing something extremely stupid, if not dangerous.'

'What are you saying?'

'I suggest that you and I go to Pettigrew Castle. We do what Ralph planned to do. That is, you pretend to be my fiancée.'

'That is a step closer to insane rather than simply mad,' Flora said aghast. 'In any event, what good would that do?'

'It would make a dying man happy for a start. He is desperate to have an heir to the estate and the title, of course.'

'But you said you don't want to inherit. Why not let Ralph do as he pleases?'

'Because he will drag you into his devious plans.'

'Are you seriously suggesting that I should go along with this wild scheme? Can't you find some other woman who would be only too happy to oblige?'

'If you are with me you would be safe from Ralph. I really fear for his sanity, Flora.'

'I would never agree to go anywhere with Ralph. I can't stand the sight of him.'

'That makes it more of a challenge as far as he is concerned. My uncle is not a good man and he certainly isn't kind, but I would like to see him die with a little dignity. Ralph can have what money there is and the castle.'

'Let me get this clear, Gabriel. You want me to go along with this charade, and then you will bring me home and we go our separate ways. Is that what you're suggesting?'

'I would never knowingly put you in a difficult situation,' Gabriel said warily. 'But time is running out. I'm afraid that my uncle will die at any moment, which makes Ralph even more desperate.'

'But if I agreed to accompany you to Pettigrew Castle it would be impossible to keep it secret. You would go back to sea afterwards and I would be left to face the world with a broken engagement.'

Gabriel frowned. 'I have the highest regard for you, Flora. I wouldn't do anything to harm you in any way.'

'But you would cheerfully use me in order to further your own ends.' Flora gave him a straight look, shaking her head. 'As I see it, you are little better than your cousin. I am going nowhere with you or with Ralph.'

'Hand on heart, I am only thinking of your safety, Flora.'

'I think I am safer away from you and your deranged cousin. You had better leave, or I shall have someone escort you from the premises.' Flora jumped to her feet and turned away, too angry to even look at him. She had thought he cared for her but it was obvious now that he was just using her in almost exactly the same way as Ralph had intended. Although at least Ralph had included marriage in his shocking proposal, even if it had been a sham. She was seeing Gabriel Cutler in a new light, and it was not flattering.

'Flora, please.'

'Go away, Gabriel. I want nothing more to do with you.'

He shrugged and shook his head, but he did as she asked and walked dejectedly towards the gates where he had left his horse tethered. Flora watched him with mixed emotions. One thing was certain – she wanted nothing more to do with either Gabriel or his cousin Ralph.

'Are you all right, Flora? Did that man say something to upset you?'

Flora spun round to see Dolly standing behind her. 'I have been better.'

'Who is he?'

'I thought he was my friend. No, to be honest, I thought perhaps he cared for me, but it seems that he was just using me.'

Dolly slipped her arm around Flora's shoulders. 'Forget him, Flora. Come and join in the rest of the party.'

'You're right. This is a happy day. I won't allow Gabriel and his wretched cousin to spoil it.' Even so, despite her brave words, Flora was upset by Gabriel's cavalier treatment. He had thought only of himself and had not given any consideration to how such a wild plan would affect her personally. Perhaps having spent most of his adult life at sea had left him naïve as far as society was concerned, but that was no excuse.

Dolly tucked Flora's hand into the crook of her arm as they strolled back to the barn. 'What was that man saying to you? If you don't mind me asking, that is.'

Flora had a sudden need to confide in someone other than Bella, who was so wrapped up in her newly found love that she had her head in the clouds. Flora found herself telling Dolly the whole sorry story, from the moment she met Ralph Pettigrew to the present. Dolly was a good listener and, apart from making sympathetic noises at appropriate moments, she waited until Flora had finished speaking. By this time they were standing outside the barn where the festivities were in full swing. Sounds of chatter, laughter and the clatter of cutlery on china plates filtered out through the open doors. The delicious aroma of the food mingled with the fumes of alcohol and the heady perfumes worn by the ladies, with a touch of bay rum and Macassar oil used by the gentlemen. The scene inside was one of joy and goodwill, making Gabriel's ideas seem bleak and totally inappropriate.

Flora finished on a sigh. 'So there you have it, Dolly. Thank you for being so patient.'

'Well, Flora, your life has been even more eventful than mine,' Dolly said, frowning. 'As I see it, you need to keep well away from your sea captain and his hateful cousin. What they are suggesting is outrageous. I've never heard anything like it.'

'That is the problem, Dolly. I have no money and no family other than the Stewarts, who have been wonderful to me. I love Bella as if she were my sister, but she has fallen for Freddie and I think he might feel the same about her. If they should marry, my position in the family is very uncertain. I can't expect Sir Arthur and Lady Stewart to keep me forever.'

'I can see that it is difficult,' Dolly said thoughtfully, then she smiled. 'But there's always a solution if you think hard enough. Forget your problems for a while and let's enjoy the wedding, but I am on your side, Flora. I will help you find a solution.'

# Chapter Fourteen

As Flora and Dolly re-entered the barn they were met by Arabella, who enveloped Flora in a hug. 'Where were you? We've been looking for you.'

'I was just getting some fresh air,' Flora said evasively.

'Flora and I were having a delightful chat,' Dolly added, smiling. 'I think she needs some food. I know I am very hungry. Weddings always give me an appetite.' She held her hand out to Freddie, who approached them carrying two glasses of wine. 'Freddie, darling. Would you be so kind as to fetch some fruit cup for myself and Flora?'

'Of course I will. Just wait here.' He handed the wine to Arabella. 'I'll be back in a moment, my dear.'

Arabella smiled sweetly. 'Isn't he marvellous? I've never met anyone like Freddie.'

'He is a wonderful man,' Dolly said earnestly. 'We all love Freddie.'

'You look rather flushed, Flora.' Arabella sipped her wine. 'Are you feeling quite well?'

'It is rather hot outside. I'll stay in the shade for a while,' Flora said, fanning herself with her hand. 'Perhaps we ought to find a table as everyone else seems to be sitting down to eat.'

Dolly took Flora by the arm. 'Come and join us. I see Uncle Tommy has commandeered the largest table. He was in the army years ago, so he likes to get everyone organised. Come along, Flora. You, too, Arabella.'

'But Freddie won't know where we are,' Arabella protested.

'He will know that you are in the care of the Careys. Don't worry, Arabella. Freddie is used to our funny little ways.' Dolly led the way to a table where Nancy and Tommy were seated with Amelia, Todd and Mariah. The children were playing hide and seek amongst the hay bales at the far end of the barn, and their laughter echoed off the rafters. Flora pushed all thoughts of Gabriel and Ralph from her mind as she took a seat next to Nancy.

'This is a lovely wedding. Everyone looks so happy and the bride is beautiful.'

Nancy nodded. 'Amelia is a lovely young woman and so very talented. She dragged herself from poverty to become a successful couturier. I really admire her, and Todd is my favourite protégé. There were twelve young boys I found living by petty crime in a London cellar. I was able to give them a second chance in Rockwood, but I must admit that Gus and Todd are my favourites. The other boys are all doing well, but Todd and Gus are special.'

'Gus is married to Dolly?'

'Yes, theirs was a real love match. It's a pity he's stationed so far away.' Nancy leaned towards her husband. 'Tommy, darling. Would you be kind enough to fetch some food for me and for Flora?'

Flora stood up. 'It's all right, Sir Thomas. I can help myself.'

Tommy grinned. 'No one calls me Sir Thomas apart from my land agent. Just Tommy will do very nicely, Flora. Come with me, I've already sampled some of the delicacies, for which I believe we have to thank Mariah.' He stood up and acknowledged Mariah with a nod. 'You, ma'am, are an excellent cook.'

Mariah beamed at him. 'Thank you, sir. I enjoy baking and my daughter Betsy is following in my footsteps.'

'I'll come, too.' Dolly rose from her seat. 'I know what I like. I don't trust you to choose for me, Uncle Tommy.' She sailed past him and made her way through the crowd to the table where the savoury dishes were spread.

'I couldn't eat a thing,' Amelia said, leaning against Todd with an ecstatic smile on her pretty face.

Todd dropped a kiss on her forehead. 'There won't be anything left soon. I've seen Nellie and the work-room women helping themselves as if food was going out of fashion. I'll be called upon to dose them for tummy ache before the day is out.'

'We must have music,' Amelia said eagerly. 'Mariah, do you know where our musicians are?'

Mariah rose to her feet. 'Leave it with me. I'll find Jim, he was organising the band.' She stood up, braced her shoulders and marched off purposefully.

'Mariah and Jim will be next,' Amelia said, smiling. 'Marsh House used to be such a sombre and unloved place, but now it's bursting with happiness.'

'It's all due to you, my darling,' Todd said, raising his glass. 'I am the luckiest man in the world to have found you.'

A murmur of agreement rippled round the table as everyone joined in the toast.

It was late evening by the time Flora and Arabella arrived back in South Molton Street. Freddie had seen them to the door. Flora chose to ignore the fact that he leaned in to brush Bella's soft cheek with a kiss before returning to his carriage. It amused Flora to see Bella walk into the house as if her feet barely touched the ground. She smiled beatifically at James as he held the door for them, and she held her hand to her cheek as she ascended the stairs.

'Goodnight, James,' Flora said with a smile as she crossed the hall, following in Bella's lovestruck wake.

'Isn't he wonderful?' Bella stopped outside her bedroom door. 'Wasn't it a beautiful wedding? I think

I would like to have one just like that.' She caught Flora by the hand and dragged her into the room, closing the door. 'I shan't sleep a wink for thinking about it.'

'It was very nice,' Flora said, stifling a yawn.

'You didn't say much on the way home. Are you feeling quite well?'

Flora had no intention of ruining Bella's euphoric state with an explanation. Bella did not need to know the depths to which Gabriel had sunk. He was no better than his cousin and in Flora's mind he was even worse.

She managed a smile. 'I'm just tired, Bella. It was a lovely wedding. No doubt you will be seeing Freddie again very soon.'

'Oh, yes. He's going to invite us all to a house party at his country estate in Devonshire. Isn't that exciting? I can't wait to see Dorrington Place.'

Flora gave her a hug. 'It looks as if you might end up as mistress of the great house, Bella. I'm very happy for you.'

'Do you really think Freddie will propose?'

'You are in a better position than I am to know that, but from what I've seen I would say, definitely.'

Bella's smile faded. 'I hope you don't feel left out, Flora. I know we rather ignored you on the way home. I'm sorry.'

'Don't be a silly goose. I was perfectly content to sit and dream, but don't tell your mama or she will say I am a very poor chaperone. You might end up with Miss Gough accompanying you on your outings with Freddie.'

Arabella's eyes widened. 'Don't say things like that. I never want to see that woman again. She made our lives miserable while she was our governess.'

'Don't worry. I'm just teasing you. I expect Miss Gough is terrorising another set of innocent children now. I promise not to tell your mama that you and Lord Dorrington held hands all the way home.'

'You saw!'

'I was seated opposite you, Bella. Of course I could see what was going on, but I am not a killjoy.'

'I really should go to bed and get some sleep or I'll look like an old hag in the morning.' Arabella sank down on her bed and took off her shoes. 'I suppose I should send for Mary, but I'm too tired.'

'I'll help you to undress, just like the old days.'

'Never leave me, Flora. Even if I marry Freddie and have a hundred people waiting on me, I will always need you.'

'I don't suppose I'll be far away, so stop worrying.' Flora pulled off Arabella's white stockings and laid them on a chair. 'Stand up and I'll unlace you.'

'Freddie has invited us both to luncheon at Kettner's tomorrow. I adore French food and so does Freddie, or so he told me this evening. I really need a new bonnet, something Parisian, don't you think?'

'Yes, well, maybe. We can talk about it in the morning.' Flora helped Arabella off with her dress, stays and chemise before slipping a cotton nightgown over her head. 'Hop into bed, Bella. Sleep well.'

Arabella snuggled down between the sheets. 'I will dream of Freddie. Who will you dream of, Flora?'

'I'm not such a romantic as you, Bella. I usually dream of Ted Tulliver shouting cooking instructions at me and poor Moses, dropping things, breaking china and getting into trouble. Goodnight, Bella. Sleep tight.' Flora blew out the candles and left the room.

She was exhausted by everything that had happened that day and it took her some time before she drifted off to sleep, but it was deep and dreamless.

Next morning Flora awoke refreshed and ready to face the day. She decided to concentrate on helping Bella with her blossoming romance. The invitation to Freddie's palatial home in Devonshire might or might not transpire, but in the meantime Flora hoped that the Stewarts would decide to return to Nine Oaks. Despite Daniel's obvious preference for the May Queen, Flora still considered him to be her friend, and she longed to see him and chat about everything that had occurred recently. She knew she could tell him anything and he would never be judgemental.

Flora washed, dressed and went downstairs to the dining room. She had eaten very little at the wedding and now she was hungry. The silver salvers on the sideboard were full of buttered eggs, crispy bacon, sautéed kidneys and grilled mushrooms. She helped herself and took her plate to the table where Ivy was about to pour coffee from a silver pot. It was all very normal and quiet.

Flora nodded. 'Good morning, Ivy. Have you seen Miss Arabella this morning?'

'Oh, yes, miss. She ate breakfast really early. I'd only just filled one salver with bacon when she came down.'

'She doesn't usually rise before me.' Flora spoke more to herself than to Ivy, but Ivy was obviously bursting with news.

'I don't wish to speak out of turn, Miss Flora, but Miss Arabella ate next to nothing. She went out at least half an hour ago.'

'On her own?'

'Yes, miss. On her own.'

'Did she say where she was going?'

'Not exactly, but she did say something about a new bonnet.'

'Did she say anything else?'

'No, Miss Flora. Although, if I'm not speaking out of turn, I thought it a little odd that she was wearing your old lace shawl around her head instead of a bonnet. That's not like Miss Arabella.'

'Thank you, Ivy. I'm sure she had her reasons. That will be all for now, thank you.'

Flora sat for a while after Ivy had left the room. She ate automatically, barely tasting the savoury food.

What was Bella thinking? Her mama would be horrified if she knew her daughter had gone shopping without at least taking a maid with her. As to the shawl, that was even more mystifying. Bella seemed to be living in a romantic world of her own. Freddie would not have asked her to meet him secretly. If anything, he was more protective of Arabella's reputation than either of her parents. Perhaps it was as innocent as a visit to Bella's favourite milliner; after all, she had said she wanted a new bonnet to wear today. Flora pushed her plate away and stood up. James might have heard her giving instructions to the coachman. She hurried from the dining room and found James in the entrance hall. He stopped polishing the brass door knocker and stood to attention.

'Good morning, James.' Flora gave him an encouraging smile. 'I believe Miss Arabella went out earlier. Did you happen to hear her instructions to the coachman?'

'She took a cab, miss. I don't know where she was going.'

'Thank you, James.' Flora walked away, even more puzzled. It seemed strange that Bella should take a cab on her own when it would have been so easy to send for the carriage, but without knowing exactly where she was going, there was nothing Flora could do other than await Arabella's return.

At first Flora did not worry too much. It was just Bella being dramatic again and daring to do something on her own, perhaps in order to impress Freddie. Although from what she had seen of Freddie, Flora thought he would disapprove strongly of Bella going out unattended. But at midday, when Arabella had still not returned, Flora was extremely worried. She was tempted to tell Constance, but Lady Stewart would only blame her, while Sir Arthur, who was more reasonable, was at his office in the City. Flora knew from the snippets of conversation she had overheard that Sir Arthur's business interests had all come to nothing. His venture into shipping had been a disaster, but that was all she knew for certain. In any event he would not want to be bothered with worries as to the whereabouts of his errant daughter. Perhaps Bella had met with a friend and had decided to spend time with them, although Flora thought this unlikely, especially as Bella was so eager to eat French food with Freddie.

At half past twelve on the dot Freddie arrived in his open landau. Flora met him in the entrance hall. His smile faded when he saw Flora's serious expression.

'What's the matter, Flora? Is Arabella unwell?'

Flora took him into the morning parlour and closed the door. 'She went out early this morning and hasn't returned.'

'She went out on her own?' Freddie's brows snapped together in a frown. 'You allowed her to do that?'

'She didn't tell me what she planned, although

last night she did say something about wanting a new bonnet to wear today.'

'Presumably she went in her father's carriage?'

'No, sir. James told me that she took a cab. He didn't know where she was going.'

'It's my fault,' Freddie said angrily. 'I mentioned the French chef at Kettner's and that led to talk of Paris fashions. I can't remember exactly what we said, but it seems to have given her the idea that she needed something special to wear today. I am such a fool.'

'Nonsense.' Flora spoke briskly in an attempt to hide her own misgivings. 'Bella is a grown woman and able to make her own decisions. But she does act rashly sometimes. I just hope nothing bad has befallen her.'

'My carriage is outside, Flora. Do you know which milliner Bella favours?'

'There are several, but I think I know the one she might have chosen. I'll fetch my bonnet and gloves. I won't be long.'

They visited all the milliners that Flora could think of without success. It seemed that Bella had left the house and vanished into thin air. It was mid-afternoon when they returned to South Molton Street and Freddie insisted on speaking personally to Lady Stewart. Jefferson showed them into the drawing room where Constance was taking tea with two other ladies, both of whom Flora knew vaguely, although they had never taken any interest in her.

'Good afternoon, ladies,' Freddie said, acknowledging them with a curt bow. 'I am sorry to interrupt, but might I have a few words in private, Lady Stewart?'

Constance smiled. 'Surely there can be nothing so secret that it cannot be said in front of my dear friends?'

Flora clutched her hands at her sides. All this polite nonsense was not helping Bella. 'Excuse me, ma'am, but it is rather urgent. It concerns Arabella.'

Constance rose to her feet. 'I will hear you out in the anteroom, sir. You, too, Flora. Excuse me a moment, ladies.' Constance made her way into a small room leading off the drawing room. She closed the door. 'What is this all about?'

'It seems that Arabella is missing, ma'am,' Freddie said gently. 'We have been out searching for her since midday.'

Constance sank down on a chair next to the escritoire where she studied the household accounts and checked menus with Cook. 'What are you saying?'

'Bella went out on her own early this morning, ma'am.' Flora snatched a vial of smelling salts from the desk and wafted them under Constance's nose. 'She hasn't returned and we couldn't find her.'

'It seems that she decided to purchase a new bonnet,' Freddie added hastily. 'But we've been to all the places she might have chosen, and she hasn't been seen.'

'Someone must fetch my husband from his office,' Constance said faintly. 'Why did you let her go out on her own, Flora? If anything has happened to my child, I will hold you to blame.'

'I didn't know what she planned. It's not like Bella to do anything without telling me.' Flora took a hanky from her pocket and handed it to Constance, whose eyes were streaming either with tears or the effect of the pungent smelling salts.

'Arthur will know what to do. Or perhaps we should send for a constable. Maybe she had an accident and is in hospital.'

It was Freddie's turn to lose the colour in his cheeks. Flora was afraid he might faint with horror at the thought of Bella being mortally injured. She looked from one to the other.

'Would you like me to summon a constable, ma'am?'

'I don't know. It would cause a dreadful scandal. She has been quite rebellious since she met you, my lord. I hope your intentions are honourable.' Constance faced him angrily. 'I would not normally say such a thing, but your philandering could ruin my poor girl.'

Freddie drew himself up to his full height. 'I am not a philanderer, ma'am. I love Bella with all my heart. I would have spoken before, but I am very conscious of her youth and inexperience and I did not want to declare my intentions too soon.'

'I'm glad to hear it,' Constance said stiffly. 'But that doesn't alter the fact that anything might have occurred. Look what happened to you, Flora.'

'I was abducted. But who would want to harm Bella?' Flora caught her breath. 'But I've just remembered what Ivy told me this morning. Bella went out wearing my old lace shawl wrapped around her head and shoulders. She might have been mistaken for me.'

'I thought your criminal relatives had received a large sum of money for you, Flora,' Freddie said thoughtfully. 'Why would anyone else want to kidnap you?'

'Ralph Pettigrew is a dangerous man. He threatened me but I refused to do what he wished, and now I fear for Arabella's safety. I'll explain everything in the carriage, if you will take me to him, Freddie?'

'Of course I will. I'll do anything to restore Bella to her family.'

'What do you want me to do?' Constance asked plaintively. 'I can't go back in the drawing room and act as if nothing has happened.'

Flora gave her a straight look. 'I'm sure you could do anything required of you if it would help Bella. If you tell them the truth it will be all around town by evening.'

Constance rose to her feet. 'You're right, Flora. I can do anything if I set my mind to it. Tell James to send someone to tell Sir Arthur he is needed urgently at home. I will deal with things here, but please hurry. Do what you have to do, my lord. Please bring my daughter home.'

'I will do everything in my power to bring Bella home safely.' Freddie held the door open for Flora. 'Do you know where to find Ralph Pettigrew?'

'As it happens, I do. He has rooms in Hay Hill. We might just get there in time if he has snatched Bella, thinking it was me.'

Freddie followed her into the corridor that led to the entrance hall. 'My carriage, please.'

James jumped to attention and opened the front door. Moments later both Flora and Freddie were ensconced in his comfortable landau, only this time it was not a pleasure outing, it was a serious attempt to find and rescue Bella. Flora was now certain that either Ralph or Gabriel was behind her friend's disappearance. Having discovered their mistake, they could hardly return her without giving away their plans. She would not put it past either of them to involve Bella as they had wanted to use her in order to secure their uncle's good will.

They arrived at the house in Hay Hill to find the housekeeper tossing Ralph's belongings onto the landing.

'Where is Mr Pettigrew?' Flora asked anxiously.

'I dunno and it's none of your business, young lady.'

'Hold fast a minute, my good woman,' Freddie said sternly. 'Why are you behaving like this?'

'No rent's been paid for three months, guv. I ain't a charity. He's done a bunk and that's it. Like I told the sea captain, Mr Pettigrew took off this morning without a by-your-leave or a thanks for me patience and understanding.' The old woman spat a stream of tobacco juice onto a pile of what appeared to be old clothes.

Flora took a step backwards. 'Did you see him this morning with a young woman?'

'Like I told the captain, I never seen nothing. Now sling yer hook and leave me be.'

'Just one thing,' Flora said hopefully. 'Do you know where the sea captain lodges?'

Freddie put his hand in his pocket and tossed some coins at the woman's feet.

She snatched them up, shaking her head. 'I dunno and that's the truth.' She eyed them slyly. 'But I did hear him mutter something afore he left.'

Freddie added another couple of coins to the heap.

'Ta, sir. You're a gent. The captain said he was going home.'

'Pettigrew Castle,' Flora said in a whisper. 'It's on the coast, overlooking the Bristol Channel, but I don't know where exactly.'

'Then it looks as if we might be heading west, Flora. As it happens, I know where Pettigrew Castle is, though I've never met Baron Pettigrew or his family.'

'Is it far away, sir?'

'About halfway to my own property in Devonshire.

271

It's on the edge of Exmoor. I was invited to a shooting party there, many years ago.'

'Do you think they will have travelled there by train?'

'It's a very out of the way place, Flora. Also, if Arabella has been abducted by Ralph Pettigrew, he would not risk public transport of any sort. He must have made other arrangements.'

'Then the sooner we go after them the better,' Flora said urgently. 'Bella's reputation will be ruined if they stay anywhere overnight.'

'I agree. I'll take you back to South Molton Street and then I'll set off immediately.'

'You are not going without me, sir.'

Freddie gave her a steady look. 'Perhaps it would be better for Bella, but what about your reputation, Flora? If you come with me, you are risking your good name.'

Flora laughed. 'I don't think I have a position in society to protect. If I did, it went when my uncle and Ralph Pettigrew conspired to kidnap me. In any event, I would do anything to save Bella and bring her home.'

'In that case we mustn't waste any more time. We'll tell Lady Stewart that we're going to bring Bella home, and you must collect whatever you need for a couple of days' stay in the country. We'll stop off at my house in Piccadilly and I'll do the same.'

Flora followed him to his waiting carriage and the footman leaped down to open the door.

'If Ralph has harmed a single hair on Bella's head, I won't be responsible for what I do next.'

Flora climbed into the landau. 'I will never forgive Gabriel Cutler for aiding and abetting his cousin. They are both as bad as each other.'

Freddie leaped in and sat down beside her. 'South Molton Street, Walton. And you need to prepare for a long journey.'

# Chapter Fifteen

It had all happened in such a rush. Flora was quite dizzy with anxiety for Bella's safety. She was anxious about the difficult journey ahead and furious with Ralph as well as Gabriel. They were both as bad as each other, and they had caused more upset in her life than almost anyone else, apart from her uncle and aunt. It seemed that she was never going to be free from any of them.

Freddie made all the arrangements and Flora set off with him in his carriage, travelling mostly in silence, immersed in their own thoughts. However, although the horses kept up a good pace they had to stop in order to allow them to rest at regular intervals. Freddie's enquiries at wayside inns drew very little information apart from the fact that they seemed to be going in the right direction. A man answering Ralph's description had called in at two of the hostelries. He had purchased refreshments but had taken them out to his carriage while the horses were fed and watered. He had not been a very talkative customer, and as far as the landlords were concerned, the gentleman was rude and impatient. That was enough to convince Flora that it was Ralph and poor Bella was his unwilling companion. According to Freddie's calculations, Ralph and Bella were at least two hours ahead of them, and there was only so much they could expect of the horses. Soon they would need to find a suitable place to stay for the night and hope that an early start next morning would narrow the gap between them.

They stopped at an inn where the landlord's wife took an instant liking to Flora and treated her like a long-lost daughter. Freddie booked a room for each of them and one for Walton and the footman. The landlady was very sympathetic and also very inquisitive, but she did remember taking a glass of water out to a young lady in a carriage who seemed to be in some distress. Despite her suggestion that the girl should rest for a while in a private parlour, the gentleman with her had refused and had told her rudely to mind her own business. She shook her head and tut-tutted.

'I didn't think the young woman looked like a runaway bride,' she added, sniffing. 'I hope you catch up with them before it's too late for her. If you know what I mean, miss.' The landlady bustled off to serve another customer. However, Flora knew exactly what she meant and now she was even more worried, but there was nothing more to be done that evening. Flora could only hope for a good night's sleep before what might prove to be a challenging day.

Next morning Flora was up, dressed and ready to leave soon after first light. She made her way downstairs to the parlour and found Freddie was already there, drinking a cup of coffee.

'Would you like something to eat, Flora? The landlord's wife has made some very palatable porridge and the coffee is good too.'

'I don't think I could eat anything, thank you, Freddie.'

'You should try, my dear. It's going to be a long day. I can only hope we will arrive at the castle before they do. If they get there first, Ralph will see to it that we are denied access. I can't allow that to happen.'

'Do you think we can get there today?'

'I've talked it over with Walton and I think the best way would be for you and I to travel on the railway. Walton is going to drive us to the nearest station and we'll go from there. I doubt if there's a direct route, but whatever there is will be quicker than by road. It's imperative that we get to Pettigrew Castle first.'

'I've never travelled by train,' Flora said eagerly. She looked up as the landlord's wife bustled into the parlour. 'I would love some porridge, please.'

'You look happier this morning, my dear. I hope

all goes well for you today. I didn't take to that young man we was talking about last evening. He's a bad 'un. You need to rescue that poor young lady before he ruins her.' She tossed her head as she left the room.

Flora smiled apologetically as Freddie raised an eyebrow. 'I wasn't gossiping, Freddie. That woman could extract information from the most tight-lipped person in the world.'

'It doesn't matter. We'll be on our way soon. With luck we should arrive at the castle before the day is out.'

'What about Walton and the carriage?'

'He's going to drive back to London. I value my horses too much to make them undertake such an arduous journey in such a short time. Ralph knows that we will follow them, so it's likely that he will take the back roads, which will lengthen their journey. We have the advantage of being able to travel together openly.'

Flora sighed. 'Yes, indeed. I am a woman of no consequence.'

'Don't ever repeat that in my presence,' Freddie said angrily. 'You are one of the most important people in Bella's life, apart from being a brave and intelligent woman in your own right. I won't allow you to think less of yourself, Flora Lee.'

His obvious sincerity and impassioned words took Flora by surprise, but she nodded and managed a tight little smile. 'Thank you, Freddie.'

'I mean it, Flora. You have been brought up by kindly people but, however unintentionally, they made you think you were second best. I can assure you that is not the case. In fact, I count myself lucky to be among your acquaintances.'

Flora was close to tears at this unexpected praise from someone she had known for such a short time. 'When will we leave for the railway station, Freddie?'

He smiled, acknowledging the change of subject. 'As soon as Walton returns with the timetable and tickets.'

It took the best part of the day to reach the coastal village where the partially ruined Pettigrew Castle stood on top of the cliffs, overlooking the sea. The carter who had given them a lift from the station pointed it out proudly.

'There've been many a battle involving the castle over the centuries. They old parliamentarians besieged it for many months, but Lady Pettigrew defended it with just her retainers and a few loyal men from the village.'

'The family were Royalists, then?' Freddie said conversationally.

'Aye, sir. Staunch supporters of the rightful king. I daresay we'd do the same today, if it was required of us. But the present owner don't have nothing to do with the village. They say as how he's not much longer for this world, but I don't know if that's the case.'

They travelled on in silence. When they came in

sight of the castle the sun was low in the sky leaving the ruined half of the ancient edifice in darkness while the battlements and towers facing the sea were tinged flame red from the setting sun. Flora suppressed a shudder. To think that Ralph had offered to make her the mistress of Pettigrew Castle. He had made it clear that he planned to abandon her there, which made his intentions even more deplorable. As to Gabriel, she was puzzled, disappointed and angry when she remembered how he had also tried to inveigle her into a deception aimed at his uncle. In her opinion, neither cousin deserved to inherit the old man's fortune, let alone the title.

Freddie tapped the man on the shoulder. 'You said there is a decent hostelry in the village. Will you take us there?'

'Aye, it's not far now. The maidy looks fair worn out, sir. If you don't mind me saying so.'

Freddie cast an anxious look at Flora. 'You must be exhausted, my dear. A meal and a good night's sleep will make you feel better.'

'But shouldn't we go to the castle first?' Flora asked anxiously. 'What if they arrive late tonight?'

The carter glanced over his shoulder, his interest aroused. 'The castle don't get many visitors these days. I remember years ago when there was all sorts of comings and goings. There was parties and shooting parties on the moor. Those were the days.'

Freddie lowered his voice. 'I doubt if they'll make

it tonight, but we'll be up and ready to greet them in the morning.'

Flora nodded tiredly. 'I must admit that I'm very weary. I'll be glad to get to bed, but I'll be up bright and early, Freddie. That's a promise.'

'I can come round to take you to the castle first thing.' The carter seemed to be entering into the spirit of their plans even though it had nothing to do with him. Flora hoped that he did not spread word of their arrival, but as they alighted outside the inn Freddie produced a pouch of coins. He tipped the carter handsomely and thanked him for his services. Flora was impressed. Freddie knew exactly how to handle people and to ensure their silence when necessary. Having a vast fortune helped, of course. It was good to know that Arabella would marry someone who could take care of her and would put her first in everything. At least they were here now and it looked as if they had arrived before Ralph and Arabella. Tomorrow would be the day that Ralph Pettigrew met his match. Flora was in no doubt that Freddie could do almost anything to which he set his mind.

Once again they were forced to spend a night at the local hostelry, but Flora was so exhausted that she could have slept anywhere. The landlord and inn servants were overtly curious but Freddie fended off their questions with a smile. Flora could only guess at the rumours that would be flying around the village by morning, but at least they would be on hand when Ralph and Bella eventually arrived.

It was not difficult to get into Pettigrew Castle next morning. What servants there might be were obviously busy elsewhere, or else still asleep. Flora and Freddie had taken their breakfast very early and had walked the half mile or so to the postern gate in the part of the curtain wall that had survived the onslaught of the parliamentarian forces. There was no one to stop them and they entered the bailey and simply walked into the castle. It was cool and the smell of must and cold stone filled the air. Rusty pieces of armour were pinned to the walls and these were covered in dust and cobwebs, as were the halberds and a couple of shields. The only furniture in the main hall was a refectory table and a carved oak dower chest. Their footsteps echoed off the flagstone floor and this brought a very elderly retainer hobbling from the depths of the castle.

'We don't welcome strangers here.'

It was hardly a good start, but Freddie stepped forward, smiling. 'Very wise, but I am an old friend of Baron Pettigrew.' Freddie produced a visiting card from a silver case and wafted it front of the old man's nose.

'An old friend? He don't have friends. You'd best leave afore I call up the dogs.'

'I am well acquainted with Captain Gabriel Cutler,' Flora said hastily. 'And Mr Ralph Pettigrew.'

'Them two!' The old man spat the words as if they left a bad taste in his mouth. 'They'll arrive soon, no doubt. They're like carrion crows just waiting to pick the master's bones when he's gone.'

'We're here to stop that, if we can,' Freddie said firmly. 'If your master is well enough, I would value a few words with him.'

'I'll enquire if the master will see you, but be warned he's not long for this world. Don't upset him or you'll have me to deal with.' The old man snatched the card from Freddie's fingers and turned to walk away. 'Stay here. Don't move an inch.'

Freddie nodded. 'We'll wait.'

'At least it looks as if we're in time to prevent Ralph from telling lies,' Flora said with a sigh of relief. 'But what will we say to Baron Pettigrew if he does agree to see us?'

'I intend to tell him the truth. We are not going to pander to Ralph or Gabriel. What they say to their uncle is up to them. All I'm concerned with is to find Bella and take her home.'

'You do realise that her good name will be compromised already, don't you, Freddie?'

'Yes, of course. Not that it matters to me. We will be married as soon as possible, if Bella will have me, that is.'

'I've no doubts on that score,' Flora said, smiling. 'I think you two are very well suited.'

Freddie swallowed nervously. 'You don't think I'm too old for her, do you? Be honest, Flora.'

'No, you are just what Bella needs, and she loves you. That's the most important thing.'

'Thank you, that means a lot to me.' Freddie turned at the sound of Bella calling his name. As if conjured up by magic, she walked into the great hall on Ralph's arm. But it was not a chivalrous hold he had on her. Flora could see that his knuckles were white as he held on to her, even though she struggled in an attempt to free herself.

'I might have known you would be here, Dorrington,' Ralph said furiously. 'Get out before I set the dogs on you.'

'That's the second time I've been threatened with those mysterious hounds,' Freddie said casually. 'You can say what you like, Pettigrew, but I am here for Arabella. Release her immediately. I'm taking her home.'

'She is at home. Bella has agreed to marry me. You can see she is wearing my ring.' Ralph raised Bella's left hand and a diamond winked at them in a shaft of sunlight.

'We are not engaged,' Bella said tearfully. 'He forced me to wear this ring. Take me home, please, Freddie.' She made another attempt to free herself, but Ralph held her even closer.

'Stop whining, woman.' Ralph twisted her wrist, making her yelp with pain. 'Your reputation is in ruins. Even a besotted fool like Dorrington won't marry you now.'

'Stop this, Ralph,' Flora cried angrily. 'Let Bella go. You can't force her to marry you.'

'What choice has she now? We shared a bed twice. I have witnesses.'

Freddie lunged towards Ralph but even as he made a move towards him there was a clatter of booted footsteps on the flagstone floor and Gabriel marched into the great hall. He lunged at Ralph and knocked him to the ground. Freddie was just in time to catch Bella as she was about to crumple to the floor.

Ralph sprang to his feet and hurled himself at Gabriel. They grappled with each other, fists flying and feet kicking, but Flora was only interested in Bella and she rushed up to her.

'Are you all right, Bella? Did he hurt you badly?'

Tears streamed down Bella's pale cheeks but she shook her head. 'I'm not hurt. Just a little sore but it's nothing.' She rested her head against Freddie's shoulder. 'I am so glad to see you, but you heard what Ralph said. I am not a fit person to be with you now.'

Freddie dropped a kiss on her tousled dark curls. 'I am the best judge of that, my love. You are safe now. I swear I'll never let you out of my sight again, if you'll have me, that is?'

Bella's answer was smothered in the folds of his jacket, but Flora smiled and nodded.

'I don't think there's any doubt about it, Freddie.' She stroked Bella's cheek. 'Thank goodness you're safe, anyway. Nothing else matters.'

Meanwhile the fight continued with Gabriel having Ralph in a stranglehold on the floor.

'He's going to kill him,' Flora observed dispassionately.

'That will save me from doing the deed.' Freddie pulled out a chair from the long refectory table. 'Sit down, Bella. I'll see if one of the servants can bring you some water or even a tot of brandy.'

Bella managed a watery smile. 'I would love a cup of tea, Freddie. I am so thirsty and hungry, too. Ralph locked me in our room and he wouldn't allow me any sustenance until I agreed to wear his ring.'

Gabriel looked up as if he had heard what Bella just said. He delivered a knockout punch and Ralph collapsed onto the stone floor. 'You deserve more than that, Cousin,' Gabriel said, rising groggily to his feet. 'I apologise on behalf of my family, Miss Stewart.'

'You're little better than Ralph,' Flora countered icily. 'You wanted me to pretend to be your fiancée so that you could inherit everything from your dying uncle.'

Gabriel brushed himself down. 'How is the old boy? Is he still breathing?'

'Show a little respect for the man who brought you up.' Freddie slipped his arm around Bella's shoulders. 'We'll leave as soon as you're feeling up to it.'

'I am ready,' Bella said, reaching out to clutch Flora's hand. 'I want to go home.'

'Trask is coming,' Gabriel said, holding up his hand for silence as the old man approached them, shuffling slowly as if every step brought pain to some part of his aged body. 'Trask, how is my uncle?'

'Only he knows that, Master Gabriel. He wants to see you.' Trask pointed to Ralph. 'What happened to him?'

'He bumped into my fist,' Gabriel said hastily. 'Don't worry, Trask. Just fetch a jug of cold water. He'll be on his feet in no time.'

'We'd best leave now.' Freddie beckoned to Trask. 'Miss Stewart is feeling unwell. Is there a carriage that could take us to the village inn?'

'After you've seen the master, my lord. He said he doesn't remember you, but he will see you anyway. I don't think he has long, so you'd all best hurry.'

'We really should go now, Freddie.' Flora could see that Bella was not feeling at all well, and an audience with a dying man might just prove too much for her, especially if either Ralph or Gabriel decided to keep up the fiction that either one of them intended to marry Bella. Gabriel had pulled Ralph to his feet.

'Wipe the blood from your nose. The old man wants to speak to us, and I want you to be there, Dorrington, when he confirms that I am to inherit everything.'

'Call yourselves grown men,' Freddie said scornfully. 'You're nothing but a pair of playground bullies – greedy ones at that. I hope your uncle disinherits the pair of you.'

Ralph wiped the blood off his face with his sleeve. 'Go to hell, Dorrington.'

'Follow me, my lord.' Trask moved painfully slowly towards the end of the great hall.

'You'd better come with me, Bella.' Freddie helped her to her feet. 'You, too, Flora. It's a dying man's wish. We've come this far, so we must see it through.'

Gabriel turned to Ralph. 'You're going to watch when the old man names me as his heir.'

Ralph grunted but did not argue and they all followed Trask as he made his way to the stairs.

The air in the large bedchamber was thick with dust and the lingering smell of decay. Bella wrinkled her nose as she leaned heavily on Freddie's arm, but Gabriel pushed past Flora, almost knocking her off her feet as he hurried to the dying man's bedside. He flung himself down on his knees.

'Uncle Peregrine. It's me, Gabriel.'

Flora was shocked to see the old man lying in the huge four-poster bed, who already looked like a skeleton with flesh drawn tightly over the pale bones.

'Where's Ralph?' Baron Pettigrew's reedy voice was little more than a whisper.

Ralph staunched his bleeding nose with a scrap of material he had torn from one of the curtains. 'Here I am, Uncle. I'm always here when you need me.'

'Liar,' Gabriel spat the word. 'He's after your money, and everything you hold dear, Uncle.'

Flora sent a pleading look to Freddie. She could hardly intervene, but perhaps a word from him might ease the situation.

Freddie cleared his throat. 'Thank you for seeing us, sir. We only came to pay our respects. We will leave you now.'

'No!' Ralph said sharply. 'That woman is my fiancée. He means to take her from me, Uncle.'

Flora had had enough. She moved swiftly to the bedside. 'Don't listen to him, sir. I beg you not to take any notice. It's all lies. Both of them want what they can get.'

'That's enough of that, miss.' Trask stepped forward to lay his gnarled hand on her arm. 'The master knows them of old.'

With a huge effort, Baron Pettigrew raised himself on one elbow. 'Listen carefully. I haven't much time left.'

'We're listening, Uncle,' Gabriel said softly.

'There is no money,' Pettigrew uttered a cackle of laughter. 'All gone, my boys. The title dies with me, I saw to that, and the castle is entailed to my distant cousin, Sir Philip de Crecy. You two get what you deserve – nothing.' He fell back onto the pillows, a rictus grin on his face. Trask moved in to lean over his master. He closed the dead man's eyes.

'He's gone. Now you two can go on your way. You heard what he said. You got nothing.'

'He can't do that,' Ralph said faintly. 'Can he?'

'There must be a mistake.' Gabriel went to give

his uncle a shake but was fended off by Trask, who curled his lips in a snarl.

'Have some respect for the dead. Go away or I'll put the dogs on you.'

Gabriel straightened up, eyeing Trask with pure hatred. 'You always were a mean brute, Trask. I don't know why my uncle kept you on. I bet you've had your share of the money.'

Ralph moved closer. 'Let's check his quarters, Gabriel. We'll probably find a tidy sum stashed away.'

Flora leaped in between them. 'You two disgust me. You heard what your uncle said. Now have some respect for the man who raised you and leave.'

'That's right,' Freddie added. 'You two are as bad as each other. Neither of you deserves to inherit. Your uncle knew exactly what you were up to. I'm ashamed and I'm not even related to you.'

Gabriel grabbed Ralph by the scruff of his neck. 'Come on, we're leaving.'

'You don't want her.' Ralph pointed a finger at Bella as his cousin manhandled him out of the room. 'She's not an innocent now, Lord Dorrington. Your firstborn will be a Pettigrew.'

Freddie thrust Bella into Flora's arms and dashed after them as they left the room.

'Don't fight, please,' Bella wailed. 'Oh, Flora, it could be true. I am not fit to marry someone like Freddie.'

Flora turned to Trask. 'I am truly sorry for this

dreadful behaviour at such a time. Is there another way downstairs?'

Trask nodded. 'The servants' staircase, miss. It's a bit steep.'

'We can manage. We'll leave the gentlemen to sort themselves out.'

Outside in the sun-filled bailey the carter who had taken them to the inn last evening was seated on the driver's seat of his cart, smoking a clay pipe. He took it from his mouth when he saw Flora supporting Bella, who was in obvious distress.

'Is the maidy unwell, miss?' He tapped the tobacco from his pipe and climbed down to the cobblestones. 'I thought she looked proper poorly when I brought her here with Master Ralph.'

'Will you help me get her into the wagon, please?' Flora said breathlessly. 'We're just waiting for our friend and then we'll be on our way back to the inn.'

'Mr Ralph hired me, miss. I should wait for him.'

'Did he pay you?'

The carter shook his head. 'No, but he will when he gets his dues.'

'I doubt it.' Flora settled Bella on a pile of sacks in the back of the vehicle. 'His lordship will tip you handsomely again if you just wait for him. He's settling an argument, but he won't be long.'

'They boys was always trouble, miss. Little devils they was when younger, always up to some mischief or other.'

'That I can well believe,' Flora said earnestly. 'Here comes Lord Dorrington. We'll go back to the inn, and then we might need you to take us to the railway station.'

The carter saluted and climbed back onto his seat.

'Are you all right, Freddie?' Bella cried anxiously. 'You're bleeding.'

'I'm fine, Bella. The other two are feeling sorry for themselves.' Freddie turned his attention to the carter. 'The gentleman won't be requiring you for a while.'

'That's all right, sir. Young miss has asked me to drive you to the inn.'

Freddie took a seat beside Bella and slipped his arm around her. 'Drive on.'

'You don't think Ralph will follow us, do you, Freddie?' Bella asked nervously.

'No, he won't. I haven't used the art of fisticuffs for many years, but it seems I haven't forgotten how to defend myself or my lady.'

Flora sat back on the wooden seat, smiling happily. She had no doubt that Bella and Freddie would make a wonderful couple. Their happiness was written in the stars. As to her own future, that was another matter.

# Chapter Sixteen

It was late evening when they finally arrived back in South Molton Street, having travelled on several different trains, and the smell of hot cinders and steam clung to Flora's clothes. It came as something of a surprise to find the entrance hall filled with trunks and valises, although Flora had known that the family would pack up the town house and retire to the country for a few months. Nevertheless, the servants were rushing around with Holland covers to protect the furniture as if the move was forever.

Constance was already in bed but Sir Arthur met them in the entrance hall. He embraced Bella with tears in his eyes.

'Thank God you are safe, my love. Your mama and I have been out of our minds with worry.' He turned to Freddie, holding out his hand. 'Thank you, Dorrington. You are a man after my own heart.'

Despite Flora's reassurances, Bella had been afraid that spending two nights in Ralph's company would sully not only her reputation but would make her a lesser person in the eyes of her parents. Flora hovered in the background, as usual. She was both touched and relieved to see Sir Arthur greet his daughter with such obvious affection.

'I should leave now, sir,' Freddie said calmly. 'But tomorrow I will return and I think you know what I will be requesting from you.'

Sir Arthur smiled and patted him on the back. 'You may be assured of my answer in the affirmative, Dorrington. But we will be leaving for the country house at noon, so don't be late.'

'You may depend on that, sir.'

'And now I think both you and Flora should go to your rooms,' Sir Arthur said gently. 'You must be exhausted.'

'Yes, Papa. I am, and I'm sure Flora is too. She has been magnificent, Papa.'

'As always,' Sir Arthur said, nodding in Flora's direction. 'I don't know what we would do without you, Flora, my dear.'

Flora nodded and smiled, but she was too exhausted to think or feel anything more than the need to go to her room and get a good night's sleep. It would be wonderful to get back to Nine Oaks where she could roam the grounds freely without fear of being accosted by either Ralph or Gabriel. Her former feelings for Gabriel had been replaced by disgust and she could only hope that she had seen the last of both him and his hateful cousin. She accompanied Bella to her room where Mary was waiting to help her undress.

'Do you think Freddie will ask Papa for my hand tomorrow?' Bella said in a low voice as Flora was about to leave.

'Do you doubt it, you ninny?' Flora brushed Bella's flushed cheek with a kiss. 'Go to bed and get some beauty sleep. Tomorrow, I can guarantee you will be an affianced woman.'

'You really think so?'

'I'd stake my life on it, Bella. Goodnight.' Flora closed the door and headed for her own room. There was no maid waiting to help her into bed, but it was good to have some time when she did not have to think or to worry about other people. Undoubtedly there would be a wedding to plan, and in the circumstances it would be sooner rather than later. That would keep everyone fully occupied for however long it took. After that nothing was certain. Still fully dressed, Flora lay down on the bed and closed her eyes.

Marsh House Modes were only too delighted to make Bella's wedding gown as well as Flora's bridesmaid's dress. She was to be Bella's only attendant and Todd was to be Freddie's best man. Everyone had decided that it would be a country wedding and Bella would be married from her childhood home, the ceremony to take place in the village church. It was not going to be a small affair. Constance seemed to be afraid that people would think it very suspicious if the event was too rushed or too quiet. The announcement of Bella's engagement to Lord Dorrington was posted in *The Times* and shortly afterward invitations were sent out to selected guests. Constance spent every morning going over lists with Cook and Mrs Fellowes, while Jefferson was given the task of organising the wine cellar for the occasion. As the ceremony would take place at the beginning of September it was planned to have marquees set up in the grounds and Flora was given the responsibility for decorating them as well as the flower arrangements for the church and the house. This would mean long consultations with Daniel and his father, although it was too late in the season to raise plants especially for the occasion. Flora was wary of facing them, especially in the light of Daniel's obvious infatuation with the scullery maid. However, Bella's wedding was more important and she must put aside personal problems to make sure that it was a truly memorable day.

Flora's first meeting with Daniel on her return to Nine Oaks happened by accident. She had spent the whole of the first day after their arrival with Bella and her mother on a visit to Marsh House. Constance was very keen on having her own outfit designed and made by Amelia, who was only too pleased to sit down with them to make sketches and discuss fabrics. Of course the bride's gown was the most important, but Flora had a feeling that Constance was more interested in how she would be seen as mother of the bride. With Bella marrying into the nobility, Constance had achieved what was the ultimate dream of even the most ambitious mothers, and of course she wanted to look her best. Sir Arthur had given them carte blanche when it came to expense, having recently secured a remunerative business deal which would restore much of the family fortune.

Flora knew better than to put herself forward, but it took all morning just to satisfy Constance. However, Bella was easier to please, and Flora was delighted with Amelia's first suggestions when it came to her own gown. Having agreed on the styles, they had luncheon in the dining room, prepared as usual by Mariah, who had just announced that she and Farmer Allen were to be married after the harvest was gathered in.

The best part of the afternoon was spent in selecting the material for the garments as well as the trimmings. It was all very taxing, and they left Marsh House tired but satisfied. The next time they came it would be for the first of their fittings. Amelia and Mariah promised that the entire staff would work on the wedding gown and outfits so that everything would be ready for the great day.

Flora arrived home with Bella and Constance just in time to change for dinner. Conversation at the meal revolved around the designs and fabric they had chosen, although Flora could see that Sir Arthur had lost interest after the first few words. He managed to make the right sounds when his wife challenged him, which Flora found quite amusing. She caught his eye at one point and he actually gave her a conspiratorial wink. After dinner, he opted to stay at the table and smoke a cigar while he enjoyed a glass of brandy. Constance and Bella retired to the drawing room for coffee and yet more talk about wedding preparations, but Flora had a sudden desire for fresh air. Despite their protests, she went out on the terrace and set off to enjoy the balmy atmosphere, with the scent of the warm grass and intoxicating aroma of roses, honeysuckle and night-scented stock wafting around her like the most expensive French perfume. The sun was setting, creating fireworks of colour in the sky and long purple shadows spread beneath the trees that surrounded the extensive lawns. Birds were rustling in the branches as they settled down to roost for the night, while a robin warbled his sweet evening song as if to lull the other birds to sleep. Flora was enjoying the solitude when she was suddenly aware of heavy footsteps behind her. She stopped and spun round, uttering a sign of relief when she recognised him.

'Daniel, you scared me.'

He touched his cap, suddenly formal. 'Apologies, Miss Flora.'

'What is this? Why are you addressing me as if I was the daughter of the house?'

'Isn't that what you are? I mean, you are so far above me I'm surprised you have the time to speak to me.'

'Daniel! I don't understand. I thought we were friends.'

'You made it clear that we aren't.'

'When was that?' Flora could see by the stubborn set to his jaw that he was not going to let her off easily. They had hardly spoken since she rejected his proposal, but that was due to circumstances and not her choice. She was suddenly angry. 'Anyway, the last time I saw you was when you were sitting with the May Queen with your arm around her. You looked very cosy, I must say.'

Daniel stared at her as if she was speaking nonsense. 'Me and Elsie Root – is that who you mean?'

'I think you understand me very well.' Flora was about to walk on, but Daniel caught her by the hand.

'There's nothing between me and her. She's a child.'

'She's a young woman and she obviously likes you. Anyway, I don't wish to argue with you. I came out to enjoy the fresh air and the beautiful sunset.'

'Where is your gentleman friend – the sea captain who came here looking for you a while ago?'

'Gabriel came here?'

'You know he did. He said you and he was engaged.'

'For one thing I have never been engaged to Gabriel Cutler, and for another thing I never want to see that person again.'

'It seems we've both been at cross purposes then, don't it?'

Flora met his gaze and saw the irresistible twinkle in his eyes that glowed amber in the last rays of the setting sun. 'Yes, it does. You should apologise for jumping to conclusions.'

'So should you.' Daniel took a step forward and when she did not move away he took her in his arms and lifted her off her feet to kiss her with breath-taking sweetness, tinged with pent-up desire. Flora stiffened at first, knowing it was inappropriate and wrong, but the feelings he aroused sparked a response in her that could not be denied. She relaxed and returned the kiss with enthusiasm, sliding her arms around his neck so that she was suspended above the ground and her head was in the stars.

He let her down slowly until her feet touched the soft springy grass. In her dazed state, she was still in another world.

'Daniel, I . . .' For once she was lost for words.

'I'm not going to apologise, Flora. I've wanted to do that for so long you just wouldn't believe it if I told you.'

'I'm sorry for the things I said to you before. I didn't mean them.'

'Yes, you did, and you was quite right. You are an educated young lady who is used to the finer things in life and I am a common gardener. How could I expect you to marry me and live in a cottage on the estate?'

'I don't know, Daniel. I don't seem to be able to think clearly.'

Daniel released her, shaking his head. 'I shouldn't have kissed you, Flora. I'm not apologising, because I love you and I'm not sorry, but I had no right to assume—'

'Rights and wrongs don't come into it.' Flora caught him by the collar of his jacket and pulled his head down so that their lips met again in a fiercely defensive kiss. She let him go again and took a step backwards. 'I love you, too. But I don't know what we're going to do about it, Dan. I really don't.' She backed away. 'I need time to think.' She turned and ran back to the house, but she stopped on the edge of the terrace, unable to resist one last look backwards. Daniel was standing where she had left him. He was looking towards her but the encroaching shadows made it impossible to read his expression. Reluctantly, Flora returned to the house, leaving part of her heart with the man she loved, but who was separated from her by the invisible but almost impenetrable barrier of their different stations in life.

Flora knew she had crossed that line as she stepped back into the drawing room and was met by a cry of delight from Bella.

'Do come and sit down, Flora. Mama and I are just going over the list of what I will need for my trousseau. Freddie has promised to take me to Paris. I wish you could come, too. I know you would love it.'

'I doubt if Freddie would want to take an extra person on your honeymoon,' Flora said with a wry smile. 'But I am sure you will have a wonderful time.'

'You and I must have a serious talk, Bella.' Constance replaced her coffee cup on its saucer, carefully avoiding Bella's curious stare. 'It will wait until a more appropriate time, but we must have our little chat before the wedding.' Blushing furiously, Constance rose from her seat. 'I am rather tired, so I will say goodnight, my dears. Don't stay up too late, Bella. You need to look your best at all times, especially now.' She hurried from the room before Bella could say anything.

'What do you think she wants to talk about?' Bella demanded, frowning.

'Wifely duties, I daresay,' Flora said casually. She had a shrewd idea as to the topic of conversation that Lady Stewart wanted to have with her only daughter, but Flora had no intention of getting involved. It was not considered appropriate for such things to be discussed among young, unmarried women. Flora had seen animals in the mating season and when younger she had questioned Daniel, who had immediately sent her to his own mother for an explanation. Down to earth and practical, Doris Robbins had told Flora what she wanted to know and had answered all her innocent questions calmly and in a matter-of-fact manner. Flora wondered whether it would be more sensible to ask Doris to tell Bella what to expect on her marriage night, but she decided to steer the conversation back to clothes – always a safe subject.

Eventually, worn out by the excitement of wedding preparations, Bella retired to bed, smiling happily. Flora was exhausted also, but as she climbed into bed her emotions were in turmoil. The embraces she had shared with Daniel had awakened desires and needs which had surprised and shaken her. She had always been able to take command of her feelings, but this was different. The time was coming, immediately after Bella and Freddie were married, when she, Flora Lee, would have to choose which path to take. Should she remain with the Stewarts and hope one day to catch the eye of a respectable man who would marry her and keep her in a way she was used to, or should she marry the gardener's son and live in a cottage for the rest of her life? She fell asleep eventually with the problem unresolved and Daniel's kiss forever in her heart.

The wedding was arranged for the first Monday in September and the banns were duly read out in church. With only a couple of weeks to go to the great day there was so much to do that Flora had little time to think about her own feelings. She threw herself wholeheartedly into the task she had been given and she planned to strip the kitchen garden of brightly coloured dahlias, Michaelmas daisies, roses and any other flowers that were in bloom. Even so there would not be enough to decorate the church, the house and the marquees. It was agreed that Dobson would drive one of the carts to Covent Garden very early in the morning of the great day and collect an order of flowers that Flora had placed with one of the suppliers.

In the meantime there were the inevitable trips to Marsh House for fittings and a day out in the West End for Flora and Bella to purchase the last items of Bella's trousseau. From being a quiet country house, Nine Oaks was suddenly a hive of activity. The aroma of baking, roasting and pickling from the kitchens wafted throughout the house. Mrs Fellowes bustled about supervising the cleaning of every room that might be used by the wedding guests. She had lists for everything, so much so that Flora was afraid she might be on one of them and find herself ticked off as being unnecessary, or, at best, saved for later. Bella thought this very funny but Constance was visibly shocked and scolded Flora for being silly. She had her own lists and these concerned the guests who had accepted and would require a room for the night; the guests who had accepted but would be leaving at the end of the celebrations, and guests who had not yet had the courtesy to respond. The latter were a constant source of annoyance to her and she complained bitterly to anyone who might lend an ear. Both Bella and Flora tried to avoid her as much as possible. At least Flora could escape to the walled garden when things became too hectic in the house. However, she tried to choose a time when she knew that Daniel would be working elsewhere. He had more duties now as he had been promoted to head gardener, his father having taken up lighter duties due to the rheumatics that regularly beset him at the start of winter.

Despite her feelings for Daniel, Flora knew that if they were to marry it would mean living in the small cottage with her in-laws. Not that she disliked either Doris or Bill Robbins, but the tied cottage went with the job, and all the other dwellings on the estate were occupied by ground staff. Flora also knew that Daniel would never seek work elsewhere while his parents relied on him to keep a roof over their heads. It was an impossible situation. She would have confided in Bella, but the bride-to-be was not only walking round in a haze of happiness, she was totally immersed in the wedding plans and could talk of nothing else. Flora kept her personal torment to herself, but she knew she would have to face her problems one day. Daniel had grown from a shy gardener's son to a man with a strong will and equally strong emotions. Even so, there was still this gulf between them which she needed to find a way to bridge or else they must part forever.

'Flora! I'm speaking to you.' Constance's voice

broke into Flora's thoughts, making her turn with a start.

'I'm sorry, ma'am. I was deep in thought.'

'That is very obvious. Anyway, I am terribly busy and Bella feels a little unwell, so I need you to go to the milliners in Bond Street and collect my bonnet for the wedding. You may take the chaise. Dobson will drive you. I know there is a lot to do, but we only have three days until the wedding. Tomorrow we will have our final fittings at Marsh House. I just hope there are no last-minute alterations, although I have a horrible feeling that Bella has lost weight yet again.'

'Could you send Mary to fetch the bonnet, ma'am? I need to start decorating the church. I can hardly finish it off on Sunday. I don't think the vicar would appreciate it if I interrupted his sermons.'

'You are the only one available, Flora. I would send Mary but she is looking after Bella and I don't trust any of the other servants enough to let them choose the silk flowers for your hair. Bella, of course, will wear the diamond tiara that her grandmama left her. She will walk up the aisle as Miss Arabella Stewart and leave the church the wife of an earl.'

Flora nodded. 'Very well. I'll go, but it will take the rest of the day.'

'No matter, dear. My bonnet and your silk roses are a matter of urgency. Please get ready. Dobson is waiting.'

*

Five minutes later Flora stepped out of the front entrance to find Daniel seated in the chaise with a carriage whip in his hand. He smiled and tipped his hat.

'Good morning, Miss Flora.'

'I thought Dobson was driving me.'

Daniel leaped down to the ground and proffered his hand. 'Allow me, miss. I believe Dobson was to drive you to town, but he was called away urgently.' He handed Flora onto the seat and climbed in next to her. 'Walk on,' he said firmly as he picked up the reins.

'You arranged this, didn't you?'

'Yes, I did. It seemed like the only way I was ever going to get near you, Flora. You've been avoiding me ever since the night you returned to Nine Oaks.'

'I've been busy. We are planning a very important wedding.'

'The whole world must know about it by now. Sir Arthur has had us mowing the lawns, tidying up borders and generally working from dawn until dusk so that the place is fit to be seen by all the important wedding guests.'

'What do you expect?' Flora said sharply. 'It's Bella's big day. She's marrying the man of her dreams.'

'He's old enough to be her father, so I've heard.'

'That's not true. He is her senior, but he's a delightful person and he adores Bella. I know they'll be very happy together.'

'Then you'll be free to marry me. I haven't changed my mind, Flora. I will always love you. But you know that, don't you?'

'Please don't make things difficult, especially so close to the wedding. You know I care deeply for you, Daniel.'

'But you can't imagine being married to a mere head gardener. You think you could be happier with a rich nobleman?'

Flora laughed. 'You make it sound enticing.' She was suddenly serious. 'You know that's not true, but we are used to different things. I simply can't see how it could work.'

'You still cling to that old excuse?'

'It isn't an excuse. Can you imagine me living in a small cottage with your parents, much as I love them? It would end in tears, Daniel.'

'What do you want, Flora? Tell me.'

She eyed him warily. Whatever she said would cause him pain, but it was necessary to be honest with him as well as with herself.

'I think I was happiest working for the Tullivers at the Play House Inn.'

'You enjoyed serving drunken dockers and sailors with ale?'

'Not really. I loved the restaurant part of the business. I didn't even mind working in a hot kitchen. I learned so much about food preparation from Ted, and Coralie taught me how to manage the bar and the actual running of the business.'

'It's hard to understand,' Daniel said slowly. 'I'm a countryman, Flora. I'm familiar with the changing seasons and I know a lot about growing plants and vegetables, but what you're talking about is foreign to me. Are you saying that you would rather work in a tavern than marry me?'

She reached out to clasp his hand. 'No, Daniel. I didn't mean that, but I suppose I would like to have both. I know it's impossible – it's like crying for the moon.'

'If only I could give it to you.' Daniel raised her hand to his lips. 'I would climb up into the sky and fetch a star for you if I could, but my feet are planted firmly in the soil.'

'Yes, I know that.' Flora sighed. 'We are too different, but perhaps you would understand me more if you were to see where I was working. I'm sure you would like Ted and Coralie and Moses, too. Maybe we could stop there briefly on the way home.'

'We'll make time,' Daniel said firmly. He leaned forward. 'Trot.' The horse obliged by quickening his pace and Daniel relaxed. 'I really want to meet these people, Flora.'

The milliner had the bonnet ready and packed in a neat bandbox, leaving them time to make the detour to Play House Yard. Daniel was unfamiliar with this part of London, but Flora knew the streets well enough to guide him to their destination without getting lost.

Moses came out to meet them as they drew up outside the inn and his face creased into a huge smile when he saw Flora.

'You've come home,' he said happily.

Flora alighted and gave him a hug. 'Just a short visit, Moses. How are you?'

'I missed you. It's not the same in the kitchen without you.'

Daniel handed him the reins. 'Will you take care of the horse while we go inside for a short while?'

Moses grinned. 'That's what I do, guv. Kind people give me a tip.'

'Do they now?' Daniel smiled. 'Well, I'll remember that when we leave. Thank you, Moses.'

Flora walked into the taproom and was greeted by shouts of appreciation. Coralie hurried into the room and her face lit up when she saw Flora. She opened her arms and wrapped her in a tight embrace.

'You've come home, girl.'

Flora drew away, smiling. 'It feels like home, but I've just brought a friend to meet you and Ted. I've told him how kind you were to me.'

Daniel stepped forward to shake Coralie's hand. 'How do, ma'am.'

'You must be Daniel,' Coralie said, nodding. 'I heard all about you, young man. Flora didn't exaggerate. You are very handsome.'

Flora was amused to see a blush stain Daniel's cheeks and he was momentarily lost for words.

'Come and meet my husband,' Coralie said, laughing.

'But don't be surprised if he refuses to let Flora leave us again. She was such a great help to us while she was here. I was sorry to see her go.'

Flora hurried Daniel out of the taproom and down the long corridor that led to the kitchen at the back of the building. The heat and steam hit her in the face as she opened the door and the tempting aroma of roasting meat made her stomach growl with hunger.

Ted greeted her with enthusiasm to equal that of Moses and Coralie. He shook Daniel's hand. 'So you are the reason that Flora abandoned us, Daniel. I should hold that against you, but life in the country obviously suits her. She was a poor skinny little scrap of a thing when I found her in Turnagain Lane.'

'She speaks very highly of you, sir.' Daniel wiped a beat of sweat from his brow. 'I don't know how you manage to work in this heat.'

'You get used to it, son.' Ted peeled off his apron. 'Come into the bar. We'll have a drink together.'

'We can't stay long, Ted.' Flora followed him from the heat into the relative cool of the passageway. 'We have to get back to Nine Oaks. I just wanted Dan to meet you and Coralie.'

'We'll sit in the private parlour and you can tell us what's been going on since you left us. I hope that Pettigrew fellow hasn't been bothering you.'

'He came here often?' Daniel reached for Flora's hand.

'I'm sure I told you that, Daniel. It was just one evening. He brought several of his wealthy acquaintances with him. They drank a lot and it ended when they threatened to throw him in the river.'

'It's a pity they didn't.' Ted opened the taproom door. 'He's haunted this place for weeks. Every day he comes here to drink himself under the table. He moans about how hard done by he is and how he missed out on his inheritance.' He glanced into the taproom. 'Hold on a minute – he's just come in now. I don't suppose you want to see him, do you?'

'Certainly not,' Flora said urgently.

'But I do.' Daniel pushed past her. 'I want to see the brute who has made your life a misery. I'm a peaceable fellow but he deserves to be horsewhipped. Let me go in there, Mr Tulliver. I'll show him what I think of him.'

# Chapter Seventeen

Ted barred his way. 'I'll have no brawling in my bar. He's a pathetic drunk these days. He's not worth bothering with.'

Daniel faced Ted with a stubborn set to his jaw. 'What would you do, sir? If the boot was on the other foot and it was your lady who had been mistreated?'

Ted was silent for a moment and then he nodded. 'Speak to him if you must, but if it comes to fisticuffs, I'll throw you both out onto the street.'

'Please leave Ralph alone,' Flora said urgently. 'Don't stir things up again.'

But Daniel was not listening and he marched into the taproom, coming to a halt in front of Ralph. He addressed him in a low voice and, although Flora could not hear the words, she could tell by Ralph's expression that they had not gone down well. He staggered to his feet.

'Get out of here, country boy.'

'I'm going,' Daniel said angrily. 'But if you ever bother Miss Lee again, I won't be responsible for my actions.'

Ralph took a swing at Daniel but missed his mark, causing him to slide to the floor. Daniel shook his head. 'You are a hopeless drunk. But I meant what I said. Keep yourself to yourself or face the consequences.'

Ted crossed the floor in long strides and laid his hand on Daniel's shoulder. 'I think he understands, son.'

Daniel fisted his hands at his sides, but he did not argue and he followed Ted into the parlour.

When they were comfortably settled with the door firmly closed, Flora told Ted and Coralie about Ralph's attempt to force Arabella into marriage in order to convince his dying uncle that he was the right person to continue the Pettigrew line. They listened with a mixture of shock and disbelief.

'And you say that Captain Cutler was involved in all this?' Ted pushed back his chair and stood up. 'It's hard to believe that the two of them could be so devious.'

'Wicked, I call it,' Coralie said, scowling. 'I've a mind to go into the taproom and throw Ralph Pettigrew out onto the street. We should bar him from the pub, Ted.'

'I agree, but I'll wait until Flora and Daniel have left.

I don't want the likes of Pettigrew on my premises.' Ted gave Flora a searching look. 'What will you do when Miss Bella is married? Might you come back here and work for us?'

Flora smiled. 'It's tempting, but I don't know yet.'

'Don't pester her, Ted.' Coralie frowned at him, shaking her head. 'Flora knows she can always come back if she wishes, but she has to make up her own mind.'

Flora rose to her feet. 'Thank you both. Whatever happens in the future, you haven't seen the last of me. I'm sorry this is such a brief visit, but we have to leave now. The big wedding is on Monday and there is still much to do.'

'Aye, that's true.' Daniel stood up, holding his hand out to Ted. 'Thank you for the ale, sir. It was nice to meet you and Mrs Tulliver.'

'Do come again soon.' Coralie gave Flora a hug. 'I miss having you here to help me.'

Flora was close to tears as they left the inn, especially when Moses clung to her like an affectionate puppy. She had to promise faithfully to return soon before he could be persuaded to let her go. She waved until they were out of sight and Daniel encouraged the old horse to trot.

'You made your mark with them, Flora,' Daniel said, smiling. 'I thought they might keep you there and I'd have to return to Nine Oaks on my own.'

This made her laugh. 'I really love them all. They were so good to me, and I felt quite at home with them, even though it was very hard work and long hours.'

They travelled on in silence while Daniel negotiated the busy city streets and it was not until they reached the outskirts of London that he turned to Flora with a worried frown.

'You aren't really going to leave us and go back to the inn, are you?'

She shook her head. 'No. Much as I love them all, I don't want to be an assistant forever. I would really like to have my own business, like Amelia.' She shot him a sideways glance. 'I know what you're going to say, and I do want marriage and children later, but not just yet.'

'I can't pretend to understand completely, but I'm trying.'

'I know you are, Dan. I love you for being so patient.'

'Let's get this wedding over and perhaps we can all return to normal.'

Flora nodded in agreement, but she dare not think too hard about what might happen when Arabella left home and began her new life as Freddie's wife. It was like standing on the edge of a very tall cliff and not knowing whether to take off like a bird or plummet to the rocks below like a stone. Flora knew that Sir Arthur and his wife would never ask her to leave, she could just say nothing and continue to do the flowers and help Lady Stewart with her correspondence, if required, remaining an unpaid companion for the rest of her days.

They spoke little after that, each absorbed in their own thoughts, but when they finally arrived back at Nine Oaks Flora was surprised to see Freddie's carriage outside the house. She leaned over to brush Daniel's cheek with a kiss. 'Thank you for taking me to the inn. It was good to see the Tullivers and Moses.'

He smiled. 'I suppose the next time I see you will be in church.'

'Yes, it will.' Flora alighted nimbly and picked up the bandbox. 'Goodbye, Dan.' She hurried up the steps to where James was holding the door open.

'I see Lord Dorrington is here, James. Is he in the drawing room?'

'I believe so, miss.'

'Lady Stewart's maid is waiting for this.' Flora handed the bandbox to James.

'Very well, Miss Flora. I'll make sure she gets it.'

'Thank you, James.' Flora knew she should go to her room to take off her bonnet and lace gloves, but she was curious. It seemed strange that Freddie should arrive when there were only two more days to go before the wedding, and she was frankly curious. She went straight to the drawing room.

Freddie was in deep conversation with Constance but there was no sign of Bella.

'Is anything wrong, Flora?' Constance raised a delicate eyebrow.

'No, ma'am. I just came to tell you that I collected your new hat and James is going to give it to your maid.'

'You took a long time. I was expecting you back at least two hours ago.' Constance eyed her curiously.

Freddie seemed to sense Flora's discomfort and he rose to his feet. 'I expect you are surprised to see me today.'

'Yes, I must admit I am rather curious.'

'Hence your slightly dishevelled state,' Constance said curtly.

'I apologise, ma'am. I should have gone to my room and changed out of my travelling costume.'

Freddie grinned. 'Well, I'm glad you did not. You can come with us now that you're home. If Lady Stewart doesn't mind, that is?'

'Where are you going? Has something untoward happened?'

'Freddie has an elderly relative who lives about half a mile away,' Constance said in a bored voice. 'He has decided to visit her and Bella is getting ready as we speak. Although I think it is rather late in the day to go calling, especially on someone of senior years and in poor health.'

'Aunt Philomena sent for me, Lady Stewart,' Freddie said hastily. 'She fell out with my father many years ago, and I must admit I have rather neglected her. But she wants to see me and the telegram suggested that it was a matter of urgency.'

'She is probably short of funds.' Constance pursed her lips. 'Anyway, it doesn't matter. You had better follow your conscience, Freddie. Although I don't think it appropriate for you to stay here tonight so close to your wedding day.'

'Of course not, ma'am. I wouldn't dream of imposing. I can see how busy your servants are with all the preparations for Monday. I would be more than happy to hire extra hands to help out.'

'No, thank you. We have a large enough staff to cope with what is really quite a small wedding.'

Freddie acknowledged the put-down with a nod and a practised smile. He turned to Flora. 'Would you like to accompany us? Or are you too tired after your trip into town?'

'I would love to visit your aunt. Where exactly does she live?'

'Not too far from here. It's a large house set in its own grounds. My late father bought it for her after her husband was killed in a shooting accident. Aunt Philomena was his only sister and so, even though they never got along, he felt a measure of responsibility for her welfare.'

'Please be back on time for dinner,' Constance said, sighing. 'You know how my husband likes to eat on the dot of half past seven. We do keep country hours when we are here.'

'I understand, ma'am.' Freddie turned with a beaming smile. 'Bella, my dear. Are you ready?'

Bella blushed and lowered her eyes coyly. 'Of course, Freddie.' She glanced at Flora and her smile widened. 'Oh, how lovely. Are you coming, too?'

'I wouldn't miss it for all the world,' Flora said firmly.

Lady Philomena's house was surprisingly modest compared with Freddie's palatial mansion in Piccadilly and the drawing that Flora had seen of his home on the border of Devonshire and Somerset. The eighteenth-century manor house was set back from the main road behind a low wall topped with iron railings. The house itself was designed in the neo-classical style with a large central portico. The white stucco was bathed gold in the setting sun and the tall windows reflected the light. Flora was instantly attracted to the friendly ambience of the building.

An elderly butler opened the door in answer to Freddie's pounding on the lion's head knocker.

'I received your telegram, Beasley.'

'Step inside, my lord. Lady Philomena has been asking for you.'

Freddie ushered Bella and Flora into the square entrance hall with a staircase rising up in an impressive sweep to the first floor.

'Is she any better, Beasley?' Freddie asked anxiously.

'No, my lord. The doctor says it's only a matter of time. If the young ladies would like to wait in the morning parlour I will show you to Lady Philomena's bedchamber, sir.'

'Of course.' Freddie nodded.

Flora and Bella followed Beasley to the parlour,

which was elegant but the upholstery on the dainty chairs was slightly threadbare and Flora noticed lacy moth holes in the curtains.

'I won't be long.' Freddie hesitated in the doorway as if unwilling to leave them. 'I don't want to tire her out with too much talk.'

'Don't hurry on account of me.' Bella stood on tiptoe to give him a kiss.

Flora was amused to see Beasley's eyes widen in surprise at such a liberty, but he held the door open with an otherwise impassive expression.

Flora went to the window overlooking the terrace and a parterre garden, which looked sadly overgrown but must have been delightful in days gone by.

'This is a charming house, Bella.'

'Freddie never mentioned his aunt before today. I wonder how many other relations he has tucked away.' Bella frowned pensively. 'It makes me realise how little I really know him.'

Flora moved quickly to Bella's side and slipped an arm around her shoulders. 'You know you love him and he loves you. That's a good start, Bella. The rest will come in time. It doesn't seem as though this poor lady has been very important in his life, anyway. Families do split up occasionally.'

'Yes, of course. I know that. I'm just a bit nervous now the wedding is so close. My whole life is going to change.'

Flora laughed. 'Of course it is, you ninny. But I'm sure it will be for the better.'

'What about you, Flora? I've been so caught up in my own affairs that I have totally neglected you. Especially after the awful business with Ralph Pettigrew.'

'You must put that behind you. Thankfully, nothing came of it and I can assure you that he has come off worst. I saw him today and he's a drunkard, spending his days in taverns and his nights on the streets, probably.'

'Little more than he deserves. He could have ruined me for life.'

'Well he didn't. You are going to marry Freddie on Monday and live happily ever after.'

'You still haven't said what you are going to do. You know you can come and live with us, wherever we are. I don't want to lose you, Flora.'

'You won't lose me. We are sisters, or as good as. I will do very well for myself, so don't worry about me. You must concentrate on yourself and Freddie. If you're happy then so am I.'

They shared a hug and sat side by side on the small and rather uncomfortable sofa until Freddie returned. One look at his face and Flora knew it was not good news.

'How is she?' Flora asked gently.

Freddie shook his head. 'The doctor is with her. He doesn't think she'll last the night.'

Bella jumped to her feet and flung her arms around his neck. 'I am so sorry, darling. Don't be sad.'

'I feel more guilty than sad, my love. I could have

been a better nephew, but she doesn't seem to bear me any malice, which makes it even harder to bear.'

'I am so sorry,' Flora said earnestly. 'Is there anything I can do to help?'

'No, but thank you, Flora.' Freddie rewarded her with a genuine smile. 'My aunt is very elderly and her time has come. She knows it and that is why she sent for me. I think I should stay here tonight, Bella.'

'Of course you must. I wouldn't expect anything less of you, Freddie.'

'My coachman will take you back to Nine Oaks, if that's all right with both of you. It's only a short drive away.'

'We will be perfectly fine,' Flora said firmly. 'Don't worry about Bella. I will look after her.'

'I am not a child,' Bella protested. 'I am soon to be a married woman and I can chaperone you then, Flora.'

Freddie smiled indulgently. 'I'll have the carriage brought round immediately.' He left the room and his footsteps echoed eerily off the highly polished floorboards.

'It's so close to our wedding,' Bella said, sighing. 'Poor Freddie.'

'At least we'll be home in time for dinner.' Flora squeezed Bella's hand. 'Your mama will be pleased.'

Bella giggled. 'You say the most dreadful things, Flora. The poor old lady upstairs is dying.'

'There's nothing we can do about that. She's come to the end of her life, which is sad but it's going to come to all of us eventually. It will be up to you to comfort Freddie – that's all anyone can do in the circumstances.'

Bella nodded sadly. 'Yes, I know you're right. Poor Freddie.'

Despite the upsetting news about Freddie's aunt, Flora slept well that night, but next morning Bella came down to breakfast looking tired with dark shadows under her eyes.

'I hardly slept a wink,' she said as she took her seat at the dining table. 'I kept thinking about poor Freddie, all alone in the big old house with a dying woman.'

Flora filled a cup with coffee and passed it to her. 'Sip this and then try to eat something. Freddie will need you to help him through this.'

'I can't help feeling things deeply. Perhaps he should have picked an older woman who could be more of a support to him.' Bella drank thirstily.

'Don't be silly, Bella. You know he adores you and you love him. You are all that he needs right now. You should have something to eat.'

'I'll be sick if I do. I can't think of anything but how poor Freddie must be feeling.' Bella turned her head as the door opened and Freddie walked into the room. She jumped to her feet and ran to give him a hug. 'Freddie.'

He stroked her hair, smiling gently. 'I'm fine, Bella darling. All the better for seeing you.'

'Would you like some coffee?' Flora picked up the silver pot. 'I'll ring for a fresh pot.'

'Yes, that would be very welcome.' Freddie guided Bella back to her seat. 'I'll have breakfast with you but I'm afraid I must get back to my aunt's house. There are formalities to go through and I need to sort out her papers.'

'It's not good news then,' Flora said as she rang the bell for Edna, who appeared almost instantly and whisked the silver coffee pot away to be refilled.

'She died peacefully at five o'clock this morning.'

'I'm so sorry,' Flora said softly.

Bella clutched his hand as he sat down next to her at table. 'Are you all right, Freddie?'

'Yes, but I should have been a better nephew. She was a stubborn woman, very set in her ways, but the least I can do for her now is to look after her servants and the estate. I need to see her solicitor, too. I'm afraid I will be busy all day, Bella.'

'I will look after Bella, so don't worry.' Flora took a slice of toast from the rack and buttered it. She placed it on Bella's side plate. 'I insist that you eat something. We don't want you fainting all over the place and scaring your mama.'

'Nothing scares Mama,' Bella said, giggling. However, a look from Freddie was enough to make her nibble a piece of toast, washing it down with sips of coffee.

'I don't think there is anything I have to do today, is there?' Freddie addressed his remark to Flora.

'No. All you have to do is to turn up at the church on Monday and marry Bella. We have enough to do here to keep us both busy today and tomorrow.'

'Thank you, Flora. That makes it easier for me. I think I am her only living relative so there is no one else to do what is necessary.'

'Does that mean the house will come to you?' Bella was suddenly alert.

'It might, but I need to see my aunt's will. It might still belong to my family as Papa bought it for her. I don't know.'

'Why do you ask?' Flora demanded suspiciously. She knew how Bella's mind worked and she had a feeling that it might involve her.

Bella smiled sweetly. 'It would make a lovely dower house for you.'

Flora laughed. 'A kind thought, but I am not a dowager and unless Freddie wants a caretaker, I see no reason for him to give away part of his aunt's estate, even supposing it is an option.'

Freddie held his cup out to Edna, who had just walked into the room with a full coffee pot. She filled the cup for him.

'Thank you, Edna.' Freddie added cream and a dash of sugar. 'Why do you want Flora to have the house, Bella?'

'What will she do when we are not here?' Bella's eyes filled with tears. 'I worry about her.'

'You must not.' Flora spoke firmly. 'I can look after myself, Flora, dear. You have your whole life ahead of you as Freddie's wife. That's enough for me.'

'You could turn it into a tavern,' Bella said in desperation. 'Why are you both laughing? I am serious.'

Freddie sipped his coffee. 'It's a clever idea, Bella. But we'll have to wait and see what my aunt's last wishes were.'

'Yes, it's a kind thought,' Flora added quickly. 'But it's a very grand house. I don't think it's quite right for a hostelry, even if it were possible.'

Freddie swallowed the rest of his coffee and stood up. 'I'm sorry, my love, I really must leave you now. We'll talk about this more when I know the full facts.' He kissed Bella full on the lips.

Flora turned away. She was not embarrassed by this display of affection; if anything, she was a little jealous, although she crushed the feeling immediately. Bella deserved to love and be loved. That was all there was to it.

Freddie released Bella reluctantly. 'I will see you on Monday, my love, at the altar.' He turned to Flora with a genuine smile. 'Look after her, Bella. And please don't worry about your future. As far as I am concerned it is assured. You are Bella's sister and an important part of the family.' He left the room hurriedly, closing the door behind him.

Bella broke the ensuing silence. 'I am being serious, Flora. You went to see the Tullivers yesterday and you enjoyed working for them. Maybe some form of hospitality is your forte, not running a village inn, but something higher class, more like the expensive restaurants that Papa used to take us to. Do you know what I mean?'

'I do, and I think you could be right, but it would cost money to do something like that. As to Lady Philomena's house, I think the old lady might come back and haunt me if I turned her old home into a restaurant or something similar. Anyway, before you argue, I haven't enough experience to do something like that on my own.'

'There are the Tullivers,' Bella said with a determined lift of her chin. 'You could do it with them.'

'You simply do not give up, do you?'

Bella giggled. 'No, you know I don't. Actually I am quite hungry now. Is there any bacon left in the salver?'

Flora rose from her seat and filled a plate from the dishes on the sideboard. 'Eat up, you'll need all your strength to get through today and tomorrow.'

Bella obliged, tackling the food with enthusiasm. Flora waited patiently for her to finish, although she had plenty to do. The largest of the marquees was being set up and she needed to be there when it was erected to make sure the tables and chairs were set out in an orderly fashion. She had to supervise the decorations, including flower arrangements, although these would be done in the coolness of the flower room and kept there until first thing Monday morning. She was just wondering what simple tasks she could come up with to keep Bella occupied, when Constance sailed into the dining room. She took one look at her daughter and threw up her hands.

'Bella, dear. You look exhausted. Did you get any sleep last night?'

'Not very much, Mama.'

'Then I insist that you rest all day today and tomorrow, too, if necessary.'

Flora opened her mouth as if to argue but Bella sent her a warning look. Bella sighed. 'Very well, Mama. But poor Freddie has lost his aunt. She passed away peacefully this morning.'

'Yes, very sad, but I gather he hasn't seen her for many years. I don't think he'll suffer too greatly. He might even inherit Hope's End.'

'Hope's End?' Flora and Bella repeated the name in unison.

Constance smiled. 'Yes, a droll name. But that's what the house is called. I believe that the first owner was called Charles Hope, a wealthy wool merchant, who fancied himself as a landowner.'

'Why give it such a sad name?' Bella asked, frowning.

'Despite all his wealth his wife fell in love with another man and ran away, leaving him with no hope of reconciliation. He was so heartbroken that he shot himself, or so the story goes. The old place is probably haunted anyway.'

'Poor man,' Bella said sadly.

'Yes, well dear, if you've finished eating, I suggest you go to your room and lie down.' Constance whipped the plate away and set it down on the sideboard. 'What are you doing today, Flora? If you are free, I have some jobs for you.'

'I was about to go to the marquee to supervise the arrangement of the tables and chairs. Then I must check that we have enough flowers. I'll go in person to Covent Garden on Monday morning if we haven't enough.'

Constance frowned. 'James can do that. I think you ought to go to Covent Garden right away, before they sell everything. You are the only one who knows exactly what we need.'

'They will probably have sold out by the time I get there.'

Constance rolled her eyes. 'Then give the wholesaler an order to be delivered here first thing Monday morning. I don't care what it costs, my daughter is going to have a splendid wedding that everyone will remember.' She rang the bell just as Edna hurried into the room carrying a fresh pot of coffee. 'Send for Dobson, Edna. Tell him he's to take Miss Flora to Covent Garden Market to buy flowers. And tell him to hurry.'

Edna placed the coffee pot on the table and bobbed a curtsey. 'Yes, my lady.' She whisked out of the room before Constance could give her any other orders.

'What are you waiting for, Flora?' Constance sighed.

'Fetch your bonnet and shawl and tell Mary to give you my reticule. You'll need money to pay the florists.'

It was late morning by the time Flora reached the flower market and there was not a lot to choose from, but she bought up most of the unsold stock and Dobson loaded it into the dog cart.

'Is that all, miss?'

Flora hesitated. 'I'll just take another quick turn around the stalls, Dobson. I might have missed something. Wait here, please.'

He tipped his cap and climbed onto the driver's seat. Flora set off again, hoping to find an outlet she might have missed. She was just passing St Paul's church when she saw a familiar figure lying on the stones beneath the columned portico. She moved closer.

'Ralph!' She prodded him with the toe of her boot, but he just groaned and turned his head away. She could smell the stale alcohol without bending over him. The temptation to walk away was almost too great, but it had rained in the night and he was lying in a puddle. She could see Dobson walking the horses up and down and she beckoned frantically. He spotted her and brought the dog cart to the bottom of the steps. He stared at Ralph in horror.

'You aren't thinking of taking that fellow up on the cart, are you, miss?'

'I can't leave him here, Dobson. He's soaking wet.'

'Got what he deserves, if you asks me.'

'I have to agree with you, but I still can't leave him. I know where we can take him and it's on our way home. I want to get all these blooms in water as soon as possible.'

Dobson hailed a porter. 'Here, give us a hand, mate.'

The porter ambled over, grinning good-naturedly. Together they managed to get Ralph into the back of the cart with the flowers stowed safely beneath the seats. Flora climbed up beside Dobson.

'Where to, miss?'

'Turnagain Lane, please, Dobson.'

# Chapter Eighteen

When Flora opened the street door in Turnagain Lane she was met with the familiar fetid smell of sewage, dry rot and rodent droppings. She was tempted to close it again and walk away, but Ralph was in the cart and Dobson was not in a good mood. Besides which she had no intention of taking Ralph back to Nine Oaks. Had she known where to find Gabriel she could have left Ralph on his doorstep, but Captain Cutler seemed to know exactly when it was politic to absent himself from the country. Ralph was definitely a problem for Gert and Syd. Flora stepped inside and thumped on the door to the basement. It was almost midday but she remembered only too well that Gert and Syd slept late after an evening carousing. Nothing ever changed in Turnagain Lane. She continued hammering on the door until she heard footsteps thudding on the stairs.

The door opened and Syd peered out bleary-eyed. He took in her elegant gown and smart bonnet with a long look, as if working out the cost of each garment, including her petticoats and chemise. A long time ago Flora would have been embarrassed but not now. She was past caring what Syd thought or said.

'I hoped we'd got rid of you,' Syd muttered, running his hand through his greasy grey hair.

'Don't worry. I wouldn't come back here for anything myself, but I've brought you a present.' She went to the front door and signalled to Dobson, who dragged a semi-conscious Ralph off the cart and manhandled him into the entrance hall.

'What's all this?' Syd demanded querulously. 'He's drunk.'

'I'm sure you recognise the symptoms,' Flora said acidly. 'He's your friend, so you can deal with him.'

'He ain't my friend. I don't want him.'

'You found me through Ralph, so don't pretend you don't know him.' Flora turned to Dobson. 'Put him down. We're leaving.'

'Yes, miss. With pleasure.' Dobson dumped Ralph on the floor, blocking Syd's escape into the hall. 'He's all yours, mate.'

'What's going on, Syd?' Gert's sharp voice echoed off the high ceiling in the hall.

'It's her, Gertie. Turned up like a bad penny. Your sister's brat.'

'I never had no sister,' Gert said crossly.

Flora was about to leave but this remark brought her up short. 'What did she say?'

'She's still out of her head. She don't know what she's saying.'

'If I'm not her niece, then who am I?'

'I'm blowed if I know. Get out and take him with you.'

Flora thought for a moment. 'If I take him will you tell me what I want to know?'

Gert popped her head round her husband, eyeing Flora with a malevolent sneer.

'Yes, take him away.'

'Only if you tell me who my real parents were.'

'Tell her, you dolt.' Gert flicked the back of Syd's head with her thumb and middle finger, making him yelp with pain.

'That hurt, damn you.'

'Tell her where you got her from.'

'I found you,' Syd said weakly as Gert twisted his ear. 'Let me go, woman.'

'She won't leave and take that drunken pig away from here unless you tell her the truth.'

'All right,' Syd said reluctantly. 'There was an accident on the river, passenger boat it was. It collided with a steamer and sank. I found you on the foreshore at low tide. You was in a large leather bag and you must have been floating round for hours, caught up between two wharves.'

'So you saved my life?'

Syd scratched his head. 'I suppose so.'

'He weren't no hero. He wanted to claim a reward, but no one knew who you was and you couldn't talk.'

'You could have taken me to a police station or an orphanage and they would have tried to trace my parents.'

Syd snorted. 'With my record, I would have been arrested. You was only about two years old. Gert thought you'd be useful, picking pockets and such.'

'A pretty child is worth a fortune,' Gert added with a gap-toothed grin. 'You was always good-looking. We called you Flora because your name was embroidered on the shawl you was wrapped in. I sold it in Rosemary Market for half a crown.'

'The leather bag I was in. Have you still got it?'

Syd laughed. 'What would I want with a peccary leather bag like what doctors use? Got a nice profit from it in the market.'

'You two are disgusting,' Flora said angrily. 'My family might have been grieving for me all these years.'

'Don't talk soft. They was all dead – drownded.' Syd snorted with laughter. 'You was lucky I found you.'

Flora was so infuriated by what she had heard that she turned to go but stepped on Dobson's foot. His cry of pain made her move away hastily, which in turn sent Ralph rolling down the stairs, taking Syd and Gertie with him. The sound of their bodies bumping on the stone steps was accompanied by yelps of pain and expletives.

Dobson put his arm around her shoulders. 'Time to go, I think, Miss Flora.' He reached out and slammed the basement door. 'Come on, I'll take you home.'

Flora was too numb to cry. Syd's words had chilled her to the bone, and she was no nearer to knowing her true identity. It seemed that she had escaped the tragedy, but had her parents survived? If so, they must have been mourning the loss of their child for more than sixteen years, but if they had died it meant that she was indeed an orphan. Either way it was too sad to contemplate.

Dobson drove on, glancing at her from time to time. It was not until they were out in the country that he slowed the horse to a walk.

'I won't say anything, miss. Your secret is safe with me.'

Flora exhaled with a sigh. 'I can't believe that they kept the truth from me, even when I was a small child. I really thought they were my aunt and uncle.'

Dobson uttered a throaty chuckle. 'It must be a relief to know they are not.'

'What would you do, Dobson? Should I tell Sir Arthur and Lady Stewart, or should I forget what I've just learned?'

'I'm not sure I'm the right person to ask, miss. But if you was my granddaughter I would advise you to wait until after the wedding. Then you can decide what you want to do. They know you was treated badly, which is why they took you into their home. Nothing has happened to change that.'

'You've always been there for me, Dobson. You taught me to ride.'

'Yes, and a very good pupil you was, too. I don't see how your position is any worse now than it was before. You didn't know who your mama was and you still don't. If it was me, I'd be glad not to be related to them two.'

The twinkle in Dobson's eyes made Flora smile. 'Thank you for that, Dobson. You've made me feel a lot better. I will do as you say and bide my time.'

'That's right, miss. Who knows, when the excitement of the wedding is over, you might be able to find out about the collision on the river. It's probably in the newspapers of that date. I'm sure they keep copies going a long way back.'

'The Tullivers might know something,' Flora said half to herself. 'Moses was found in the river and he must be about my age.'

'Moses, miss? Not the one found in the bulrushes?'

Flora laughed. 'Not quite. He was saved from the river by Ted Tulliver and brought up by him and his wife. I lived with them in the Play House Yard Inn for a while. I was very fond of Moses.'

'You was both saved from the river?' Dobson took a clay pipe from his pocket. 'Do you mind if I have a pipe of baccy, miss? It's been a difficult morning.'

'There's a tea garden further along. I remember

passing it on the way into London. We'll stop there and you can have a smoke, and a cup of tea if you wish. I could certainly do with a cup myself. Maybe they have cake, too. I'm starving.'

'What about them flowers? Her ladyship won't be too pleased if they're wilting when we get home.'

'I'll put them in buckets of water overnight. They'll freshen up, but we need to have a short break, and the poor old horse could do with a drink.'

'Very well, miss.' Dobson gave a croak of laughter. 'I wonder if them two are still stuck underneath that drunkard?'

'I have no sympathy for them whatsoever.' Flora pointed to the cottage ahead. 'There it is. We won't stay for long, but we all need some refreshments.'

Flora need not have worried about being late back. Everyone was so busy that no one seemed to know what time of day it was. She was able to unload the flowers outside the servants' entrance and Dobson carried a huge armful while she took the rest into the flower room. Buckets were duly filled with water and the blooms placed into them to soak up as much as they needed. Flora looked into Bella's room but she was asleep on her bed and best left to rest. Flora went on to inspect the marquee and found that James had done a very good job of setting out the tables and chairs. She need not have worried on that score, but she was still reeling from the information she had received as to her origins.

Dobson had been like a kind uncle with his words of wisdom, but she still wanted to confide in someone who would understand.

She found Daniel supervising the erection of a smaller marquee in the area of parkland that was once home to a herd of deer. He met her with a smile that made her feel light-headed with pleasure. Nobody else had that effect upon her.

'It's all going splendidly,' Daniel said happily. 'We still have tomorrow after church to finish what we can't do today. James said you went to Covent Garden to get more flowers.'

'I did and they are in the flower room recovering from their journey.'

'I would have liked to go with you, but I was needed here.'

'Yes, of course. The wedding is more important than anything at the moment.'

A shout from one of the groundsmen made Daniel look round. 'I'm sorry, Flora. I have to sort this out. We'll talk later if you have time.'

She managed a smile. 'I'll probably be with Bella for the rest of the day, attempting to calm her nerves, and there is a family meal with some of the wedding guests this evening. I'll see you after church tomorrow.' Flora felt oddly deflated as she walked back to the house. She would tell Bella her news when the right moment arrived, but until then she had to hug her secret to herself.

Flora was on her way to her room to change out

of her travel-stained clothes when she was met by Constance, who looked pale and fraught.

'Is anything the matter, ma'am?'

'I fear I'm having one of my megrims. My head is pounding and all I want to do is to lie down. Bella has gone to sleep, but she is so nervous for Monday, especially with Freddie not being here today.'

'I believe he is seeing Lady Philomena's lawyer, ma'am. I'm sure he has a lot to do.'

'Yes, of course, but Bella doesn't really understand that. Will you look after her for me, Flora? She always listens to you, and I really must go to my bed.'

'Yes, most definitely, ma'am. You need to rest and I will make sure that Bella doesn't fret.'

'You are a good girl. I don't know what I would do without you.' Constance walked away, clutching her hand to her forehead.

Flora made her way to Bella's room and found her awake now and staring at the ceiling.

'Where have you been, Flora? I've had Mama giving me good advice about being married until I could scream. I pretended to be asleep in the end.'

Flora perched on the edge of the bed. 'She thought she was comforting you. Now she's gone to bed with a megrim.'

'I suppose that means we won't see her until it's time for church tomorrow,' Bella said with a sigh. 'I know she means well, but she makes matters worse.'

'She said you are unhappy because Freddie isn't here today.'

'Not unhappy, but I do wish he didn't have to go into town to sort out his aunt's business. I know I'm selfish, Flora. I can't help it. I want him all to myself.'

'That's love, I suppose. I hope you always feel that way, Bella.'

Bella snapped into a sitting position. 'What's wrong? I know you, Flora. You can't hide anything from me. Why did it take you so long to buy flowers?'

Flora could see that Bella was not going to be put off with a weak excuse and she decided to tell her the truth. Bella sat open-mouthed as she learned about Flora's miraculous survival and the part that Syd and Gert Fox had played in her early years.

'My goodness! That's unbelievable, Flora. I mean, it was amazing that you survived the accident, but how unlucky you were to be rescued by those awful people. I can't imagine how you must be feeling.'

'Rather shaken if I were to tell the truth.' Flora shook her head sadly. 'I don't know if my parents are alive or dead, and I still don't know who I am, apart from my name. Did I say that?'

Bella was instantly alert. 'Is there more?'

'I was wrapped in a shawl with "Flora" embroidered on it, so that's what they called me.'

'Perhaps there is a passenger list for the boat that sank,' Bella said thoughtfully. 'There must be a way to find out. I'm sure Freddie could help. He knows everyone and everything.'

'I'm sure he does,' Flora said, smiling. Bella's absolute faith in her intended was touching, but it was also naïve. However, she had no intention of disillusioning her. 'At least I have something to go on now, and the best thing is that I am in no way related to the hateful Foxes.'

'Yes, I can see that must be a relief. So what will you do now?'

'I think I might go and see Ted Tulliver again. He saved Moses from the river. For all I know, he might have survived the same accident. If so then maybe Ted can tell me the name of the vessels involved.'

'But I won't know what's going on if I'm in Paris with Freddie.'

Flora laughed. 'You will be having such a marvellous time with your husband that you won't spare a thought for me. Anyway, I'll tell you everything when you return.'

'I will miss you, Flora. We've been together all our lives, or the best part of them anyway.'

'I will never be far away, you may depend upon that. Anyway, you will have a family of your own before long and that will keep you busy.'

Bella's eyes filled with tears. 'Mama tried to tell me what to expect on my wedding night, but she got so embarrassed she made it sound dreadful. I don't think I will like that part of being married. She said I would have to be brave and think of something else.'

Flora eyed her warily. 'But you spent two nights in Ralph's company. He made it sound as if you had been more than just travelling companions.'

'I was so afraid that I might be in that way, Flora. He kissed me and it was horrible.'

'And that's all?'

'He slept on the bed, outside the covers, but he was with me for two whole nights.' Bella mopped her eyes on a scrap of lace handkerchief. 'I am a ruined woman, but Freddie still wants to marry me.'

'You are nothing of the sort. He put you in a compromising situation, but that is all.' Flora sighed. She was not the best person to advise Bella on the facts of life. The time had come for Bella to have a heart-to-heart chat with Doris Robbins. She pulled back the coverlet.

'Get up and put your shoes on and your bonnet and shawl. I'm going to take you to someone who will tell you exactly what you need to know, and that will put your mind at rest. You and I are going for a walk, Bella.'

Doris was taking in washing from a line stretched across the cottage garden. She stopped when Flora led Bella round the side of the house.

'Miss Arabella and Miss Flora,' Doris bobbed a curtsey. 'You caught me by surprise.' She smoothed her pristine white apron with both hands. 'Won't you come into the parlour? It's too hot to stand in the sun for long.'

'Wait there a moment, Bella,' Flora said firmly. 'I'll explain everything and then I'll stay outside while she talks to you.'

'I feel so silly.' Bella glanced over her shoulder as if looking for the easiest way to escape.

'Doris won't embarrass you. I had this conversation with her last year. She puts things much better than I ever could. I only know what she told me, so I can't speak with any authority. Wait here, Bella, I'll only be a moment.' Flora strolled over to help Doris unpeg a large white sheet from the line. 'Bella needs your advice, Doris. Lady Stewart apparently tried to tell her what will happen on the wedding night, but she only made matters worse. Bella needs some reassurance and a measure of your good common sense.'

Doris nodded sagely. 'They all come to me. I don't know why when it's the most natural act in the world, as I told you. Have you forgotten what I said?'

'No, Doris. But I couldn't put it as well as you did. I would only make Bella even more embarrassed than she is already.'

'Leave it to me, miss. When I've done I'll call you in and we'll have a nice cup of tea and a slice of my seed cake.' Doris bustled across the grass to usher Bella into the cottage, leaving Flora to take in the rest of the washing.

*

On the walk home Bella was smiling. 'She is such a wise woman, Flora. She put me at ease, and she makes the most delicious seed cake.'

'Yes, she does. I'm very fond of Doris. She's a good woman and very down to earth. You look much happier now.'

'I am. Thank you for taking me to see Doris.' Bella stopped and turned to look towards the road. 'That sounds like a carriage approaching. I hope it's Freddie.' She started towards the road and broke into a run when she recognised the equipage tooling up the drive. Flora followed more slowly.

The coachman reined in the pair of greys and the carriage came to a halt. Freddie leaped out to embrace Bella before helping her into the vehicle. He held his hand out to Flora.

'Do accompany us for the rest of the journey.'

Flora hesitated, but Bella urged her to get into the carriage and she acquiesced. It was easier to give in sometimes when Bella had her heart set on something.

Bella clutched Freddie's arm as he sat down beside her and the vehicle moved forward.

'What did your aunt's solicitor say, Freddie?'

'As I suspected, she has left her entire estate to me. It doesn't amount to much in monetary terms, but there is Hope's End and grounds, and also the contents. Although I doubt if there is anything of great value. When the will is probated I will have to decide what to do with the old place.'

'I know what you can do with the house,' Bella said with an arch smile.

'What is that, my love?'

'Give it to me as a wedding present.'

Flora stared at her in amazement. 'Bella! Surely you don't mean that.'

'But I do. Can't you see? It's a very sensible idea. I do have good ones occasionally, Flora.'

'Of course you do, darling,' Freddie said gently. 'Tell me why you want Hope's End?'

'It's an obvious solution, Freddie. We can stay there when we visit my family. That way we will be very close but not too close, if you know what I mean. Also, we can let Flora live there so that she doesn't feel she has to stay with my parents forever.'

'You don't have to do that, Bella,' Flora protested. 'I am quite capable of looking out for myself.'

'Of course you are.' Bella smiled smugly. 'But can't you see, Flora? You will be there whenever I choose to visit home. It will be like old times.'

'Bella, my love. Perhaps Flora has plans of her own.'

'No, she would have told me about them if she had. Wouldn't you, Flora?'

The carriage drew to a halt outside the main entrance and the footman leaped to the ground to open the door and put the step down.

'I'll think about it, Bella.' Flora took the opportunity to be first to alight. Freddie came next and proffered his hand to Bella.

'You must admit that it's a good idea,' Bella said hopefully. 'Do consider if carefully, Flora. I don't want to lose you.'

'That will never happen.' Flora took a step away from them. 'I'd better take a look at the flowers. You won't want to see faded blooms on your wedding day.'

The flowers had revived in the cool water and Flora went to her room happy in the knowledge that the floral arrangements would be perfect on the day. She was seated at the dressing table, brushing her hair, when Bella burst into the room.

'Darling Flora. Have you had time to consider moving to Hope's End? I think we'll have to change the name of the house, but Freddie is in total agreement with me. He will be happy for you to live there for as long as you like, and I can come and stay with you when I want to visit Mama and Papa.'

'I haven't said yes, Bella. Don't put words into my mouth.'

'But you will agree, won't you? It solves all our problems.'

'I said I will think about it, Bella. You are giving me a headache, please let the subject drop for now. We have more important things to think about. You are getting married the day after tomorrow, or have you forgotten?'

'Don't be silly. Of course I haven't. But thank you for taking me to Mrs Robbins. I feel so much happier now, and Freddie is such a darling. I can't wait to be his wife.'

'That is how it should be. Now, do you want me to help you get ready for dinner? Or is Mary going to be there for you?'

'Mama has excused herself from dinner so Mary is free to dress me. Just think, when I'm married to Freddie I will have my own personal maid. I won't have to share with anyone.'

'Such luxury,' Flora said with a smile. 'I'll see you at dinner.'

'Yes, you're right. I'm so excited. Everything is falling into place, Flora. When I am married to Freddie you will be mistress of Hope's End for most of the time, anyway. I promise not to interfere when I come to stay. It will be wonderful.' Bella breezed out of the room leaving the door to shut of its own accord.

Flora sighed. She was desperate to discover her true identity but this was Bella's special time and nothing must be allowed to spoil it for her. She gazed at her reflection in the mirror and shook her head. It did not matter how much she wanted to rush back to Play House Yard and discuss things with Coralie and Ted, she must put all that aside until after the wedding. As to Hope's End – the name was enough to put anyone off. Flora understood Bella's reasons for wanting her to live there, but if she accepted it would make her a virtual prisoner. It would be as if her worst fears had come true and she was destined to remain the girl who had been rescued from Turnagain Lane, living forever on charity.

Flora put up her hair and changed into a dinner gown before going downstairs to the drawing room. Freddie was already there, chatting to Sir Arthur. They both rose to their feet when Flora entered and sat down again when she perched on the sofa.

'Freddie has been telling me about his aunt's house, Flora,' Sir Arthur said, smiling. 'I wish I had a relation who would leave me all their worldly goods.'

'Surely you don't mean that, sir?' Flora said, puzzled. Bella had said airily that her father's financial affairs had been settled satisfactorily.

'No, not really.' Sir Arthur shook his head. 'Although things are much better now. However, a few months ago I would have been grateful for anything. It was Freddie who put me back on the right path. I'm forever grateful, Dorrington.'

'Not at all. I have no business interests myself, but I know plenty of people who are experts in trading on the stock market and setting up new companies. They are always asking me to invest, but I prefer to look after Dorrington Place and the estate.'

At that moment the door opened and Bella wafted into the room, a picture in pale pink organdie and lace. Her face lit up with joy when she smiled at Freddie, and he rose from his seat to pull a chair closer to his so that they could sit side by side.

'What are you talking about?' she demanded cheerily.

'Have you told Papa about our plans for Hope's End, Freddie?'

He shook his head. 'Not yet, my love.'

'Papa, Freddie has inherited an estate just a few minutes away from here. Hope's End. Do you know it?'

'Of course I know it, my dear. I knew Lady Philomena quite well years ago, before she became a recluse.'

'I don't recall you ever mentioned her, Papa.'

'Her name would not necessarily have come up in conversation, Bella.'

'Well, Papa. I want Freddie to give me the house as a wedding present. Then we can keep it in the family and Flora will be able to live there and keep house for me when I choose to visit Nine Oaks.'

'I haven't agreed to anything,' Flora said hastily. She was aware that they were all gazing at her, as if waiting for her to qualify Bella's bold statement. There was an awkward silence.

'But it's the solution to everything, Flora.' Bella pursed her lips in a pretty pout. 'Surely you won't deny me this little request?'

'I said I would consider it, Bella.' Flora tempered her words with a smile. 'And you have more important things to think about at this moment.'

'Flora is right, my darling.' Freddie took Bella's hand in his. 'We can settle the details when we return from Paris.'

Flora began to relax as Freddie skilfully steered

the conversation away from Hope's End to other subjects equally dear to Bella's heart. It was the same all through dinner that evening and Flora was beginning to envy Constance, who was still suffering from a headache and chose to dine alone in her room. Freddie took his leave after dinner, having decided to spend the night at Hope's End, although he promised to join them for morning service at the village church. Flora tactfully left them saying a long goodnight and although she had intended to go straight to her room, it was not yet dark and she stepped outside, taking deep breaths of sweetly scented air. After the hive of activity during the day it was a pleasure to stroll into the velvet shadows, listening to the rustle of a gentle breeze as it rippled through the branches of the oak trees, but the sudden crunch of booted feet on the gravel made her turn with a start.

'Flora, wait. It's me.'

# Chapter Nineteen

Daniel hurried towards her. 'I'm sorry. I didn't mean to scare you. I was hoping you might take a walk after dinner.'

'You made me jump, that's all,' Flora said evasively. 'What do you want, Dan?'

'I needed to apologise for leaving you so abruptly this morning, but there is so much to do before the big day. You obviously had something to tell me and I didn't have time to stop and listen.'

'It's all right, Dan. I understand. The wedding is taking up all our time.'

'What happened this morning? I thought you just went to Covent Garden to get more flowers.' Daniel proffered his arm. 'Hold on to me. We can't have the chief bridesmaid tripping over something in the dark and hurting herself.'

Flora laughed as she slipped her hand through

the crook of his arm. 'If you'll stop talking nonsense I'll tell you everything.' It was always so easy to talk to Daniel and he was a good listener. Even so he interrupted occasionally with a horrified groan when she told him about finding Ralph and what subsequently had passed between her and the Foxes. She could feel the tension tautening his muscles and she patted his hand. 'I will never see Syd or Gert again. I promise you that, Dan.'

'Why couldn't you have left Pettigrew outside the church? Perhaps some good Samaritan would have come along and helped him.'

'It gave me a chance to challenge Syd. He and Gert had always told me that my mother was a slut beyond redemption and they were doing me a favour by bringing me up as their child. At least I now know the truth, or part of it.'

'So what do you plan to do next?'

'I need to visit the Tullivers again. If what Syd told me was true and I was found in a leather doctor's bag, floating on the water like Moses, then we might have both been involved in the same tragedy.'

'There should be accounts of such a dreadful accident in newspapers of that time.'

'Yes, exactly. I believe the newspapers keep copies of past editions and *The Times*'s printing office is close to the inn.'

Daniel stopped and twisted her round so that she was in his arms. 'Are you sure you want to find out who your parents were? I mean, are you prepared to accept the fact that they died?'

'They could still be alive, Dan.'

'Don't you think they would have moved heaven and earth to find their baby daughter, especially as they did what they could to save your life?'

'I have thought about it, Dan. I must know who I am, even if I am still an orphan, at least I will have a real name. Although, my first name is Flora. Apparently it was embroidered on the shawl that was wrapped around me.'

Daniel nodded. 'I understand. And of course I will come with you.'

'I wish I could go tomorrow but it's Sunday, and there is too much to do. Monday is out of the question so it will have to be Tuesday.'

'Tuesday it will be.' Daniel drew her closer and kissed her gently but with increasing fervour until she wrapped her arms around his neck and responded with equal ardour.

'I love you, Flora,' Daniel said in a low voice in between kisses. 'I don't care if you come from a good family or villains like the Foxes. I will always love you.'

Flora drew away, looking up at him with misty eyes. 'Thank you, Dan. I love you, too. I think I always have and I know I always will.'

'But you won't marry me?'

She held him at arm's length. 'Everything is going

to change after Bella is married. I don't know what I will discover about myself . . .'

Daniel laid his finger on her lips. 'Don't say any more, Flora. I'm a patient man. I've waited a long time to tell you how I feel. I can wait even longer for the right answer. There is always a way, if you look hard enough.'

Flora laid her head against his shoulder, comforted by the warmth of his embrace. 'I want to find the right way, Dan. I don't want us to end up hating each other.'

'That could never happen.' Daniel slipped his arm around her waist. 'I'll take you back to the house. You need a good night's sleep and so do I.'

Sunday morning passed in a blur of activity. The church service was followed by luncheon, after which Freddie said a reluctant goodbye to Bella, having decided to return to his mansion in Piccadilly. Bella was whisked away by her mother and Freddie took Flora aside.

'I want you to know that Hope's End is yours if you want it, Flora. I've given it a lot of thought, and while I don't want to make you feel obliged to take up the offer, it is sincerely meant.'

'I realise that, Freddie,' Flora said cautiously. 'It is a very generous offer, but I would still be totally dependent. If Bella decided that she did not wish to visit so often or you wanted to sell the property, what would happen to me then?'

Freddie nodded. 'I know, and I've thought of that. Of course Bella wants to keep you near, that's totally understandable. You two are like sisters and I would never wish to come between you. My suggestion is for you to become my tenant, at a peppercorn rent.' He held up his hand as Flora opened her mouth to speak. 'I know you want to be independent and there are ways to make money from the house and the considerable grounds. You could let some of the rooms, or even run it as a small hotel.'

'I don't know what to say, Freddie.' Flora bit back tears. 'You are so kind.'

'Actually I'm being quite selfish, Flora. If Bella is happy that's all that matters to me, and you are very important to both of us. I won't press you for an answer now. Think about it and you can let me know your decision when Bella and I return from Paris.'

Flora reached up to kiss him on the cheek. 'Bella is a very lucky woman. I know you will be very happy together.'

'And you will think about my offer?'

'Yes, of course, and thank you. I do appreciate it.'

Freddie gave her a hug. 'I think I'm allowed that liberty as you will be my sister too, from tomorrow onwards.' He turned away and hurried down the steps to climb into his carriage.

There was so much to think about but Flora had no time to worry about her own future. The flowers were waiting to be arranged and that would take the best part of the afternoon. Flora set off for the flower room, which was a haven of peace and quiet away from the frantic last-minute dusting, polishing and cleaning supervised by Mrs Fellowes with the enthusiasm of a regimental sergeant major. There were several interruptions when Flora was summoned to Bella's room to give her advice on trivial matters to do with the wedding apparel, most of which were imagined by the nervous bride-to-be. In the end Flora had to be quite sharp with Bella and Constance stepped in to tell her daughter that she was over-wrought and should rest. Surprisingly Bella agreed and went to lie on her bed, leaving Flora free to return to finish decorating the entrance hall and main reception rooms. Having done that, she took the remaining blooms to the main marquee and made small table decorations. Swathes of greenery had been pinned to the canvas walls, and Flora added bright spots of colour with broken-stemmed blossoms that would otherwise have been cast aside.

It was late evening by the time she finished and was satisfied with the results. She managed to avoid being drawn into conversation with anyone on the way to her room and she stripped off her clothes, leaving them in a pile on the floor. The laundry maid would be busy for days after the wedding, but that was not Flora's problem. She slipped on her night-gown and fell into bed.

*

Next morning the whole house hummed with excitement. Flora ate breakfast alone in the dining room before going upstairs to Bella's room, where Mary was fussing around laying out the wedding gown and the lace-trimmed undergarments. Bella seemed reasonably calm as she sat up in bed, sipping a cup of hot chocolate. She sent Mary away, telling her to return in half an hour.

'I don't want to be ready too early,' Bella said as the door closed on her maid. 'What about you, Flora? Did Freddie speak to you about Hope's End?'

'Yes, he did.' Flora eyed her warily. 'What did he tell you?'

'Don't worry, you won't hurt my feelings. Freddie thinks it would be best if you were to be independent and rent the house from him, and I agree.'

'You do?'

'Of course I do, Flora. I am going to be so happy with dear Freddie, and I want you to be happy, too. If you are the tenant of Hope's End you will be as close to me as if you were still living here. Better still, you might think of a way to make money from the old house. You are so clever, I am sure you will do very well for yourself.'

'And you really don't mind?'

Bella laughed. 'Of course not. I think I will have enough to do being mistress of Dorrington Place as well as the house in Piccadilly. Besides which, Freddie and I plan to travel a lot. He is going to take me to all sorts of exotic places. I can't wait.'

'I'm sure it will all be wonderful.' Flora glanced at the untouched food on the breakfast tray. 'Perhaps you ought to eat something. We don't want you fainting at the altar.'

Bella put her cup down and took a slice of toast. She took a small bite, chewed, swallowed and smiled. 'There! Are you happy now?'

Flora laughed. 'I think Freddie will have his hands full with you, miss. I hope he's prepared for an exciting time ahead.'

'I can't wait to be his wife. Anyway, it's not long now so you had better get yourself ready. I have Mary to help me, but you need to look beautiful, too. You are my chief bridesmaid.'

'I am your only bridesmaid.'

'True, but that makes your job even more important. Ring for Mary before you go, Flora.'

Flora felt like a bride herself when she put on her new gown. The bodice moulded to her figure, emphasising her tiny waist, and the skirt was drawn back into a fashionable bustle. The heavy silk in the palest shade of blue-green reminded her of the sea, and was almost exactly the same colour as her eyes. Her matching hat was small and perched perkily on top of her auburn hair. Mary had found time to put it up for her in between taking care of the bride, with a little help from Elsie, who had been promoted for the day. A dashing ostrich feather finished off the hat to perfection. Flora could hardly believe that it was her reflection gazing back at her from the mirror. However, it was Bella's day and she went to her room to help with the finishing touches.

Bella was undoubtedly a beautiful bride and her pure silk gown was elegant in its simplicity. Marsh House Modes had triumphed both in design, cut and in the tiny details that made the gown unique. Constance was ecstatic when she saw her daughter looking so regal. Her own outfit was a masterpiece in itself. The cut and peachy colour suited and flattered her and yet it did not detract from the bride's costume, in fact it complimented it beautifully.

It was just a five-minute drive to the village church and onlookers lined the route, cheering when they spotted the bride and bridesmaid in the open landau, which Daniel and his assistants had garlanded with greenery and white satin bows. Flora was very touched by their efforts. Sir Arthur and Lady Stewart had gone first and were already at the church when the bridal party arrived.

Flora looked for Daniel in the crowd but he had made his way to stand close to the church entrance. He tipped his cap as she walked past but it was the admiration in his amber eyes that sent a thrill down her spine. She smiled back as she followed Bella into the cool interior of the church. But as they joined Sir Arthur in the nave, Flora could see that Bella was nervous and her posy of flowers shook in her hand. However, a few whispered words of encouragement from Flora and a tender smile from her father made Bella hold her head high as she laid her hand on her father's arm. They processed up the aisle to the organist playing the Wedding March with gusto.

The church was packed with guests and Freddie stood at the altar with Todd Taylor as his best man. He had, according to Bella, chosen Todd in preference to any of his close friends at Rockwood Castle to avoid showing favouritism. Amelia, Mariah and the children were all seated in the front pew together with Freddie's friends. They turned to gaze at the bridal party as they reached the altar. Flora was deeply moved by the look of love and admiration on Freddie's face when Sir Arthur gave him his daughter's hand in marriage. The ceremony progressed without a hitch and almost too soon the bride and groom were leaving the church to be bombarded by handfuls of rice from well-wishers, clapping and cheering.

Daniel was standing by the lychgate as the wedding party left the churchyard. He doffed his cap to Flora, smiling tenderly in a way that went straight to her heart. She knew that he thought her even more beautiful than the bride without the need for words, but she felt a sudden chill and it was not just the fresh breeze that tugged at ladies' bonnets and gentlemen's top hats. If she accepted Freddie's offer to rent Hope's End it would raise yet another barrier to her and Daniel spending the rest of their lives together. She knew she must tell him quickly before the gossip mongers spread the story around the village. She would find an opportunity before the day was out, but for the moment there was nothing Flora could do but climb into the family carriage with Sir Arthur and Constance while the newlyweds drove off in the garlanded landau. The rest of the guests followed in their own carriages or on foot.

When they reached the house Bella and Freddie were in the entrance hall ready to receive their guests. Flora had never seen Nine Oaks so crowded with people, but her part in the proceedings was over. The flower arrangements were attracting a lot of compliments and their scent was even more intoxicating than the expensive perfumes and pomades worn by the guests. Flora was satisfied that she had done her bit, leaving her free to enjoy the reception. When everyone had arrived Jefferson announced that the wedding breakfast would be served in the largest marquee. Flora was about to follow the last guest but Bella caught her by the hand.

'Thank you for everything, Flora,' Bella murmured. 'You have done so much for me.'

Flora hugged her, taking care not to crush the beautiful gown. 'Nonsense. You deserve all of this, Bella. I know that you and Freddie will have a wonderful life together.'

'You will still be a part of our lives. Don't talk as if I am going to go away and forget about you.'

'I know that won't happen, but you will have

362

other things to occupy you, Bella. That's entirely normal.'

'But I must know that you are taken care of, dear sister. Please say you will accept Freddie's offer of Hope's End. He says he will still pay for the gardeners and for the old butler who took care of Lady Philomena until she died. Freddie won't expect you to pay the rent until you have an income of your own.'

'Can I think about it some more, Bella?'

Bella shook her head vehemently. 'No. You've had enough time. I want an answer before I go away today. I know that Mama and Papa would be happy to have you stay here, but I also know that you don't want that. I have to be certain that you are safe and well in your own home, or I simply can't leave.'

Flora stared at her in amazement. 'You really mean that, don't you?'

'I do. I don't want to spend my honeymoon worrying about you.'

Freddie had been in conversation with Sir Arthur but he walked over to them and placed his arm around Bella's waist.

'That seemed like a very earnest conversation. Is anything the matter?'

'No, darling.' Bella smiled up at him. 'I was just asking Flora to make up her mind about the house before we leave later today.'

'You were insisting upon it, Bella.' Flora laughed.

'I hope you realise what a determined person Bella is once she makes up her mind to something.'

Freddie smiled tenderly. 'I'm learning things about Bella every day, and it just makes me love her even more.'

'I am only stubborn when I know I am right.' Bella tossed her head. 'I can't enjoy myself unless I know Flora is taken care of.'

Flora could see that Bella was deadly serious and she nodded. 'I will think about it during luncheon and I will tell you my decision before you leave.'

'I won't go unless you agree, Flora.'

'Come along, my love,' Freddie said, smiling indulgently. 'Our guests are waiting for us. They can't eat until we join them.' He tucked her hand in the crook of his arm and led her out of the house with Flora following them.

The offer of a real home of her own was almost too tempting to turn down, but she needed to tell Daniel before she agreed.

The opportunity occurred after the cake had been cut and the speeches had been made, although thankfully they were quite short. Outside in the warm sunshine, the orchestra was playing and couples wandered off to explore the gardens and the rest of the grounds, or else they sat on chairs placed in the shade of the old oak trees. Flora had spotted Daniel, who had eaten in the smaller marquee with the rest of the servants, something she deplored but could do nothing about. She waited for him to join her some way away from anyone who might overhear their conversation.

'It's all gone very well,' Daniel said, smiling. 'You must be very happy.'

'Yes, of course. I know that Bella and Freddie are going to have a wonderful life together.'

He gave her a straight look. 'But, what? You are very serious.'

'Shall we walk? I have something to tell you.'

'Of course, but it doesn't sound promising.'

'It could be a very good opportunity for me, but I want to know what you think and feel before I accept or reject the offer.' Flora shot him a sideways glance. 'Freddie has suggested that I might like to occupy Hope's End at a peppercorn rent.'

'You haven't any money. How could you accomplish that without a steady income?'

'That's true, but Freddie thinks I could run a business of some sort from there, and I would like to try.'

'You want to set up a business in Hope's End?'

'Yes, that's what I said. I could take in lodgers or try to run it like a small hotel, or I could hire a chef and maybe run it as a high-class restaurant. There is very little competition round here.'

'You want to be a businesswoman. You don't want to marry me and live in a cottage on the estate. That's what you said before.'

Flora came to a halt at the edge of the parterre garden. 'You never actually proposed, Dan. But can you imagine me living in your cottage with your ma and pa? Not that I don't love them both, I do, but living like that would end in tears all round.'

'If we were married perhaps Sir Arthur would allow us to have one of the larger cottages on the estate.'

'It's not just that, Dan. I have to discover who I really am, but I know I won't be happy to simply keep house and bring up a family.'

'It seems to be enough for Bella. Look how happy she is.'

'Bella has loving parents and a wealthy husband who can give her anything she wants. I just want to be myself, whoever she is.'

Daniel sighed. 'How are you going to do that?'

'I'll go to Play House Yard tomorrow and speak to Ted. If he knows the names of the boats in the fatal collision I will visit *The Times* printing house and ask to look at the relevant newspaper. Maybe there was a passenger list, or some sort of clue as to who were on board.'

'I'll come with you. It's my day off anyway, so there won't be a problem.'

Flora hesitated. 'You haven't said what you think of the idea, Dan. I mean, I would hope to run a business from Hope's End.'

'It doesn't seem to include me, Flora.' Daniel turned away but she caught him by the sleeve.

'Of course it does. You would always be part of my life, whatever I do.'

'Are you saying you would marry me if this plan went ahead?'

A wry smile curved her lips. 'You would have to propose in order to find out.'

'Perhaps I'd better wait until we discover who you really are. If you turn out to be the daughter of a duke or an earl, I might not reach the high standards you set.'

Flora met his amused gaze with a toss of her head. 'Now you are making fun of me, Daniel Robbins.'

Dan seized her hand and raised it to his lips. 'You look like a duchess anyway. Have I told you how beautiful you look in that gown? It's the exact colour of your eyes.'

'Now you're flattering me.'

He drew her into his arms. 'I've never been more sincere.' He kissed her until she could hardly draw breath.

'Someone will see,' Flora said, wriggling free.

'I hope they do. I don't care if you are a lady or the daughter of a criminal. I love you, Flora Lee, or whatever you name is. One day I hope it will be Flora Robbins, but I'm prepared to wait as long as it takes.'

Flora knew he meant what he said and she brushed his lips with a kiss. 'I don't deserve you, Daniel.'

He put his head on one side, listening. 'They're playing a waltz. May I have this dance, Miss Lee?'

'We're not on the dance floor.'

He swept her into his arms. 'We managed to dance

in a forest clearing on May Day. I like it here. I have you all to myself.' He whirled her round the paths in the parterre garden and her feet hardly touched the ground. When the music stopped she leaned against him inhaling the heady scent of crushed lavender on his coat sleeve as they had brushed past the purple-headed spikes that filled the flower beds. She glanced across the gardens to the rest of the party who were clustered together beneath the oak trees.

'It looks as if the bride and groom are ready to leave, Dan. We'd better get there to see them off.'

'I'd rather stay here with you.'

'If I'm being honest, so I would, too. But I know that Bella will be very upset if I don't wish her bon voyage. Not only that, but she insists on me giving her my answer, and it is only polite to let Freddie know.'

'And what is your decision?'

'I won't accept if it will make things difficult between us, Dan.'

'Nothing will ever change how I feel about you, Flora. But this is important to you and the answer must be made by you. I won't interfere.' He took her by the hand. 'Come on. We'll go and wave goodbye to the happy couple. Maybe one day it will be us departing on our honeymoon.'

# Chapter Twenty

Coralie welcomed them with open arms. She hugged Flora and then Daniel. 'This is an unexpected pleasure. It seems you can't keep away from us.'

Flora smiled. 'I was very happy here with you, Coralie. But I think I might have a clue as to my true identity and I need your help.'

'Come into the parlour, dear. I'll fetch Ted and you can speak to us together.' Coralie cast a knowing look in Daniel's direction. 'I expect a glass of ale wouldn't go amiss, Dan. It's still quite hot considering we're in September now.'

'Thank you, that would be nice, but you must allow me to pay for it.'

'Nonsense. You are my guests. What about you, Flora?'

'I need to keep a cool head. Perhaps a cup of tea?'

'I'll get Moses to make a pot. That is something

he can do on his own.' Coralie ushered them past the curious drinkers in the taproom. She settled them in the parlour with a tankard of ale for Dan before going off to find her husband.

With a cup of tea clutched in her hands, Flora glanced from Coralie to Ted. 'Syd Fox and Gert brought me up to believe that my mother was Gert's sister and a thoroughly bad person. I've since discovered that, like Moses, I was found floating in the river after the tragic accident when so many lives were lost. I was in a peccary leather doctor's bag.'

'It's possible that he was lying,' Coralie said gently. 'It sounds so similar to how we found Moses.'

Ted frowned. 'But it's a possibility. Did he keep the bag?'

'He sold it,' Flora said bluntly. 'As well as the shawl with my name embroidered on it.'

'Do you recall the names of the boats in the collision?' Daniel looked from one to the other. 'There might have been a passenger list.'

'There was certainly an account of the tragedy in all the newspapers,' Ted said thoughtfully. 'There was considerable loss of life. But Moses was a babe in arms sixteen years ago. How old are you, Flora?'

'I'm eighteen.'

Ted turned to his wife. 'Would a two-year-old child fit into a doctor's bag?'

'A small girl might. Looking at Flora now, I

370

would imagine that she was a delicate child. It's not impossible.'

'I know several of the fellows who work in the print room at *The Times*. They drink here regularly.' Ted rose to his feet. 'I'll come with you, Flora, and we'll ask to see the old copies of the newspapers around that date. You can come with us, Dan, unless you'd prefer to stay here and enjoy my superior quality ale.'

Dan swallowed a mouthful before placing his tankard firmly on the table. 'I wouldn't miss this. It means a lot to both of us.'

Ted kissed Coralie on the cheek. 'I won't be long, darling.' He left the parlour with Flora and Daniel hurrying after him.

The inn was virtually next door to the print room and Ted seemed to know most of the staff. Flora was excited and yet nervous as they waited for one of the workers to fetch the relevant newspaper. This could be the day she would discover who she really was, or it could be another dead end.

He returned, carrying a carefully folded paper. 'Here it is, guv. Terrible accident, so many lives lost.'

Ted nodded. 'Thanks, Tom. Yes, I agree. I remember it well.'

'The ship owner lost his wife and two nippers.' Tom shook his head. 'Should never have happened.' He laid the newspaper on the table in front of them, but Flora's hands were shaking too much for her to do anything but stare at the newsprint. The account was all over the front page detailing the tragic accident that happened sixteen years previously. However, the numbers of casualties and fatalities did not include any names and there was no mention of a passenger list.

'This is very disappointing,' Flora said tearfully. 'I was really hoping it would give me more information.'

'It does give the names of the two ship owners, Flora. I know where their offices are on the docks. We'll go there next.' Ted turned to the man who had brought the newspaper from the files and shook his hand. 'There's a free drink for you any time, mate.'

The man grinned and touched his cap as he walked away.

'Don't give up, Flora.' Ted slipped his arm around her shoulders. 'We'll go to the first one right away.'

Two hours later they returned to the inn with a list of names from both shipping companies copied from the official documents. They had whittled the possibilities down to as few as possible, eliminating people who were least likely to be Flora's parents. Ted had been eager to discover Moses' background, too, although he insisted that it made no difference. As far as he and Coralie were concerned, Moses was their son and they would continue to care for him no matter what.

They sat round the table in the inn parlour with Coralie, who provided them with bread and cheese to be washed down with ale or tea. They pored over the lists while they enjoyed their meal.

'It's going to be more difficult than I thought,' Flora said wearily.

Coralie leaned forward, pointing with her index finger. 'There are several families with small children who are not named. I suppose they didn't bother much about tiny children – they thought their parents were responsible for their wellbeing. But, look. There are two doctors, although one of them seems to be a single man.'

Daniel looked over her shoulder. 'There's a married woman with two children but no mention of a husband.'

'There were at least two hundred people altogether,' Ted added, frowning. 'Assuming that all the children on board were listed, we eliminated the fatalities, of course, so the ones left are all possibilities, according to age.'

Coralie produced a pencil and they went through the lists again. Eventually they had five possible families to which Flora and Moses might belong.

'I'm sorry we can't help more.' Ted smiled sympathetically. 'But it must be possible to trace these people. You could still discover your identity, Flora.'

She nodded. 'I won't give up now, but at least I can be fairly certain that I was part of that terrible disaster. Moses and I have so much in common.'

Coralie sat back on her seat, sipping her tea. 'What

are you going to do now that Bella is married? You could always come back to us, Flora.'

'As a matter of fact, I have something I was going to ask both of you.'

Coralie and Ted exchanged amused glances.

'Tell us, Flora.'

'I've had a stroke of good fortune. Freddie, Lord Dorrington, owns a house close to Nine Oaks. He's prepared to let me live there for a peppercorn rent.'

'Very generous of him,' Ted said, smiling. 'But what will you do with a large house? I gather it must be quite grand if it belongs to your friendly aristocrat.'

'I was thinking of turning it into a restaurant, but not the ordinary sort of place where people come just to eat.' Flora looked from one to the other to try and judge their reactions, but they all seemed stunned rather than enthusiastic.

'What would that entail?' Ted asked warily.

'I thought that, as it's in the country, people could enjoy the best of part of a day at Hope's End. They could come for luncheon and spend the rest of the time in the gardens or sitting by the fire in the winter, with a nice meal before they left in the early evening.'

'But Flora, to set the house up for that sort of thing would cost money,' Daniel said, frowning.

'I'm sure that Freddie would invest in the idea. Bella wants to stay with me when they visit her parents. It would mean that they would be waited on and have meals prepared especially for them, just as they do at home.'

'I suppose it does make sense in a very roundabout way.' Ted gave her a searching look. 'I feel that you are going to ask for our help?'

Flora smiled. 'Just to set it all up. I have a good idea how to run a restaurant and I'm prepared to work hard. I would need to hire staff, but a good cook will always attract custom and I want to make the old house beautiful again. The gardens would be Dan's creation, if he's willing to take on the task?' Flora turned to him eagerly. 'You could make them into a paradise, Dan.'

'You're forgetting I have a job at Nine Oaks, Flora.'

'No, I'm not. You are head gardener there, you have plenty of groundsmen to do the hard work. We could do this together, you and I.' Flora looked around the table. 'What do you say?'

'It might be possible,' Daniel said slowly. 'I'd have to consider it carefully. But I'm afraid you would be taking on too much.'

'I agree with Dan.' Coralie reached out to clasp Flora's hand. 'I think it's a wonderful idea, but very ambitious. You would be under a degree of obligation to Lord Dorrington, too. Do you really want that?'

'I can see no other way, but if I'm successful I will repay Freddie, and maybe even purchase Hope's End from him.'

Ted eyed her speculatively. 'I think you're quite capable of doing well, Flora. I'm willing to help you start up, but I can't spare too much time away from here. On the other hand, I'm always ready to give you good advice, and you learned a lot when you worked for me.'

'Yes, I did. And that's why I would value your help just at the beginning.'

'Perhaps Coralie and I ought to come and view the house before you make a start. I'll be quite honest with you, Flora. If I don't think it's a good proposition I will say so.'

Daniel nodded. 'I second that, sir. I don't want to see Flora wasting her talents on something that will never work out.'

'What will you do about this, Flora?' Coralie held up the two lists of survivors.

Flora shook her head. 'I don't think there is much I can do. There are too many names, even after cutting out the ones we thought unlikely. I wouldn't know where to start, especially after sixteen years. I have to think to the future now and try not to look back.'

'Well said.' Ted clapped his hands. 'Now I'd better get back to the kitchen. We have a party of well-heeled gentlemen coming for dinner this evening.' He gave Flora a quick hug and shook Daniel's hand as he left the parlour.

'It will be a rowdy do, but they will spend well,' Coralie said, sighing. 'I just hope that Ralph Pettigrew isn't one of them.'

'Has anyone heard what happened to Captain Cutler?' Flora asked casually. Not that she had any desire to see Gabriel again, but she was curious.

Coralie shook her head. 'No, but he was never a regular customer. Putting up with his cousin was quite enough for me.'

'We'd better go now, Flora,' Daniel said firmly.

'Of course.' Flora picked up the lists and folded them. 'I hope to see you again soon, Coralie. Give Moses a hug from me. I don't want to disturb him while he's working.'

'He was very fond of you, Flora. We might give him a treat and bring him to see your new home.'

'I haven't moved in yet, but I'll let you know as soon as I am there.' Flora kissed Coralie on the cheek. 'Goodbye for now.'

Daniel shook Coralie's hand. 'Thank you again. You and Ted have been so good to Flora. I hope to see you again soon.'

That night in the seclusion of her own room, Flora studied the passenger lists, but she was still none the wiser. None of the names jumped out at her, and even had they done so, finding those people seemed like a gargantuan task. She tucked the documents away in a small writing case that had been a present from Bella, and decided to put the search firmly behind her. Now she would concentrate on making Hope's End into a home for herself and for Daniel, if they ever managed to come to a compromise, which at this moment seemed unlikely.

Next morning after a solitary breakfast in the dining room at Nine Oaks, Flora put on her bonnet and shawl and walked to Hope's End. The rheumy-eyed butler opened the door.

'Good morning. It's Beasley, isn't it? I am Miss Lee. Perhaps you remember me?'

'Yes, miss.'

'May I come in?'

Beasley opened the door wider and stepped aside. Flora entered and was met once again by the smell of must and dampness. She turned to Beasley with a smile. 'Lord Dorrington has agreed that I can be the new tenant, Beasley. Perhaps you would show me around and introduce me to the rest of the servants.'

Beasley sniffed. 'Yes, miss. This way, please.' He walked stiffly opening the doors that led off the square entrance hall, giving Flora a view of darkened rooms filled with furniture draped with Holland covers. When she had first seen the house Flora thought it very dilapidated, but on closer inspection it was nothing that a good spring clean and a fresh coat of paint would not overcome. Beasley spoke very little, answering her questions in monosyllables.

Flora followed him upstairs at a painfully slow rate but she soon realised that he was suffering from what Dora Robbins described as her 'niggling rheumatics'. Beasley came to a halt at the top of the stairs, turning to Flora with an agonised look.

'Do you really intend to live here, miss?'

'Yes, I will move in as soon as the house is ready.'

'Then I'd best pack my bags.'

Flora stared at him in surprise. 'Why would you do that, Beasley?'

'You won't want an old codger like me serving you, miss.'

Flora realised why he seemed so reluctant to acknowledge her as the new lady of the house. 'I understand you were Lady Philomena's right-hand man, Beasley. I would not want to lose someone of your experience and loyalty.'

He eyed her suspiciously. 'You want me to stay?'

'Of course I do. I need you to help me run this house. I am totally inexperienced when it comes to dealing with such things. I will have to rely on you.'

'Thank you, miss. I don't know what to say.'

'You should call me Miss Lee or Miss Flora, I don't mind which. You can show me the servants' quarters before we go upstairs and inspect the bedrooms. How many people work here?'

Beasley took a hanky from his pocket and blew his nose loudly. 'Begging your pardon, Miss Flora.' He stuffed his hanky back in his pocket and took a deep breath. 'There's just me and Cook, and the young girl who is learning to be a housemaid.'

'Very well. I would like to meet them.'

'Yes, Miss Flora.' Beasley braced his shoulders and walked on with his head held as high as his rheumatism would allow.

Below stairs in the vast and very old-fashioned kitchen, Flora was introduced to Mrs Carlton, who had been Lady Philomena's cook for thirty years, and Mattie Briggs, a young girl from the village who seemed to do everything, including scrubbing the flagstone floor.

Flora sensed that Mrs Carlton was suspicious and did not like change. Mattie was constantly smiling, which was equally unnerving, but Flora was determined to establish herself as mistress of Hope's End.

'I will be moving in as soon as the house is ready,' Flora said firmly.

'Have you any instructions for us, Miss Lee?' Cook sniffed and folded her arms, as if ready for an argument.

'I would like you to hire some scrubwomen from the village, Mrs Carlton. I want the whole house spring-cleaned.'

'That's a housekeeper's job, Miss Lee.'

'I would have thought it in your interests to select women you know and trust, Mrs Carlton. I am not yet in a position to take on a housekeeper, and I'm sure you are used to running the kitchen without anyone telling you what to do.'

'Yes, Miss Lee.'

'Good. I think we understand each other. Things will change, Mrs Carlton, but it will be for the better and I hope you will continue to be in charge of the kitchen for the foreseeable future.'

'Yes, thank you, Miss Lee.'

'I will be here every day from now on, so any problems you have, please come straight to me.' Flora left the room before either of them had a chance to speak. She was so used to servants behaving in a professional manner that it was a shock to find a simmering mutiny in the kitchen before she had even moved in. However, it was nothing that she could not handle. Flora followed Beasley back upstairs.

'How did I do, Beasley?' Flora said with a smile as they reached the entrance hall.

'You did well, Miss Flora. I'm afraid Winnie Carlton has ruled the roost for too long. She needs taking down a peg or two.'

'I appreciate that it's difficult when a new mistress walks in, especially as you have all been loyal servants to Lady Philomena, but you will find me fair-minded, Beasley. I will rely on you to keep peace below stairs. By the way, have we many ground staff? Or is that a silly question?'

'There's Tompkins the head gardener and his boy. That's all, Miss Flora.'

'Thank you, Beasley. Please show me the rooms upstairs now, including the attics. I want to get a picture of the whole house in my mind.'

'Certainly, miss.'

When she had finished the tour of the house Flora went outside to explore the grounds. To her surprise she discovered that Freddie's property shared a boundary with Sir Arthur's land. She wondered if either of them realised that, and in fact it made sense for Freddie to give the estate to Bella, who would one day inherit Nine Oaks. With that in mind Flora walked home, but her visit to Hope's End had not turned out as she had hoped. If she were to be honest she had to admit that her grand plans for the old house were impractical. It was simply a country residence and totally unsuited for a business premises. Even with Ted Tulliver's help and expertise she could not hope to make a living there, and to set it up and bring the house and particularly the kitchens to the standard required would take a small fortune. She could not keep asking Freddie for money nor could she impose such a problem on Ted and Coralie. Perhaps the old place really was Hope's End, at least for her. But to admit defeat was not in her nature. She decided to continue with her plan to bring the house back to its former glory, if only for Bella's sake. Perhaps she could settle for life keeping house for Bella and Freddie whenever they chose to come home. If only Bella were here now they could talk about it together, but this was something that Flora knew she must face on her own. She could not even share her disappointment with Daniel, at least not yet.

Back in her room she turned to the passenger lists, longing for a distraction to take her away from fretting about her broken dreams. Two names came to her attention, both doctors. After all, according to Syd, she had been found in a doctor's bag. It was the only clue she had to go on. Even if the gentlemen in question were not related to her, they might have loaned the bag to a desperate parent. She knew their names but that was all and sixteen years was a long time, they might have retired or worse. Flora was not in a mood to be beaten. There was only one person she knew who might be able to help and that was Todd Baker, Amelia's husband. She had spoken to him briefly at the wedding and he might be able to tell her how she could trace the two other doctors.

Flora had no particular duties to perform these days, and she doubted if she would be missed until dinner that evening. It was an easy matter to change into her riding habit and walk to the stables to instruct one of the grooms to saddle her horse. A long ride would brush away the cobwebs and with a definite purpose in mind she set off for Marsh House. It was a pleasant day in early autumn and the morning mist had evaporated leaving the air crystal clear. The dusty leaves on the trees were beginning to turn all shades of copper, gold and brown, tinged with red, but the sun was warm on her face and the horse was eager for an outing. It was just past midday when she arrived at Marsh House and was greeted by Betsy, who held the horse while Flora dismounted.

'What a lovely animal,' Betsy said, stroking the horse's muzzle. 'I'll take him to the stables for you, miss.'

'Thank you, Betsy. I really came to see Todd, is he at home?'

Betsy nodded. 'He's finished his morning surgery. You'll just catch him before he goes out on his rounds. I think he's in the kitchen with Mariah.'

Flora was acquainted with the layout of the old house, having been for many fittings for her bridesmaid's outfit. She went straight to the kitchen and was met by the delicious aroma of hot bread and a savoury stew bubbling on the range.

Todd was seated at the table with a cup of tea in front of him. He rose to his feet and met Flora with a wide smile.

'This is a pleasant surprise, Flora.'

'Would you like a cup of tea?' Mariah picked up the teapot. 'It's freshly made.'

'I would love a cup, thank you. It's quite a long ride from Nine Oaks.'

'Take a seat.' Todd eyed her curiously. 'Did you want to see Amelia?'

'No, it's you I came to see. I won't take up much of your time, but I wonder if you would take a look at these.' Flora put her hand in her skirt pocket and pulled out the folded passenger lists. She spread them out on the table in front of Todd. 'You know I was found floating on the Thames in a doctor's bag? I think everyone is aware of my origins by now, but it seems that I might have been involved in the tragic accident when two ships collided on the river.'

Todd sat down again. 'These are passenger lists. How did you come by these?'

'It's a long story, but there are two doctors listed. I have nothing to go on apart from the fact that it was a doctor's bag that saved me from drowning. I really want to find out who I am, and I thought if I could trace these doctors, one of them might have given his medical bag to my parents or whoever was with me that fateful day.'

Mariah filled a cup with tea and placed it on the table. 'So you want to trace those doctors?'

'I don't know how to go about it, Mariah.'

'It was a long time ago,' Todd said thoughtfully. 'I don't know that fellow, but Dr Paul Hadley was a physician at the London Hospital when I trained there. If it's the same person, you might be able to find out if he is still working there.'

'Dr Sutton would know,' Mariah said thoughtfully. 'He is Amelia's pa. He still works at the London Hospital.'

'Could you give me his address? Maybe he can help me?' Flora looked from one to the other.

'Why not leave it to me, Flora?' Todd refolded the lists and passed them back to her. 'Emmie and I have dinner with Dr Sutton and his wife once a month, and it so happens that we're seeing them tomorrow. I'll ask him and let you know what he says.'

Flora flung her arms around Todd's neck and kissed him on the cheek. 'Thank you, so much. I haven't had anyone to talk to about this. It's such a relief to know you are going to help me.'

Todd disentangled himself, laughing. 'I can't promise anything, Flora. It might come to nothing, but I can see it means a lot to you.'

'More than I can say.' Flora clasped her hands together. 'Thank you, Todd.'

Mariah laughed. 'Why don't you stay for luncheon, Flora? I know that Emmie would love to hear all about your attempts to find your real family.'

'Thank you, I would love to, but only if you have enough. I don't want to impose.'

Todd rose to his feet. 'I have a patient to visit before I eat, but I'll be back later. Don't worry, Flora. If we can find out if Dr Hadley is still at the hospital or better still, where he lives, I will let you know.'

'I can't thank you enough.' Flora sat down and sipped her tea.

Todd picked up his hat and medical bag as he left the kitchen.

'You must miss Arabella,' Mariah said as she stirred the contents of the large saucepan. 'Are you planning to stay with the Stewarts?'

'Freddie has offered me the tenancy of his late aunt's house and I accepted. But now I've had second thoughts. My original idea was to run a restaurant from Hope's End. I had some experience at the Play House Yard Inn, but I realise now that it wasn't enough to take on such a huge project. I want to be able to earn my own living, but being brought up to be a lady has left me at a disadvantage.'

Mariah nodded. 'Yes, I can see that. Young ladies wait for a suitable husband to come along. Is there someone you care about?'

'Daniel wants to marry me. He's the head gardener at Nine Oaks.'

'You don't sound as though that's what you want.'

Flora met Mariah's sympathetic gaze with an attempt at a smile. 'I do love him, but our situations in life are so different. I simply can't see myself living in a small cottage with my in-laws. Can you understand that, Mariah? Or am I being a hateful person?'

Mariah sat down at the table, opposite Flora. 'I do understand. My first husband died very young and Percy's pa was a brute, who forced himself on me. But I've been independent for a long time now and I will have to stop working for Amelia when I marry Jim. He has a large family and they need me to take care of them.'

'But you love him enough to make the change, Mariah?'

'Yes, I do. You will have to decide what is best for you, Flora. Maybe it will be easier if you can find your real family, although you and Miss Arabella seem more like sisters than just friends.'

'I love Bella, and she wants me to live at Hope's End. It was her idea for me to keep house for them, and I would always be there when she visited her parents. I only agreed because I had a plan to run a business at Hope's End, but I've come to realise that it's virtually impossible without a large amount of capital. I know I have a big decision to make. Maybe if I know who I really am it will all become clear to me.'

Mariah laid her hand on Flora's as it rested on the table. 'I know you will make the right choice when the time comes, Flora. Let's hope that Todd will have some good news for you.'

# Chapter Twenty-One

Flora waited eagerly for news from Todd, but in the ensuing days she found herself relegated to the position of housekeeper at Hope's End. She was still living at Nine Oaks, but she spent all day every day at the old house. She threw herself into the task of bringing life back to Hope's End, organising a small army of women from the village who came to clean the rooms from top to bottom. The back-yard was criss-crossed with washing lines hung with the curtains that were salvageable, and a little further from the house the carpets were strung over taut lines and beaten to free them from years of dust and fluff. Flora spent much of her time in a small office below stairs where she wrote out orders for supplies of food that Cook needed to stock up the pantries, as well as lists of cleaning materials, and wines to restock the cellar, according to Beasley.

Try as she might, Flora could not dissuade the existing servants from the idea that Freddie and Arabella were going to reside at Hope's End, if only for a few weeks in the year. They seemed to think that her position was that of housekeeper and they brought their petty squabbles to her door.

The interior was improving, but the gardens were another matter. Lady Philomena had kept on a rather elderly gardener and an undergardener, but they were not a match for the onward march of brambles, weeds and wildflowers. Freddie had thoughtfully left a fairly generous amount of money to pay for the servants and the upkeep of the house, but it was not nearly enough to pay for more ground staff. Flora took the problem to Sir Arthur after breakfast one morning. He seemed to have only a vague idea that his land and that of Hope's End actually shared a boundary, but he listened intently and when Flora had finished explaining the situation he nodded.

'I've always left the management of the estate to my land agent, but you may tell Robbins to send some of our men to put the place to rights. I know that Freddie has given the house and land to my daughter, which makes me in part responsible. I don't want her to return from her honeymoon to look out at a wilderness.'

'Thank you, sir.' Flora smiled gratefully. 'I will speak to Robbins.'

Sir Arthur gave her a discerning look. 'You are a good girl, Flora. Are you sure that you want to move into that old house? You know we think of you as our daughter and would be more than happy if you continued to live with us.'

'You've always been so kind to me, and I wish we were related. I do think of Bella as my sister and I am happy to be doing something for her, if she truly wishes to keep on Hope's End. After all, what else is there for me to do?'

'I've never given it much thought, my dear, but you must find it odd not knowing who your parents were.'

'I didn't think much about it at all while I was growing up, but recently it's become very important to me to discover who I really am.'

'I understand that, but we know very little about you. The rogues who claimed to be your aunt and uncle spun us a story that was apparently a pack of lies. Bella told us that you were rescued from the river as a very small child. That disaster was in all the newspapers.'

'You know about it, sir?'

'The whole of London knew what had happened. It was a terrible loss of life. You were one of the lucky ones.'

Flora smiled. 'I think my lucky day occurred when you found me in Turnagain Lane. Those people are not my relations, I know that now.'

'I never thought for a moment that they were. The woman in particular was very keen to sell you to the highest bidder. No mother does that to her child.'

'They did sell me in the end, but it was Ted Tulliver who paid the asking price. I was extremely fortunate that he's a good, kind man. I owe him and his wife a lot.'

'I would like to meet him and thank him for saving you from the Foxes. They should be locked up in prison for what they did to you.'

'I'd prefer to forget them, sir.' Flora glanced out of the window. 'If you have no objection, I would like to find Robbins and pass on your instructions regarding the grounds of Hope's End. We need to take advantage of the fine weather, and I'd love the old house to look its best when Bella and Freddie return from their honeymoon.'

'Yes, of course. Do that, Flora. Tell Robbins he has my permission to do what is necessary. I know I can trust him. He's a good reliable fellow, just like his father before him.'

'Thank you, sir. I'll go at once.'

As luck would have it, Flora found Daniel in the walled garden. The last of the summer root crop was being dug up and stored ready for the winter, and the beds dug over and weeded, ready to sow spring vegetables and flowers. Daniel's smile was a welcome in itself. He walked towards her holding out his arms, but she avoided his embrace.

'Flora, what is it? You look troubled. I haven't seen you for days.'

'I'm quite all right, Dan. I've been very busy at

Hope's End. The house is being cleaned from top to bottom but the grounds and the old gardens need a lot of work. Sir Arthur has given his permission for you to take some of the ground staff to clear the land before Bella and Freddie return.'

'We can do that. We're up to date with all the work on the estate. When do you want me to start?'

'As soon as possible. Apparently, Sir Arthur had no idea that his land abuts that of Hope's End. It means that Bella will own both estates one day.'

'I can see that, but where does it leave you with your fine ideas about opening a restaurant so far from the centre of town?'

'I've given it a lot of thought, and I realise that it was too ambitious. I've neither the experience nor the funds to start up a business.'

He grasped her hand and squeezed it gently. 'I am sorry, Flora. I know how much it meant to you.'

'It was just a dream. At least I realised that before I had gone too far. I'm disappointed, but I will think of something else.'

'Marry me and forget all your grand ideas. I love you and I'm sure I could make you happy.'

She smiled. 'You know it isn't quite as simple as that.'

'Are you still intent on finding your real parents?'

'More than ever. I've asked Todd Baker to find out all he can about Dr Hadley, who was on one of the passenger lists. I have to start somewhere.'

Daniel nodded. 'I'm in favour of anything that

makes your life easier, my darling girl.' He smiled and lifted her off her feet, twirling her around. 'Take me to Hope's End and I'll see what needs to be done, and how many men it will take to do it quickly.'

Breathless and laughing as he set her back on her feet, Flora took a step away from him. 'I'd challenge you to a race as we did in the old days, but that would be unladylike. I am a sober housekeeper now, so I'll lead the way very sedately. Follow me, my man.'

Daniel caught up with her and tucked her hand in the crook of his arm. 'Sedate never, and I have no intention of allowing you to become Miss Arabella's housekeeper. You are worth more than that.'

'We'll see,' Flora said, sighing. 'Maybe Todd will find out that I am really an heiress, with a huge fortune awaiting me. In the meantime let's get to work on Hope's End. Although I wish that Freddie would change the name of the house.'

'What would you call it, Flora?'

She shot him a mischievous sideways glance. 'Flora's Folly.'

Daniel and his men set to later that day and worked until dusk. They had already made great strides in clearing the waste ground with scythes and sickles, as Flora noted with pride when she went to inspect their work. When Daniel had finished for the day, Flora walked back to Nine Oaks with him, having sent the groundsmen on ahead. Flora knew she ought to move into Hope's End but she kept putting it off, unwilling to leave her comfortable bedroom where she had slept since a child. Becoming the housekeeper would quite literally break the bonds she had formed with the family and place her forever in the position of a servant. Bella might not agree, but Flora knew instinctively that this would be her future, and she was not prepared to settle for such a fate.

Daniel saw her to the main entrance, but they arrived at the same time as a man on horseback. Even before he dismounted Flora recognised him. 'Todd! What brings you here at this time in the evening?' She hurried to meet him.

'I have some news for you, Flora. It's not definite, but I think I might have found out who you are.'

Flora clutched her hands to her heart as it beat a tattoo against her ribs. She could hardly breathe. 'Tell me, please.'

'Maybe we should go inside,' Daniel said hurriedly. 'You look as if you need to sit down, Flora.'

'I can't stop,' Todd said hurriedly. 'I need to get home for dinner, but I've written down the details.' He took a folded sheet of paper from his pocket and handed it to Flora. 'I'm sorry it took so long, but I had to wait until Emmie's pa had made enquiries at the hospital. We found Dr Hadley and he remembered you and your family, Flora. It was his bag they put you in when the ship started to sink.'

Flora leaned against Daniel for support. 'It's unbelievable. After all this time.'

'Neither my father-in-law nor myself chose to follow this up, Flora. We both thought it should be done by you. It's all there on that piece of paper.'

Flora flung her arms around him and kissed him on the cheek. 'I can't thank you enough. I still can't believe that who I really am is written on this single sheet.'

Todd patted her on the shoulder. 'Let us know how the reunion goes. I'm sorry I can't stay but I really have to go home or Emmie will be frantic with worry. I came straight here from her father's house.'

'Thank you.' Daniel shook his hand. 'This means so much to Flora.'

'I know it does. I have no idea who my parents were, so I have a fellow feeling with Flora.' Todd mounted his horse. 'I hope it goes well, Flora.' He rode off at a trot, breaking into a canter.

A shaft of light from the oil lamp held in James's hand illuminated the steps and Daniel propelled Flora into the entrance hall. He glanced at James and smiled.

'I know I should use the servants' entrance, but Miss Flora has just had some news, which I hope will be good.'

James nodded and pulled up a chair. 'Sit down, miss. You look done in.'

Flora sank down on the seat. 'Hold the lantern closer, please.' She unfolded the paper but the words danced up and down in front of her eyes and she handed it to Daniel. 'I can't focus on the words. Will you read it for me?'

He studied it for a moment. 'It's an address in the West End, I only know because I've delivered flowers to the house in South Molton Street.' Daniel handed the paper to James. 'Here, mate, you know the place better than I do.'

James studied the writing, frowning. 'This is one of the restaurants that the toffs go to and spend a fortune on eating out.'

Flora snatched the paper from him. 'I know this restaurant. I've been there several times with the family. It is very expensive, as you say, James.' She frowned, racking her brain to bring the passenger lists to mind. 'I think I saw this name on one of the passenger lists, but I didn't pay much attention to it at the time.'

'Is it the owner, or one of the chefs, or a waiter?' Daniel looked over her shoulder. 'Peter Calvert.'

'I don't know. I've never heard of him, but there's only one way to find out.' Flora rose to her feet. 'Tomorrow I'm going to drive into London and visit Chez Marcel in Brook Street. I'll find out one way or another.'

'I'll take you,' Daniel said firmly. 'I'm sure Sir Arthur would allow me to drive you in the chaise. I'll put someone in charge of the gardens at Hope's End. We'll find out once and for all if you are related to this person.'

*

Flora hardly slept that night. She was excited, nervous and amazed. She tried to imagine what Peter Calvert might be like. If she was closely related to him and he was a chef or even a waiter it might explain her desire to open her own restaurant and the fact that she had enjoyed working for Ted Tulliver. It was interesting but also rather scary, and what would she say to Mr Calvert when she met him? She ran through a series of scenes in her mind as if watching a play at the theatre, and in the end she fell asleep and dreamed of being thrown out of a very exclusive dining room with the maître d' calling her a fraud.

She almost fell out of bed at the crack of dawn and splashed cold water from the washbowl on her face. She dressed in a pale grey travelling costume and confined her hair in a snood at the back of her neck. Stubborn auburn curls refused to be contained and in the end she had to give in and allow them to frame her pale face. Dark shadows underlined her eyes but she chose to ignore them. A brisk walk in the parterre garden before breakfast failed to give her an appetite and in the end she only managed a cup of strong coffee and a bite of toast.

At nine o'clock on the dot Daniel brought the chaise to the front entrance and James opened the door. 'Good luck, Miss Flora,' he said, grinning. 'Or should I call you mademoiselle?'

Flora managed a weak smile. 'Don't be cheeky, James.'

He winked at her, something he would never have dared to do with anyone else in the family. 'I hope it goes well, miss. And don't worry, I haven't breathed a word of it below stairs.'

Flora nodded and stepped outside into a glorious autumn morning. She had a feeling that this was going to be the most momentous day of her life, so far.

The restaurant in fashionable Brook Street was not yet open but Daniel knocked on the glass-fronted door until a waiter came. He opened it, glowering at them. 'I'm sorry, we do not open until midday, sir.'

Flora stepped forward. 'I would like to speak to Mr Calvert. It's very important.'

'Have you an appointment, miss?'

Flora eyed him warily. If she needed an appointment to see Peter Calvert he was unlikely to be one of this fellow's workmates or even a busy chef. She decided to brave it out.

'My name is Flora Lee. Please tell him that Dr Hadley sent me.'

'I'm not sure if Mr Calvert has come in yet, miss. I'll check if you will kindly step inside and wait here.'

Flora and Daniel did as he asked and stood in the foyer while the waiter hurried off presumably looking for Mr Calvert.

'Do you suppose he might be the manager of this

establishment?' Flora said in a low voice. She could see waiters polishing cutlery before setting it on the tables, which were covered in pristine white cloths.

'Maybe he's the head waiter or something.' Daniel followed Flora's gaze. 'I wish I'd put my Sunday best on. This is not the sort of place I'm accustomed to.'

'It's just an expensive fish and chip shop,' Flora said, giggling. 'Only they cook the fish in fancy sauces and they serve the potatoes dauphinoise.'

'Beyond me.' Daniel shrugged. 'I'll stick to eel pie and mash.'

'He's coming back,' Flora said in a low voice. 'Please don't mention chips or jellied eels.'

'Mr Calvert will see you now. Please follow me.' The waiter led the way to an office at the back of the restaurant.

Flora followed him, acutely aware of the covert attention of the staff. The waiter showed them into the office and backed away, closing the door behind him.

A distinguished-looking gentleman rose from his seat at the desk. His dark hair was winged with silver but his lean features were smooth and unlined. His hazel eyes fringed with thick lashes took in Flora's appearance with an appraising glance.

'Good morning, Miss Lee. I understand you are a friend of Dr Hadley's. Won't you both take a seat?'

Flora hesitated, suddenly nervous and unsure of the best approach. 'I've never met Dr Hadley, at least not knowingly.'

'You and he were on the passenger list of one of the ships involved in a serious collision on the river sixteen years ago,' Daniel added impatiently. 'Flora was rescued from the river that day, or so we think.'

Calvert's smile faded as he fixed his attention once again on Flora. 'You must have been little more than a baby.'

'I don't remember anything,' Flora said hastily. 'I believe I might have been two years old. I was found floating in a doctor's bag that probably belonged to Dr Hadley.'

Calvert resumed his seat. 'Only probably? Do you have the bag in your possession? Has he identified it?'

Flora shook her head. 'It's a long story, sir. I fell into the wrong hands and the person who found me sold the bag and the shawl that had been wrapped around me. It had my name embroidered on it.'

'Are you claiming to be related to me? Is that why you are here, Miss Lee?' Calvert narrowed his eyes. 'I am a wealthy man and for that reason I have had other people trying to convince me that they were my offspring, or had knowledge of them. They all wanted payment for the information.'

'I don't want your money. I didn't even know you existed until a friend found Dr Hadley, who passed your name so that I might try to find my real family.'

'A little late in the day, isn't it, Miss Lee? Why did you leave it so long?'

Flora took a deep breath. This was not going as well as she had hoped. 'I was told a different story, sir. The criminals who found me said they were my aunt and uncle. I was a small child. Why wouldn't I believe them?'

'But they are not your relations?'

'No, thank goodness. But they did eventually admit that they had lied to me.'

Calvert eyed her curiously. 'You neither look nor sound like someone from the criminal classes. Why should I believe your story?'

'I was rescued from the couple by Sir Arthur and Lady Stewart when I was about six years old. They raised me with their own daughter.'

'You seem to have had a comfortable life. Why are you not satisfied with what you have been given?'

Flora could feel Daniel getting impatient by her side and she laid her hand on his arm to calm him. She decided to go in on the attack.

'Why didn't you look for your child after the accident?'

'Not that it's any business of yours, Miss Lee, but I suffered a serious injury in the shipwreck and I spent many weeks in hospital. When I recovered I put advertisements in all the London newspapers and I offered a reward. If your so-called aunt and uncle wanted to make money out of you, why didn't they come forward?'

Flora shrugged. 'I can't answer that, Mr Calvert. I just want to know who my parents are. Dr Hadley must have thought it a good chance that you were my father.'

'How do I know that you haven't fabricated this story?'

Flora was suddenly angry. 'I think we had better leave, Dan. This is obviously a waste of time.'

'What did you expect?' Calvert demanded coldly. 'It's quite a few years since I had anyone claiming to be my long-lost son or daughter.'

'You had a son as well?' Flora stared at him in amazement. 'Did you place him in a wooden crate in the hope that he too would be found?'

'I had a son, a year younger than my daughter. But you could have found that out from the newspapers. My children died in that terrible disaster, as did my beloved wife.'

'I think you are mistaken,' Flora said eagerly. 'I think I know where your son is. He was pulled from the water, too.'

'I don't believe you.' Calvert's voice shook with emotion. 'Stop this cruel charade. It still gives me pain even after so many years.'

'Think what you like.' Flora backed towards the doorway. 'If you don't wish to acknowledge me, I am no worse off than before. But if Moses is your son you will find him working for Ted Tulliver at the Play House Yard Inn.' She opened the door and hurried into the restaurant, making her way to the front entrance with Daniel on her heels.

'Wait, Flora,' he said as he caught up with her

outside in the street. 'Don't leave it like that. Can't you see that the fellow was finding it as hard to accept as you are?'

'He just didn't want to know me, Dan. He thought I was an imposter after his money. You know that's not true. Where is the chaise? I want to go home.'

'Are you certain? That man really could be your father.'

'He didn't seem to think so. Anyway, I've told him where to find Moses. He can go to the inn and see for himself.'

'But that would mean that Moses is your brother. You're very fond of him, aren't you?'

'Yes, of course.'

'Would you like to call at the inn on the way home? You could tell Ted what you know.'

Flora thought for a moment. 'No, I think it best to leave Mr Calvert to think things over. If he doesn't want to acknowledge Moses it would be cruel to raise the poor boy's hopes. He's happy with Ted, maybe it's better that way.'

'All right, I understand.' Daniel whistled to attract the attention of the young boy who was walking the horse. 'I'll take you home, but I still think it's a pity to leave on a sour note.' He waited until the boy drew the chaise to a halt. 'Thanks, mate. You did well.'

The boy pocketed the tip with a cheeky grin. 'Ta, guv. But the toffs pay better.'

Daniel laughed. 'They've got more money than sense. Get on with you.'

The boy hurried off as Daniel assisted Flora into the chaise and climbed in to sit beside her. 'Walk on.' The horse obliged and Daniel skilfully handled the reins as they negotiated the busy street. He shot a sideways glance at Flora. 'Maybe you should have left your address with Calvert. He might change his mind. After all, it must have been a shock to have a grown-up young lady walk into his office and claim to be his long-lost daughter.'

Flora smiled and shook her head. 'I don't think he felt anything for me, Dan. I imagined that if I found either of my parents they would recognise me instantly.'

'And you felt nothing for him?'

'He made me very angry. I wanted to throw something at him.'

'So you felt something?'

'Yes, I'm very disappointed. Although I find it hard to believe that my pa could be the owner of an exclusive restaurant.'

'That makes perfect sense to me, Flora. You have been trying to do exactly that. The only thing stopping you is lack of funds. Maybe Calvert will set you up in business when he gets used to the idea that you are his daughter.'

Flora sighed. 'That's enough. I don't want to talk about it, so can we just go home? I'll give up my grand plans and settle down to being housekeeper at Hope's End.'

'You might believe that, but I don't. You have

never given up on anything in your whole life, Flora Lee or Flora Calvert. It doesn't matter who your parents were, it's what you are that counts and that's why I love you.'

Flora turned her head to give him a watery smile. 'I don't deserve you, Daniel. But I'm not going to let Monsieur Calvert make me miserable. I'm going to forget all about him and put all my efforts into making Hope's End a suitable home for Bella when she and Freddie decide to visit.'

# Chapter Twenty-Two

Two weeks later Flora was preparing the house for the newlyweds' return, which was expected within days. Hope's End had been scrubbed, polished and small repairs had been made. The paintwork had been touched up and the parterre garden was weeded with the box hedges trimmed and the grass cut. Daniel and his team of workers had tidied up the entire grounds and cut back overhanging tree branches, opening up distant views that had not been seen for years. Flora was delighted with the result of all their labours. She had taken on two more housemaids and a boot boy who would help Beasley with some of his tasks. Hard work helped to soothe Flora's hurt feelings, and the disappointment she had experienced when the man who might be her father refused to even consider the idea. She lived resolutely for the moment, refusing to think further than the end of the month when Bella and Freddie were to return.

With everything pristine inside and outside and the larder fully stocked, as was the wine cellar, Flora had little to do. Despite her mixed feelings towards Calvert, she could not help wondering if he had visited the Tullivers and if so, had he accepted Moses as his son? Curiosity burned in her heart and in her head and in the end she decided she had to find out for herself. She was still living at Nine Oaks and she walked to the stables to ask a groom to saddle her horse. It was comforting to be Miss Flora of Nine Oaks rather than Miss Lee, the housekeeper at Hope's End.

She arrived at the inn and a ragged child offered to look after the horse while she went inside. He was skinny and Flora was worried that he was too small for the task, but he was obviously eager to earn a penny or two and she handed him the reins.

'Where is Moses?' she asked urgently, although she knew the answer before it was spoken.

'Gone away, miss. Gone to live with 'is pa, so I heard.'

Flora inhaled sharply as the news hit home much harder than she would have imagined possible. She managed a brief smile of thanks as she turned to walk slowly into the taproom.

Coralie was behind the bar and she greeted Flora with a cry of delight. 'This is an unexpected pleasure, Flora.' She lifted the hatch in the bar counter and crossed the floor to give Flora a warm hug. 'You look sad, dear. Is anything wrong? We'll go and sit in the parlour and you can tell me all about it.'

'The boy who is looking after my horse said that Moses has gone away.'

'It's a most extraordinary thing, Flora.' Coralie hurried on to open the parlour door. 'Come in and take a seat. Can I get you a glass of wine or lemonade?'

'No, I'm fine, thank you. Where did Moses go?'

'It was only a few days ago, a gentleman walked into the taproom and it turns out that he's the famous Peter Calvert who owns Chez Marcel in Brook Street. You could have knocked me down with a feather.'

Flora nodded. She could guess at what was coming but she did not trust herself to speak.

'Anyway, he had a simple meal,' Coralie continued cheerfully. 'Although Ted was nervous when it came to feeding someone who is a brilliant chef in his own right. Well, the conversation somehow turned to the accident on the river and Mr Calvert told us that he had lost his son, having placed the baby in a wooden crate while he tried to save his wife.'

'He acknowledged Moses as his son?'

'Not exactly. He said he had been searching for his child for years and had only recently heard of a boy who was found in the river. Ted told him how Moses had been floating close to the shore and how we had tried to find his family, but without success.'

'He didn't mention he had a daughter, too.'

Coralie's eyes widened in surprise. 'No, dear. I'm afraid not. Do you think he might be your papa, too?'

'I'm sure of it, Coralie. And Moses is my brother. Oddly enough I wasn't too surprised when I found out. I've always been fond of him and now I know why. What happened when Mr Calvert met Moses?'

'Mr Calvert spoke to Moses for quite a long time and they seemed to get on really well, which surprised us. You know how difficult Moses finds things, but it was obvious that they had something in common. Ted and I could see the likeness between them.'

'So Moses went off quite happily with Mr Calvert.'

'Exactly. That was the biggest surprise of all. But it's only for a few days. If Moses doesn't settle well, he will come back to us. We made it clear to Mr Calvert that Moses will always have a home here.' Coralie eyed Flora with raised brows. 'You don't seem surprised. Was it you who told him about Moses?'

'Yes, that's really why I came here today,' Flora said with a heavy sigh. 'I've been trying to trace my family ever since Syd Fox told me that they had lied about my mother. It's a long story, but I was given Mr Calvert's name and I went to see him in his expensive restaurant.'

'That must have taken courage, Flora.'

'He didn't seem inclined to believe that I could

be his long-lost daughter because I had no proof,
thanks to Syd and Gert selling off the only two things
that came with me. I was shocked when he told me
he had lost two children, but then I knew it had to
be Moses.'

'So you discovered you have a brother.'

'That was the only good thing to come from the
interview.'

'And you told Mr Calvert where to find Moses?'

'Yes, I did tell him at the very last minute. He
might not want a daughter but I sensed that his son
was more important to him.'

'I am so sorry, Flora. Being rejected by the man
who is your papa must be even worse than not
knowing.'

'I don't want anything from him, except recognition. That would be enough for me.'

Coralie's eyes flashed with anger. 'He ought to be
proud to have a daughter like you, especially as you
have clearly inherited his culinary talent, and not
only that, but you know how to set everything up
to be attractive and welcoming. Ted and I were very
impressed by the way you handled things here. Mr
Calvert should be ashamed of himself.'

'Well, that's the way it is. I can't force him to
accept me as his daughter. I have no proof, Syd and
Gert Fox saw to that.'

Coralie enveloped her in a hug. 'My dear girl,
if only I could make things right for you I would
do so.'

Close to tears, Flora laid her head on Coralie's shoulder. 'Thank you, I know you would and I'm grateful.'

Coralie released her gently. 'Tell me, does Mr Calvert know where you live now?'

'I can't remember if I told him. Daniel was with me, he would know. Why do you ask?'

'Maybe Mr Calvert will have second thoughts when he has had time to get used to the idea. It must have come as quite a shock.'

'I suppose so.'

'What will you do now, Flora?'

'I'm not sure. I have had to give up the idea of running a business for lack of the necessary funds. I could stay with the Stewarts like a poor relation, or else I will be the housekeeper at Hope's End.'

'You could marry Daniel. He's a good man and he loves you.'

'I know and I love him, but I fear the ambitious side of my nature would come between us. I would feel trapped, and I'm neither meek nor submissive.'

'Then don't give up, girl. You survived the terrible accident that took your ma and so many others. Don't let your pa get away with treating you like this. Show him what you are made of.'

'You are right, Coralie.' Flora felt the fire of ambition burning inside her. She had survived so much and she was not going to give way now. She took a deep breath. 'I am not going to be ignored just because I have no way to prove who I am. I will show my pa that he has a daughter to be reckoned with.'

Coralie kissed her on the cheek. 'I'm so proud of you, Flora. I would be delighted to have a daughter like you.'

Flora rode back to Nine Oaks going over every possible way in which she could prove to her father that she was worthy of his respect, even if he could not love her. By the time she reached home and was changing out of her riding habit she had gone through every possibility in her head, and had come to one conclusion. She had, quite literally, to beat him at his own game. She knew that there was no chance of a woman being hired to do anything at Chez Marcel other than menial tasks, but that was not going to put her off.

Having changed into a plain cotton gown she went in search of Daniel and found him chatting to Jenkins, Sir Arthur's land agent. She waited until they had finished their conversation.

'Can you spare a moment, Dan?'

'Yes, of course. Anything for you, Flora.'

His smile warmed her chilled heart and she responded eagerly. 'I need your help.'

'All right, just tell me what you want me to do.'

She could see Jenkins loitering close by as if intent on listening and she linked her hand in the crook of Daniel's arm. 'Walk with me. I don't want anyone to hear what I am about to say.'

'Go on. This must be something very important.'

Flora related her conversation with Coralie in detail. 'So you see, Dan. I need to prove to Mr Peter Calvert that I am his daughter and I am just as important as his son, even if he doesn't think so.'

'He might be nervous about accepting you at face value, Flora. Have you thought of that? You can't prove anything, as you said.'

'Not by material things but I am going to do it my way. I intend to work as a cleaning woman in the kitchens at Chez Marcel. I need you to take me there first thing in the morning and leave me at the door.'

'What?' Daniel stopped walking to twist her round so that they were face to face. 'That's madness, Flora. What good will that do?'

'I haven't formed a plan, but if I can work in the kitchens for a few days I might be able to find a way to impress him. I am very good at organising and I have wonderful ideas for serving food and making the dining area look even more splendid than it does now. Heaven knows I've visited enough expensive restaurants to know what guests want.'

Daniel nodded. 'All right,' he said slowly. 'I can see that nothing will dissuade you. I'll do as you say, but am I to leave you there to fend for yourself?'

'Yes, most certainly. If I get into difficulties I can always go to South Molton Street. There are a few servants there keeping the house ready for Sir Arthur and Lady Stewart should they decide to return to

London. I will be quite safe, Dan. I have to do this. You do understand, don't you?'

'I know you so well, Flora. If I tried to keep you safe by my side it would be like caging a tiger.'

Flora laughed. 'I am not so fierce, surely?'

He kissed her gently on the lips. 'Not as long as you get your own way. But I do understand and I just want you to be happy. I know you won't rest until you've proved yourself to your pa. You've survived everything that fate has thrown at you so far. I've no doubt you can make Mr Calvert see sense.'

'Thank you, Dan.' Flora wrapped her arms around his neck and reached up to kiss him. 'That means more to me than anything. And you will take care of Bella for me if I'm not back by the time she returns from her honeymoon?'

'I can't promise anything but I'll do my best. Although, you know Bella, if she discovers what you are doing she will make Freddie purchase Chez Marcel so that you own it.'

'I'm not sure Mr Calvert would agree to that,' Flora said, giggling. 'I think it would be a battle of the giants and probably my pa would win.'

'I wouldn't bet on it.' Daniel shook his head. 'I think Freddie is made of sterner stuff than anyone gives him credit for. Anyway, I'm not happy about this, Flora, but I will do as you ask.'

First thing next day, Flora made Daniel drop her off a good distance from the restaurant and she set off on foot, looking for the staff entrance in a service alley at the back of the buildings. She was wearing her oldest clothes, covered with a large pinafore she had taken from the kitchen laundry basket at Nine Oaks. She had tucked her hair into a mobcap, taking care to hide every giveaway auburn curl, and for good measure she had reddened her pale hands with rouge paste that Mary kept for polishing Lady Stewart's jewellery. The paste had washed off but the stain was quite convincing, not that Flora had actually scrubbed any floors but she was prepared to do anything to get across the threshold of Chez Marcel.

It was still very early in the morning and the servants in the large houses were busy polishing door furniture and generally setting everything up for the coming day. Cleaning women trudged along the pavements, their booted feet sounding like a marching army. Flora joined in at the end of the line and only stopped when she reached the backyard of the restaurant. The gate was unlocked as a potman hefted crates of wine and ales into the storehouse. His gaze flickered over Flora but nothing registered and he turned away. So far so good. Flora was encouraged by this lack of interest and she crossed the yard to enter the building. To her surprise it was very quiet with only one woman bustling about with a mop and bucket, grumbling beneath her breath.

'Where shall I start?' Flora asked casually.

'Who are you? You ain't one of the usual.'

'She's sick. I come in her place.'

'I hope you work harder than what she did. Lazy cow.' The grumpy woman pointed to a bucket and a scrubbing brush. 'You can do the kitchen floor. It's a hands and knees job. I've got the miseries in me back, so I'll mop the dining area.'

'Don't you have to polish the floor?'

'Nah! I get the mess up and then I heat a tin of lavender polish over a candle. Works a treat. Smells like I've done it proper. I'm Meg. What's your name?'

Flora was about to tell her but she stopped herself in time. 'F-Fanny.'

'My eldest boy stammers.' Meg wandered off with her mop and bucket, leaving Flora to scrub the red tiled floor in the kitchen. The night staff had swept up the rubbish that had accumulated but they had not been very thorough and Flora had to sweep the floor before she could even begin. The work surfaces were long wooden benches and these looked clean enough, but the two large black ranges were in definite need of attention. However, Flora had been given the task of scrubbing the tiles and she filled a bucket from one of the hot water tanks. She hitched her skirt up and went down on her hands and knees working with a will. She was not going to allow this menial work to beat her, hard though it was. She scrubbed, rinsed and dried the wet tiles until the entire floor shone in the early morning sunlight as it filtered through the tall windows.

'Don't work too hard, duck,' Meg said tersely.

417

'You'll show the rest of us up.'

Flora scrambled to her feet. Her back and knees were on fire and her hands were genuinely reddened now. 'Isn't it what we get paid for?'

Meg uttered a croak of laughter. 'You won't last long, Fanny. I can tell you're new to this sort of work. Take a tip from me, love. Do just enough to get by and no more. You won't get paid no more for killing yourself. They'll just walk all over you and hire the next muggins to do the work. Anyway, I'm off. See you tomorrow.' Meg sashayed past Flora and dumped her mop and bucket in the scullery. The back door opened and slammed shut, leaving Flora on her own in the kitchen. She emptied her bucket as well as Meg's and left the mop and scrubbing brushes outside to dry in the sun. Returning to the kitchen she found a pile of dirty plates that had been left in the sink. Unable to leave them alone she made sure they were washed, dried and replaced in the cupboard before turning her attention to the dining room.

Sure enough the scent of lavender polish filled the air but the floor was dull and patchy. Although she had never polished a wooden floor in her life, Flora had seen the maids at Nine Oaks working and she simply could not rest until she had used the entire tin and polished all the boards that were visible until they gleamed. She was standing back admiring her work when the front door opened and Peter Calvert strode into the dining area.

He came to a halt, sniffed the air and gazed down at the floor, frowning. 'You should be gone by now,' he said slowly. 'You're new, aren't you?'

Flora kept her head bent and her eyes lowered. 'Started today, sir.'

Calvert walked past her on his way to the kitchen. Flora followed him, hoping he was not going to study her as carefully as he was checking her work.

'You've done well. What's your name? I'll ask the cleaning company for you again.'

'It's Fanny, sir. I come as a favour to Meg. I don't work for the cleaning company.'

'You're hired,' Calvert said firmly. 'I need someone reliable and thorough. Lawson is my manager, he usually gets in early and he'll be here soon. Give your details to him and he'll put you on the payroll. He will assign you your tasks and you do everything he says. I'll be in my office if anyone needs me.' He walked away without looking at her.

Flora heaved a sigh of relief but almost immediately staff began to arrive. They walked past her as if she were merely a piece of furniture and soon the kitchen was a hive of activity with the head chef shouting orders. In the dining room the maître d' was bellowing at the waiters as they set up for the lunchtime session. Flora decided to clean and polish the glassed front door and the brass handles. She was just finishing when a man in a smart suit stepped out of a hansom cab and walked up to the entrance. She opened the door and held it.

He came to a halt, staring at her. 'I don't know you.'

'I'm Fanny Jones, sir. Mr Calvert took me on this morning.'

'I'm Mr Lawson the restaurant manager. We'll see about that.' He hesitated, eyeing the sparkling glass and the shiny handle. 'Impressive. Who told you to do that?'

'No one, sir. I just saw it needed doing.'

He nodded. 'Interesting. I need to speak to Mr Calvert, but don't go yet. I can find more work for you. We've been plagued by poor cleaners. You seem to be the exception.'

Flora picked up her dusters and polish and took them through to the scullery. Every bone in her body ached and her hands were so sore she could hardly make a fist, but she felt a glow of satisfaction at a job well done. However, she would never take the servants for granted again. They were more than worthy of respect.

'You look like you could do with a cup of tea, love.' One of the chefs winked at her. 'I've just made a pot. Come and join us. We don't often get the company of a pretty girl. What's your name?'

'It's Fanny, what's yours?'

'I'm Ben. One day I'll be head chef.' He grinned. 'Come and meet the others.'

Flora was drinking tea with the kitchen staff when Mr Lawson entered the kitchen and they all scattered, picking up their utensils as they peeled, chopped and sliced vegetables, poultry and cuts of beef.

'Come with me, Jones.'

Flora almost forgot that she had given him a false name and she hesitated for a second but then she remembered and she followed him out of the kitchen and down a corridor leading to a small office at the back of the building.

'I take it you can read and write, Jones?'

'Yes, sir.'

He passed her a sheet of paper and a pencil. 'Write your name and address.'

Flora thought quickly. She had to put something and she wrote down her assumed name and the address in South Molton Street. She had to sleep somewhere and she did not have enough money to pay for lodgings.

Lawson took it from her and raised his winged eyebrows. 'This is a very grand address for a cleaning woman.'

'I used to work there, sir. The housekeeper, Mrs Fellowes, is allowing me to sleep in the servants' quarters until I can find somewhere of me own.'

'Very kind of her, I'm sure. She must have valued your services, Jones.'

'Yes, sir.'

'That's all, Jones. You've done well this morning. Go home now and return at four o'clock this afternoon. You will clean the dining room ready for this evening.'

'Yes, sir.' Flora realised that she was limping as she left the restaurant and headed in the direction of South Molton Street. She knew she would have to return later, but every muscle and sinew in her body cried out for rest. Her next problem would be to convince the few staff left in the town house that she was simply playing a part and had not taken leave of her senses. Although it was not going to be easy. Her clothes smelled of lye soap and beeswax mixed with turpentine plus a hint of lavender, and her apron was filthy. She scuttled along the street praying that she would not meet anyone who might recognise her. When she reached the house she went round to the servants' entrance and stepped inside, hoping to get to her room before anyone saw her, but unfortunately Cook was standing in the kitchen doorway talking to Mrs Fellowes. They stared at her as if dumbstruck.

Mrs Fellowes was the first to speak. 'Miss Flora, is it really you?'

'What happened to you, miss?' Cook gazed at her in horror. 'You look like you've been run over by an omnibus.'

Flora felt a bubble of hysterical laughter rising in her throat but she managed to control herself. 'I would like a bath, please. I'll explain later.'

'Of course, Miss Flora.' Mrs Fellowes shooed Cook back into the kitchen. 'I'll send hot water to your room.'

'Thank you, Mrs Fellowes.'

'If you don't mind me asking, does the master know you are staying here, miss?'

Flora knew better than to lie. Mrs Fellowes had been a part of her life for as long as she could remember and would instantly spot a lie.

'To be honest, Mrs Fellowes, no one knows I am here. It's only for a few days and then I'll return to Nine Oaks or Hope's End, depending on when Miss Arabella returns home.'

Mrs Fellowes pursed her lips. 'You mean Lady Dorrington, miss. I take it that you have your reasons for whatever it is that you are doing.'

'Yes, you're right, and you know that I would never do anything to compromise the family name. You won't say anything at home, will you?'

'As far as I'm concerned you are invisible, Miss Flora.'

'And Cook?'

'She is the soul of discretion when she needs to be. I'll have hot water sent to your room, Miss Flora.' Mrs Fellowes walked away, heading for the green baize door.

Flora ascended the stairs, painfully and with difficulty. She would have to rest and return to Chez Marcel, but it would take every ounce of strength she possessed. All she wanted to do now was to soak in a hot bath.

Rested and with renewed energy, Flora returned to Chez Marcel on the dot of four o'clock. Lawson was in his office and he glanced at the clock on the mantelshelf as Flora entered the room.

'Punctual. That is good.'

'What do you want me to do, sir?'

'Start in the dining area and then go on to the kitchen. You have just under two hours to make the whole place ready for the evening service. The chef and his underlings will arrive at six o'clock and you should be gone by then.'

'Yes, sir. I understand.'

'You will be here by six o'clock tomorrow morning.' Lawson dismissed her with a flick of his fingers.

'Yes, sir,' Flora murmured as she left the office and headed for the kitchen. Lawson, like his employer, had not once looked her in the face. She was beginning to feel like a ghost or an inanimate object, and she wondered if all servants felt this way. It was not a pleasant thought, but she had work to do and she intended to do it well, leaving no room for anyone to complain.

Flora made a start in the dining room where all the chairs had been upended and left on the tables, which enabled her to clean the floor quickly and efficiently. The kitchen was next and that was more of a challenge but Flora knew exactly how it should be when the head chef arrived and she worked to her own high standard. She had finished earlier than Mr Lawson had predicted and she returned to the dining room where she rearranged the chairs, setting them neatly around the tables. She found a pile of newly laundered white cloths, which she laid on the

424

tables, smoothing out the creases with her hands. She stood back and admired her handiwork, but she was still not satisfied. There was a large and badly arranged display of hothouse roses, lilies and ferns, which did nothing for the ambience and she could not resist the temptation to interfere. She found small glass vases in a store cupboard and filled them with water, adding a couple of well-chosen rosebuds, plus a spring of fern. She placed them in the centre of each table next to the silver candlesticks, which she polished with a soft cloth until they shone. She was so busy with her task that she did not hear the kitchen door open and Ben, the chef who had spoken to her earlier that day, stood in the doorway, open-mouthed.

'What are you doing, girl?'

Flora stood back with a guilty start. 'I'm sorry. I just thought the tables needed something extra.'

'You're right, Fanny. The tables look splendid,' Ben said, grinning. 'But I'm not sure that the maître d' will appreciate your help.'

'Should I take them out?' Flora stared at him in dismay. 'I didn't mean to interfere.'

Ben laughed. 'I think you did, though. You felt you could do better, and you're right. Anyway, you've done a good job in the kitchen and I need to start work. Chef will be here soon so you'd better get going or he'll have you peeling spuds and carrots.'

It was so good to see a friendly face that Flora could have hugged him, but she was also worried.

'I hope I didn't go too far. The tables just looked so plain, like hospital beds.'

'You are funny, girl.' Ben cocked his head on one side. 'Best scarper. Go out the front way, I'll lock the door after you.'

# Chapter Twenty-Three

When Flora arrived back at the house in South Molton Street she used the servants' entrance as before. She was about to walk past the kitchen when Cook called out to her.

'Yes, Cook. What is it?'

'Have you eaten anything today, Miss Flora?'

Flora thought for a moment. She had been surrounded by food in the restaurant kitchen but she had neither eaten nor drunk since the cup of tea with the cooks that morning. She shook her head.

'I thought as much. You were the same as a little girl. If you were busy doing something you always forgot to eat. Miss Arabella had to tempt you with my strawberry jam tarts.'

Flora was suddenly very hungry. 'I don't suppose you have any in the larder, do you?'

Cook beamed at her. 'As it happens I made some today. Now if you would like to go to the dining room, I'll bring you some supper and a couple of jam tarts, too.'

Flora glanced down at her dishevelled and grubby appearance. 'I'm not exactly dressed for the dining room, Cook. May I eat in the kitchen? I am really exhausted and I need to go to bed very early.'

'Come and sit down, dear. It's just me and the stupid scullery maid. She won't repeat anything she hears, and you can tell me what mischief you are up to. You could never hide anything from me even when you were growing up.'

Flora stepped into the kitchen and was enveloped in delicious aromas. She sat at the table like a dutiful child and Cook served up a large slice of chicken pie and roast potatoes, followed by strawberry jam tarts and a cup of tea.

Cook leaned her elbows on the table. 'Now, Miss Flora. I want the truth. What on earth is going on?'

Flora laughed. 'Did Mrs Fellowes put you up to this?'

'She might have said something to that effect before she left for Nine Oaks this afternoon. You know we all love you like you was one of our own, so don't be shy of telling me the truth. Rose and I were here when Sir Arthur brought you home, you poor mite. Skinny you was and bruised, too. You was like a scared rabbit and we all took to you that instant.'

Flora ate hungrily, talking in between mouthfuls

while Cook listened patiently. When she had eaten the last crumb of jam tart, Flora sipped her tea. 'That was a wonderful meal. I haven't enjoyed anything so much for an age.'

'I'd like to try the food at Mr Calvert's restaurant,' Cook said wistfully. 'I know I'm good, but I've heard that his food is wonderful.'

'If I can convince him that I really am his daughter I will personally invite you to Chez Marcel for the banquet of your life. That is if I am not given the sack tomorrow for interfering in the restaurant, but the flowers did look so pretty on the tables.'

Cook puffed out her cheeks. 'If you get trouble from that Mr Lawson, just say the word and I will come to Brook Street and give him a piece of my mind.'

'I'll remember that,' Flora said, trying not to laugh. 'Thank you for everything, Cook, but I really have to go to bed now. I need to be at the restaurant at six o'clock in the morning.'

'Lady Stewart would have a fit if she knew what you were doing.'

'Yes, but I hope she won't find out,' Flora said hastily. 'It's our secret, Cook. I know I can trust you.' She left the kitchen and made her way wearily to her room.

Next morning Flora was at work on time and she started as before in the kitchen. When she was satisfied that she had done her best she moved on to the dining room and was pleased to find that the vases of rosebuds had been spared and were lined up neatly on a side table. She had half expected to find them emptied and put back in the cupboard and she took it as a good sign, however, when the front door opened and Lawson entered, she was suddenly nervous. He came to a halt and peeled off his gloves, placing them in his top hat.

'So, you decided to take matters into your own hands, Jones.'

'Do you mean the flowers, sir?'

'Of course I mean the flowers. You had no right to interfere in the organisation of the dining room. That is my job.'

'Yes, sir. I apologise. I just thought it looked a bit bare.'

'You are paid to sweep up and scrub floors, Jones. However, as it happens, the diners thought the flowers were a delightful touch, and Mr Calvert also approved. But do anything without my consent in future and you will find yourself looking for another position.'

'Yes, sir.' Flora tried not to sound too pleased. 'If you want my opinion, Mr Lawson . . .'

'I don't,' he said sharply. 'Now get on with your work. When you've finished in here, Mr Calvert wants his office cleaned. He won't be in today as he's spending time with his son. You can do mine as well, but don't touch anything on either of our desks.'

*

Flora worked tirelessly, ignoring the aches and pains she was experiencing, as well as sore hands and feet. However, she did everything that was asked of her and found time to enjoy a cup of tea and a chat with Ben and the other sous chefs in the kitchen. All thoughts of home went out of her mind as she concentrated on her work, but when she was walking back to South Molton Street she could not help but wonder if Bella and Freddie had returned, and if they had what must they be thinking of her? Cook had a meal waiting and seemed intent on spoiling her, which made a pleasant change after the rigorous routine at the restaurant. After Flora had eaten she went to her room to rest until she had to return to Brook Street later that afternoon. However, she could not settle as she tried to think of more ways in which to impress Peter Calvert. It seemed that he had liked the flowers on the tables, which was a very small thing, but Flora was not prepared to spend the rest of her life attempting to gain her father's recognition and good opinion. If, she decided, she had not managed to convince him in the next few days, she would return to Hope's End and take up the position of housekeeper. She had hoped she might see Moses but it seemed that Mr Calvert was keeping him away from the restaurant. She could only hope that Moses was not pining for the Tullivers, and that their father had managed to see what a sweet-natured and kind individual Moses was. He might be different from most boys of his age, but in Flora's mind that made him special and even more loveable. If Mr Calvert had been less than patient with Moses he would have her to deal with. It was all very worrying.

After a while, she gave up trying to rest and set off back to the restaurant. It was only a short walk and she dawdled on the way, not wanting to arrive before the luncheon guests had left. She was almost there when she spotted a young man sitting on the pavement amidst a pile of canvases, some of which were propped up against the railings of a town house. The landscapes were so vivid and fresh that she had to stop and admire them.

'Are these your work?' Flora asked eagerly.

'Yes. D'you want to buy one? I could let you have one cheap. Business has been bad lately.'

'But they are really beautiful. May I?' Flora pointed to the pile on the pavement next to him. 'What's your name?'

'Adam Brown. A good name for a painter, except that it doesn't help to sell my work.'

Flora examined each one in turn. 'They really are very good. I can't imagine why people aren't buying them. I would,' she added quickly. 'But I haven't any money.'

Adam peered at her from beneath the brim of his felt hat. 'You sound like a rich person but you dress like a skivvy.'

'I can assure you that I am not a rich person, but I know someone who is very wealthy and he might be interested in buying your paintings, or at least putting them on the walls in his restaurant with a price on them. I am sure some of the clientele would want to purchase them.'

'Sounds unlikely, miss. What's your name?'

'I'm Fanny Jones,' Flora said hastily. 'I'm just a cleaning woman at Chez Marcel.'

Adam curled his lip. 'And you think the owner would take notice of a charwoman?'

Flora could see that he was not going to believe her unless she told him the truth, but she was genuinely impressed with his work, and they would certainly brighten up the dining room, which at present she thought too dark and oppressive for comfort.

'All right, Adam Brown. I'll tell you the truth, but you must promise to keep it a secret.'

His blue eyes sparkled with sudden interest and he scrambled to his feet. 'All right, Fanny. I promise.'

'That isn't my real name. I am Flora Lee, although I think I am really Flora Calvert. I and my brother were rescued from the river after a terrible accident when hundreds lost their lives. Mr Calvert has accepted my brother as his son, but he doesn't believe that I am his daughter and I'm having difficulty in proving it, mainly because I was lucky enough to be taken in and brought up to be a lady. Or maybe I should say unlucky because it hasn't done me much good so far.'

'I thought you sounded like a toff.'

'Never mind that now. If I can impress Mr Calvert, he might take me seriously. You can help by letting me put your paintings up in the restaurant. It might do you some good, too.'

Adam shrugged. 'I think you are mad, love. But I've got nothing to lose. I'm behind with my rent and I haven't eaten properly for days.'

'Come with me, then. I can find you some food while you put your canvases on the walls in the dining room. We have to do it while the restaurant is closed.'

Adam picked up the canvases. 'Lead on, Miss whoever you are.'

When they reached Chez Marcel, Flora held back. 'That's Mr Lawson, the manager. Wait until he's gone and then we'll go in by the back entrance.'

When it was safe to do so, she steered Adam and his paintings to the rear of the building. The kitchen was empty and silence echoed throughout the ground floor. She showed Adam through to the dining room and he walked round, eyeing the wall space critically.

'What do you think?' Flora asked eagerly. 'Would they show up to their best advantage in here?'

Adam nodded. 'If you're certain that Mr Calvert won't rip them down and put them out for the dust collectors.'

'He's too clever to do that,' Flora said emphatically. 'You put them up and I'll find you something to eat before I start work. We only have an hour so there's no time to waste.'

Flora started in the dining room, paying extra attention to refilling the vases with fresh flowers that Lawson purchased daily from the child flower sellers who plied their trade in the more affluent streets. In the past arrangements had been left to the most junior of the kitchen staff and these consisted of ramming the blooms in a large vase filled with water. Flora considered it an insult to the flowers and she took pleasure in rescuing them and showing them off individually. When she was satisfied with the dining room, she went on to make the kitchen ready for the evening service. She had just finished mopping the floor when Adam strolled into the kitchen.

'I think they look good, even if I say so myself,' he said proudly. 'Come and look.'

Flora went to inspect his efforts and she nodded in agreement. 'They look splendid. A touch of colour is exactly what this area needed.' She turned to Adam, smiling. 'I've made you some sandwiches, but you'll have to eat them quickly before Ben and the other sous chefs arrive.'

'I'm starving. Thank you, Flora.'

Flora watched him eat in silence. She kept glancing at the wall clock to make sure they did not clash with the kitchen staff.

'That was wonderful,' Adam said, having swallowed the last mouthful of bread and cheese. 'Just one thing, though. How will I know if any of my paintings have been sold? I can't afford to leave them here indefinitely, and if I don't pay my rent at the end of the week I will be living on the street, again.'

'Come here tomorrow afternoon at half past four. I'll find out in the morning if Mr Calvert accepts what we've done. I have as much to lose as you, or perhaps more. All I want to do is to impress my father. I just want him to acknowledge me.'

'Is that all? Don't you want him to look after you, as a father should?'

'No, but I would like to be a part of Chez Marcel, or if I could learn from him then one day I would like to run my own restaurant.'

Adam shook his head. 'I've never met a woman like you, Flora Lee. If I had you behind me I think I could make a fortune as an artist.'

'Let's wait until tomorrow, Adam. If my plan works it will help both of us. If it fails you are no worse off and you can take your paintings back.'

'I'll settle for another plate of sandwiches if that happens. They were delicious, Flora. You have a magic touch.'

'With sandwiches?'

'Yes, definitely. Maybe you should cook something for your pa. If that doesn't convince him that you're his daughter, nothing will.'

Flora laughed, but his words struck home. She had learned a great deal in the short time she had spent with the Tullivers, and she had eaten in some of the finest restaurants in London. If she could re-create one of Peter Calvert's dishes perhaps that would be enough to convince him.

'You could be right, Adam. But we'd best be gone. The kitchen staff will be here soon, and I prefer not to be here when Mr Lawson arrives. We need to give him time to get used to the new art on the dining room walls.'

'What if he tears them down and throws my paintings out on the street?' Adam fingered his collar nervously. 'They are my livelihood, Fanny. Not only that, they are part of me.'

Flora hustled him out of the back door. 'Mr Lawson won't do that. He's a mean man but he's far from stupid. Anyone can see that your work is remarkable. I am sure the diners will agree with me.' She waited until they were a safe distance from the restaurant before stopping and taking Adam aside. 'Where can I contact you if Mr Calvert insists on taking the paintings down?'

'I rent a room in the basement of an old house near Paddington station, but I'll come round tomorrow afternoon when you are here on your own.'

Flora nodded. 'All right. Let's hope I have some good news for you.'

Next day, Flora started work even earlier than usual. She finished the kitchen and dining room before starting on Mr Calvert's office. She was dusting his desk when the door opened and Calvert himself strode into the room. Flora's hand flew automatically to her head as she attempted to tuck her hair out of sight but she was too late.

'So it is you. I had my suspicions, especially when the vases of flowers appeared on the tables, and last evening the walls were hung with paintings. I take it that was your idea, too, Miss Lee.'

Flora clutched the duster in both hands as if it were a lifeline for a drowning person. She faced him boldly. 'Yes, I'm guilty. The paintings, which I think are beautiful, came about by a chance meeting with an artist who is desperate to earn his rent money.'

'So why the elaborate pose of pretending to be a charwoman? Did you plan to steal from me or to sell my culinary secrets to another chef?'

Flora stared at him in horror. 'Such things never crossed my mind. I wanted you to give me a fair chance. I think you must be my father, but I can't prove it. Although perhaps I was better off not knowing.'

'You don't seem to have a very good opinion of me.'

'What do you expect? You dismissed my story without giving me a chance, and yet you accept Moses as your son.'

'His name is Oliver, but he only answers to Moses.' Calvert paused, eyeing her warily. 'He's not happy with me, despite all I've done for him. He wants to return to the Tullivers.'

'You agreed to take him back to them if this

happened. He's not like other boys of his age. You need to know how to treat him.'

'You were close to him at the inn?'

'Yes, I'm very fond of him, and even more so now I know we're brother and sister.'

'All right. Perhaps I should have believed your story, but you must admit it sounded very unlikely.'

'Yes, I do. That's why I came to work for you.'

'Perhaps you could persuade Oliver to stay with me. He might settle down if he sees a familiar face, otherwise I'm afraid I will have to lose him for the second time.'

'That might be better for everyone,' Flora said thoughtfully. 'The Tullivers raised him from a baby and he's like a son to them.'

'Nevertheless I would like you to try. He is my flesh and blood, after all.'

'If you believe that Moses is your son, why did you doubt me?'

'He looks like me, to put it simply. Others have tried to convince me that they were my offspring and that's made me suspect everyone.'

'I'll do it for Moses.' Flora picked up her cleaning materials. 'I'll put these away and then I'm ready. You will have to explain to Mr Lawson, although now you know who I am there is little point continuing this charade.'

A wry smile curved Calvert's lips. 'It's a pity to lose you, Fanny Jones. You are the best cleaner we've ever had.'

Flora laughed. 'I'll take that as a compliment, coming from you, sir.'

'I see some of myself in you, Flora.'

'Does that mean you think I am your lost daughter?'

'I admire your courage and your persistence. My carriage is waiting outside. Leave those things. Lawson will see to them when he's found a replacement for you.'

Flora took off her mobcap and tucked it in her pocket as she followed him out of the office and through the dining room to the street door.

'What about Adam's paintings? He's desperate to make his rent money.'

'It's not something I approve of, but two of them were bought by one of my best customers, and, according to Lawson, they attracted a lot of favourable attention. I will see this young man at some point.'

'He'll be here this afternoon expecting to see me, but perhaps Mr Lawson could look after him?'

'I'll deal with it.' Calvert opened the restaurant door. 'My carriage is waiting. You'd better come with me, Flora.'

The carriage drew up outside a terrace town house in Half Moon Street. A footman opened the door and Calvert ushered Flora inside.

'Is Master Oliver in his room?' Calvert demanded urgently.

'Yes, sir. We had to lock the door to stop him from harming himself.'

Flora stared at him in horror. 'What have you done to Moses?'

'He's been extremely well treated but he has these sudden temper tantrums when he doesn't get his own way. I want you to talk to him, Flora. Calm him down, please.'

'Show me to his room. I don't know what you've done to him but to my knowledge he's never been violent.'

Calvert thrust his top hat and gloves into the footman's hands. 'Follow me, please.' He strode off, taking the stairs two at a time, and Flora followed him. She could hear the sound of Moses beating his fist on the bedroom door before they had reached the second floor.

'Just unlock it and let me in to talk to him,' Flora said firmly.

'He might lash out at you.'

'No, he won't. Just open the door, please.' Flora stood back while Calvert turned the key in the lock.

'Oliver, you have a visitor.' Calvert stood back to allow Flora to open the door.

She went inside and found Moses curled up on the floor with tears running down his cheeks. She went down on her knees beside him.

'Moses, my dear. It's me, Flora.' She held him close until he became calmer. 'That's better. Can you stand up?'

Moses wiped his eyes on his sleeve. 'I want to go home, Flora.'

She helped him to his feet. 'And you shall. Mr Calvert hoped you would be happy here, but I can see that you are very sad.'

'Very sad,' Moses said, nodding vehemently. 'I want to go home and see Ted and Coralie.'

Flora turned to Calvert. 'You can't break your promise.'

'I've done everything I could to make him comfortable. I've taken time to be with him, but it isn't enough.'

'I think we should take him back to the inn straight away. He's calm now.' Flora kissed Moses on the cheek. 'You will be good now, won't you?'

Moses sniffed and nodded. 'Want to go home.'

'I'll come with you,' Calvert said firmly. 'I need to speak to Tulliver. It's obvious that the boy won't settle here.'

Flora took Moses by the hand. 'Come with me, Moses. We're going to the inn straight away.' She led him unprotesting downstairs to the waiting carriage.

Calvert sat opposite them, his expression one of bewilderment and sadness. 'I don't understand it, Flora. I gave him everything he asked for and I took him to all the attractions, but he still wasn't happy.'

'He doesn't know you,' Flora said gently as Moses leaned his head against her and closed his eyes.

'Maybe if you visit the inn regularly and take him out you could get to know each other properly.'

'You are so much like your mother, Flora,' Calvert said reluctantly. 'I saw it from the start but it was too painful to admit that you reminded me of Marianne. The red hair and sea-green eyes were so like hers that it shocked me to the core. I shut out the image because to think of losing her was unbearable. I'm sorry, Flora.'

'You really think I'm like my mother?'

'You are the image of her in every way. I could hardly believe it when I saw you standing behind my desk this morning, I thought for a moment that I had slipped back into the past.'

'But you still didn't admit that I am your daughter.'

'I developed a hard shell around my heart after the accident. I devoted myself to making my name as a chef and restauranteur. It was easier for me to accept Moses as my son because he doesn't present a challenge to my authority. You did from the start.'

'Perhaps I am more like you than you care to admit.' Flora eyed him warily. She was still coming to terms with the sudden about-face from the man she had been working so hard to convince of her identity. The fact that he knew all the time but refused to admit it, even to himself, was even more astonishing.

'Can you forgive me for not believing you?'

'I suppose it did seem like a tall story, although it's not something that anyone would be likely to make up. Perhaps we can start again, but let's get Moses settled first.'

'Most certainly. I will speak honestly to Tulliver and we'll come to a mutual agreement. Maybe one day Moses will come to look at me in a different light.'

'I'm sure he will. He is a very loving boy, just give him time.'

'And you, Flora. What can I do to make it up to you?'

'You can keep Adam's paintings on the walls of Chez Marcel, and make sure he gets paid for his work.'

'Of course. It was clever of you to think of displaying them in such a way, but do you need money? Would you like to come and live with me in Half Moon Street?' Calvert gave her a searching look. 'You were obviously brought up to be a lady and I wouldn't expect you to work.'

Flora laughed. 'There is so much you don't know about me.'

'And I want to learn. I was arrogant and self-centred before. I know now I made a terrible mistake and I want to make it right. Just tell me what you really want and I will do my best to make it happen. I have sixteen years of lost fatherhood to make up for and I will be more than happy to grant your wishes.'

'Well, one thing you can do for me is to invite me and Cook from South Molton Street to dine at

Chez Marcel tomorrow evening. Cook has been kind to me ever since I can remember and she's been looking after me while I've been working for you. It's her desire to dine in your restaurant.'

'Now that is something I can do. Tomorrow evening you and Cook will dine like royalty, and that is just the beginning. I will give you anything in my power to make up for the lost years.'

'It will do for now, Pa.' Flora shifted to a more comfortable position with Moses sound asleep at her side. 'I must tell you that I want more than being just the daughter of a rich and famous man. I didn't know why I took so easily to working at the inn, but now I know. I want to follow in your footsteps and open a restaurant of my own, preferably in the country.'

Calvert stared at her in amazement. 'What gave you that idea? It's unheard of.'

Flora laughed. 'Perhaps that is why it appeals to me. Are you saying it can't be done?'

'No, but it wouldn't be easy and it would take a huge investment. Tell me your ideas, Flora.'

# Chapter Twenty-Four

Moses was overjoyed to be back with the Tullivers, and they were equally happy to have him restored to them. Calvert had promised to visit regularly and take time to get to know his son. However, he acknowledged, with obvious reluctance, that Coralie and Ted were the boy's surrogate parents, although Flora could see that this was hard for him. Peter Calvert did have a heart after all and leaving his son with the Tullivers was obviously painful for him.

That evening Calvert entertained Cook and Flora royally in his restaurant. Cook was somewhat over-awed but delighted to be an honoured guest and the evening was a huge success. Flora knew that Cook would talk about it for years to come and that Mrs Fellowes would be extremely envious. Maybe a similar gesture for the Stewarts' kindly housekeeper would not go amiss at a future date. Flora would have liked to spend more time with her father but she knew she must return to Nine Oaks and Daniel. She realised now how much she missed him. If there was one thing she had learned from posing as a simple charwoman, it was that fame and fortune were not what she had been seeking. She had found her father but she was not going to lose the one person who had loved her since she was a child. She had another life and she was eager to return to the place and people she cared for most. Her relationship with her father would take time to develop and become meaningful, but at the moment she admired and respected him, and he in turn seemed prepared to work hard and be patient in order to earn her affection. He insisted on taking Flora back to Nine Oaks, as he was determined to meet Sir Arthur and Lady Stewart and thank them for everything they had done for his daughter. Flora was delighted but slightly dazed by the sudden turn of events. She sent a telegram advising the Stewarts of her return.

They arrived at Nine Oaks in the early afternoon. As the carriage drew to a halt in front of the main entrance the door opened and Bella ran down the steps to fling her arms around Flora as she alighted.

'I was so disappointed to find you weren't here or at Hope's End. We returned three days ago but it wasn't the same without you.'

'It's good to see you, too. You look wonderful.'

'It's happiness, Flora. Being married to Freddie is the most wonderful thing that ever happened to me.'

Bella glanced at Calvert and a frown puckered her smooth brow. 'I seem to recognise you, sir. You are the owner of Chez Marcel, my favourite restaurant.'

Calvert bowed over her hand. 'How kind of you to say so, Lady Dorrington. Flora has told me all about you.'

'You're right, of course,' Flora said hastily. 'But may I introduce you to my father, Peter Calvert. We've only just come to terms with the truth ourselves.'

'How do you do, Mr Calvert,' Bella said, smiling. 'Daniel told me why he took you to London, Flora. No doubt he'll be waiting to hear your good news.'

'I will find him later. I want to introduce my pa to your parents, Bella. Are they at home?'

'They're waiting for you in the drawing room.' Bella turned to Calvert with an engaging smile. 'My husband will be here later. He's at Hope's End at the moment, but he's looking forward to meeting you at dinner. You aren't rushing back to London, are you?'

'That would be my pleasure. I thought I would stay for a couple of days, but I can't impose upon your parents' hospitality. Is there a local inn where I could book a room?'

'You might like to have a room at Hope's End, Pa,' Flora said cautiously. 'I would like you to see how much I've done to it in a very short time.' She glanced at Bella. 'Unless you and Freddie are staying there?'

'No, we are stopping here for a few days. Mama and

448

Papa were adamant that they wanted to spend as much time with us as possible before we go to Devonshire. I have yet to see Freddie's ancestral home and to be honest I'm a little nervous.' Bella mounted the steps. 'Do come inside, Mr Calvert.'

Flora slipped her hand in the crook of her father's arm. 'Come along, Pa. I've dreamed of this moment and now it's here I can hardly believe it.' She gave James a bright smile as they walked past him and entered the great hall. Flora could see that her father was impressed and she puffed out her chest. She loved Nine Oaks and it was like showing off a prize possession, even though it would never be hers to own. Bella led the way to the drawing room where Sir Arthur and Lady Stewart were waiting.

Sir Arthur rose to his feet. 'Welcome to Nine Oaks, Mr Calvert. We are delighted to know that Flora has found her own family at last.' He shook Calvert's hand vigorously.

'Yes, indeed,' Constance added graciously. 'Won't you take a seat, sir? I've sent for a tray of tea and cake, but we dine early here in the country. You will stay with us, I hope.'

'Mr Calvert is going to stay at Hope's End,' Bella said firmly. 'I thought that Flora might have some ideas regarding the old house.'

Flora stared at her, frowning. 'I had abandoned that plan, Bella.'

'It must have been while Freddie and I were on our honeymoon. I know it was dear to your heart and it's amazing what you did to the house in such a short time.'

The conversation paused while Ivy brought in a tray of tea and Elsie followed with another of cake and biscuits. They left as silently as they had come.

'You may pour, Bella,' Constance said, smiling tenderly. 'I must get used to having a countess waiting upon my commands, or should I say my requests?'

'Very droll, Mama.' Bella poured the tea and handed round the cups and saucers. 'I think I will enjoy being the hostess in Dorrington Place as well as the house in Piccadilly.'

'What about Hope's End?' Flora asked anxiously. 'Are you going to keep it so that you can stay there when you come home, Bella?'

'I really don't know. It's true that Freddie gave it to me as a wedding present, but it really is up to him what happens to the old place. Do you still wish to try to make it into a business, Flora? I'm sure we could come to some arrangement if you do.'

'Really, girls,' Constance said sharply. 'This is neither the time nor the place to discuss such things. Leave that to the gentlemen. They can talk it over after dinner this evening.'

'You have a beautiful home, Lady Stewart,' Calvert said conversationally. 'And what I saw of the grounds looked superb.'

'I'm sure Flora would take pleasure in showing you round,' Constance said, smiling. 'We are proud of our gardens and the parkland. We have an excellent head gardener, who has also been supervising the restoration of the gardens at Hope's End. But you will see all that later.'

Bella put down her cup and saucer with a clatter. 'I suggest we go there now, while there is still plenty of daylight.' She rose to her feet, holding her hand out to Flora. 'I hope you are not too tired after the journey from town, but I know there is someone at Hope's End who is longing to see you.'

Flora gave her a grateful smile. Bella might be a countess but she was still able to read Flora's thoughts, especially when deep feelings were involved. Flora stood up, acknowledging Constance and Sir Arthur with a nod of her head. 'Thank you for the tea. If you will excuse us now, I will take my father to Hope's End and we will see you at dinner.'

'Of course,' Sir Arthur said cheerfully. 'I look forward to getting to know you better, Calvert. I was thinking of investing in a business similar to yours. Maybe you can give me some tips.'

'I have restaurants in most of the major cities, Sir Arthur. I would be delighted to share my knowledge of the trade with you, sir.' Calvert rose from his seat. 'I can't thank you enough for what you have done for Flora. Until recently I thought I had lost both my children. Flora has told me what she went through before you rescued her from those villains. I am forever in your debt.'

Flora linked arms with him. 'Come along, Pa.

Let me show you what I have done. I hope you'll be justifiably proud of me.'

They arrived at Hope's End just as Freddie was about to leave. He came towards them with a welcoming smile.

'Flora, it's good to see you and your father.' Freddie held out his hand. 'Good afternoon, Calvert. We met once before when I called you out of your kitchen to congratulate you on your cooking, but that was many years ago, before you were famous.'

Calvert shook hands. 'I remember it well, my lord. It was at the start of my career.'

'You can chat about that later,' Bella said impatiently. 'I've come to take you home, Freddie, so we can leave Flora and her papa to settle in and we'll see them at dinner.'

'If you say so, my love.' Freddie kissed her on the cheek. 'But first I must congratulate you on what you've done to the old house, Flora. I don't know how you managed on such a small amount of money, but it's amazing. You must be very proud of her, Calvert.'

'I'm learning more about my daughter every day. I really don't deserve her.'

Bella tugged at Freddie's arm. 'Let us leave them in peace, darling. Mr Calvert wishes to stay for a few days so there will be plenty of time to talk.'

'Excellent, Calvert. I look forward to getting to know you.' Freddie kissed Flora on the cheek. 'There is

someone in the kitchen who is eager to see you, Flora.
He refused to come above stairs, but I'm sure you will
be able to change his mind.'

'Thank you, Freddie. I must say it's good to be
home.'

Freddie was about to answer but Bella guided him
gently towards the front door and Beasley moved
with surprising speed to open it for them.

Flora turned to her father. 'Let's find you a room.
I haven't actually stayed here yet, but I chose one
at the back of the house overlooking the gardens.
But if that's your choice I will happily pick another.'

Calvert smiled. 'I tell you what, Flora. I haven't
completely forgotten what it is to be young and in
love. I suggest you go and find Daniel. I assume that
is the person who is waiting for you in the kitchen.
Make him come upstairs because I want to meet
this young man.'

'But you need me to show you round the house,
Pa.'

'My dear, I think I can find myself a bedroom
without a guide.' Calvert beckoned to Beasley. 'How
do you do? You must be Beasley. Flora has told me
all about you. I'm glad she has a man of such experience to help her here.'

'Thank you, sir.' Beasley's pallid features flushed
pink with pleasure and Calvert slapped him gently
on the back. 'Don't worry about my valise. I can
manage.'

'I'm always happy to serve a true gentleman, sir.'

Beasley picked up the case and trudged up the stair-case, clutching it in one hand as he grabbed the banister rail with the other. Calvert gave Flora a wry smile as he followed Beasley upstairs.

Free at last, Flora headed for the kitchen at the back of the house.

Daniel rose to his feet as she rushed into the room and he swept her off her feet, kissing her until she wriggled free at the sound of a giggle from Mattie, the young housemaid.

'Go about your duties, girl,' Mrs Carlton said crossly. 'Mind your manners.'

'I'm sorry, Flora. I didn't mean to embarrass you.' Daniel caught Flora by the hand. 'Let's continue this conversation outside and let Mrs Carlton get on with whatever she's doing.'

'Don't mind me, miss.' Mrs Carlton hurried into the pantry and began rattling the jars and bottles on the shelves.

Flora and Daniel exchanged amused glances and hurried outside into the yard before they burst into laughter.

'You should be sorry, Daniel Robbins,' Flora said with mock severity. 'You've made a show of me in front of the servants.'

'I am a servant.' Daniel caught her round the waist and drew her closer. 'I've missed you so much, Flora. I was terrified that you would find your pa and stay in London with him and I'd never see you again.'

Flora slid her arms around his neck, looking him

in the eyes with a hint of a smile. 'I did find my pa, but I also found myself. Does that sound silly?'

He shook his head. 'No, not at all.'

'I learned that being close to those you love is the most important thing in the world. My pa lost his beloved wife and he thought his two babies were drowned, too. Now he knows he has a son, even if Moses is going to be difficult to win over, and he has a daughter who thought she knew what she wanted.'

'And what does she want, Flora?'

'I can't answer that, Dan. Not yet, anyway. I need to get to know my father better.'

Daniel took her by the hand. 'At least you are home now. Come with me, I want to show you how much work we've done to the gardens in your absence. Sir Arthur has been very good and allowed me to have a team of men to work under me.'

They left the yard surrounded by outbuildings and Daniel led her to what had once been a formal garden but had gone wild.

'What a transformation,' Flora said, clapping her hands. 'You've cleared it completely and you've even managed to plant young box hedges.'

'I thought you would be pleased. The grounds are much more extensive than it would seem at first glance. It could be made really splendid with more work.'

Flora looked up at him, smiling. 'Doing this makes you happy, doesn't it?'

'Yes,' Daniel said simply. 'It does. I'm never more

content than when I'm working with nature. What about you, Flora? Has finding your father made a difference to your hopes and dreams?'

She smiled ruefully. 'That's probably what they were – just figments of my imagination making me think I could achieve success in whatever field I chose.'

'I believe in you.'

'Yes, you do, don't you? You've never told me I was being stupid or over-ambitious.'

'Because you are neither of those things.' He took both her hands in his. 'You can do whatever you set your heart on and I will help in any way I can.' He bent his head and kissed her lightly on the lips.

Flora drew away at the sound of footsteps. She turned to see Calvert striding towards them.

'If you'll excuse me, Flora. I have work to do.' Daniel backed away but Flora caught him by the sleeve.

'You are not the servant here, Dan. I want you to meet my papa as an equal. He worked his way from nothing to being a very successful man.'

'Quite right,' Calvert said seriously. 'Flora has told me all about you, Daniel. From what I've seen so far you have handled this estate brilliantly.'

'I am just a gardener, sir.'

'Was Capability Brown just a gardener? No, Daniel. You have knowledge, vision and you know how to encourage those under you to work. You should be proud of your abilities, as I am of mine.'

'You won't win this argument,' Flora said, laughing. 'It's better to know when to give in, Daniel. Take advice from me. The only person I know who is as stubborn as my pa is me.'

Calvert pulled a face. 'You will be a brave man if you can take the pair of us on, Daniel.'

'It would be my honour, sir. I've loved your daughter since we were both children.'

Daniel returned home at the end of a long day, and Flora and her father were left in the drawing room at Hope's End.

'You have good friends, Flora.'

She smiled. 'Yes, I was very lucky to be found by the Stewarts. Everything I am today I owe to them.'

'Well, not quite, my dear. You inherited beauty and wit from your late mama, and I can see a lot of myself in you. Your desire to prove yourself and become someone to be reckoned with has come from me. I was determined to succeed in life and I have, at least in financial terms. I try to be a good and fair employer and now I need to prove myself as your father and one day I will win Oliver's confidence, or so I hope.'

'I'm sure you will. He's very loving and kind, but give him time.'

'So what about you, Flora? I like your young man, Daniel. I can see that he is very much in love with you.'

'We've known each other since childhood, Pa.'

'Unless I'm mistaken, I think you have feelings for him, too.'

'Yes, of course I do. But again, it's not easy. I've been brought up to be a lady, not the wife of a humble gardener, and I don't mean that in a patronising way. I don't think I could marry him and live in his parents' cottage on Sir Arthur's estate. I would go mad.'

'Of course you would, but you are an intelligent woman. There is always a way, you just need to find it.'

'Is that all you are going to say to me?'

Calvert laughed. 'For now, yes.'

'Perhaps we should change and get ready to dine at Nine Oaks?' Flora rose to her feet.

'Before we do that I want you to tell me exactly what you planned for Hope's End before you gave up the idea as being too costly.'

Flora sank back onto the sofa, folding her hands in her lap. 'Well, it wasn't just the amount of money it would take. I realised that we are too far in the country to make it worthwhile.'

'I don't agree, at least not entirely. At the moment this village is very much on the outskirts of London, but there is a railway station only about a mile away.'

'Are you suggesting that people will get on a train to come here for a meal?'

'Not exactly, but new housing close to London is being built at an alarming rate. Soon all these small villages will become suburban areas with people travelling into town to work. It has happened to some places already. You have to think ahead, Flora.'

'Even if that were true, and assuming that Freddie would allow me to turn his property into a smart restaurant, where would I get the money to allow me to go ahead?'

'Freddie might be interested in it as a business proposition, or Sir Arthur. Failing that I would be prepared to do my bit to set your feet on the road to success. I believe in you, Flora. We were parted for sixteen years but I am going to make that up to you in one way or another.'

'You really think it is possible?'

'I am certain of it, my dear. You can do it, Flora. And I think you might have a stalwart person at your side, and I don't mean me. Don't say anything now, just think it over carefully. Now perhaps we had better change for dinner. I'm looking forward to having a meal prepared for me other than by my chefs.'

Dinner at Nine Oaks was a great success. Flora had been slightly nervous about introducing her father to the Stewarts as well as Bella and Freddie, but he charmed them all. She had only seen him in such an ebullient mood when he entertained Cook from South Molton Street at Chez Marcel, and on this occasion he exceeded himself. Even Constance, who could be prickly with people she did not know well, was charmed by him. He praised the food and threatened to steal Cook and take her to Brook Street, and he told harmless jokes that made everyone laugh. Flora had been afraid that he might bring up the subject of Hope's End, but he did not mention it once, other than to praise her for making it into such a delightful place to live. Constance said she hoped that he would remain in the area for as long as possible and Calvert replied that he had no intention of leaving for a few days. He ended the evening by telling them all of the horrors of losing his beloved wife and two small children in the tragedy on the Thames, and of his struggle to come to terms with life without his family. There was hardly a dry eye in the drawing room when he came to the part of how Flora had come into his life and his sincerity in thanking Sir Arthur and Constance was undeniable. Flora had heard it all before but even she was impressed.

As they drove back to Hope's End in Calvert's carriage she found herself thinking of Daniel, still living with his parents in the small cottage, and she knew then what was more important to her than life itself.

'Stop the carriage, Pa.'

Calvert turned to her in astonishment. 'What for? Are you going to be sick?'

'No, Pa. Please tell the coachman to stop. I have to see Daniel now.'

'But, my dear, it's very late. He and his family will be sound asleep.'

'I don't care. I must speak to him.'

Calvert banged on the roof and the carriage slowed to a halt. Flora opened the door and leaped out. 'Don't worry about me, Pa. I will make my way back to Hope's End.' She did not wait for an answer but picked up the satin skirts of her dinner gown and raced down the lane to the head gardener's cottage. She hammered on the door.

'Daniel, Daniel. I must speak to you.' She kept on until he opened the door, his shirt open to the waist and his hair tousled as if he had just risen from his bed.

'What's happened? Are you all right?'

Flora threw her arms around him and kissed him on the lips until he responded. He lifted her off her feet and carried her into the kitchen.

'What is this all about? Are you sick or dying? Why have you come here in the middle of the night?'

'I love you, Daniel. I never want to be parted from you again. Do you still want to marry me?'

'Flora! This won't do. It's very late. Please get back in the carriage.' Calvert stood in the doorway, glaring at them both.

Daniel set Flora back on her feet. 'Your pa is right. You should go with him. We'll talk in the morning.'

'But this is between us, Dan. I want to stay here and sort things out between you and me.'

'Flora, please.' Calvert held the door wide open. 'Daniel is right. You need to leave this until morning.'

# Chapter Twenty-Five

Flora slept badly that night and awakened early. She was still angry with her father for following her to the Robbins' cottage, and interrupting her important moment with Daniel. He had insisted on taking her home and irritatingly Daniel had agreed with him. Both of them seemed shocked to the core that she had taken matters into her own hands, and nothing she had said made either of them change their minds. In the end she had climbed back into the carriage and had refused to speak for the rest of the ride home. Last night everything had seemed so clear. She had known that there was a big decision to be made as to her future and she had finally acknowledged that it would be nothing without Daniel at her side. Now it was all a terrible muddle. Her father had treated her like a wayward child and Daniel had allowed him to spirit her away without an argument.

She rose from her bed, washed in cold water and dressed in a serviceable blue cotton gown before making her way downstairs to the dining room. To her surprise she found her father seated at the table enjoying a plate of buttered eggs and fried bacon. She hesitated in the doorway, unsure of her reception, but he looked up and smiled.

'I can recommend the eggs, Flora. Your cook is excellent.'

'I inherited her from Lady Philomena. She's been here forever. But about last evening—'

Calvert held up his hand. 'Before you say anything, Flora, please allow me to speak. I wasn't going to tell you last evening because I wanted to think it through.'

'It's a little late to act like the stern father,' Flora said angrily. 'I am glad we have found each other but I'm not a child, sir. You will go away again and I will have to decide my own future. I realise now that Daniel is more important to me than my some-what childish dream of becoming a successful businesswoman.'

'Hear me out, Flora. Last evening when you ladies had retired to the drawing room, I had a very inter-esting chat with Sir Arthur and Freddie.'

'Doubtless you were all deciding my future for me.'

Calvert smiled and patted his lips with a snowy white table napkin. 'I'm afraid that is the way of the world. You are young and unmarried and therefore my responsibility, but I have your best interests at heart, Flora.'

She sighed and picked up a rather battered silver coffee pot. Her hand was shaking as she filled a cup and added a dash of milk, but she forced herself to remain calm. 'Go on then, Pa.'

'I've seen a little of what you can do when you put your mind to it, Flora. I know how resourceful and determined you are, and I think you have the makings of a good businesswoman. Although I also think that love and marriage are foremost in your thoughts, as proven by your actions last evening.'

'I don't normally behave so rashly, but I've kept Daniel waiting for an answer for long enough. I am ready to settle down to be a head gardener's wife.'

'Hear me out. I have the backing of Sir Arthur, who has been more of a father to you than I ever could be, and Dorrington, who adores his wife and wants to make her happy by taking care of your future.'

Flora rolled her eyes. She knew she was trapped, for the moment anyway. 'Go on, Pa.'

'Dorrington has agreed to let you have Hope's End on a long lease, but the freehold still belongs to his wife. Sir Arthur is more than happy to have you and your business as his close neighbour, and I am willing to put up the money to start a restaurant here. It will take time to build up a clientele but that will enable you to gain the experience needed to handle such an undertaking. I will always be available to help and advise you, and I'm sure that your friends the Tullivers will be happy to add their expertise to yours.'

'You would allow me to manage the restaurant on my own?'

'I believe in you, Flora. I hope one day you might take your brother on to help you, and Sir Arthur has agreed to allow Daniel to manage the grounds here as well as those at Nine Oaks. That is if the plan suits him, although from what I witnessed last evening I think he would be more than willing.'

Flora sipped her coffee as she struggled to come to terms with the size of the proposed undertaking, and yet it was only what she had had in mind from the start. However, put in such stark terms she was excited by the idea as well as slightly nervous.

'I need to speak to Daniel, Pa. I took him by surprise last night, and you barged in before he could tell me how he feels.'

'I think it's obvious that he loves you deeply, Flora. I've only met him briefly, but it was obvious by the way he was with you and the tone of his voice, in fact everything, that he has deep feelings for you. I see myself in him as I was twenty years ago when I first met your dear mama. I've never loved another woman and I never will. I think Daniel feels the same.'

'I must speak to him before I give you my answer, Pa.'

'He's here already. I saw him before I came into

breakfast. We spoke briefly, Flora, and I told him what has been suggested. It's up to you now.'

Flora rose to her feet. 'I can't imagine my life without him.'

'Then tell him that, my dear girl. Everything else will fall into place. From what I've seen of him, he's a fine young man.'

Daniel was supervising the men as they hacked their way through the undergrowth to reveal a red-brick wall that surrounded the old kitchen garden. Flora wanted to run to him, but she was suddenly shy and unsure of herself. Perhaps she had gone too far the previous evening. She felt that she was seeing him for the first time. His strong profile, weathered complexion and nut-brown hair that curled around the back of his well-shaped head made her heart beat faster and she was suddenly tongue-tied. He turned his head as if sensing her approach and his amber eyes shone gold in the early morning sunlight.

'We have a secret garden, Flora.' He stepped forward and lifted the rusty latch. The door stuck but a nudge from his booted foot opened it to reveal what must have once produced the food for the entire household. The warmth encased in the brick walls and the sweet-smelling soil came out to greet them like an old friend. Daniel held out his hand and Flora allowed him to lead her into the tangled mass that had once been a productive kitchen garden. He closed the door and swept her into his arms.

Flora did not resist. She parted her lips and gave herself up to the tidal wave of emotion aroused by his kiss. She knew she would always remember their first embrace in the newly discovered walled garden that was now theirs to save from the rampant growth of brambles, nettles and encroaching grass.

Daniel released her lips but he held her so close she could feel his heart matching its beat to hers. 'I've always loved you, Flora. I didn't get a chance to answer your question last night.'

Flora brushed his hair back from his forehead, raising herself on tiptoes to brush his lips with a kiss. 'It's still the same question this morning.'

'You always have to be first in everything, but not this time.' He went down on one knee in the dusty soil, still clutching her hand. 'I love you now and forever, Flora Lee, or Flora Calvert, whichever name you care to use. Will you marry me?'

She nodded vigorously. 'Yes, with all my heart. I will be Flora Robbins forever. We'll make this place into a home and a business, too.'

Daniel stood up, wrapping his arms around her. 'I think we'll have to change the name of the house.'

'You're right. It's no longer Hope's End. This is just the beginning.'

Their story had begun in the walled garden at Nine Oaks and Flora knew instinctively that the next chapter would start here.

# The Rockwood Chronicles

High upon the beautiful cliffs of the Devonshire coast, the once proud
Rockwood Castle is crumbling into ruin. Can the Carey family save
their home and their family before it's too late?

In this spellbinding six-book series, Dilly Court opens a door into Rockwood Castle –
chronicling the changing fortunes of the Carey family...

## Book One: Fortune's Daughter

Abandoned by her parents, headstrong Rosalind must take
charge of the family. Until the appearance of dashing
Piers Blanchard threatens to ruin everything...

## Book Two: Winter Wedding

Christmas is coming and Rockwood Castle has once again been thrown into
turmoil. As snowflakes fall, can Rosalind protect her beloved home?

## Book Three: Runaway Widow

It is time for the youngest Carey sister, Patricia, to seek out her own
future. But without her family around her, will she lose her way?

## Book Four: Sunday's Child

Taken in by the Carey family when she was a young girl,
Nancy Sunday has never known her true parentage.
Now eighteen years old, can she find out where she truly belongs?

## Book Five: Snow Bride

The course of true love does not run straight for Nancy. Her life is filled with difficult
choices – but with Christmas around the corner, which path will she choose?

## Book Six: Dolly's Dream

The eldest daughter at Rockwood, Dolly, dreams of a bigger life
beyond the castle walls. But with the family's future under threat,
will Dolly's heart lead her astray – or bring her home?